M000289816

KILLING SEASON

KILLING SEASON

a Violet Darger novel

LT VARGUS & TIM MCBAIN

SMARMY PRESS

KILLING SEASON

PROLOGUE

The Jeep scuttled up the hill, tires slipping a little in the mud. The rain and runoff had washed out the dirt trail here, baring a mix of rocks and a reddish layer of clay that lay beneath the topsoil — a craggy wound slit into the earth.

His whole body rattled along with the bumps, hands strangling the steering wheel as if gripping it hard enough could steady the vehicle, help it find traction.

He hit the steepest section, the windshield pitching to point him straight into a lifeless gray sky. A dead swirl of clouds above. The heavens totally without shape.

And then everything evened out again. The Jeep reached the flat ground of the hilltop, and it was over. He was there.

He killed the engine and sat a moment.

His skin sheened. Glistened. The surface of his arms and face moist from the heat inside.

It didn't feel real.

All of the planning. All of the hours of fantasy and frustration. All of his will channeled into this.

One moment. One time and place to make his mark.

It almost felt like going into battle.

He lowered himself from the vehicle, careful to avoid the mud. Though the rain had died off hours ago, the ground was still soggy underfoot, water puddling around his shoes with every step.

The roar of the traffic on the highway was loud but somehow indistinct. The distance smeared all of the noises together into an endless drone like the sound of the ocean in a shell.

He walked to his spot under the transmission tower — 180 feet of latticed steel that hoisted the power lines up above the tallest of the trees. From the vantage point on top of the hill, he could look into the distance at the line of identical towers, a strange path of grass slashed into the woods to make room for the steel structures, to make way for electricity.

He lowered himself to the ground, belly down, and the wet saturated his jeans up to the shins straight away. The military issue rain poncho kept the rest of him dry. He was thankful he'd worn it after all. He'd felt silly taking it to the counter at the army surplus store — the oversized, hooded thing almost looked like a green Klan robe — but now it felt right.

He'd always wanted to be a soldier when he was a kid, had planned all through school to join the Marines. He dreamed of a lifetime spent fighting for his country, for his people. The feel of the rifle settling into place against his shoulder brought those old feelings back all the way. An old dream. An old version of himself. The someone he used to be.

But things change. People change. And the world wasn't worth fighting for. The people weren't worth saving. Not anymore.

The wind kicked up, moaning softly where it cut against the metal of the transmission tower. He waited for it to pass.

He sucked in a big breath, and his chest felt clammy inside and out. Heavy with the wet.

He peered through the scope, pinching the off eye closed.

Traffic swarmed. Sedans and mini-vans jockeying for position on the strip of asphalt below. He watched them, measuring out how much he'd need to lead his moving targets. Predictable targets weren't too bad. He'd practiced for it.

His hands were blocks of ice gripping the rifle. Cold and moist and numb. But he could feel the trigger, if only a little.

If the people weren't worth saving, what did that mean? He'd let the thought twist his guts into knots until the tension got to be too much. The pressure inside him ached to find release. He had to do something about it. Had to.

So here he was. It was time.

He squeezed the trigger, and the gun cracked and bucked against his shoulder. His chest lurched and pulled in air, wet lips and throat and lungs greedy for the wind, some attempt to fill the strange emptiness between the shot and impact, and then the bullet punched a hole in the windshield of a Ford Explorer.

The opening was small. Neat. It looked to be in line with the driver — possibly even a headshot — but it was hard to say for sure.

The SUV remained steady for a moment and then careened off to the right. Black lines of rubber trailed behind as the vehicle dumped itself into the ditch, rolling onto its side, the windshield spider-webbing from the fall.

He could read the panic in the movements of the surrounding vehicles like a pack of animals jerking away from some horror.

It felt good. It felt right. The clammy nervousness fled his body, and heat flushed his face.

He fired again and again and again, a burnt smell surrounding him, the stock battering the hell out of his shoulder.

CRACK-CRACK-CRACK-CRACK-CRACK

Hatred focused him. His movements gained confidence. Quickness. Machine-like precision.

The damaged vehicles swerved, and the frenzied cars behind

them bashed into each other, the lanes of traffic like serpents lurching and slowing before him.

Chaos achieved. Just like that.

He hesitated. Licked his lips. Stared through the scope.

An older Escalade jammed its passenger side fender into the median wall and scraped along it a while before it veered back to sideswipe a Prius, pushing it across the other two lanes. The hybrid's door crinkled and folded around the hood of the SUV, and black smoke fluttered out of the wounded place where the two vehicles meshed.

And now the traffic stopped entirely. All four lanes rendered motionless.

Everything quiet. Everything still.

And he waited. And his heart thundered, restless in his chest. And the darkness inside of him seemed to grow, seemed to reach out now to touch the face of the deep.

His finger found the trigger. Brushed it lightly like a butterfly kiss.

When the first good Samaritan climbed out of the driver's seat of his Mustang, he squeezed. The man waddled out of the sports car in the distance and stood, graying hair pruned into a crew cut, sunglasses adorning the pudgy face, and the gun cracked and kicked and sheared off most of that flat-topped head all at once, body toppling to the blacktop totally limp.

And the heat flooded him again. Hate pulsing in his face. Blotching his vision with floating pink spots.

He scanned the highway for movement. For targets.

If mankind wasn't worth saving, it should be destroyed.

CHAPTER 1

Violet reached for the champagne bottle and filled her flute. A groomsmen took the stage and began tinking his fork against his glass. Nearly everyone in the room followed suit, a musical clamor filling the space like hail rattling against the windows of a house. The bride and groom kissed for what had to be the twentieth time, completing the ritual.

It had been a weekend full of strange formality. It started with the bachelorette party — complete with Jell-O shots, feather boas, and penis-shaped paraphernalia. Next came the rehearsal dinner, which seemed less like a rehearsal for anything and more like a mini-wedding before the real wedding. Then came the wedding day itself. The morning started early with the bridal party being shuttled to a nearby salon to be primped and prodded and manicured.

She couldn't help but think of one of Leonard Stump's journal entries:

Human beings like to think of themselves as sitting higher up the chain than animals. More evolved. But what is a social custom other than an animal habit meant to serve some baser instinct? If things were reversed, if we sniffed each other's asses in greeting and dogs were the ones that shook hands, we would surely still consider ourselves the superior beings.

As much as she was loath to admit it, some of Stump's observations about human behavior resonated with her. She wondered if that's what Loshak meant when he referred to the journal as "educational." Educational or not, she didn't like feeling in communion with a serial murderer.

Violet took a swig from her glass. She wasn't sure why she was in the bridal party to begin with. She and her stepsister had never been close. When Jenna first called and asked her to be a bridesmaid, Violet wondered if her mother and stepfather had put her up to it. An attempt to bring the family closer together or some other such misguided logic. Was she supposed to be flattered? Was it an honor being bestowed upon her? Violet tried to feel it but couldn't. Standing at the front of the church during the ceremony, all she could think was that she would have much preferred being one of the nameless faces sitting in the pews. At least then she probably wouldn't have gotten blisters.

She looked down at the strappy torture devices masquerading as footwear. The blasted shoes had rubbed away the flesh on her feet in at least three places already. At this angle, she also couldn't miss the dress. It was a short, empire waist number in pistachio green with wisps of chiffon that billowed about the skirt. The other bridesmaids cooed with joy when they stood to admire themselves in the mirror earlier that day. When Violet saw her reflection, all she could think was: Ice Capades.

The excited chirping of the bridesmaids continued throughout the day, and the other women might as well have been speaking a foreign language as far as Violet was concerned.

Currently, the one named Morgan was saying, "So I was waiting for my order at Panera, and this woman standing next to me started asking about my bag. It was the new Chloe Faye-"

"Did you get the mini or the medium?" Lauren interrupted.

"The medium. Tan leather and suede."

"Ohmygawd, jealous," Lauren said.

"Yeah so, this lady turns to me and goes, 'I love your bag. What kind is it?' I told her it was a Chloe, and she's like, 'Oh, is that like Kate Spade?' I almost choked on my iced tea. Like, seriously. To first of all *not* know Chloe bags? But then to think that a Kate Spade would be on the same level? Um, no."

Lauren snorted.

"Snob."

"I'm not denying it," Morgan said with a shrug.

Violet downed what was left in her champagne glass and reached for the bottle on the table. Upending it, she found it was empty. Damn.

Just as she turned to see if the table behind them had a bottle she might be able to snatch, she heard a flurry of activity from the birds, err, bridesmaids. Morgan's chair squeaked over the floor as she pushed it back from the table and rose.

"You coming, Violet?"

"Huh?"

"She's about to throw the bouquet," Lauren said.

"Oh," Violet said. "That's OK. You guys go ahead."

The two women exchanged a glance.

"But you're single, aren't you?" Lauren asked.

"Yeah."

"Then you *have* to come," Morgan said. "All the single ladies!"

Lauren and Morgan began singing what Violet figured to be some popular song. She wasn't familiar with it.

"I'm good. Really," Violet said, but it was too late. They descended upon her like robins defending a nest from a crow.

They each took an arm and yanked her in the general direction of the dance floor where a crowd of young women gathered.

"Alright, alright!" she said, nearly tipping out of her chair.

Really, they should have been happy to let her stay in her

seat. If they were so eager to catch the damn bouquet, it would be one less person competing for the prize. Tradition defied logic, she supposed. That was what made it a tradition, wasn't it? We do it because we do it. Not because it makes sense.

Christ, maybe she *had* been reading too much of that Stump journal. She was starting to think like him. Or had she already thought like him all along?

The two women stood guard while Violet got to her feet. Like they thought she might try to make a run for it. She took one step in agony and stopped, tearing the evil shoes off and tossing them back under her seat.

When they reached the group waiting for the bouquet to be thrown, Lauren and Morgan immediately elbowed and jostled their way closer to the front. Violet hung back.

Jenna clicked across the dance floor in white satin heels, bouquet in hand. Standing with her back to the gaggle of women, the rest of the crowd counted down in chorus.

"FIVE! FOUR! THREE! TWO! ONE!"

Violet watched the cluster of flowers somersault through the air, stepping sideways as it passed over her head. Half a dozen women dove for it. Violet saw a flutter of mint green chiffon among the scuffle as Morgan set her sights on the bounty. Violet wasn't sure if the women were just playing at being so enthusiastic or if it was genuine. She wasn't sure if it mattered.

She took advantage of the momentary distraction to edge closer to the bar. The bartender was stooped over a cardboard box, organizing the empties. When he saw her approaching, he straightened and gave her a broad smile. She wagered he earned himself a lot of tips with those big, perfect teeth and that dimpled chin.

"What can I get for you?"

"Is there more champagne? Our table is out," Violet said.

He reached under a table and produced a fresh bottle, then set about opening it for her.

"Got anything stronger back there?" Violet stood on her tiptoes in an attempt to peek over the edge of the bar.

"Not having fun?"

The bartender's eyes twinkled as he asked the question. He was pretty cute, despite the ridiculous man-bun he was sporting on top of his head. Darger figured him for maybe 25, at the oldest. Cute, but too young for her.

"I'm not really a wedding person, I guess," she said.

Without a word, he set a shot glass on the bar and filled it with tequila.

"Straight to the Patron, huh? You must have dealt with my kind before."

He winked and slid the glass toward her. "I don't like to half-ass these things."

"A man who takes his job seriously," she said, lifting the shot to him.

Violet threw her head back and downed it, almost choking when the burn hit the back of her throat. A tear escaped the corner of her eye, and she wiped it away before replacing the glass on the bar top.

"Don't you?" Manbun asked.

"Don't I what?"

"Take your job seriously?"

Violet smirked. "It'd be bad news if I didn't."

"Why? What do you do, fly planes or something?"

She thought about telling him the truth — that she was an FBI agent, one who specialized in profiling violent criminals, one who'd made national headlines just last year for her fight to the death with a serial killer — but decided against it.

"Something like that."

His eyebrows reached up in an attempt to high-five his bun. "For real?"

She nodded, and the million-dollar smile returned.

"Wow. Sounds bad-ass." He tilted the bottle side to side, liquid sloshing gently against the glass. "Another?"

Violet held up a hand. "I think I'm good."

A cheer erupted toward the front of the room. The groom had a garter clenched between his teeth. Violet turned back to the bar.

"For now," she added.

The bartender grinned at her, and she made a mental note to return with a generous tip for him. She grasped the fresh bottle of champagne by the neck and hoisted it.

"Thanks for this," she said, then nodded at the shot glass. "And the other."

"My pleasure."

When Violet got back to her table, Morgan and Lauren were huddled together, chattering excitedly. Violet slid into her chair and saw the wedding bouquet laid out on the table.

"So who got it?" she asked.

Lauren pointed at Morgan, who beamed as if she'd won some kind of award.

"Congrats."

"Where'd you run off to?" Morgan asked.

Violet let the bottle thump onto the table.

"We were out," she said and stood to refill their glasses.

"To Morgan and her magical bouquet," Violet said, lifting her champagne flute by the stem. "May your future husband be both well-endowed and blessed with little back hair."

Lauren and Morgan snorted into their glasses as they all drank.

"Oh!" Lauren said, putting her hand to her nose to keep champagne from squirting out. "Your phone buzzed when you were gone."

Violet's hand groped behind her, reaching for the bag slung over the back of her chair. Her fingers slithered amongst lip balm and old shopping lists and a tin of mints before finding the phone. Pulling it out, she woke the screen and found she'd missed a call from her partner.

The DJ had returned after a brief break, and Violet had to hold a finger in her ear to hear the voicemail over speakers that were now blaring "SexyBack." An old one. It turned out that Loshak hadn't left much of a message.

"I suppose you're still out there for the wedding, but call me when you get this."

Violet scooted her chair back at the same moment the other bridesmaids got up.

"Yes!" Morgan said. "You're coming to dance with us?"

"What? No," Violet said, almost recoiling in horror. "I have to make a call."

Morgan pretended to pout.

"You better get your butt out there when you're done," she said.

"Uh, sure. Absolutely," Violet said, thinking that she'd need about a dozen more shots before that happened.

Taking her phone in hand, she stepped into the relative quiet of a hallway beyond the ballroom, though she could still hear the thumping bass through the walls.

Loshak answered before the first ring ended.

"When's your flight back to Virginia?" he asked, forgoing

any sort of greeting.

"Tomorrow night. Why?"

"Save yourself the flying time and switch it to Atlanta."

"What's in Atlanta?"

"We've got an active shooter situation."

"Where? What happened?"

"Freeway sniper. Shot fourteen people during rush hour on Interstate 20. Five confirmed dead so far."

"Jesus."

Darger heard a voice announcing something via intercom over the line.

"Listen, my flight's boarding, so I gotta go. Gimme a call when you get an arrival time, and I can pick you up at the airport."

"Will do," she said.

The background noise she could hear from Loshak's end clicked out, and her phone's screen blinked out the message, CALL ENDED.

She pushed through the steel doors that led back into the ballroom, the music swelling as the gap between door and threshold widened. Her heart thumped along with the pulsing beat, and by the time she reached her seat, she'd already made her decision.

A normal human being would probably at least wait until the end of the reception to leave, but it had been a long time since anyone had accused Violet Darger of being normal.

CHAPTER 2

If she hurried, she could make it.

Maybe.

There was one more flight leaving Denver that could get her a connection to Atlanta tonight. With the amount of time it took to get through airport security these days, it was a gamble. Since it was one of the last departing flights of the night, Darger hoped luck would be on her side. But if she was going, she had to go now.

She had her phone in one hand, scrolling through the list of upcoming departures. With the other hand, she raced from one end of her hotel room to the other, tossing everything in sight into the gaping jaws of her suitcase.

It wasn't until she was snatching her toothbrush from the bathroom that she realized she was still wearing the pale green bridesmaid dress.

Shit.

She glanced at her watch. No time now. She could change at the airport after she got through security.

Except for the shoes. No way was she wearing those damn things another second. She stuffed the offending things into her suitcase along with her remaining toiletries, stepped into her boots, and glanced around the room one last time. Tucking her trench coat over her arm, she realized it was probably long enough to mostly conceal the frilly dress. Thank god for small favors.

The wheels of her suitcase squeaked and bumped over the floor as she hurried down the hallway to the elevator. The inside of the metal box smelled strangely chemical, like a dentist's office. It chimed when she reached the ground floor, and the doors slid open.

Darger went to the front desk in the lobby. She turned in the key cards for her room and checked out. Passing the glass doors at the main entrance, she could see the car she'd called was already waiting. She had one more task left to do. The one she'd been avoiding since making the choice to leave for Atlanta immediately instead of waiting until tomorrow.

She was half-tempted to just go. Slip out into the cab and call to break the news from the airport. But if she did that, she'd end up feeling even crappier.

After the brightness of the lobby and the hallway, stepping into the ballroom was like entering a cave. Darger stood and squinted around the darkened space. A disco ball spun over the center of the dance floor, casting a constellation of glittering reflections over the walls and ceiling. It was a bit disorienting, but after a few moments, she located her mother.

She stood near one of the tables toward the back, talking to another guest. She'd be disappointed, of course. There was a "family brunch" scheduled for tomorrow morning, and Violet knew her mother expected her to be there.

Oh well, she thought. Duty calls.

She left her suitcase and coat by the door and started toward the back of the ballroom. On her way, she passed by the bar. The strapping young bartender was busy with another guest but glanced her way. He smiled when he saw her. Violet gave him a nod and then slipped a twenty from her wallet and into the tip jar.

Drawing up next to her mother, Violet reached out and placed a hand on her arm.

"Hi, honey," her mom said.

She slid her arm around Violet's waist and pulled her close.

"I'm so glad you're here. I miss you."

An ice pick of guilt stabbed at Violet's heart.

"Me too," she said, hugging back.

They stood for a moment, watching the dots of light from the disco ball whirl around them. Violet tried to decide how to segue into breaking the news, but the words wouldn't come.

Finally she turned to her mother and blurted out, "I have to fly back early."

Her mother's head tipped to one side.

"You aren't going to miss the family brunch, are you?"

Violet picked at the chipped polish on her nails. They'd all had manicures done that morning, and Violet's nail polish was already destroyed.

"That's the thing. I have to go tonight. Right now, actually."

Liar, liar, pants on fire, she thought to herself. You don't have to go anywhere, Violet Darger. You're bailing by choice.

"Tonight?"

Violet nodded.

"I came over to say goodbye."

"Oh," her mother said, frowning.

She gazed into Violet's eyes.

"This job, Violet… Are you sure they don't ask too much? It seems so demanding. After everything that happened with that last one…"

They'd had this discussion at least a dozen times since her mother found out exactly what went down in Athens, Ohio. She hadn't been wild about Violet joining the FBI in the first place, even when she was working in OVA counseling victims of violent crimes. When Violet decided to try for a special agent position, her mother had asked (with a straight face) if there were any special agents that didn't carry guns, and if so, maybe Violet could be one of those.

Violet's go-to line — the one where she insisted the job wasn't non-stop danger like they showed in movies and on TV — kind of fell flat after she'd been kidnapped and nearly drowned last year.

"That's the job, mom. It's what I signed up for."

As creases formed between her mother's eyebrows, Violet added, "But what happened in Ohio isn't going to happen again. That was a fluke. You don't have to worry."

Her mother watched her for a time and then kissed her cheek.

"But worrying about you is my job, don't you know that?"

They hugged, and then Violet's mother stepped away.

"How are you going to get to the airport? I should drive you—"

"No, mom. I already called a cab. Besides, you can't leave yet. The party isn't over."

Her mother reached for her hand and gave it a squeeze.

"Will you call me to let me know you got home safe?"

"Sure," Violet said, omitting the fact that she was flying into an active shooter situation and not back to Virginia. Sometimes Violet felt it was better to give her mother the grisly details only after she could assure her she'd gotten out safely.

They exchanged a final embrace, with Violet promising she'd get in touch if she ended up stranded at the airport. After Violet ducked out of the ballroom for the last time, she shrugged into the trench coat. With the belt tied at the waist, an onlooker would barely see the frothy hem of the green chiffon peeking out from underneath. Not bad.

The telltale screech of the steel ballroom door opening sounded behind her, and then a hand fell on her shoulder. She turned, expecting her mother. It was the bartender.

"You never came back for another shot," Mr. Manbun said.

She smiled. "Yeah, I think one was plenty."

He was grinning back at her until his gaze went from her coat to the suitcase by her side.

"You're leaving?" he asked, and Violet almost chuckled at the cartoon expression of disappointment on his face.

"Afraid so."

"But the reception's not even over," he said, gesturing back at the double doors and the throbbing music within. "I was working on a whole routine to give you my number. It was going to be very smooth."

That got a laugh out of her.

"I'm sure it was. But duty calls. And you know how that goes, being a man that takes his job seriously."

He nodded at their little inside joke. "Serious business, eh? With that trench coat on, you look kinda like a superhero in disguise. Do you have to run off to catch a bad guy?"

"Actually, yes." She said it with a straight face, because it was true.

"Shit, I was only joking. Really?"

"Really."

"That's crazy." He shook his head in disbelief. "I'm Mark, by the way."

He put his hand out, and Violet took it.

"Violet."

His grip was firm but somehow gentle. This Mark was either a genuine sweetheart or a very practiced heartbreaker. Either way, he was still too young for her.

And yet, she had an urge to rip the hair tie from his head. To push him up against the wall and kiss him with his hair all tumbling free. That was the tequila talking, of course. That, and the adrenaline still coursing through her veins from Loshak's call. The remembrance of where she was going and why was enough to tear her from her indecent thoughts. She had a plane to catch.

"It was nice to meet you, Mark. But I really have to go now."

"Can I give you my number, sans smooth moves?" he asked, patting his pockets and then pulling out a piece of paper with a phone number scrawled on it.

She thought about shooting him down based on the age difference but decided against it. He'd been sweet. She could let him down easier than that.

"I'm from out of state."

He held it out to her.

"In case you're ever back in town."

Her phone buzzed. Probably her driver getting antsy. She took the piece of paper, glancing at it before she tucked it into her bag.

"Thank you," she said. "Now you better get back to your post. If I know some of those people as well as I think I do, they're helping themselves to the top shelf stuff. You don't want them to end up too shitfaced to pay you at the end of the night."

"I hope you catch him. The bad guy, I mean," he said as she started to wheel away with her suitcase.

He was still watching when she passed through the glass doors at the front of the lobby and got into the car waiting at the curb. Violet raised one hand in a final farewell as the car started toward the airport.

CHAPTER 3

It wasn't until she'd checked her bag at the ticket counter and passed through security that Violet realized the opportunity to change out of the froofy dress was gone. She was stuck looking like a garnish of celery foam on the plate of some pretentious chef for the next seven hours, at least. Longer if she didn't make her connecting flight in Minneapolis.

She kept her trench coat buttoned up in the airport terminal, only loosening the belt after a flight attendant offered her a blanket and pillow. She accepted both, settling in for the first half of her red-eye to Georgia.

A magazine in the seat pouch caught her eye, tucked in with the emergency exit instructions and air sickness bags. All Violet could see was an ad for Quaker Oats on the back. She reached out and slid the magazine free, flipping backward through the pages with a thumb and only pausing long enough to get a vague idea of what each story was about. She wasn't really in the mood to read, but turning pages gave her something to do with the extra energy still crackling through her nerves.

She passed by a fashion spread featuring pregnant celebrities on the red carpet and an interview with the star of the most recent blockbuster superhero movie. Violet couldn't remember the last time she'd seen a movie in the theater. She hurried past a stinky perfume sample that made her nose wrinkle and itch.

When she caught a glimpse of her own face smirking back at her from the glossy paper, she almost let out a groan. She managed to keep it to a disgruntled sigh and glanced at the man in the seat next to her. He was fiddling with his phone and hadn't noticed, thankfully. How embarrassing would that have been? To get caught appearing to read a story about yourself?

She slapped the pages shut and stuffed the magazine behind a SkyMall catalog. Now that it was concealed from view, Violet relaxed a little. She'd managed to avoid seeing the article up close until recently. It had come out three weeks ago and was mostly going to pass under the radar, she thought. Except with her mother. Her mother had bought a whole stack so she could give them away to friends. She even tried to get Violet to autograph some of them.

What she couldn't avoid was the copy her mother had clipped, framed, and affixed to the refrigerator in her home.

Violet found herself frozen in front of the fridge the other afternoon, staring into the dot-matrix print of her own eyes, wondering to herself: Is that what I look like? How people see me?

A bolded pull quote caught her attention.

"There isn't much time to think about the profile when someone's got a gun to your head. All I was really thinking was that [Clegg] killed the girls quickly after abducting them, so I didn't have a lot of time. If I was going to act, I had to act now."

And act she did, hitting Clegg with everything her FBI training had taught her, ultimately fighting him to the death.

Violet cringed as she read it. It wasn't quite as bad as hearing a recording of her own voice or seeing video footage of herself. But there was still an uncanniness to seeing her words and thoughts typed up and printed in black and white. It was like seeing a version of her that wasn't quite her. Or was it?

This was how people saw one another, wasn't it? Boiled

down to quotes and snapshots. Filed into boxes. Sectioned off into the appropriate partition.

The journalist kept bringing her questions back to being a female in a male-dominated field. Darger didn't know how to answer. She didn't think about it like that. To her, it was a job. It was her purpose. Her gender had nothing to do with it. If other people thought it did, that was their problem.

But still, she'd kept asking.

"It's obvious that James Clegg hated women, and that was part of what motivated his crimes. Do you think being a woman yourself is part of what helped you catch him? The unique way you could perhaps identify with the victims? A level of empathy that your male colleagues might have a harder time with?"

Maybe that was true, Darger thought. Maybe it *had* been a factor in catching Clegg. But even if it were, Darger didn't know what to do with that information. Or how to comment on it.

"I don't think it was any one thing that caught Clegg. Or any serial killer, for that matter. It's a delicate balance of science and instinct, patience and persistence. And probably a whole lot of being in the right place at the right time," she answered finally.

Ugh, so trite. And naturally the reporter had cut out everything she'd said about Loshak and Detective Luck and the other people that had been instrumental in finding Clegg. That wasn't what they wanted. The media wasn't interested in painting a picture of cross-departmental cooperation and teamwork. They wanted a star. A hero. A lone avenger, fighting for justice. Another archetype to be indexed and labeled.

Just before take-off, Darger rifled through her bag in search of gum to battle the imminent ear-popping she was about to endure. Not finding any, she settled on the tin of mints. Her quest also turned up the phone number of Mark the Bartender.

She ran her finger over the writing, wondering why she should feel so flattered that he'd given it to her. Was it because he was young? Or because he was attractive? Or was it the mere fact that she'd been wanted?

She suddenly remembered an article she'd read a few months ago in one of her psychology journals. The topic was one-night stands. A recent study had found that women — contrary to what is commonly suggested — do not enter into such a fling thinking it will turn into a long-term relationship. Instead, the women generally reported that they were pleased to be wanted. Flattered to be found attractive.

The psychologist performing the study had noted the irony in that the men interviewed admitted to drastically lowering their standards when it came to one-night stands.

"What's so flattering about a man wanting casual sex?" the researcher wrote.

Violet wondered what Leonard Stump would have to say about it, with all of his theories about animals and ritual.

Attraction is lust and lust is a nice way of saying that we're all just rutting beasts.

Fuck, she thought. She really was starting to think like him.

Darger crumpled the bartender's number in her fist and stuffed it in the seat pocket next to the barf bags. Pulling the blanket up to cover the silly dress, she thought that if she were lucky, she'd be able to sleep for most of the flight.

CHAPTER 4

Potential targets drifted over the blacktop. A white-haired couple loading bags into the back of their Mercedes. A young black mother with a toddler resting on her hip. A bum wearing a tattered flannel shirt, raising a tallboy wrapped in a brown paper bag to his lips. All ages. All races. All walks of life.

Some would live, and some would die.

He watched them all, watched the grocery store parking lot through the driver's side window of a beat up Ford Focus, arms draped over the steering wheel. He tried to keep still, but his legs bounced, his hands twitched, his intestines squished and gurgled deep inside.

Intensity. That's what this was. Physical intensity. Some force, some passion that held him in its grip, made the synapses smolder that little bit brighter in his head, turned the volume up on all of his sensory perceptions.

He felt every follicle of hair on his body, sensed the lingering moisture in his armpits, smelled the stale French fry stench that clung to the upholstery. His pupils dilated into black pits, eyelids opened wider than usual, almost stinging from the electrical sizzle of the energy burning just behind them, and he saw every movement in the lot like it was happening in slow motion.

Men, women and children and shopping carts and bulging plastic bags and gallons of milk with that film of sweat beading up on them. Every satisfied shopper coming and going with no idea that a predator looked upon them. Judged them. Deemed them worthy of life or death.

The sensation matched what he'd experienced when he parked the Jeep on the hill overlooking the highway. He'd never felt more alive than he did in these moments just before the event, just before the violence. His whole body woke up, his awareness, his state of being lurching toward some plane beyond normal existence, some form of divinity that he couldn't hold onto for very long.

His eyes drifted over the lot again. The Publix nestled in a suburban neighborhood. A land of polo shirts, minivans, Starbucks, and cleanliness. A soft energy pervaded the parking lot itself. Smiling faces that wouldn't look out of place on Food Network. Even the bum had straight white teeth.

The neighborhood reduced the risk, Levi felt, of anyone else in the vicinity packing a weapon. In the inner city, he'd probably run into some gang banger. Out in the sticks, it would be some NRA freak's dream come true to put him down. But here in the middle ground, in the suburbs, it was all sheep and no wolves. Or so it seemed.

Again, he fidgeted in his seat, fingers writhing on the steering wheel, liquid thrashing in his stomach.

He checked his phone. Chuckled under his breath. Only two minutes since he'd last looked, though that felt impossible. 9:16 AM. It wasn't hot yet, but even this early he noted that stickiness creeping into the air, that mugginess eagerly waiting to make everyone miserable. Not so different from his own plans, now that he considered it.

That thought seemed as good an omen as any. He pulled around the corner to park out of sight and slid the ski mask over his face.

Heat shimmered a little over the parking lot. It wasn't as prominent this early, but he could see it better now that he was on foot, that slight blurring of all things just above ground level.

He stepped onto the blacktop, his abdominals flexing against that bulk of cold steel tucked into his waist band, acrylic fabric forming black rings around each of his eyes. He had to resist the urge to scratch the places where the ski mask made his eyelids itch.

The parking lot swarmed with life all the more now that he was up close, the people in motion everywhere around him — pushing carts, climbing in and out of cars, walking through the rectangle where the automatic doors swung open. From what he could tell, they took no notice of the masked intruder sauntering their way. Sheep, indeed.

He pushed his forearm into the gun, the hard edges pressing into his flesh.

This hadn't been the plan. Not originally.

He'd removed the backseat of the Ford Focus — one of the backup vehicles — so he could lie in the trunk and fire his rifle out of a hole above the license plate. The car's body would serve as something of a silencer, at least enough to obfuscate where the shots were coming from. And he'd be ready to scramble into the front seat and be gone in seconds, probably without anyone seeing him at all.

But after going through with the first shootings along the highway, things had changed. He didn't do as much damage with the sniper rifle as he thought he might, but it was more than that. He needed to walk into the parking lot, to plod toward the grocery store on foot, to meet his victims face to face.

He needed it to be personal, needed to feel it.

He didn't know why.

He remembered hearing a boxing announcer once mention

that during the truly great fights, it was an honor to get spattered with a little of the fighters' blood while sitting ringside. Even as entertainment, violence was sacred somehow, the blood itself made precious. Almost religious. That. He needed to be close enough to feel *that.*

As he drew up next to the cars parked toward the back of the lot, his perspective shifted. The people in motion before him became individuals, no longer moving pieces of an abstract whole.

A fat man with sunburned cheeks checked that his Volvo was locked and then fished something out of his pocket and dropped it into the partially opened sun roof.

A woman with freckled shoulders protruding from her tank top wrangled two toddlers into the child seat of a shopping cart.

A young couple held hands as they moved into the automatic door. They looked so much more fit than everyone else. Lean and taut. Time and gravity hadn't yet pulled their bodies into saggy wads of flab. Maybe it never would.

Moments ago they'd been distant. Indistinct. Almost like ants in an ant farm. Now they were real live human beings with lives and families and faces that expressed great depths of emotion with the faintest change in the wrinkles around their eyes.

He kept his pace. Swallowed. A spaghetti taste lingered at the back of his tongue, acidic and sour. His throat contracted again, an attempt to flush it, but no amount of swallowed spittle could wash it away.

And his eyes darted to a college-aged kid in a wife beater and powder blue mesh shorts. Skinny and pale and heading this way. He drank Powerade, neon yellow fluid glugging around in the bottle when he tipped it. It looked like he'd been playing basketball. An early morning practice or something. Maybe that was true. Maybe not. It didn't matter anymore.

The kid was about to get…

He grasped after a word, mentally flicking past the usual choices in his vocabulary for something appropriately exotic to match the drama of the occasion.

Smoked.

The kid was about to get fucking smoked.

Icy fingers plucked his t-shirt out of the way, and he drew the gun from his belt as he closed the last few paces. His nerves steadied as soon as he felt the grip in his palm. All fear, all anxiety, all shakiness fled his body at once, replaced by a calm, a coldness.

Power. He felt powerful.

He didn't hesitate.

He lifted the gun and pulled the trigger, the crack loud enough to make it feel like his ear drums had imploded.

He could tell by feel that he'd let the muzzle drift high, and this sense was verified when the window of the grocery store shattered in the distance, white lines carving the safety glass into little shards. His recoiling ear drums could just make out the tinkle of the window coming apart, the sound so small and somehow musical.

He steadied himself to fire again.

In this fraction of a second, the kid in the mesh shorts jumped a little, arms folding in front of himself out of instinct. But he didn't have time to think, let alone run.

The second shot put a neat hole in his forehead and a big sloppy one where the brain sludge exited the back of his skull. The propulsion of the exit wound snapped the head forward, and the limp body followed the momentum, smacking the ground face first.

Powerade spread over the blacktop like a piss puddle.

He blinked and moved on, back straightening a little, pushing him up a little taller. The electricity surged in his skull, arcing brighter and brighter. The sizzle intensified in the wet of his eyes.

He closed on a cowering old man crouched between a pair of mini-vans. He was black with a hunched back and one of those cabbie hats, the trembling palms of his hands obscuring most of his face. Good. He wanted diversity. Wanted his work to represent the chaos of absolute hatred, no bullshit political message. No lines drawn based on race or class or creed.

Kill 'em all.

The Glock lifted again, and it strained against his arm, jerked in his palm, and two shots put the man down. One in the head and one in the chest. He was dead before he landed from the looks of it. Face all blank and slack.

And he could feel the way the hate contorted his own face beneath the mask, the way it wrinkled his nose and snarled his lip, the way the heat of it seethed in his cheeks. But inside he felt only the power, the animal satisfaction of dominating this scene, this swath of land, mounting it and gouging away, just gouging the fuck away. And lusting after more and more and more.

The people in the lot screamed now, little feminine mews and moans all around him. They responded like puppets to his every move, to his every whim. Some ran for the store, but many froze like frightened rabbits, twitching in unison whenever he took a step or turned his head.

Total power. Total control.

The tall man strode over the concrete land, and the lesser beings cowered in his presence, waiting their turn to die.

Levi Foley.

They would know his name after this. The whole world would know his name. Soon.

He fired wildly into a cluster of sedans ahead and to the left, having sensed movement there. People cowered in some of the vehicles, he knew. And based on the fresh screams, he also knew he'd punched new holes in a few of them.

He paused there a moment, jammed a fresh clip into the gun and pressed forward again.

A woman was next. Judging by the streaks of gray in her hair, she was probably about his mother's age. He didn't wait to get within arm's reach this time, gunning her down from a distance, watching the floppy body topple to the ground in a heap, maintaining his slow but steady momentum toward the storefront with the broken out front window.

He'd need to turn soon, to walk the well-planned route of his escape, but not yet. One more.

This was it. The fantasy made real. The power he'd dreamed of for all of those years. The release of a lifetime of pent up aggression. They'd talked about it so many times. Dreamed about it so many times.

It felt good.

A blur took shape in the corner of his eye, but he didn't get a chance to turn his head that way before something struck him about waist high. Hard.

His feet kicked out from under him, shoes scuffing a little before lifting off. And he hovered, his body made weightless in this slow motion moment. Some dark object latched onto his middle.

His vision tipped skyward. Pointed him toward the indifferent blue stretched out above. Wisped with clouds.

He looked down to see the greasy head of blond hair tucked under his arm. And it occurred to him that he was being tackled, though he couldn't quite believe it. That wasn't possible, was it?

A hero.

The ground rushed up to throttle him, his brain rattling around in his skull, cutting his vision out to black for an instant and fading it back in. And then an emptiness filled his torso, a feeling like the walls of his chest had contracted, his lungs rendered concave and motionless, his rib cage unable to expand to draw wind. In a way, he thought the only thing that kept him from getting knocked out was the intense pain of biting his lip upon landing. The blood pooled in his mouth, salty and warm.

The greasy-haired hero drove his legs into Levi's impact with the ground, adding a little torque. Probably a wrestler or football player. Some daring athlete here to save the day.

Well, his brains would splatter the same as all the rest.

It wasn't until he went to pull the trigger that he realized the gun had skittered away from him when he landed.

His shoulder blades scraped against the ground, and all of that power vacated his being as though sucked out by the asphalt. That animal swell of alpha pride he'd been drunk on drained rapidly. It left him small and vulnerable.

The football player squirmed against him, a lean and hard muscle cinched around him like a boa constrictor. The hair obscured the face. Gave the eerie impression that the thing attacking him wasn't human.

He tried to scramble back, hands and legs pistoning in a crab walk, but every motion seemed only to tighten that sinewy grip of the thing adhering to him.

Time slowed and slowed as they writhed in this hateful

embrace. The seconds fragmented into minutes.

Levi never saw the punch. It came from nowhere and cracked him in the crook of the jaw, snapped his head to the side and knocked the props of his arms out from under him, laying him out flat once more. His vision dimmed, smudged black along the edges, and his thoughts got slow and distant, his consciousness retracting into its shell some. It didn't quite put his lights out, but damn near.

In that dazed moment, eyelids fluttering, he saw it.

The gun. It lay directly beneath the gas tank of a Mazda, shrouded in the shade there. It was ten feet from him. Maybe more. He'd never be able to reach it.

Nausea welled in his gut at the sight of it. Jesus. He was on the bottom in this fight, getting bullied — getting his ass kicked — by what looked like a high school kid. He'd gone from the predator to the prey. This would be his legacy.

Another punch glanced off the side of his head, the near miss actually sharpening his senses some. Time to fight or die.

His hands scrambled out of instinct, finding the football player's forearms and clenching. His grip should be enough to at least slow any more punches.

The kid sat up, trying to pull back enough to wrench his arms free, and his face came into view. The sparse stubble confirmed it. He couldn't be eighteen, even.

Levi rocked forward, bashing his forehead into the kid's nose as hard as he could.

The blood seemed to appear there all at once. Gushing red. Strangely thick. It spread over the kid's fingers when he brought them up to cover the wound.

And the hero's resolve seeped out of him. His grip loosened, and he scrambled back, hands and knees scuffing over the parking lot in a hasty retreat.

Levi tottered to his feet and moved. He found his legs a little wobbly from the tackle and headbutt, but he leaned into the dizziness and jogged.

As soon as he got around the corner of the building, he ripped off the ski mask and jacket and dumped them in the trash can there.

With the disguise gone, he slowed, no longer jogging. He walked those last few paces to the car, taking even steps. He had to force his legs to keep the slower rhythm, the nonchalant beat.

He couldn't breathe, chest all tight and clammy. His mind fumbled for something routine he might be doing, some fantasy he could concentrate on to try to keep calm. He imagined he was some dad who had run in to grab some baby formula and had to get back to the little one. He even tucked his arm up against himself as though he were toting the can of powdered, artificial breast milk.

And then his hand reached out, found the door handle, opened it. He slid into the Focus, started it, hitched in one noisy breath.

Someone could have seen, but he didn't think so.

As he drove away, his eyes danced from the rear view to the driver's side mirror, waiting for the twirling police lights to appear in one or the other, sure the cops would come ripping out of nowhere and grab him the way the football player had.

Nothing happened, though. All the traffic around him behaved itself, acted like it was any other day.

Six blocks later, he ditched the beat up Focus in the parking lot of an abandoned gas station and climbed into his Jeep, which was parked in the East Coast Subs lot next door.

The vehicle switch seemed to ease that tightness in his chest some. He took a few deep breaths. He'd gotten away. He even smiled at himself in the mirror, but his teeth were all covered in blood.

CHAPTER 5

Her luck held, in that she was able to sleep for most of the first leg of her flight, and she made her connection in Minneapolis. Barely. She sent Loshak a text from the tarmac, giving him her flight details and time of arrival.

She slept a little more on the way to Atlanta, but she was keyed up now. She'd had a chance to look into the sniper reports before the plane took off, and her head was filled with unanswered questions. Questions that rattled around until the plane finally touched down a few hours later.

The morning was bright and warm as Darger disembarked in the Peach State and headed for the luggage claim. The saccharine smell of cinnamon goo and frosting wafted from one of the food stalls she passed, and her stomach rumbled. She hadn't eaten for hours. It was tempting to stop, to dive headfirst into a cinnamon roll the size of a bowling ball, but she wanted to get her bags and meet up with Loshak as soon as possible.

When she reached the baggage area, the crowd seemed agitated. As she wove between the clusters of her fellow travelers and picked up bits and pieces of their conversation, she realized it should have been obvious why.

"Guy's a fucking coward, you ask me," Darger overheard one man saying. He was a bulky man in a rumpled, travel-worn suit, who stood with his spine ramrod straight and his chest puffed out like a strutting rooster.

"Who is?" the man next to him asked. He had a slighter build and kept reaching up to fiddle with the knot in his tie.

"Fuckin' sniper. Jesus, haven't you been watching the news?"

"Oh yeah," the fidgeter said. "Right. I just-"

"I mean, if he's any kind of man, he wouldn't be skulking around in the shadows. Pickin' off random folk as they drive home from work? Coward."

The smaller man tugged at the neck of his shirt.

"Right. I guess so."

The words were barely out of his mouth when the rant continued.

"Even the goddamned jihadists are at least willing to die for their cause. But this guy? He doesn't have the stones. He's a pussy."

The fidgeter, sensing now that he was being talked *at* and not *to*, didn't bother responding this time.

"You want a fight? I'll give you a fight, brother. Man to man. But no. He's after innocent civilians, doing nothing but going about their daily business. It's fucking sad. And you know what? I guarantee you something. In the end, we're going to find out that this guy is a loser. Bitter at the world for his own shortcomings. Too gutless to just do us all a favor and off himself. No, he's gotta take us all down with him."

His companion cleared his throat, perhaps relieved that the diatribe had seemingly come to an end.

"Fucking coward," the bigger man muttered one last time before falling silent.

The group shifted and murmured, and Darger thought she could feel their restlessness infecting her like something contagious. Like the grooming behavior in a group of monkeys. *The flock is nervous, so I should be too.*

She swallowed and stood straight, resisting the impulse to fidget or check her watch. Finally, the soft babble of voices was interrupted by the shrill cry of an alarm, warning that the rotating conveyor belt was about to start moving. A mechanical whir filled the air as the luggage carousel started up, and the first bag soon slid through the gray flaps over the small door at one end.

Darger waited, keeping an eye out for the length of bright orange yarn she kept tied to the handle of her bag to distinguish it from the rest of the small black suitcases. She fought the tide of anxiety that rose each time a black bag trundled by that was not hers. It was here. She had to be patient.

The herd thinned, finding their luggage and moving on to greener pastures. Only a handful of bags remained in the rotation now. She couldn't hold back the flood any longer. Dear God, what if her bag was lost, and she was stuck in this ghastly dress for eternity?

She felt herself beginning to plunge into a pit of desperation when she saw it glide through the plastic flaps and join the rest of the circling bags. As she stooped to grab it, someone called her name.

"Darger!"

She turned to see Loshak crossing the terrazzo floor, his mouth set in a grim line. He looked stressed.

"You got your bags. Good. Got a car waiting upstairs. Let's roll," he said and took off in the direction he'd come.

Darger extended the handle on her suitcase and hurried after him. She caught up at the escalator.

"I don't know what you have planned, but I'd like a chance to stop in at the hotel-"

He cut her off.

"No time. And I hope for your sake that you got some sleep on the plane."

The same grave expression was still on his face, but this time she saw something else as well. A sharpness in his eye. He was on high alert.

"Why? What's going on?"

His chest rose and fell with a sigh.

"There's been another shooting."

At the top of the escalator, they stepped off and headed for a set of automatic doors. The doors whooshed open and the balmy Georgia air wasted no time introducing itself. The humidity was so thick she felt like she was swimming through it. Darger reached down and undid her coat, and she caught a wayward glance from Loshak.

"What?"

He shook his head.

"Nothing," he said. He blinked a few times and then added, "I was only wondering where your date was, is all."

"My date?"

There was a strained expression on his face as he said, "For the prom."

The tense set of his mouth loosened a little, and then she heard the unmistakable hiss of Loshak's laugh.

"Hysterical," she said.

This elicited another round of wheezing laughter.

"It's perfect. Just what I wanted, really," Darger continued. "To show up at a crime scene dressed like a blob of mint toothpaste."

Loshak's chuckles subsided, and he eyed her as they approached a large black SUV. The engine was idling, and Darger could see two silhouettes occupying the front seats.

"Don't sell yourself short, Darger. You look more like a… pistachio cupcake."

"That reminds me," she said, reaching for one of the jacket pockets. "I got something for you in Colorado."

She removed her hand from the pocket and flipped Loshak the bird. He responded with an impish wink, then helped her load her suitcase into the back of the Chevy Suburban.

Inside the vehicle, Darger assessed their party. The man in the driver's seat wore a black suit and a plain gray tie. The top half of his face was obscured by a pair of sunglasses, but beneath that she saw a strong jaw and a square chin. His hair was dark and cropped close to his head. He did not smile. She figured him for about her age, early thirties.

In the passenger seat sat a black woman in a nylon FBI jacket. She was older than the man, probably in her mid-forties, with a smattering of freckles dotting her cheeks and forehead. When she turned to extend a hand to Darger, dozens of braids swung about her shoulders like a curtain.

"I'm Karla Dawson from the Atlanta field office," the woman said. "And this is my partner, Ethan Baxter."

The man regarded her from the rear view mirror, nodding once. He did not turn to shake Darger's hand.

So much for southern hospitality.

"We're glad to have you joining the team," Agent Dawson said, probably trying to make up for her partner's aloofness.

The man's hands tightened their grip on the steering wheel. A tell, perhaps, that he didn't agree with Dawson. There was definitely a strained feeling in the cabin.

Darger tried to lighten things with a joke.

"Does he ever shut up?" she asked, aiming a thumb at the silent driver.

After a beat, Agent Dawson let out a deep, resonant laugh. Baxter didn't so much as smirk. And while Darger couldn't see his eyes, she swore she felt him glaring at her from behind the shaded lenses. Not much of a sense of humor either, it seemed. Something about his whole demeanor reminded her of a bratty six-year-old being forced to share his toys with another child.

Whatever his problem was, she didn't have time to worry about it. She reached for her seatbelt and buckled it across her chest.

Satisfied that all passengers were secured, Agent Baxter guided the Suburban down through the spiraling levels of the parking structure.

Darger cleared her throat and spoke up.

"So what do we have?"

"A clusterfuck of epic proportions," Loshak said, running a hand through his gray-blond hair.

Agent Dawson gave her a quick summary, swiveling in her seat so she could make eye contact with Darger as she spoke.

"There are fourteen victims from yesterday evening's attack. Eight dead, last we heard. Several of the wounded were not out of the woods as of this morning. The crime scene spans almost a mile of freeway. Once he started shooting, there were multiple chain-reaction crashes. So on top of the shooting, we have a massive pile-up on one of the busiest stretches of highway in the country."

The ticket booth drew near. Rolling down the window, Agent Baxter flashed his ID at the attendant. The yellow arm of the gate rose, and then they were sailing out of the artificial midnight of the parking garage and into the blinding light of day.

Loshak took a breath and picked up where Agent Dawson left off. "That brings us to this morning. Guy unloads in the parking lot of a busy supermarket. Stalking from car to car, shooting at anyone and everyone he comes across."

"Jesus. How many?"

"Three killed, five wounded. Would have been worse, but a good Samaritan jumped him."

"No shit?"

"Yeah, a seventeen-year-old kid, actually. Honorable Mention All-District Strong Safety." Seeing the glazed look in Darger's eye, Loshak added, "Football. Got in a few good punches from the sound of it. And wrestled the gun away from him."

"We got his gun?"

"One of them, anyway. I imagine he's the type to keep quite a collection."

"Description?" she asked.

Agent Dawson shook her head. "He was wearing a ski mask, so we only got enough to say average build, probably white."

Darger noted then that Agent Baxter had yet to utter a word. She didn't know why, but the whole too-cool-for-school routine was starting to irk her.

Get a grip, Violet, she thought to herself. You have a job to do.

But she had a feeling that Agent Baxter was going to end up being a real pain in her ass.

CHAPTER 6

The sheet covering the woman's body had been solid white once. Not anymore. Now it was awash with red. One of the bottom corners hung into the pool of congealing blood. Through osmosis, the crimson stain spread upward, wicking through the white threads, the fabric soaking it up.

Darger couldn't stop staring at it. The shade of red changed the further it got from the source, growing lighter, fainter.

A pair of feet clad in white canvas sneakers poked out from under the sheet. The woman was sprawled in an awkward position with the upper half of her body slumped in the backseat of her Honda Fit, like she'd tried to crawl inside after being shot.

Two crime scene techs bustled by, carrying a measuring tape. The parking lot was flooded with first responders — two fire engines, three ambulances, and easily twenty police cars, not to mention FBI, ATF, and a task force from Homeland Security.

Overhead, she could hear news choppers hovering.

The medical examiner was running through the list of injuries sustained by the victim, but Darger could barely hear him. He murmured clinical terms like "severed aorta" and "hypovolemic shock." Words that right now, in the midst of all the carnage, were meaningless to her.

Her mind was clouded with her own thoughts. She imagined the people going about their day. This woman, coming to get eggs and milk and bread. That man, coming to pick up a prescription from the pharmacy. Had the killer watched them before he started? Did he stand in the shadows, waiting for the perfect moment to strike? Did he set his sights on someone in particular? A carefully chosen victim? Or did he stride up without hesitation and just… begin the massacre?

Massacre. The word echoed in her mind. There was no other word to describe what happened here.

The scene left her speechless. How could anyone do this?

She felt a rising anger in her chest. That someone would get enjoyment from this destruction. This chaos.

And now she understood the man at the airport. The one ranting in the baggage claim about how unmanly the shooter was. He was angry. Angry at the wrongness of it all. Angry at the fear he felt in his own heart.

Her eyes roved over the cars parked in the lot. She picked a vehicle that seemed right. A dark green GMC Yukon with a patch of rust emanating from below the gas cap. That would do. And then Violet began to picture it as if she were the killer. Sitting in the driver's seat. Parked off to one side, partially obscured by a canopy of crabapple trees. Surveying the lot. Waiting for a moment of peak activity. Maximum impact. Highest fatalities.

In her lap, a semi-automatic handgun. She lifted the pistol, ejected the magazine, and double-checked that it was full. She knew it was, but couldn't resist confirming one last time. It was part of the ritual. And besides, she liked the feel of a gun in her hand. The cold, hard sound each movement elicited. *Snick, scrape, clack.* Metal on metal.

Satisfied, she reinserted the magazine and gave the gun a tap against her palm. She disengaged the safety and racked the slide. Her heart rate was accelerating now. It was time. She could smell it in the air like the ozone before a thunderstorm.

Only one final preparation. She reached over to the

passenger seat and grabbed the black ski mask. She stretched it over her head, adjusting so that her eyes lined up with the holes properly. A cursory glance in the rear view mirror confirmed what she already knew: she was ready.

Her hand found the door handle without fumbling. The door peeled open. She swung one leg down and then the other, boot heels hitting the pavement with barely a sound. Her motions were fluid. Certain. She felt a sort of electric charge running through her now, as if she were a machine on autopilot, each move perfectly balanced.

She held the pistol at her side, finger already on the trigger. Ready to strike. But first, she needed to get closer. Wanted to get closer. That's what this morning was all about.

Movement to her right caught her eye. A gangly kid in a white tank top and athletic shorts, chugging from a bottle of sports drink. He would be the first.

Darger stalked between cars, her footsteps confident, her path clear. The kid was ten yards away, then five. The gap closed. The kid didn't even look up from his phone to peer at the shadow that fell over him. The darkness that had come to blot out the sun.

Darger did not speak. She simply raised her right arm and fired. The bullet missed and shattered the front window of the store, the surge of adrenaline coursing through her causing her aim to go a little high.

The kid barely had time to react. His eyebrows came up and then his face was blown open by the second bullet, flesh and bone exploding into a spray. His body went limp and collapsed forward, liquid glugging from the Powerade bottle as it hit the ground. He was dead before he'd even had a chance to wonder at what was happening

With the sound of the gunshot, the atmosphere of the parking lot changed. Most people screamed and ran. Others froze, searching for the source of the sound, unsure of what they had heard.

An elderly man saw her coming, opened his mouth as if to protest when her hand came up, but he was silenced by two bullets. One to the chest and the other to his neck.

She emptied the rest of the clip without really aiming at anything or anyone in particular. She didn't really need to. There were so many people in the lot, she was guaranteed a few hits. *Boom, boom, boom, boom.* Reload.

The last target was a woman, early fifties, loading groceries into her Honda. The sunlight hit the part in her hair, illuminating a speckle of gray hairs where her roots were growing in. It lit her head like a beacon. Like a lighthouse shining above the sea.

Before she could pull the trigger, someone bumped against her, and Darger blinked twice, snapping out of it.

Loshak drew his sunglasses down and studied her for a moment.

Before he could ask, she said, "I'm alright."

His head bobbed once, and he moved on.

Her thoughts wrenched free from the spell that had come over her. Time to change perspectives.

Her gaze lifted to take in the scene as a whole. The neat grid of parked cars. The endless rows of glass and chrome and metallic finishes glinting in the morning sun. The heat distortion rippling off the asphalt. The smell of fried food coming from the Wendy's across the way.

The end result was the same, and yet this felt much different than a serial killer. Why? Was it the fact that the murders were done in the open? For the world to see? Plenty of serial killers coveted the attention their crimes received, but this was something else.

Glancing back at the small crowd, she thought she detected something different even with the reporters. They looked… grim. She thought back to wading through the news vans and cameramen during the mess in Ohio, during their hunt for the Doll Parts Killer. The media folk she'd crossed paths with then had an almost hungry gleam in their eyes. A desperation to get their own piece of the action. Not so with the crews out today.

Scared. That's what it was. They seemed scared.

And there weren't many civilian gawkers, she noticed. A serial killer drew them like flies, but this guy repelled them.

Everyone felt like they could be next. Even she felt it. The vulnerability of being out in the open. Like he could be watching.

He probably would have been, too, had he not been attacked by the good Samaritan. He would have fled after that altercation. Gone back to whatever hidey-hole he was currently calling home.

What would his home be like? The first thing that popped into her head was a run-down trailer in the middle of nowhere. A "No Trespassing" sign nailed to every tree and fence post. A fence, yes. And a gate. He'd drive a rusty pick-up truck with a Confederate flag bumper sticker.

Careful, she thought, stopping herself. She was letting anger cloud her assessment. Letting her bias against the crime lead her down a road full of clichés.

After all, he was probably just like her. Just like most people. Working or middle class. Late twenties to middle thirties. He probably lived in a clean apartment with white walls and beige carpet and drove a mid-sized sedan. An office job. The picture of American mediocrity.

That's what he was so pissed off about, wasn't it? How meaningless his life felt. How boring and pointless.

He'd probably picked the supermarket on purpose. First, people often shopped near their homes, in their own neighborhoods. It was within their inner circle. Familiar. Safe. On an animal level, it was where they got food. Sustenance. Like a watering hole on the African plains.

Damn. There she was, thinking Leonard Stump thoughts again.

Except it was true, wasn't it?

Here was the herd of zebra, approaching the oasis. And somewhere in the long grass, a predator stalked.

But at least the lion and the jaguar killed to eat. It was survival.

She wouldn't be surprised if he fancied himself some kind of kin to a big cat or a wolf. But this man killed for sport. For vengeance. It was anger. Desperation. He wanted the world to hurt.

There was nothing animal about that, Darger thought. That was pure human.

CHAPTER 7

Loshak gestured at her from the shade of an awning, and Darger crossed the way to meet him.

"Any initial thoughts?" he asked.

"I think you had it right when you called it a clusterfuck of epic proportions."

He nodded, a half-smile playing on his mouth even if his eyes looked grave.

It was then that Darger noticed Agents Baxter and Dawson standing a few yards away. They were having what looked to be a heated discussion. A lot of hand-waving and head-shaking.

"What do you think that's all about?" Darger asked with the barest tick of her head.

Loshak scratched at his temple.

"I'm sure you've already sensed that we're not exactly wanted here, if you know what I mean."

"You mean Agent Bastard over there?" She'd come up with the nickname on the ride over, in between being 100% focused on the job at hand. "What's his deal anyway? Did you take a dump in his All-Bran or something?"

"All-Bran?"

Darger scrunched her shoulders into a shrug. "Seems like the kind of guy that would eat something boring like that for breakfast. Every day. Plus, it could be that his sour disposition is a result of constipation. The extra fiber would do him good."

Loshak plucked his sunglasses from his shirt collar and slid them over his eyes.

"Whatever his problem is, you've seen enough of it by now.

Delicate egos. Territorial BS. FBI politics. The usual nonsense."

When Darger looked up again, Agent Dawson was approaching. Baxter followed behind, looking like he'd been sucking on a lemon.

Loshak was right. She *had* seen enough of it. She'd seen so much that she was getting a little sick of it now. Never mind that they were always ready to drop everything to fly out wherever they might be needed. They were all supposed to be working together.

Darger filled her lungs, counted to three, and let out the breath. She needed to focus. Agent Baxter's shitty attitude was *his* problem. Not hers.

"I had a question for you, if that's alright?" Agent Dawson said, resting her hands on her hips.

Agent Baxter stayed a couple steps behind his partner, not quite willing to join their little huddle. Even so, he emitted a sigh loud enough for all to hear. The set of his mouth gave him the appearance of seeming perpetually unimpressed with everyone and everything in his surroundings.

"Ask away," Loshak said.

"Is it unusual for him to change tactics like this? To go from sniping to shooting up close? It seems like an awfully big shift," Agent Dawson said.

Loshak removed his sunglasses and pinched the bridge of his nose.

"I don't know if I'd call it unusual. Nothing about this type of crime is *usual.* I'd use the term 'unique.' The shift to face-to-face violence suggests an emotional escalation. He's like a rage addict. The same dose won't do it for him the second time around. The frantic beating of his own heart as he crouched on that hilltop wasn't enough. He wants to see the terror in their faces as he pulls the trigger. Wants to revel in the destruction up close and personal," he finished, replacing his sunglasses on his face.

"Well," Agent Dawson said, taking a moment to find the words. "That's a comforting thought. Will he keep escalating?"

Darger and Loshak exchanged a glance. They both nodded.

"These guys… they tend to keep going until they get caught. I think a good lot of them are hoping for suicide-by-cop. Though this guy apparently wants to drag it out. Inflict the maximum amount of destruction," Darger said.

"What about the kid that tried to stop him? Any chance that'll give him second thoughts? Change his mind about continuing on with his plan, I mean?"

Loshak took that in for a moment before answering.

"Maybe. But I doubt it. He might get more cautious for a few days. Lay low. But the rage in this guy, it's not liable to burn itself out. If anything, he might be emboldened by the fact that he made it through the conflict. Proved his mettle and all that. We're talking about someone who will be very difficult to catch, very difficult to stop. And he will only push the scale of these attacks to something grander, something even more dramatic. You think he seems dangerous now? Think bigger."

Agent Dawson turned back to the parking lot and extended her arm toward the scene.

"How do you get bigger than this?"

Loshak had a fist to his mouth. Darger knew what he was thinking, but she got the impression he didn't want to be the one to say it.

She licked her lips. Cleared her throat.

"A big public event. Or kids. Or both," she said.

"Excuse me?"

Darger could see in Agent Dawson's face that she was horrified at the suggestion.

"He'll probably contact us or the media and threaten us first. With a note. Or an anonymous call. He'll say he's going to target a large sporting event or a concert, blow up a hospital, take a school bus hostage. Something like that."

"Why would he contact us first? So we try to stop him and kill him in the process? Suicide-by-cop, like you said before?"

"It's the same reason he's doing all of this," Loshak said. "Because our collective fear makes him feel in control. The threats and the violence are the way he reassures himself that he has power, and we — the general public, all of us — are the props he needs to actualize this control fantasy. It's not real for him until he can watch us squirm."

Agent Baxter's voice cut in.

"This is all based on the pattern of the guys in DC?"

"Pardon?" Loshak said.

"Isn't that what the DC snipers did? Left notes? Threatened to kill kids?"

Loshak sniffed.

"They did. But this profile isn't based purely on that one case."

"No? You might as well be quoting from the case file to me. And I can guess where the profile will go from here. You'll say he's a fringe anti-government type, radicalized by his military history. Because war turns us all into psychotics, right?"

Darger was a little surprised at how calm Agent Baxter looked throughout his rant. Given the amount of venom he was spouting, she would have expected at least a touch of foaming at the mouth. But his face remained as placid and unimpressed with the world as ever.

Darger's attention flicked over to Loshak, curious to see how he'd handle this. His eyes narrowed, but they were more inquisitive than threatening.

"Look, we're not here to take anything from anyone. We're all on the same team."

"Like the way things went down in Ohio last fall?"

Agent Dawson tried to cut in, her voice a warning tone. "Ethan."

"I'm not sure what you mean by that," Loshak said, and now Darger thought she detected a note of anger.

"I've seen the press, the feature in *Vanity Fair*," Baxter said, forming the words as if they had a bad taste.

Darger felt the hair on the back of her neck prickle. The article about *her*, that's what he was talking about. Practically sneering. Was that why he'd been such a dickhead since they'd arrived? Jealousy and resentment? Fear that she and Loshak would get all the credit?

"It's not hard to figure out how your unit operates," Baxter continued. "If you get it wrong, you're nowhere to be found. On to the next city to spout your theories while we get left behind picking up after you. If things work out, you guys are there at center stage, taking your bow, doing photo shoots for glossy magazines."

"Look, if you're that worried about getting your fucking picture in a magazine, I suggest you go see a modeling agent," Darger said, practically lunging toward him.

Before Baxter could say anything in response, Loshak was pulling her back by the forearm.

"Violet, hey," he said, "let it go."

She was still locked on Agent Baxter as Loshak dragged her away. She shook free from his grip and stalked off to be alone. It wasn't until she'd taken a few steps that she realized she was shaking.

Arrogant prick, she thought, squeezing her hands into fists.

Everywhere they went, it was just more bureaucratic baloney. More pissing contests. How had Loshak put up with it all these years?

Her foot crunched through some of the glass from the shattered front window of the supermarket, and she turned to stomp back the way she'd come. When she whirled around, Loshak was there.

"That was bullshit," she said, not waiting for him to speak. Her voice wavered with emotion. "Neither one of us was even on the DC sniper case."

"Forget it. It's not about that anyway," Loshak said, smoothing the sides of his hair. "I swear to Christ it's contagious."

"What is?"

"The chaos that comes from a crime like this. Stirs everything up," he said.

Loshak turned to scan the horizon, one arm crossed over his chest, the other hand clenched into a fist and pressed to his mouth.

"You think he's watching?" she asked.

"Had things not gone awry with that football player, I'd put money on it. But I think that probably spooked him enough to duck and cover. For a little while at least."

He waved a hand indicating that she should follow.

"If you're ready to go, Agent Dawson offered to drop us off at our hotel."

Darger nodded, hoping that meant Agent Baxter wouldn't be along for the ride. She wasn't sure she'd be able to resist punching him in that big movie star chin of his.

Loshak was right again. It was going to be one of those trips.

CHAPTER 8

The adrenaline waned in time, the numbness of the shock faded, and the humiliation settled over him in waves. Embarrassment. Shame.

The Jeep weaved through the traffic, its movements restless, agitated. There was nowhere to go, he knew, but he hurried to get there nevertheless. He drove on as the day wore into the afternoon, winding his way around the city, licking his wounds.

He tongued the jagged split in his lip, still tasting the salty blood there. The wound had ceased bleeding from what he could tell, his gum line no longer ringed in red when he bared his teeth in the mirror, but it still stung to lick and jab and prod at the torn flesh like he did.

Maybe that was why he couldn't stop.

The pain. That sharp tendril snaking its way into his chin and cheek with every movement. It felt right somehow. The hurt inside brought out into the real world and injected into the lining of his mouth, made corporeal, made concrete.

The Glock-18c had been a holy grail of sorts — a fully automatic version of the gun that was technically illegal for civilians to buy or own. Luke had been the one who told him about it, way back before any of this started, before either of them had even fired a gun, and it had become something of an obsession for the two of them.

The Jeep stalked up to a red light and waited. Waited. He watched an overweight woman in the Volkswagen Jetta alongside him, her eyeliner smeared, her mouth working, jaw chawing endlessly like a grasshopper's. Even through the glass, he could almost hear the gum smacking.

How could he let it happen? Some kid plastering him like that? Disarming him. Flinging him to the ground like a rag doll and grinding him into the pavement. A goddamned kid.

He ground his teeth a moment, and then went back to flicking his tongue over the gash in his lip.

Losing that gun of all guns. The rage welled in him when he pictured it there, nestled under the gas tank of the Mazda.

Forever out of reach.

He still remembered the day they got it. They were so excited. Like kids. They couldn't resist. They fired a few rounds in the backyard just to feel it. He shot through a bush at the back of the yard, the bullet disappearing into the empty lot beyond. Luke thought that was particularly hilarious. Just shooting a bush.

When it was his turn, Luke set an empty Dr. Pepper can on the picnic table and fired, the exit wound curling shards of the metal outward, a little explosion preserved in aluminum.

It was the first time either of them had fired a gun outside of the range, and it got Levi's heart banging pretty good. Loud as fuck, too, of course, so they scrambled inside right away out of fear of a neighbor calling it in.

But they had something now. Something that could do real damage.

They had power. Real power. For the first time. Power made all the more alluring by the fact that the gun was illegal, undocumented, obtained through back channels.

Some part of him wanted to go back for it, wanted to at least drive by on the very slight chance that the police had overlooked it, but no. It was hopeless and far too risky. He'd lost it.

The light flicked to green, and the Jetta throbbed to life next to him. The overweight grasshopper woman sped away, veering off to the left. His Jeep lurched forward a beat after she was gone.

He couldn't be sentimental about the gun, about any of this. In a way, he should consider himself lucky, shouldn't he? That kid came close to ending it right there in the parking lot — damn close — but Levi had found his way out of it. He was still here, still going, and one gun made no difference one way or the other.

The plan could still go on, could go bigger and bigger still. He could move on. Move forward. It's what Luke would want.

Again a red light made him wait, made him restless. He watched an ugly couple sing along with their stereo, tilting their fat heads in unison, smiling a little at each other. He wished he could brandish the sawed-off shotgun right here and now. Just roll down his window as if to ask for Grey Poupon and open fire. He licked his lips at the thought, palms and fingertips itching for the feel of the weapon, the jerk and throttling vibration as it blew the ugly people away. All of them, preferably. All of the ugly, stupid people all around him.

When the traffic got moving again, the fire inside died back if only a little.

He drove on, replaying the events in the parking lot in his head over and over again, steeling himself for what would come next — what would have to come next.

He was pretty sure of what he'd do, even if thinking about it made him sick.

CHAPTER 9

Agent Dawson eased the Suburban up in front of the hotel entrance.

"I'd like to apologize on behalf of Ethan. He was part of a sniper team in the Marines, so I think he's taking this all a little personally. Which is why he probably came off a little… strong-willed."

"I think the word you're looking for is asshole-ish," Darger said and Loshak shot her a withering look from the front seat.

"Let's just drop it," he said.

Darger knew he was right. As usual.

"Apologies, Agent Dawson. I mean no offense to you, of course."

Dawson nodded.

Darger hopped out, eager to be out of the car. Violet caught sight of the frilly hem of her dress as she hauled her suitcase out of the back. And doubly eager to finally be out of the frou-frou gumdrop dress.

"I'll call or text if there are any developments before the meeting," Dawson was saying as Loshak climbed down from the passenger seat.

"Thank you, Agent Dawson," Loshak said. "We'll see you then."

The SUV began to roll down the drive, and Darger set her sights on the hotel lobby. In less than ten minutes, she could be showering — better yet, soaking in a bubble bath — and then putting on fresh clothes in colors that did not belong in an Easter basket.

Loshak tugged at her sleeve.

"Come on, Darger. I'll buy you breakfast."

She planted her feet, resisting. She was still stuck on thoughts of luxuriating in the bath tub.

"It's almost noon. Isn't it a little late for breakfast?"

Loshak hooked a thumb over his shoulder.

"Sign says breakfast all day."

"Well, I'm not really hungry," she said.

Hands on hips, Loshak studied her from behind his ever-present reflective shades.

"Bull. When was the last time you ate?"

Darger looked up and squinted at the glare of the sun.

"Does the little packet of pretzels they gave me on the flight count?"

Loshak scoffed.

"Not on your life."

There was a voice in her head that wanted to argue. Wanted to tell Loshak to quit fussing over her like a mother hen. But she knew that wasn't really what it was. It made sense, getting some food in her. Plus, she hadn't had any coffee this morning. That was likely the main source of the grouchy voice.

"Oh alright," she said and followed Loshak past the hotel entrance and into the restaurant.

Loshak pointed at her with his fork.

"What's up with you?"

Darger didn't look up or stop buttering her toast.

"You mean aside from the bloody massacre we just picked over? Or the part where the lead agent inferred that we're a couple of histrionic hacks?"

After washing down a bite of egg white omelet with a gulp of orange juice, Loshak shook his head.

"Nah, you've been acting squinky since you got off the plane."

"Squinky? Is that your professional diagnosis, Doctor?"

He narrowed his eyes.

"Just trying to figure out if you're all pensive and morose for a reason, or if it's only jet lag."

"I am not pensive and morose."

Shrugging, Loshak reached for a bottle of Tabasco. He uncapped the lid and liberally splatted the red sauce over his plate.

"Why are you so worried about it, anyway? Shouldn't you be using all that profiling brain power in a more productive way? Like, figuring out the best way to catch this guy?"

"Have it your way, Sullen Sally. I'm only trying to help," he said, then wiggled his fingers at his head. "Besides, you gotta let this stuff stew sometimes, you know? Give it a chance to percolate."

Yeah, right, Darger thought. Loshak was like a hound that was supposed to be duck hunting but caught the scent of a skunk and just couldn't resist.

She shoveled a mound of hash browns into her mouth. Chewed. Swallowed.

Then again, he *had* asked. And it *was* bugging her.

"Don't you get sick of being treated like the outsider wherever we go? I feel like every new case is another boulder stuck at the bottom of the hill. We're on one side trying our damnedest to get it up the slope, and the locals are on the other side pushing back the other way."

"Ah. So this *is* about Agent Baxter."

"Not just him. Everyone."

"You against the world. Is that it? You're not the type that has to be liked by everyone, are you?"

"No. Nobody has to like me. But if they aren't going to be productive, then the least they could do is stay the fuck out of my way. *Our* way."

Loshak raised his coffee cup in a sort of toast.

"I do admire your tenacity."

"But?"

"No buts," he said. "Well, maybe a small one. Don't get so fixated on proving people wrong that you forget what the real job is."

"I won't."

"And look, if you're upset about his little dig about the *Vanity Fair* article, don't be. He's probably jealous. I know you didn't really want to do it."

Darger narrowed her eyes across the table.

"You're just trying to butter me up because you ditched me."

"Ditched you?"

"We were *both* supposed to be in that feature, remember?"

He pursed his lips, the picture of innocence.

"Guess they must have decided they didn't need me after all. I'm sure once they interviewed you, they realized they had all they need."

She scoffed.

"You are so full of crap, Loshak. The reporter specifically asked me how to get in touch with you, because you weren't answering your phone or returning her messages."

"Messages? I didn't get any messages."

"Liar."

"What do you want from me? A pound of flesh? A pint of blood? Name it."

Darger squinted at him, then snatched a piece of bacon from his plate.

"This is a start," she said and popped it into her mouth.

Violet stifled a yawn on the elevator ride up to her hotel room.

"You should try to get a little sleep before the meeting," Loshak said. The bastard never missed anything, did he? "I have a feeling we're going to be putting in some long hours on this one."

"Don't have to tell me twice," she answered as they exited the elevator and moved into the hall.

She slid her key card through the scanner. The light turned green, and she heard the click of the door unlocking. Loshak gave a farewell wave before disappearing into his own room down the hall.

Inside, Violet didn't bother to fully unpack. She only unzipped her suitcase to grab her toothbrush, and then she made a beeline for the shower. She felt a palpable sense of relief when she finally slid the bridesmaids dress off. Part of her had started to worry she might never be able to change clothes again.

As the hot water soaked into her hair and onto her scalp and down over her shoulders, it occurred to her that it had felt that way, in part, because these attacks seemed almost apocalyptic in nature. Chaos pushed to the nth degree. Violence and wrath raining down upon them as if from a vengeful god.

But the world wasn't ending. Not yet.

The thought of trying to live out the rest of her days in a post-apocalyptic landscape dressed like a beauty pageant reject made Violet snort, and then the hot water lulled her into a daze for a time.

Fluffed and dried and dressed in fresh clothes, Darger flopped onto her bed. The memory foam squished pleasantly beneath her.

She closed her eyes and saw the red and white of the blood-stained sheet covering the woman from that morning's crime scene. Her eyelids snapped open.

She'd have that image burned into her mind for a good long while.

She sat up, leaning her back against the scratched and pocked MDF headboard. So much for sleep.

Instead, she got her phone and did the same thing she'd done every spare minute for the past week: pored over Leonard Stump's journal.

The remains of the first two Stump victims were found burned in the trunk of the family car, a mother and her teenage daughter. They were tourists, in town for the week at a ski resort in Telluride, Colorado. Presumably, they'd been abducted four days earlier in a parking lot outside of a nearby state park.

This set the pattern for Stump's crimes. Always pairs. Always abducted and held onto for three to four days before the murders were carried out and the bodies burned.

Over the next three years, Stump claimed twelve more victims officially, though speculation among law enforcement put the total as high as 37. Many of the bodies were never found, which made it difficult to be certain.

Of course, he discussed none of these details in his journal. He was, he claimed, an innocent man.

A sharp rap at the door startled her upright and out of her reading. A glance at the clock revealed that she'd been at it for over an hour and a half. Jesus, had she really lost that much time? She scolded herself. She needed to be focused on the active shooter. Not a serial killer from nearly twenty years ago.

The peephole showed an oddly distorted version of Loshak waiting in front of her door. She turned the handle and opened it wide.

"Manage to get any sleep?" he asked, handing her a cup of coffee before breezing past.

"A little," she lied.

She didn't know why, but she didn't want Loshak to know how deep she'd gone into the Stump file. She had a feeling he wouldn't approve. Not just because of the potential distraction from their current work. He would say something like, "We see enough, read enough, hear enough gruesome shit in our work life. You need boundaries or the work will consume you."

As if he would apply that same rule to himself.

"Good," he said and crossed the room to settle into a chair. "Ready to sketch out a profile before we head out?"

She picked up her phone and closed the Stump journal file.

"Ready."

CHAPTER 10

Darger's gaze flitted about the conference room. There were no windows, just the artificial glow of fluorescent lights. Rows of tables were arranged classroom style, all facing the front of the room, and Darger felt a little bit like she was back in one of her agent trainee classes at the Academy. At least the chairs were fairly comfortable, she thought, leaning into the padded backrest.

A flat screen monitor on the wall showed a map of Atlanta with red dots marking the two crime scenes. Assistant Special Agent in Charge, James Fitzgerald, gestured at the screen. He had a hooked nose that ended in a sharp point, a combination that brought to mind a bird's beak. A pair of cold gray eyes peered out from beneath his heavy brow.

Again Darger's eyes flicked to the people sitting around her. She picked out Agent Dawson and Agent Baxter, and from the ID badges affixed to every shirt and jacket in the group, she determined it was only FBI personnel, no police. She frowned and leaned over to Loshak.

"I thought this was a multi-jurisdictional task force. Where's the local PD? ATF? Why is it only us?"

"You got me," Loshak said quietly.

ASAC Fitzgerald continued his briefing from the front of the room.

"Right now we're channeling tips through our standard office lines, but we are setting up a dedicated call center for the shootings. I have been assured that it will be ready to go live first thing tomorrow morning. Local police have their media liaison contacting the TV stations, radio, and newspapers with that information as we speak. Because of the public nature of the attacks, coupled with the fact that we're in a major metropolitan area, we're expecting a high number of calls. To give some perspective, the FBI logged over 15,000 calls with the DC sniper case. Our hope, of course, is that we'll catch these guys before we reach that volume."

Fitzgerald's fierce gaze fixed on her then, and Darger resisted the urge to twitch like a field mouse.

"Agents Loshak and Darger, I'd like you to take the lead on the call center. We'll need to put together a screening process to assign priority to the calls, based on your profile. I understand you have some prior experience in this area."

Loshak nodded assent for the both of them, and Fitzgerald went on.

"Quantico is sending us twelve trainees from the Academy to answer phones and log calls. You'll also have a smaller team of four analysts to help you run through the high priority calls. If you find that you need more bodies or have any special requests, please let me know, and I'll do my best to arrange it."

Loshak cleared his throat.

"I actually have one request right off the bat. There's a particular analyst in DC I'd like to have assigned to our team in addition to those already assigned. His name is Rodney Malenchuck."

Fitzgerald pulled a silver pen from his pocket and took down the name.

"I'll see to it."

After verifying there were no further comments from either her or Loshak, Fitzgerald moved on to the next order of business. Darger watched those hawkish eyes scan back and forth over his notes.

"Local police are pulling security footage from all businesses that share the parking lot with the Publix store, as well as the available traffic cams in a quarter-mile radius. We'll be running plates on all vehicles—"

Loshak raised his hand.

"I don't mean to interrupt, but based on the profile, my suggestion would be to narrow that down to SUVs and pickups, starting from thirty minutes before the attack. If that brings up a goose egg, we can broaden the search."

"Thank you, Agent Loshak. I'll pass that on to Chief Hogaboom," Fitzgerald said and made another note with a flourish of his pen.

"About that," Darger cut in, "where *is* Atlanta PD? Aren't we working together on this?"

Two lines formed in the center of Fitzgerald's sharp brow line.

"We are. But Chief Hogaboom and I have agreed that we'll each issue commands to our own people."

"Right, but in terms of our profile, for example, isn't that something everyone on the task force should hear?" Darger asked.

"As I made clear a moment ago, anything pertinent will be passed on to Atlanta PD."

With a satisfied nod, Fitzgerald prepared to push on to the next order of business. But Darger wasn't done yet.

"I mean no disrespect, sir, but that seems inefficient. And prone to error, in my opinion. A profile changes over time. Plus, the task force should be given the opportunity to ask questions. If we can't offer clarification—"

Fitzgerald held his pen aloft now, as if it were some kind of magical staff or wand that gave him the power to speak above all others.

"I know that you and Agent Loshak are used to running your own show, but that's not how it's going to work here. As I said before, all coordination with the local PD will go through me. Should Chief Hogaboom and I decide at a later juncture that a joint meeting is required, we will revisit the topic at that point."

Darger thought about pressing further, but it was obvious he wasn't interested in hearing her out. She settled back in her seat.

Great. More bullshit.

Fitzgerald's voice droned on.

"Early forensics: We found a black ski mask and jacket dumped in a garbage bin near the Publix."

The screen switched from the map to a picture of the clothing laid out on a white table.

"Trace is going over both with a fine-toothed comb, and I know they've come up with some brown hairs. DNA will take a while, of course, if we can get it."

Now the monitor flipped through a series of evidence photos.

"We've pinpointed the shooter's location from the highway scene. One of the hills to the west that looks down on the overpass. We recovered some shell casings, and the muddy conditions left us with some good tire tracks and tread impressions. We also have a few boot prints. The lab is analyzing those now."

Someone's phone chirped out a ring tone, and Darger noticed Agent Dawson ducking into the hallway to take the call.

"What was he using?" Baxter asked, drawing the room's attention back to Fitzgerald.

"Fifty-caliber BMGs."

Baxter whistled then said, "Talk about overkill."

The door opened and Dawson bustled back in. She signaled to Fitzgerald.

"What do you have, Agent Dawson?"

"That was the ballistics lab," she said. "Ammo from this morning's shooting is Speer Gold Dot. Jacketed hollow points, 124 grain weight. Fairly common among law enforcement, but it's also popular with civilians for self-defense ammo. Obviously, everything is being run through IBIS to determine if either weapon was used in a previous crime. But the real kicker is the gun he was using this morning. The one he dropped in the scuffle."

Darger thought she felt everyone in the room collectively hold their breath.

"He was packing a Glock-18c."

"Well, well," Fitzgerald said. "That *does* make things interesting."

"What's the big deal?" Darger asked.

"The Glock-18 is fully automatic," Baxter explained, then turned to Dawson. "Capable of what? A thousand rounds a minute?"

"Twelve-hundred," she answered. "Only legal for law enforcement, military, and Class III dealers. Though I think we can rule out our guy getting this gun through legitimate means."

"How's that?" Loshak asked.

"Serial numbers were filed off."

"So he stole it," Darger suggested.

After exchanging a knowing look with Dawson, Baxter said, "Or he bought it from someone who stole it."

Loshak brought a hand up to his face and stroked his chin.

"Can I assume that suggestion means you have an idea of where one would acquire such a weapon?"

Before Agent Baxter could answer, Fitzgerald raised his hands in the air like a marching band conductor.

"Let's not go down that rabbit hole just yet. I'd like to hear your profile first."

She and Loshak stood and shuffled to the front of the room. Darger scooted behind the podium. She hated this part. Public speaking was not her forte.

Thankfully, Loshak started.

"Our subject is likely a white male, late twenties, which fits the witness statements from this morning. Works a blue collar job, maybe menial white collar. He's probably been married at least once, possibly has children, but I would expect him to be estranged from his family, which is a major influence on his current behavior. A history of domestic violence wouldn't be surprising."

With the barest bob of his head, Loshak indicated it was her turn.

"He probably has a military history," Darger said.

Though she kept her focus on her notes, she sensed Agent Baxter shifting in his seat. It wasn't her fault if that was part of the profile. It just made sense.

"To narrow the search, especially when cross-checking the license plates from the surveillance footage, look for someone with combat experience. Possibly a sharpshooter, but not necessarily. He may have attempted to join some sort of elite unit but probably would have washed out because of his underlying psych issues — paranoia, resentment of authority figures. Despite that, I'd expect that wherever he wound up, disciplinary problems would have been minor, and he would have been honorably discharged. He's good at smoothing things over when he needs to."

Loshak broke in again.

"He is extremely paranoid and antisocial, especially when it comes to the government and law enforcement. Anyone approaching a suspect should use special caution. He will not hesitate to use deadly force. In fact, he's probably hoping he'll get a chance to. To that end, he'll contact us or the media at some point. He'll want to taunt us, to make the public even more fearful. He'll probably threaten to specifically target children and women in crowded places. The chaos in his personal life makes him feel out of control, so this is where he attempts to reclaim that power."

Fitzgerald rubbed his palms together when they'd finished.

"Alright. I think we're off to a good start. I'll get this information to Atlanta PD so they know what to look for with the video footage. Assignments: Agent Baxter and Agent Dawson, I'd like you to put together a list of people that would have had legitimate access to that gun, just in case. We need to look at all angles. Agent Loshak and Agent Darger, you'll meet your tip line team tomorrow morning, so start preparing a script for the operators and a means to separate the wheat from the chaff."

Baxter raised his hand in the air.

"Excuse me, sir. I understand putting together that list, but shouldn't we go straight to the most likely source? Our guy was carrying a Glock-18, a gun that by all rights he shouldn't have access to. It's not a big mystery where he probably got his hands on it."

"Don't get tunnel vision, Agent Baxter. We need to be thinking big picture," Fitzgerald said.

Darger waited for someone to explain what the hell they were talking about. But the two men only stared at one another, and it brought to mind two rams preparing to bash their heads together in a battle for dominance.

"Sorry to interrupt," Loshak said, "but could someone explain what you're talking about?"

"The Nameless Brotherhood," Baxter said.

Fitzgerald pressed his lips together in an angry pout.

"Who's that?" Loshak asked.

"Local motorcycle club," Baxter answered. "One-percenters all the way and the biggest illegal arms dealers in the metro area."

Darger didn't know much about bikers, but she knew enough that the one-percent label was a reference to an old quote that said 99% of motorcyclists were law-abiding citizens. The remaining 1% were outlaws, and it was a badge of honor some clubs wore quite literally on their vests.

The silver pen tapped out an angry beat on the edge of the podium.

"And what exactly do you suggest, Agent Baxter? That we waltz into their clubhouse and ask if they'll set aside three decades' worth of actively fighting law enforcement to do us a little favor?"

Baxter twitched one shoulder. An annoyed tic, Darger thought.

"Obviously I was thinking we'd be a little more discreet than that. Start pulling in some of the guys on the fringe, see if they've heard anything."

"At this time-"

"Time," Baxter interrupted, "is exactly my point. We don't have it. So why pussyfoot around when we have a solid lead we can actually do something proactive with?"

The words came out strained. Agent Baxter was trying his damnedest to keep his emotions in check and nearly failing.

How very interesting, Darger thought. She would have pegged an uptight son of a bitch like Baxter for a bootlicker, but judging by this exchange, she would have been wrong. Agent Baxter's esteem went up a hair in her mind. She supposed the contrarian in her couldn't help rooting a little for the rebel.

ASAC Fitzgerald didn't raise his voice, but his tone was firm and absolute.

"That's a hard no, Agent Baxter. I don't think anything more needs to be said on this topic."

With that, they were dismissed. Fitzgerald gathered his notes and hurried out of the room, phone already pressed to his ear.

As Darger and Loshak exited the conference room, Agent Baxter called out.

"Agent Loshak," he said, "can I trouble you for a moment?"

Darger hung outside the door, turning to the bank of windows that lined the hallway. No need to wonder why she hadn't been invited to the clambake.

This end of the building overlooked a wooded area with a creek winding through it. It wasn't a half bad view.

"What's your take on the biker angle? From a profiling point of view, I mean."

Darger wasn't looking, but she imagined Loshak fluffing his hair with his fingers.

"From a profiling angle, the gun could have come from anywhere."

"No," Baxter said, "I'm saying, what if he's a member of the motorcycle club?"

"Wouldn't fit," Loshak said.

Darger smirked to herself. Never one to parse words, ol' Loshak.

"Why not? He hates law enforcement and the government. Check. He's anti-social. Check. These guys are scumbag extraordinaires. Drugs, guns, girls. They peddle it all. Definite ties to the Aryans, though they like to keep that under wraps. What I'm saying is… maybe that's where all this started. The violence. Maybe he's developed a taste for it. Built up an appetite, so to speak."

Darger watched a hawk being chased by two smaller birds. They flapped along after the larger bird, pecking and dive-bombing at every opportunity. She wondered why the hawk didn't fight back.

"This is a summation of rage that he's been bottling up for a long time," Loshak was saying. "If he were in a gang, he'd have too many opportunities to… sate his appetite, to use your term."

She heard a puff of breath expelled in frustration.

"What about you?" Baxter asked.

It was a moment before Darger realized he was addressing her. She pivoted away from the window.

"Me?"

"Do you agree with Agent Loshak's assessment?"

Well, well, well. So *now* he wanted her opinion… after Loshak shot his little pet theory down. How interesting.

"Sorry," she said, though she wasn't. "I have to agree with Agent Loshak. I also don't see him as the type to join a group like that. Any group, really. His experience in the military would have really soured him on that. He's probably mostly a loner now."

She watched the bundle of muscle on either side of Agent Baxter's jaw clench. Someone didn't like being told he was wrong. After the way she'd seen him dressed down by Fitzgerald, she decided to throw him a bone.

"That being said, I wouldn't rule out him *associating* with people in such a group. Friend-of-a-friend. That kind of thing."

She shot Loshak an apologetic look, not sure if he'd take that last part as a contradiction to his assessment. He gave a noncommittal shrug.

"Fair enough," Baxter said, then excused himself.

Darger waited until she and Loshak were alone before she asked, "What was that all about?"

"Hm?"

"All that Nameless Brotherhood stuff. I mean, I'm with you in terms of him not being a member. It doesn't feel right. But if that *is* a likely source for the weapon, it just seems like Fitzgerald was pretty quick to write it off."

Loshak was gazing down the empty corridor, seemingly lost in thought. She was starting to wonder if he'd heard anything she'd said when finally, he spoke up.

"We've got plenty to sort through already," Loshak said. "Diving headlong into this whole biker thing is premature."

She opened her mouth to say more, then decided against it.

CHAPTER 11

Shapes moved in the dark places where the streetlights couldn't reach. Shadows stirring on porches here and there. Some part of his brain could discern the movements as animal — as human — even if his conscious mind didn't understand how. It was a part of his lizard brain that just knew things, knew how to hunt, how to kill.

The whole area looked much different than he'd remembered. So much had changed since they were kids.

The Jeep crept through a suburban neighborhood now. McMansions and upscale apartment complexes and trees and neatly cropped landscaping replaced the concrete sprawl of the city. Tufts of exotic grasses poked up from behind sculpted shrubs and beds of red wood chips. Every yard looked as manicured as the front of a dentist's office, Levi thought. Weirdly artificial.

The humidity blew in through the window like bad breath, hot and thick against his face. It clung to his skin, slicked him in its soggy heat, pressed its fever deeper and deeper into him.

God forgive him for what he would do next. What he'd promised to do next. God forgive him.

He mopped the back of his hand over his top lip, already moist with sweat, and in that moment he smelled the vodka on his breath. It took a lot to be able to do this, the kind of drunk that obliterated even the faintest inhibitions. The adrenaline kept his mind and movements sharp, though. Funny how it all worked together, he thought. The cocktail of chemicals sloshing around in his brain. You can't have a brutal killing machine without a few stiff drinks.

The sawed-off lay across his lap, ready and waiting. He pressed the heel of his left hand into the stock now and then, just to feel it maybe.

He checked the time. 10:19 PM. If it got much later, he didn't know if he'd find what he needed. And surely part of him wanted that, he knew. Part of him wanted to puss out. To stop at the highway and grocery store incidents. To leave it at that.

But he wasn't done yet.

The progression was accomplishing what he wanted — what *they* wanted — and now he would take the next step.

If you kill people on the highway, they're scared to head out on the road.

If you kill them in a parking lot, now they're scared to leave the house.

If you kill them in their homes, though, they have nowhere left to hide.

The throb of the traffic waned as he crept deeper into the suburbs, fewer and fewer cars accompanying the Jeep on the streets, and that sour taste ascended his throat once more to coat his tongue.

He was close now. Very close. He could feel it.

He watched the shadows again, peering through the darkness for what he needed to find, what this mission required.

He promised. He promised he would.

And maybe part of him even wanted it. A part that was embarrassed about getting tackled back at Publix. A part that wanted to reassert that demonic power he'd felt, the fleeting moment when he wielded death at the end of his arm, dealt it from the barrel of his gun, the moment when he felt like Luke.

His Adam's apple bobbed, the muscles in his throat twinged,

and for a split second he thought he might be sick, but it didn't come.

And then he saw it. Saw her. Feminine curves in silhouette, the shadowy figure framed in the yellow light streaming through the doorway.

He pulled over, mopped his hand over his sweaty lip again, watched for lights in the rear view.

He saw nothing on the road. No one.

He watched her there, alone, just standing from the looks of it. Like she'd been waiting around for his arrival.

His arms and legs were numb as he stepped from the car. Distant and strange. All of his consciousness filtered down to the beat of the blood in his temples, that tart pizza sauce taste in his mouth, and the field of vision focused on the doorway where the pregnant woman stood.

He didn't want to, but he'd promised.

Apart from turning her head a little, she never moved, never turned to run, never backpedaled off the threshold upon which she stood.

And he leveled the shotgun at her. Felt its heft settle into his hands. His finger finding the trigger. Squeezing.

Flame plumed from the snubbed barrel. The boom split open the night. Loud and deep and violent.

The recoil throttled him, wrenched at the muscles in his arms and chest, tried to push him back.

And the shadow figure dropped. At first he could only see the wetness of her chest in the dark. A shimmering black surface. Moving liquid on her front. Flowing. Like the churning water of a river.

But the light found her as she went down. Revealed her at last. The red showing now where the buckshot tattered her flesh.

Opened her up.

She sat up partially. Lifted her head. Their eyes met. Locked onto each other.

Her eyelids fluttered. He saw no real understanding in her gaze. Only shock. Confusion. Fear and remoteness.

Noises crackled from her lips. Meaningless syllables whispered.

She leaned against the doorway. Her chest heaving. Her blood seeping. Gushing. Faster and faster. She looked so small. Those terrible wounds. So vulnerable. Bleeding and dying and confused.

He took a breath. Racked the shotgun. Finished her.

Red spattered the wall. A violent final twitch.

It was a mercy. He knew the second shot was a mercy. But it didn't feel like it.

And then his numb legs carried him away from the scene. Hurrying. He felt like he was hovering. Floating.

And he was in the Jeep. Shifting gears. Gliding back onto the street.

Drifting away and away and away.

He was panting, he realized. Pink splotches flickering before him.

Three and a half blocks later, he had to pull over to vomit into the gutter. Vodka and fruit punch spurting out of him.

The nausea didn't depart with the puke. It stayed. Dug itself deeper into his abdominals, into his skull.

The sickness only got worse. Something beyond sickness, something beyond bodily suffering.

Damnation, he thought. This was the physical manifestation of damnation — a divine sickness unto death and beyond.

Suffering without end.

Maybe God truly was merciful. Maybe He could forgive almost anyone for almost anything.

But Levi knew in his heart that God would never ever forgive this.

CHAPTER 12

The flashing lights of the police and other first responders cut through the black of night, tinting everything in a strobe of red and blue. Loshak caught sight of the scene from half a mile away. As he got closer, he pulled the car to the side of the road. Loose stones pinged up from the shoulder, ringing out against the undercarriage. He parked and stepped from the vehicle.

"Agent Loshak," a familiar voice called.

He turned and saw Agent Dawson and Agent Baxter climbing out of their Suburban down the street. Dawson raised a hand in greeting and paused to wait for him.

Loshak didn't bother locking the rental. He pocketed the keys and jogged across the asphalt to catch up with her. Agent Baxter had already gone ahead without them.

Agent Dawson's eyes did a quick search behind Loshak and came up empty.

"Agent Darger isn't with you?" she asked.

"Nah, I left her at the hotel," he explained. "She's been up for going on forty hours. Figured she could use the extra shut-eye."

Dawson shrugged and led the way toward the nexus of the crime scene.

She'd be pissed, of course, Loshak thought. He'd get all manner of grief from her tomorrow morning. But it was the smartest move. She was running on what, three hours of sleep? At most. And this shooter wasn't showing any signs of letting up. They'd have to pace themselves, or they'd burn out before the end.

The end.

What was the end? Where was he headed with all this? Toward more death and destruction, surely. But why hadn't they received any contact? Where was his manifesto? This type always had one. Maybe not written down, but it would be there. A list of wrongs committed against him. A case laid out against humanity. His warped reasons for perpetrating these crimes.

As if any sense could be brought to this.

Loshak followed Dawson up the sidewalk to the front of the house. Free-standing screens had been set up around the perimeter to block the view of news cameras, and they had to turn sideways to step between two of the barriers. As he did so, a uniformed officer bowled through the gap holding a hand over his mouth. He made it a few stumbling steps past Loshak before throwing up into a patch of daylilies.

Loshak and Dawson exchanged a glance before proceeding. That was never a good sign, and he readied himself for whatever horrors lay ahead.

The first thing he noticed was the blood. A tremendous amount of blood. It pooled around the body, seeped over the boards of the front porch, dribbled off the top step in thick, gummy drops.

The body sprawled over the threshold of the open front door. From the height of the blood spatter on the door, he'd shot her once as she stood in the doorway, and again after she'd fallen and lay slumped against the door frame.

She had not been covered yet. The crime scene photographer was still taking pictures.

A large, jagged wound covered most of the chest. Flaps of skin were indistinguishable from the torn bits of her dress.

And the face… well, it wasn't much of a face anymore.

Everything above the lower jaw was a mess of shredded tissue and bone fragments.

But the most disturbing part was the unmistakable swell of the woman's belly.

"How far along was she?" Loshak asked.

Agent Baxter was muttering something to Agent Dawson, and he broke off to answer.

"Almost eight months," he said, the faintest crack in his voice.

Loshak didn't blame him. Nor did he fault the uni for losing his lunch over this one. The body was in bad enough shape, but the fact that the victim had been pregnant added a deeper level of profanity to the whole scene.

The amount of gore, the yellow light pouring out from the interior of the house, the incessant strobe of the police lights — all of it gave the feel of a cheap haunted house. Except that it was real. Loshak wasn't looking at corn syrup and chicken guts.

No sir. Tonight the horror was 100% genuine.

CHAPTER 13

As soon as Levi entered the motel room, Luke jolted upright from his seat and moved to the window.

No hello. No how are you.

He just stared out at the parking lot, head twitching back and forth like a squirrel, cigarette dangling from his lip.

Levi moved to one of the beds and sat, lying back after a few seconds. All of the muscles in his neck and shoulders released, some small euphoria accompanying the slack feeling, and it occurred to him that he'd rather not move again, if possible.

The room was a dump. Wood paneling everywhere. Bedspreads worn and frayed. One corner of the carpet featured a dark splotch that smelled faintly of puke, so they'd steered clear of that.

Images flickered on the TV screen, a seemingly endless stream of commercials, though at least the sound was turned down.

Bored with that, he swiveled his head to watch the figure standing in the window, seeing the twitchy face in profile.

He and Luke looked so much alike that it was weird to look upon this other. It was like looking in a mirror that somehow thinned him out, etched intense lines around his brow and eyes, painted tribal tattoos onto those sinewy arms all roped with veins. Luke was the version sprinkled with crystal meth, educated in martial arts classes, perpetually stubbled and clad in a wife beater.

In contrast, Levi looked like the wholesome version, the clean-cut rendition, baby faced, muscles somehow smooth in appearance instead of fibrous, like he was raised on a strict diet of milk and pot roast in Utah or something.

"Anybody follow you?" Luke said, smoke coiling out with his words.

"No."

"How can you be sure?"

"Because we're in some bullshit motel in the middle of nowhere. You're the one lookin' out there. The Jeep is the only car in the lot, isn't it?"

Luke nodded and Levi went on.

"No one's out here. No one wants to be. I mean, I didn't see any headlights on the road for the last ten minutes or so."

Luke didn't answer. He sucked on his cigarette, blew smoke against the glass, and peered out at the gravel lot.

"So," the standing figure said, finally, not turning from the window. "Did you do it? Like we talked about?"

Levi's gaze drifted up the wall toward the ceiling, and his tongue clucked against the roof of his mouth. He tried to say "yes," but nothing came out.

The wallpaper peeled everywhere above him, flaps hanging down, weird sticky lines and grooves of dried glue the color of snot peeking out from behind. The humidity was relentless out here, he supposed. Corrosive. A destructive force.

When he looked back toward the window, his brother was looking at him.

"I'll take that as a yes," Luke said, flicking ashes onto the carpet.

Levi shrugged, bobbed his head once.

"Well, you did good. You did the right thing."

The pregnant silhouette flashed in Levi's mind. He closed his eyes, but he knew there was no escape. The movie played on, projected onto the insides of his eyelids.

The snort of flames exhaled from the barrel. The weapon jerking and cracking. The blood. The tattered flesh. The yellow light. All of it.

Luke walked to the edge of the bed, and when Levi sat up, his older brother clapped him on the shoulder.

"You set everything up, you know? And now? Now we can finish it together."

By design, Levi had carried out the first wave of attacks on his own. That way if he did get caught — either in the act or fleeing — the mission could still go on, with Luke taking over. It was all part of Luke's master plan, and whenever he talked about it, it all started to make sense. A lot of sense. Hate — genuine, passionate hatred — was pretty infectious, maybe.

"I been watching on TV. You went national after the grocery store, of course. Not only cable news, either. ABC and CBS interrupted their regularly scheduled morning programming and everything. Pretty nuts."

"So they connected them?"

"Yep. Told you they would, didn't I? You're the *active shooter* that'll be the top story coming up on the 11 o'clock news here in a minute."

They both looked at the TV screen. A commercial for a hearing aid played, a cartoon of the little flesh-toned device being inserted into an ear. The animation dissolved into old people standing in a studio, their mouths moving, their smiles all coming off that much more saccharine with the sound muted.

"The next step is the big 'en," Luke said. "It locks everything into place."

Levi let his head drop back onto the bedspread.

"I know."

Long after Luke's breathing slowed, Levi lay awake in the dark, twisting and turning in bed. He'd been up for 42 hours or so, and his eyes stung like someone had flung sand in them. Even still, sleep would not take him.

Some pit opened in his gut now that he felt alone. An emptiness. A vacancy. It quivered inside of him. Throbbed. He knew it was some physical manifestation of anxiety or guilt or dread. Trauma. Stress. Some combination of all of the above, probably. He'd never experienced anything like it before.

How empty can someone feel? Is this as far as it goes? This he wondered as he stared at those flaps of wallpaper, the places where the room itself was sliding apart, coming unglued.

But they hadn't hit bottom yet, had they? Luke's plan was only beginning. It would rage on and on and on. Until one of them was dead, perhaps.

No.

Until both of them were dead.

He adjusted his limbs, sliding a leg to open up his hips, to stretch his sore quads and abductors a little. It offered no comfort, no relief for that roiling in his belly.

Maybe all stories end in death. He'd heard that somewhere, and it was true, one way or another.

When Luke first got back from Iraq, he was in pretty bad shape. Physically, he seemed fine — if anything, a little leaner and meaner than when he'd left. His wounds were mental.

PTSD grew in him like cancer. What started as a little twitchiness and social anxiety blossomed into a crippling condition. By the time he'd been back for six months, Shelly had kicked him out of the house. After that, he barely got out of bed, barely would let anyone into his apartment. He just sat alone in the dark, in the silence, wasting away.

Levi would go there to be with him whenever he wasn't working, would sit on the foot of the bed and play video games while his brother rotated between chain smoking and sleeping. Even when he was awake, Luke often didn't talk for hours. It was hard to imagine he'd be alive much longer.

As the weeks went by, the apartment felt more and more funereal. The body laid out on the bed, wrapped in dark sheets. The stale smell. The creeping gray stillness that settled over everything within its walls.

Levi was playing The Last of Us when his brother said it.

"You know I'm going to kill myself, right?"

The words croaked out of him, thick with sleep, barely louder than a whisper.

Levi didn't say anything. What could he say? He stared into the TV screen like any other day, kept right on killing video game zombies.

But he was there. He was present. It was all he could do, and so he did.

He sat in the room.

What seemed to bring Luke back to himself was talking about what he'd seen. The horror stories about IEDs blowing off legs and late nights storming into civilian homes and making everyone lay flat on their bellies based on tips of terrorist locations. The clatter of distant assault rifles most every night. The tension of riding out on patrol in total silence, riding out of the calm and into the storm over and over and over.

Luke seemed to wake up when he recapped those moments of conflict, those moments of violence. His voice sounded fuller, clearer, more solid.

Levi couldn't remember anymore when the talk transitioned from memories to plans, when his brother started turning his pain outward. But that revitalized him even more. It was a goal. A dream. Even if it was more of a nightmare.

And when he talked about it, it made sense. Even still, there were moments when it made perfect sense.

In some ways, Levi thought, maybe that's how all of this got started. His brother needed him.

CHAPTER 14

The thin strings of morning light threaded their way between the gaps in the curtain. It woke Violet a little after dawn.

She stretched and yawned. She'd had a surprisingly restful sleep. In fact, she couldn't remember waking even once during the night.

Her bare feet stomped over the carpeting on her way to the shower. She soaped up, rinsed off, and wrapped herself in a towel.

Brushing her teeth, she padded to the window and threw the curtains wide. Looked like it was setting up to be another scorcher judging by the clear horizon.

From the vantage point of the eighth floor, Violet gazed down at the city. Her room overlooked a park, and she watched the specks of people moving on the brick paths. Was that how he saw them, looking down through the crosshairs of his gun sight? As moving targets, barely more than an ant crawling over the floor?

The first time — along the highway — it would have felt that way, maybe. But that hadn't been enough, it seemed.

She passed the TV and flipped it on, craving something to disrupt the silence.

"The community remains absolutely shaken by what appears to be a string of random violence perpetrated by one man on a rampage. A man some are calling the Georgia Sniper," a newscaster was saying.

Violet rolled her eyes as she wiped toothpaste foam from the corner of her mouth. The media just couldn't resist coming up with a nickname, could they? They just couldn't fucking help themselves.

Bunch of hacks, she thought and spat into the drain.

"Police are saying this murder may be related to both the sniper attack on Interstate 20 on Tuesday and the massacre in a crowded Publix parking lot yesterday morning, making it the third such attack in two days. Many residents of the city are in a state of dread, fearing where and when the madman might strike next."

Violet's head snapped up from the sink in the bathroom, and she stared at her reflection with wide-eyed bewilderment.

Third attack?

She leaned around the bathroom wall to get a look at the screen. The reporter stood in front of a green sign with gold lettering that spelled out *Pheasant Brook.*

"The latest episode in this ongoing nightmare played out right here, in the quiet subdivision of Pheasant Brook. Last night at a little before 10:30 PM, Carol Jones was shot at point blank range while standing in her own front doorway."

Darger tuned out, eyes staring at the wall above the TV but seeing none of it. How could this happen without her knowing? Had she slept through a call?

She reached for her phone, scrolling through the recent calls. Nothing.

Was this Baxter's doing? Trying to cut them out? She wondered what Loshak would have to say about that.

Then it occurred to her.

Loshak.

That son of a bitch.

She dressed hurriedly, the anchor on TV still yammering on.

"Over the next hour, we'll be bringing you live team

coverage from every possible angle—"

Darger jabbed the power button on the remote and the voice cut out.

Loshak stretched his arm across the seats as he backed out of the parking space.

"Hopefully Rodney will have his stuff installed by the time we get there. The sooner we get the tip line set up, the better."

She didn't respond.

"You listening, Violet?"

"I heard you."

"Aww, come on. You're not still pouting about last night, are you?"

"Pouting, huh? Interesting choice of words. I suppose last night you felt I needed my nap, and that's why you didn't call?"

He smirked.

"So you're *not* mad about last night?"

"Of course I'm mad. I'm pissed. I wouldn't leave you behind like that, you…"

For some reason, she hesitated to actually swear at Loshak. Out of respect or intimidation, she wasn't sure.

"You poophead," she finally finished.

That got a laugh out of him.

"Look, I had my reasons, OK? You needed the sleep more than I did."

He rubbed a bloodshot eye and yawned.

"This tip line detail is going to be as close to a round-the-clock thing as we can muster. With the twelve trainees we have coming in, we can easily divide them up into standard eight-hour shifts. Same with the analysts. As for the two of us… probably makes the most sense if we split up and take different shifts. After we get things set up down there, I'll take the first shift. You can take off. If you want, go take a look at the new scene. But you should also try to get some more sleep. If we do it that way, it'll mean you're on the night shift for now."

She considered it for a time, then nodded. It made sense.

"I can handle that. Twelve-hour shifts?"

"Or close to it," he said, adjusting the sun visor to cut the glare. "I hate to do it, really. Longer shifts are inefficient. You can't help but get sloppy toward the end. But I don't anticipate either one of us being happy with the idea of an eight-hour stretch where we don't have eyes and ears on what's coming in. Let's be honest, Darger. We're both control freaks."

She didn't deny it. No matter how good their team of analysts might be, Darger wanted to know that either she or Loshak were skimming the majority of the tips.

In the DC sniper case, she knew that one of the shooters had called in weeks before they were caught, but the operators on the tip line had written it off as a crank call. And there were other tips that had been ignored. There were those that said the shooters could have been caught sooner, had the tip line been better managed. Darger wasn't about to let mistakes like that happen on her watch. And Loshak was pretty much the only other person she trusted enough to do the same.

"What if we rotated eight-hour shifts instead?" she suggested. "Eight on the tip line, eight for sleep. If we're being honest, you know neither one of us is going to be taking any extra time for R&R."

"True," he said.

"We'll split the nights evenly that way. For all we know, the calls will slow way down then, and it'll be a chance to get some extra rest. I don't want to hog that all to myself."

Loshak smirked.

"More like you don't want to miss out on the peak hours during the day."

She grinned back, the picture of innocence.

"Who, me?"

The turn signal beat out a rhythm like a metronome as Loshak steered the car into the lot of a Dunkin Donuts.

"Breakfast of champions," he said. He unbuckled his seatbelt and climbed out. Darger followed.

It was busy inside, and Darger picked up bits of chatter relating to the shootings.

"When I woke up this morning and saw the news, saw about that poor girl last night," a woman was saying, "I almost couldn't get myself out the door. I stood in the foyer, peeking out the window, looking for anything suspicious. Any cars on the street I didn't know. Finally, I got up the nerve to make a run for my car. I felt foolish, but… I can't help it. I don't feel safe in my own front yard."

"Makes me glad I park in the garage. You know, I told my wife, don't be opening the door for anybody. Don't get the mail, I'll do it when I get home," he said, then leaned a little closer to the woman. "And you can be damn sure I'll be bringing my friend Mr. Sig Sauer along for the trip."

The woman clutched her styrofoam cup with both hands.

"I don't understand how he hasn't been caught yet. Are the police even trying?"

"Probably too busy eating donuts," the man responded, and the two of them chuckled.

While they waited in line, Loshak glanced over at her.

"Take a look at the Stump journal yet?"

Violet didn't want to admit that she'd already read it

through twice and was working on the third pass, so she said, "A few glances, yeah."

"Was it what you expected?"

"He really loves his animal analogies. Probably could have been a good veterinarian if he wasn't, you know, a sadistic serial killer."

Loshak chuckled.

"Yeah, I think he fancies himself some kind of philosopher. I also don't think he left the journal behind by accident. Probably still eatin' away at him that it never got out. If that little manifesto of his had been published he probably would have turned himself in and confessed to everything, just to get the credit he'd think was due. The interviews. Documentaries."

"You really think so?" she asked.

"Maybe. But nah. Not really. He's an egomaniac and a narcissist, so as much as he loves the attention, his sense of self-preservation is still number one on his list of priorities."

When they reached the counter, Loshak smiled at the girl in the Dunkin Donuts hat and apron.

"I called in an order. Should be under the name Victor Loshak."

The girl nodded and grabbed a receipt from next to the register.

"Four boxes of Munchkins and two Box o' Joes, one dark roast, one decaf?"

"That's it," Loshak said, reaching for his wallet.

The girl finished ringing up the order and then disappeared into a back room to retrieve it.

"Someone's hungry," Darger said.

"It's a very delicate management technique I've picked up over the years."

"Oh yeah?"

"If you want the undivided attention of a group of rowdy greenhorn trainees, arrive bearing baked goods and hot coffee."

CHAPTER 15

In a large room on the fourth floor of the Atlanta field office, Loshak stood front and center and addressed the crew of agent trainees and analysts that would staff the tip line. Behind him, Darger added a list of words and phrases to a white board. If any of the calls contained these keywords, they would immediately be marked as the highest priority. That had been Darger's idea, her hope being that if the shooter called, they wouldn't miss it. If he called, he would inevitably leave clues that would, at the very least, improve their profile.

As the marker in Darger's hand squeaked over the board, Loshak gave the group a Cliff Notes version of the crimes thus far. He used the same map she'd seen in the meeting the day before to highlight where the shootings had taken place.

"The sniper attack took place here, on this hill," Loshak said, using a laser pointer to pinpoint the spot. "The hill can only be reached by this unmarked access road. Chief Hogaboom of Atlanta PD is holding a press conference this morning. He'll be releasing the attack location, so be especially vigilant for any callers reporting they were near that area around the time of the shooting. We're waiting on tire track analysis from the lab, but we might be able to get a vehicle description more quickly if there are any eye witnesses."

He ran through summarized versions of the Publix shooting and the Pheasant Brook murder, pointing out locations on the map and giving time frames for each incident. When he finished with that, he pocketed his laser pointer and picked up a sheaf of paper.

"Has anyone here ever worked a tip line before?" Loshak asked.

Two trainees raised their hands, and Loshak raised the pages in the air.

"Then you're probably familiar with this."

It was one of the standard forms the FBI used to log tip line calls. It had a simple questionnaire on the front and several sheets of carbon paper to make copies on the back. The two trainees nodded.

"For the rest of you, I'll explain. The standard procedure for a tip line organized by the FBI is for each operator to take down the calls *by hand* onto one of these forms. You can imagine how efficient that is."

A few of the trainees chuckled.

"Here's what we're doing with the standard procedure," Loshak said.

He wadded the paper into a ball and made a free throw shot at the garbage can. He made the basket.

"Now I'd like to introduce you all to Rodney Malenchuck, who's going to take you through the newest innovation in tip line technology."

Rodney sat off to one side of the group, and bright pink splotches formed on his cheeks at the sudden attention. He unfolded his long, bony frame and stalked to the front of the room, reminding Darger of a stork.

He cleared his throat nervously and began.

"Hi, my name is Rodney, uh, Malenchuck. Which I guess Mister, I mean, Agent Loshak already said, so… Anyway, I'll get to it. The program I designed is called Autological, and what it essentially does is combine voice-to-text software with call logging and recording."

Darger thought he was fairly young, maybe only 22 or 23, but a large part of that assessment was his childlike nature. He was soft-spoken, fidgety, and had a habit of blinking rapidly when he talked. His eyes had a sort of perpetual wetness that gave him the appearance of being just on the brink of an emotional outburst.

"How Autological works, without getting too technical," Rodney said, and his moist eyes glanced over at Loshak, who gave an encouraging nod, "is that as a call comes in through the tip line, the program grabs it and logs the basic information — time, location, etcetera. The next step is that Autological determines whether or not there is a human operator available. If so, the call is routed to one of them. If all lines are busy, the program has an automated voicemail backup."

Rodney seemed to grow more comfortable once he was talking about his program.

"Both the live calls and the automated backup systems are set to record the calls in audio and voice-to-text, similar to the way a 911 call center works. What that allows us to do is add the calls to a searchable database. As the case progresses, we'll be able to organize calls by common keyword, location, and so on. Each live call will also be given priority rankings by the operators, which should allow for a more effective workflow for the analysts."

By the time Rodney was through giving a demonstration of how to use the program, Darger had completed her work at the whiteboard. Loshak resumed control of the meeting and directed the attention of everyone in the room to the matrix of words scrawled on the shiny surface.

"There is a real chance the shooter will call into the tip line. Agent Darger and I put together a list of things to listen for. For example, calls that sound rehearsed, recorded, or utilize voice modification. Because he's likely been in the armed forces, use of military or law enforcement jargon should raise a red flag. Also religious terms, racial slurs, or mention of negotiating or demands. This is by no means an exhaustive list, so if you have questions, or you get a call that gives you any kind of gut feeling, anything that sets your Spidey Sense a-tingling, please don't hesitate to call me or Agent Darger over."

They broke then, the operators moving off to private cubicles where they would start getting acquainted with the Autological interface. Rodney approached, giving an anxious flap of his elbows, and again Darger was reminded of a tall, spindly bird.

"I should remind you, Agent Loshak. The system is still in beta testing."

"I know, I know. You told me on the phone." Loshak gave him a reassuring pat on the shoulder. "Don't worry, kid. This is light years ahead of the pencil-and-carbon-paper method. It's worth a few bugs."

Loshak chuckled to himself as Rodney wandered off to help the trainees, and then his gaze turned to Darger.

"You heading out to the crime scene now?"

"As long as you're sure you've got everything covered here," she said, feeling a little guilty leaving him here alone.

"Go on. I know you're chomping at the bit to get out there."

CHAPTER 16

The latest crime scene was still crawling with investigators and representatives from the various media outlets when Darger arrived. An officer from the Atlanta Police Department stopped her at the entrance of Pheasant Brook. She recognized the green and gold sign from the TV footage that morning. Across the street, a dozen news vans loitered in the parking lot of an apartment complex.

Darger rolled down her window.

"Morning, ma'am," the policeman said.

She wondered if he was this polite to every car that rolled up, or if he possibly recognized her.

Flashing her badge, she said, "FBI."

He nodded once, resting his hands on his duty belt.

"Go on ahead."

She thanked him and guided her car around his cruiser, which blocked the entrance from any unauthorized traffic.

She parked behind a Chevy Impala marked with the emblem of the local sheriff's office and got out. Judging from the activity and crime scene tape, the real action had taken place a block further up the street.

The neighborhood was quiet and clean. A dog barked somewhere in the distance, and faint traffic noise filtered through a stand of pines off to the west. But for the most part, it was a serene little nook hidden in the midst of the bustling city.

Most of the homes were two stories tall. They weren't identical, but it was clear it was a planned community by the similar tones and textures used on the exteriors: creamy beige, sage green, or slate gray for the paint, limestone brick or mixed river rock for the stone accents. Each lot looked to be about half an acre. Many were landscaped in front with palms and azaleas nestled into curved beds lined with wood chips. Swaths of green lawn in back left plenty of room for pools, sandboxes, swing sets. It was a picture-perfect example of the upper middle class suburban American dream.

Which was why he'd chosen it, of course. He was an overgrown child, stomping through someone else's carefully erected sandcastle. If he couldn't have it, no one could. The "it" in this case being: Happiness. Peace. Life.

She pivoted on her heel at the foot of Carol Jones' sidewalk and passed through a pair of screens set up in front of the house. Darger sucked in a breath when the porch came into view. The body had been bagged and moved to the morgue by now, but evidence of the savagery remained aplenty. The telltale spatters on the door and the siding. The dark red-brown stains on the deck boards.

A fly buzzed past Darger's face, and she swatted it away. It landed in the congealing puddle just inside the Jones residence, rubbing its legs together as if sitting down for a picnic lunch. A sickly heat crept over Darger's face, and she turned her back on the carnage.

Agent Baxter stood beneath a cluster of palms, the fronds overhead casting shadows over him. He had his phone pressed to his ear and wore the same humorless expression as always. Darger wondered if he ever smiled.

As Darger moved closer, he ended the call and stepped from beneath the canopy. The sun shone on his face, hitting him like a spotlight. He looked like hell. Rumpled suit. Bags under his red-rimmed eyes. His hair was dark and thick enough that not shaving for even a day meant that a good crop of stubble had already taken root. He pawed at his jawline, producing a grating noise she associated with sandpaper.

She closed the gap between them, and her feet left wet prints on the dew-covered grass.

"I had a feeling you'd still be here," she said and held out a cardboard cup like an olive branch. "I took a wild guess that you drink it black. No sugar."

He frowned at her like he didn't know if she was poking fun at him or not. But he accepted the cup and took a sip.

"Appreciate it," he said.

She noted that he did not use the words *thank you.*

"So was I right?"

"About what?"

"How you take your coffee?"

"You want a prize or something?"

He really is Agent Bastard, she thought. It occurred to her that she was probably not the first one to think it.

"There it is again. That effervescent personality of yours."

He didn't answer, only further illustrating her point. Not a fan of small talk? Fine. Back to business.

"So take me through it. What happened here last night?"

Without needing to consult his notes, Baxter began a recap of the prior night's events.

"Carol Jones, 31. Running theory is she was already out here on the porch when he arrived."

"He didn't knock on her door first?"

Agent Baxter shook his head.

"We think not. Judging by the position of the body, she was standing outside the door. Do you live alone, Agent Darger?"

The question struck her as an abrupt change of subject, and

she stuttered out an awkward, "Yes… why?"

"If a strange man came knocking at your door at night, would you step out onto the front porch with him?"

Not without my gun, she thought.

"What if she knew him?"

"We're looking into that possibility, of course. But there's more that suggests it might have been a case of wrong place, wrong time. From the trajectory reconstruction, he didn't even get all the way up onto the porch. He was standing on the bottom step when he fired the first round."

He jerked his head toward the street.

"There's outgoing mail in the box down there. My personal theory is that she takes the mail down, flips up the little red flag, heads back up the walk, and she's almost back inside when he comes up behind her. He says something, or maybe she hears his footsteps, but whatever it is, she turns around and…" He gestured to the darkening smears and speckles in the entryway.

And *boom*, Darger thought.

"If you want to see inside, it's better to come around back to avoid stepping in the… mess."

He led the way to a rear entrance. The interior of the home matched the generic suburban exterior. Polished stone countertops, white cabinetry, a contemporary chandelier over the dining room table.

"Victim's husband is a corporate attorney for Turner Broadcasting. He's been in L.A. all week. Apparently, it's not unusual for him to be out of town several times a month."

"He's been notified, I assume?"

"Yeah, he's on the first flight back. We've got an interview scheduled for this evening."

"And what about her?" Darger asked and pointed at a

portrait of the victim in her wedding gown. "Did she work?"

"She did hospitality design up until about a year ago."

Darger raised an eyebrow.

"I have been informed that it's a fancy term for interior decorating for hotels."

"Ah," Darger said with a nod.

"According to her sister, she left her job when they decided to start a family."

At that moment, Darger's eyes came to rest on another frame on the wall. It was a series of seven black and white images. Each one had a date written in looping, feminine handwriting, followed by an inscription. The first read, "One month!" The second, "Two months!" One sonogram for each month of the pregnancy, all the way through the seventh month. Months eight and nine were blank spaces, never to be filled.

Violet's gaze remained glued to the ultrasound images for a long time.

Two kills in one.

What kind of person got off on that?

She considered the prospects of the rest of the day ahead. Hours spent poring over the phone calls that were surely flooding in by now. Most of them would be useless. A waste of time. Bored housewives glued to the daytime news circuits who wanted nothing more than to be part of it all — from a safe distance, of course. And so they would convince themselves they'd seen the gunman. Knew it was their downstairs neighbor or the brother-in-law they hated.

Then there were the cranks. Mostly adolescents who didn't understand the gravity of the situation and thought it was funny to call in with bogus stories and obscene jokes.

After that, the drunks and the mentally ill. They would blame their sons, their fathers, their bosses. Some of them would confess that they were the gunman.

Finally, Violet tore her eyes from the grainy black and white pictures. She swiveled around. Agent Baxter had moved farther down the hall, conversing with one of the detectives. When he finished, she called him over.

"Baxter," she said.

His response came as a series of lines running across his forehead.

"This biker gang…"

"The Nameless Brotherhood," he said.

"Right. Do you know why Fitzgerald was so intent on quashing that? Surely the bureau has a few CIs that might have some intel. And if not us, then ATF or even the local vice cops. I don't understand why we're not at least putting out some feelers."

He watched her for a time, pondering perhaps whether he should share his thoughts on the subject or not. Whether he could trust her.

"I have my suspicions," he said finally.

"Like?"

"Like I think someone higher up the chain might be running some kind of undercover operation. This is 100% speculation and obviously doesn't leave this room. But I think whoever it is might be worried that we'll blow whatever they're working on."

"And that's worth more innocent civilian deaths?"

He shrugged.

"Fucking bullshit FBI politics," she muttered, more to herself than to him.

He scratched at the stubble on his chin as if its presence

irritated him. The words that came out of his mouth next were not what she'd expected.

"You hungry?"

CHAPTER 17

Stifling heat swelled in the Jeep. Levi cracked the door, leaned his head into the opening. It was a little better, maybe, but the mugginess had descended upon the day. The kind of sticky air that wrapped itself around him and squeezed gently at all times.

The grass to his left sheared off into a steep hill. It flattened out at a sharp angle far below, and cars rushed past on the freeway there.

The endless stream of traffic flowed on and on, the teeming masses of humanity, loaded into metal boxes and hurtling from place to place as fast as legally possible. Apart from the background noise, however, these vehicles concerned him not at all.

He kept his eyes on the flat grassy area atop the hill in the distance. *The* hill. The one with the latticed steel of the transmission tower protruding from it. The one where he'd hunkered down with his sniper rifle and started all of this.

It felt like that had taken place weeks ago, maybe longer, but no. It had only been a couple of days and nights. So much had happened since then. So much had changed. And it was irreversible. Time he couldn't have back. Violence and death he could never undo.

A trickle of sweat sluiced down from the corner of his brow, and he mopped at it with his knuckles. The moving liquid brought him back to the moment, made him realize that sweat slicked the surface of his being, every inch.

It was too hot for all of this. Too hot for Luke's plan. Too hot to run through these memories. Too hot to think.

And the heat only enhanced the tension he felt about being here. On one hand, he wanted this wait to be over. On the other, it wouldn't be over until more people died, and that notion filled him with a different kind of dread.

He blinked a few times and refocused on the scene on that distant hill. Nothing stirred there, but he told himself that was OK. He'd wait. Wait and sweat. That's what he'd do. If someone showed up? Well, he'd burn that bridge when he came to it.

Black clouds roiled to the west. A storm was heading this way, would be here in a few hours. And somehow he knew it would offer no relief. Not from the heat. Not from the pressure.

He looked at the rifle resting on a diagonal in the passenger seat. The instrument of death just waiting to go off once more.

Luke probably had it worse, he figured. His older brother was likewise waiting around, except he was camped out near the Publix parking lot. All of that concrete and asphalt reflecting the heat everywhere? At least Levi was on grass. There were even patches of woods and lesser-foliaged areas sporting brush and thickly leaved undergrowth close by. Did any of that diminish the humidity? Fuck no. But it was better than sitting on blacktop. After thinking about it a while, he decided to take advantage of the setting.

He got out of the vehicle, noting the streaks of vomit trailing down the driver's side door. He hadn't quite gotten his head out the window in time for that first heave last night. Last night? Was it really so recent? Even the episode of nausea seemed like forever ago, seemed distant and somehow indistinct like the fading memory of a dream.

The mugginess relented when he stepped away from the car, if only a little. The air moved some out here at least, rippling against his soggy t-shirt and the moisture on the back of his neck.

He walked along the edge of the hill where the land had been cut to make room for the freeway. It made him a little lightheaded to stare down that steep slope. When he'd gotten a few paces on, he turned to look at the Jeep.

Leafy branches lay over the hood of it. Just enough camouflage to keep the vehicle from sticking out, at least from a distance. If someone on the opposite hill wasn't looking for it, they wouldn't see it. Or so Levi hoped. It was hard to be sure from this vantage point, but he thought it possible.

Something about gathering and setting out the sticks had reminded him of his dad. They ultimately hadn't spent much time together, but he remembered playing in the yard when he was three or four. They each had sticks which became the hilts of imaginary light sabers, the duels always ending with Levi force-choking his father who played along by buckling at the knees and pantomiming some gagging. It was, for no reason he could think of, his second most prominent memory of his father.

The most prominent, of course, was the fight.

When Levi was six, his dad knocked his mom's two front teeth out. He'd never forget the image of that overhand right catching her clean in the mouth. And the sound. The clatter of her teeth on the linoleum, bouncing and skittering along. He didn't know something could sound so wrong as the enamel of her incisors tapping the floor like that. And it took a few seconds to fully register what he was seeing and hearing. Those trembling white chunks on the floor couldn't be her *teeth*, could they? It seemed too disgusting to be true. Too permanent.

He saw his dad just three times after that. Brief episodes of strife, heated exchanges that he had a hard time recalling context for. Fever smeared vignettes that didn't connect to the rest of his life in any way. Interludes.

Abusive to his mother or not, losing dad was not a good thing — not for him and not for Luke. Their dad had been the defender, in the community and at home.

They grew up in a rough neighborhood — a violent, thieving, awful place. Rape and murder happened monthly. Home invasions and muggings were closer to weekly. Some of it was gang related. Almost all of it was drug related. The narcotic of choice fueling the crimes changed over the years as heroin, crack, and meth went in and out of fashion, but the violence remained the same.

And the two scrawny boys took beatings often. No dad. Mom working two jobs. It was like the predators could smell that they had no one looking out for them. Like blood in the water. They got their shit stolen repeatedly — wallets, shoes, and even toys — until they were big enough to stave off attackers or at least run away.

Thinking back, it was probably around fifteen years old that Luke went fully psycho, Levi thought.

A shoving match with one of their mother's boyfriends pushed him over the edge. He tried to slit the guy's throat with a kitchen knife. Technically, his brother *had* cut Russel's throat. It broke the skin at least, the blade kissing the flesh just enough to draw little red lines, zigzags stretching from one ear to the other.

Levi helped his mom wrestle Luke away before he could spill the man's blood onto the welcome mat and all over their shoes. It was a close thing. And everything was different after.

Before that incident, they got it worse at home than they did on the street. Mom's string of loser boyfriends beat on both of them. Black eyes. Busted lips. Rib cages mottled black and blue and yellow. One guy — a mean drunk named Kenny — even put a cigarette out on the back of Luke's hand when he was nine. The losers came and went, none staying around for more than six or nine months. That was the one thing that pretty much all of her boyfriends had in common — they reveled in beating on the boys.

But everything changed after the close call with Russel's jugular. Luke stopped taking shit after that, and he made sure Levi didn't have to, either.

"The world will make you eat shit your whole life if you let it," he'd said at one point. "You gotta kick it in the teeth until it backs the fuck down."

The next guy who tried to mug them got his head kicked in. A fractured skull. Three days in a coma. He came out of it and survived, but he was too scared to press charges.

The story got around. It cemented Luke's reputation, and all of the predators kept their distance. Now when scuffles erupted, it was if and when Luke sought them out.

Levi could still remember what Luke said about it some months later.

"It was like before that, I didn't exist. Now I do."

Maybe that's what they were still doing in a way — kicking heads in to assert their existence, to prove that they were here, that they were alive, their hearts full of napalm. To prove it to the world and to themselves. Except they'd traded up in terms of weapons, swapping fists and feet for a rifle, a handgun, a sawed-off shotgun.

A semi screamed by on the highway, the pitch of its engine standing out from the others, catching his attention. He let the memories go and looked over at the hilltop some ways off.

Still nothing. For now.

CHAPTER 18

Holy Smokes BBQ was located in an unassuming building on the edge of the city. Nestled between a BP gas station and a municipal parking lot, the place had a definite greasy spoon feel to it, complete with a neon light declaring the restaurant to be OPEN. A giant fiberglass pig adorned the roof, decked out in angel wings and devil horns.

Darger could see smoke rising from behind the restaurant, the scent of burning wood and charred meat mingling into a drool-inducing aroma. She supposed she should have expected casual when it came to barbecue. But it wasn't exactly the kind of place she would have pegged as a favorite of Agent Baxter. She had a hard time imagining him in anything but his full suit and tie. Judging by the other patrons, Holy Smokes was more of a board shorts and flip-flops type of establishment.

Despite the humble appearance, the line of hungry people waiting to place an order stretched almost out the door.

"Popular place," she commented.

"Used to be kind of a secret, but I guess they got featured on that show. *Diners, Dives, and...* something or other. Anyway, it's pretty much packed every day around noon now. Even worse on the weekends."

Darger sniffed the air again, taking in the mouth-watering odors wafting about.

"Well, it smells good. That's for sure."

"You ever had Georgia barbecue, Agent Darger?"

"We *do* have barbecue in Virginia, you know."

He scoffed. "So you've had chicken mull?"

"Chicken what?" Darger asked.

Baxter smiled enigmatically. It was possibly the first time she'd seen his mouth do anything but frown or sneer.

"Exactly."

When it was their turn at the counter, the cute young thing behind the register grinned up at Agent Baxter. She had honey-colored eyes and one perfect dimple per cheek.

"Hello, Mister FBI," she said. She batted her eyelashes from underneath the brim of a visor embroidered with the restaurant's name.

"Afternoon."

He nodded politely, barely seeming to notice the girl's shameless flirting. Arrogance or obliviousness? Maybe a little of both. Darger had met more than a handful of good-looking people who were so used to the extra attention the world gave them that they developed a sort of blasé lack of acknowledgment of it.

"Two Butt Plates with slaw and chicken mull," Baxter said, ordering for her without asking. It took some cheek, but ultimately, she didn't mind. Everything on the menu looked good, and when she was away from home, she always trusted a native's judgment.

They found an empty table near the front with a 5-star view of the auto parts store across the street.

"What you said earlier… about putting out feelers?" Ethan said. "Gave me an idea."

"Like what?"

"Well, I'm hesitant to ask anyone tied to the FBI. Too much risk of it getting back to Fitzgerald. I'm sure it will come as a great shock to you to learn that we tend to lock horns fairly frequently."

Darger almost snorted sweet tea out of her nose, thinking back on how she'd imagined almost exactly that image during their argument about the biker gang the day before.

"Right."

"But I might know someone outside the FBI that I trust to be discreet."

"Someone in another agency?"

"You could say that," he answered.

"ATF? Or a local cop?" Darger said, then realized he was probably being intentionally vague. He had no reason to reveal his source to her.

Agent Baxter didn't dignify her guesses with any kind of response, and they were soon interrupted. Instead of calling the name on the order like she did for everyone else, the dimpled counter girl brought the order out to their table. Darger doubted the special treatment even registered with him.

The girl set the trays down. Each one was laden with so much food, Darger could barely see the styrofoam plate underneath. Steam coiled above a bowl full of some sort of primordial ooze. The aforementioned chicken mull, Darger supposed.

"Thank you, ma'am," Baxter said, and the girl flashed a glowing smile at him.

"I confess that I came over with an ulterior motive."

"Oh?"

"I was wondering what cologne it is that you wear. You smell so good," she said, biting her lip.

Darger looked on, amused and curious. It was such a blatant pick up, she wanted to see how he handled it. To start with, she didn't know how the girl could possibly smell him over the various meat and sauce scents drifting through the place. She lifted a fork-load of slaw and shoveled it into her mouth. It was crunchy, creamy, and delicious.

"Oh, I don't wear cologne. I guess it's just my natural musk," he said in absolute seriousness.

Darger choked as she tried to stifle a laugh at the same moment she was swallowing her mouthful. Both Baxter and the girl turned to regard her. She buried her face in her napkin to continue her choke-laughing with a little privacy.

"Excuse me," she finally gasped. "Wrong pipe."

Her outburst must have ruined the moment, or maybe the girl suddenly remembered she had a job to perform. With a final wistful glance at Agent Baxter, she turned on her heel and traipsed back to her post behind the register.

"You are ridiculous," Darger said after the girl had gone.

"Beg your pardon?"

"Your *natural musk*?" she repeated.

"What?"

Darger chuckled and licked her spoon. "Where to begin…"

"It's the truth," he said. "I don't wear cologne."

She could see a little color in his cheeks now. Like he was annoyed or embarrassed. Violet leaned closer to whisper.

"She was hitting on you, dummy."

He frowned. "How do you know?"

"How do you not? It was obvious."

Baxter forked a piece of pork butt and studied her. The combined effect of his chewing and the ruminating look he now gave her brought to mind a particularly intelligent-looking cow.

As he sawed through another piece of pork with his knife, he said, "Anyway, she's not my type."

Darger couldn't resist.

"You have a type?" She sipped at her tea. "Wait, let me

guess."

She squinted as she considered him.

"You're what, 6'1"? 6'2"? So your type is gonna be 5'10". Works out six days a week. Naturally blonde, bottles need not apply. Big, white teeth to set off her impeccable tan. College-educated, but once you get married you'll expect her to give up her career to be a full-time housewife and mommy. She had some ambition before that. Law school, med school, astronaut."

He stared at her for a long time, not even the faintest flicker of a smile in his steely gray eyes. Had she offended him? He really needed to lighten up.

"Is this seriously what you do?"

He shook his head, disappointed.

"I can't believe the Bureau pays to fly you all over the country to spout that kind of nonsense."

Ouch, she thought, regretting every word. She'd only been teasing, really. Well… mostly. But apparently Agent Baxter wasn't the teasing type.

They ate in relative silence after that. There was the occasional scrape of a plastic knife or the crinkle of a napkin, but the banter ceased. When she'd had her fill, Violet wiped her fingers on the paper napkin spread in her lap and took a long drink of sweet tea.

"Well?" Agent Baxter asked.

So he was still talking to her, at least. She had begun to wonder if he was giving her the silent treatment after the discussion about his "type."

"I concede your point. Georgia barbecue is not Virginia barbecue."

He raised his fork in the air.

"But did you like it?"

She tipped the now empty styrofoam bowl of chicken mull toward him.

"I know you Southerners are sticklers about manners, and that is the only thing that kept me from jamming my face into this bowl to lick it clean."

The rare smile returned, transforming his face into something softer. Warmer. He really was pretty handsome when he smiled, she had to admit.

Had he forgiven her for mocking him earlier? She still wasn't certain if he'd been insulted or if he just didn't appreciate her sense of humor.

He dabbed at his lips with his napkin and dropped it on top of his tray.

"Ready to go?" he asked.

"Sure."

They crossed the parking lot, heat distortion rippling from the baking macadam.

"I have a favor to ask," she said.

The interior of the Suburban was stifling after sitting out in the heat for an hour, even with the windows cracked. Baxter cranked up the AC, and Violet directed one of the vents directly at her face.

"What's that?"

"I never got a chance to check out the first scene," she said. "Could you take me there?"

"I can drive you past it, but it's a freeway, you know. Can't really stop and take in the scenery."

They rolled through a residential area, white picket fences and petunias passing by in a blur.

"What about where he shot from?"

"The hill overlooking the freeway?"

Darger nodded.

"I've seen it on a map, but I'd like to be there in person. To see it how he saw it."

"What time do you have to be back at the call center?"

Darger glanced at her watch. It was a few minutes after 1 PM.

"Not until four," she said.

"Should give us plenty of time to head out there and back," he said and hung a left at the next cross street. "I have to make a quick stop before we go."

They passed a squat house made of tan brick. A moment later, they went by an identical brick cube. And then another, and another. Even the scrubby little yards with the gravel driveways were the same.

"Imagine coming home after a few too many drinks and trying to figure out which house is yours," she said, thinking out loud.

Ethan shot her a look that she could only interpret as disapproving.

"Not that I would ever do something so… irresponsible," she said.

He didn't reply. The car slowed and rolled up to the curb in front of one of the brick dwellings. This one happened to have one distinguishing landmark: a rather large statue of Mary cloistered under half an upended bathtub. Violet had seen bathtub Madonnas before, but never one this large. Or perhaps the house being so small was what made the statue appear oversized.

Violet had been wondering if this was Ethan's neighborhood. After seeing the statue, she was certain it wasn't. Even if he were a religious zealot, no way would he have that thing in his yard. Now that she thought about it, this whole neighborhood had a very un-Baxter vibe to it. She tried to imagine who he might know that would live here. His enigmatic contact perhaps?

He turned off the ignition and unbuckled his seatbelt.

"Is this the guy?"

"Don't worry about it," he said.

Violet paused with her thumb on her seatbelt release button.

"Whoa. I thought we were teammates now. BBQ buddies."

"Just stay here," he commanded.

The hard, unfriendly tone was back in his voice. Maybe he hadn't forgiven her for the teasing after all.

He exited the vehicle and crossed the crispy-looking grass on the front lawn, then entered the screened porch area and disappeared from view.

"Damn," Darger said.

Agent Baxter's reticence about his source only increased her curiosity. She was just naturally nosy that way.

She tried to imagine who it could be. An ex-biker? An old lady on the outs? Would a biker guy or gal be the type to install an Our Lady of the Bathtub in their front lawn?

She didn't have long to ponder the mystery. Baxter had barely been inside for two minutes when he was striding back to the car.

"That was quick," she said as he climbed into the driver's seat.

"Yep," was all he said.

Agent Bastard, we meet again, she thought to herself as he started the car.

CHAPTER 19

As they drove on to the scene of the first shooting, Darger noted a distinct darkening of the sky off to the west. The low bank of clouds hugging the horizon there had a bruised look. A storm was coming.

Agent Baxter took a right onto an unmarked service road. It was unpaved, a gash of dirt running up and around a small hill that overlooked the freeway. Despite being a stone's throw from downtown Atlanta and in clear view of the freeway, it had a remote feel to it.

"He must have picked this spot out pretty carefully."

He grunted in what she thought might be agreement.

"I bet most people that drive past the entrance to this road never even notice it," she continued. "But he did."

Baxter brought the Chevy to a stop just shy of the police tape still strung between two bushes. It shuddered and swayed in the breeze that warned of the oncoming weather.

"I don't know if anyone mentioned it to you, but Lake Street bridge is a — well, I don't like using the word *popular* — spot for jumpers."

"Jumpers? You mean suicides?" she asked.

He dragged a knuckle over the edge of his prickly jaw and nodded.

"Have you run any of the names? What if he's a family member of someone who—"

"Already on it," Baxter said. "I can email you the list if you'd like."

"Yes, please. And thank you."

She was appreciative that he'd offered to share and felt like maybe they'd regained some of the ground lost when she'd teased him about his "type."

"That stuff I said earlier — about the kind of woman you date — I was only screwing around. I meant no offense."

He shrugged.

"None taken," he said. "And for your information, my last girlfriend was a short brunette who taught the seventh grade."

Last girlfriend, Darger noted, wanting to point out that maybe she wasn't his *current* girlfriend because she wasn't actually his type. But for once, Violet had the sense to keep her mouth shut.

"Although, I did date a blonde pre-Med in college," he admitted.

"Ha!" Darger clapped her hands. "How you like them profiling-nonsense apples?"

Baxter smirked and started to climb out of the car. He angled his head to look in at her.

"You know what they say about blind hogs," he said.

Darger paused, one foot out the door. She didn't know what they said about blind hogs, but she supposed she was about to find out.

She did not.

There was a loud peal of thunder. From their position on the hill, the crack and rumble of it echoed ominously over the terrain.

Ethan hadn't finished his thought yet. In fact, he hadn't said anything for the last few seconds. Swiveling her head to where he still stood next to the vehicle, she peered up at him.

"Well? What do they say?"

Ethan's mouth was pressed closed like he was thinking hard

on something. His lips parted when she spoke, but still he said nothing. In what looked like slow motion, his chin dipped down to touch his chest.

That was when she saw the dot of red on his white shirt. A nosebleed, she thought at first. And then the red spread before her eyes, growing like a puddle to color more and more of his chest.

"Baxter!"

His left hand was resting on top of the roof, and his fingers squeaked against the polished exterior as he slid downward, knees buckling. He crumpled in a heap next to the truck, curled up on his side, one leg splayed beneath the undercarriage.

For a second, she could only watch the stain on his shirt growing ever wider. It was wet. Thick. The fabric settled against his chest as the red saturated it.

Darger spun out of her seat and jumped to the ground. Her fingers were already reaching into her pocket for her phone when a loud crack sounded and the window of her passenger side door burst into a thousand fragments. She instinctively dropped to her knees and cupped her arms over her head. Frozen in that position, she stared up at the shattered glass, her thoughts finally catching up to her panic.

The sniper had shot Ethan, and now he was gunning for her.

CHAPTER 20

She dove away from the vehicle, sailing over the edge of the hill, and coming down hard on her elbow. Violet's momentum carried her into a barrel-roll the rest of the way down the incline. She bumped over rocks and tree roots and dry grass before she came to a stop in a cloud of dust. A fork of lightning lit the sky in the distance. The thunder barely registered over the thrum of her pulse in her ears.

She was ten or fifteen feet below the hilltop now, crouched behind a bush. She peeked up at the front end of the Suburban, at the shattered window she'd been standing beside only a few seconds ago. Could the shooter still see her? She figured he was positioned somewhere to her left, looking down on the back of the vehicle. She surveyed the surrounding landscape but found nothing out of the ordinary. Glancing farther down the hill, she found a dismaying lack of shrubbery to use as cover. She was stuck here.

Loshak, she thought, fumbling for her phone. She had to call Loshak.

No, 911 first.

Her hand shook as she dialed 911.

"911, where is your emergency?"

Darger's head whipped around, remembering then that the road, as far as she knew, didn't even have a name.

"It's a service road. There's no name. It's just off I-20. Exit 50-something. 52?"

"Pardon me, ma'am? I couldn't hear that last part. Can you tell me where you are?"

Darger pressed her lips to the speaker of the phone, as if that might get her point across more clearly.

"I'm an FBI agent, and I have another agent down with a gunshot wound to the chest. Tell the first responders to go to the hill next to the first sniper crime scene. They'll know where it is."

It wasn't until the words came tumbling out of her mouth that Darger fully realized that Ethan was still up there. Alone. She'd just left him there.

"Ma'am," the 911 operator's voice came through the ear piece. "I need an address for your location."

Darger's attention snapped back to the phone call.

"I told you, there's no address! I'm on top of a hill. The hill near the first sniper shooting—"

There was a crackle over the line, and Darger pulled the phone away from her ear. A red phone icon blinked with text that read: CALL ENDED.

"Shit!"

Darger tried to redial, but a message blipped at her that she was out of service range. No wireless networks found.

"No, no, no," she muttered to herself.

How long had it been since the last gunshot? A minute? More? Had the shooter given up? Or was he waiting for her to come out from her hiding spot?

Her mind was racing, and she struggled to reason through it.

He would have to assume she'd call for backup. As soon as word got out that an agent was down, they'd have helicopters swarming the area within minutes. Roadblocks.

He wouldn't stick around. He would run.

She stood from behind her cover, holding her breath. She

counted to ten. And nothing happened. Still not sure if she was walking to her death, she began to claw her way back up the slope.

She was not going to let Ethan Baxter die on this hill.

CHAPTER 21

She scrabbled over the lip of the ravine and hurried to Agent Baxter's side. The sharp edges of stone and loose gravel bit into her knees as she knelt beside him, but she barely felt it.

Ethan's eyes stared straight up at the murky Georgia sky, unblinking. But for the rise and fall of his chest, she might have thought he was already dead.

The bloodstain was even bigger now, the size of a dinner plate and growing still. Darger held her hand to the wound, applying pressure, but she could feel the blood pulsing out in bursts.

"Agent Baxter, can you hear me?"

He still didn't look at her. She fumbled with the buttons on her blouse, ripping the last few off in her impatience. She folded the shirt into a rough square and pressed it to his chest.

"I called for help. Just stay with my voice now," she begged him, leaning forward to keep pressure on the hole in his chest.

He was not responsive. His eyelids were barely parted and his mouth hung open, but she could see that he was still breathing, though his breaths were rapid and shallow.

"Ethan?" she said.

The shirt she held over his injury was quickly sodden with blood, and she pulled it away for a moment to try to find a dry spot. As she did that, Ethan wheezed.

No, she corrected herself, he hadn't made any noise from his mouth. The noise had come from the wound. She removed the bloody wad and again noted the strange sound. Half hiss, half gurgle. And the blood was frothy and pink. Bubbles.

Something tickled in the back of her mind. That sound and those bubbles meant something. What was it? She'd taken an advanced first aid class only a few months ago, but the details eluded her. Her mind was a swirling torrent of fear. What if the ambulance couldn't find them? What if the 911 operator decided it was a prank call and never sent anyone at all?

Stop it, Violet. Think.

She tried a centering exercise.

I'm Violet Darger.

I live at 437 West Walnut Street, Apartment 1.

And right now I'm stranded on top of a goddamned mountain with a dying man.

Fuck!

But it must have been enough, because the correct sequence of words came to her. She said them out loud.

"Sucking chest wound."

Also known as a pneumothorax. Or was it a hemothorax? She couldn't remember just now, and it didn't matter. She knew it meant that the bullet — or perhaps a bone fragment from a shattered rib — had punctured his lung. That meant it couldn't inflate properly, and precious oxygen was leaking out of the wound every time he took a breath.

She needed an occlusive dressing. She glanced at Ethan's face, noting his pallor and the blue tinge to his lips. She needed that dressing now.

She dove into the truck, digging around for a First Aid kit. Come on, she thought as she checked the center console. A meticulous bastard like Ethan had to have a First Aid kit in his car. Her fingers fumbled at the glove box, practically ripping the door off in her haste. There was a rectangular white box nestled underneath the user manual for the vehicle. She tugged it free, immediately recognizing the red letters and large cross on the lid.

She popped it open, hustling back to Ethan's side to continue compressing the wound while she searched. Her free hand sifted through the contents of the box: Band-Aids, alcohol and Betadine pads, medical tape, exam gloves, antiseptic wound spray, a pair of scissors, an Ace wrap. Finally she reached a stack of large bandages on the bottom. There was a plastic baggie filled with gauze bandages in a variety of sizes and two large abdominal pads. No occlusive dressings.

She ripped open the two abdominal pads and pressed them to the wound while she thought. Her wadded shirt made a wet splat as she tossed it aside.

Occlusive was just the opposite of absorbent. She needed something to block the flow of air from the wound. Airtight. Waterproof.

She looked down at the contents of the First Aid kid again. The plastic baggie. She opened the zipper at one end and shook out the gauze squares. Next, she collected the medical tape and the scissors. She removed his tie, stuffing it into her pocket, and used the scissors to cut away the front of Ethan's shirt. The scraps of fabric came in handy for cleaning up the blood in the surrounding area. She needed a dry surface for the tape to adhere to.

Then, quickly, she pressed the plastic bag to the wound and taped it down. Remembering that the real occlusive bandages were open on one side, she left the lower end of the plastic bag unfastened.

When Ethan took his next breath, she leaned closer to listen and watch.

His chest rose on an exhale. When it started to fall, Darger could see the bag pucker as the wound pulled at it, suctioning the plastic and sealing the hole. The gurgling sound was gone, and his breaths seemed more even now.

"Ethan, are you with me?"

His eyes rolled slowly over to where she crouched next to him. They were glassy and out of focus. She was probably not much more than a dark blur looming over him.

He responded with the slightest nod of the head. With her hands free, she found his fingers and gave them a squeeze.

"You're going to be OK. Hold on."

What next?

A little voice in her head spoke up: exit wound.

Right. She hesitated to move him. A shot to the chest meant a risk for spinal injury. Shifting his position could make things worse. Then again, if he had another gaping hole in the back of his lung, he'd be dead soon for certain.

"I need to roll you on your side to check for an exit wound."

There was a lot of blood staining the white shirt underneath him, and she was sure that meant another wound. But after she cut and peeled the crimson fabric away and lifted him enough to get a look at his back, she didn't find anything. She wrapped her hand in the remaining gauze and wiped as much of the blood away as she could, to be certain.

Ethan was quite a bit taller and a lot more heavily muscled than she was, and Darger grunted as she gently rolled him back into a supine position. As limp as he was in his current state, he was damned heavy.

"Good news," she said, though she wasn't sure how good it actually was that the bullet was lodged somewhere in his body. "No exit wound."

She considered the lack of an exit wound for a moment, and

recalled that the shooter used hollow points in the Publix attack. Less penetration. More tissue damage.

Ethan's eyelids rolled closed again. His face looked still and almost peaceful now.

Christ, was he still breathing?

Darger reached out to take his pulse. Just as her fingers made contact with the point under his jaw, she heard them.

Sirens.

CHAPTER 22

The ER waiting room was chaos. Dozens of voices talking, shouting, muttering at once. Shoes squeaking over linoleum. Gurneys rolling by, bumping through swinging doors. Metallic instruments clinking against trays.

Violet heard none of it. She hunched there, playing it over and over in her head: Baxter climbing out of the car, pausing next to the door. The way he pitched forward and then slid to the ground. The frothy blood running into the dirt.

"Darger!"

Loshak's voice broke through the racket.

She looked up, saw him approaching, then let her gaze fall back to the floor.

He took the empty seat next to her and laid a hand on her shoulder.

"You OK?"

She searched for an appropriate word or gesture and settled on a nod.

"Baxter?" Loshak asked, running his fingers through his hair.

At the name, she lifted her head again to stare him in the eye.

"In surgery. They wouldn't tell me much, but it's not good."

The hand in his hair clenched into a fist, tugging at the strands caught in his grip. His fingers released and fell into his lap.

"How did you know I was here?" she asked.

She could barely muster more than a whisper, and given the

noise level of the hospital floor, she was surprised Loshak could hear her at all.

"What are you talking about?" Loshak pawed at his face and gave her a worried look. "You called me."

Darger frowned down at her lap, noticed her phone there. The screen was covered in reddish-brown smears.

Had she called him? She didn't remember. Everything after the moment Baxter had been shot was all mixed up in her mind. She couldn't remember calling 911, but she recalled talking to a woman and trying to explain where they were, so she must have. And the ambulance ride. She vaguely recalled a paramedic hustling her into the back of an ambulance, and now she was here at the hospital. But the details were gone. Had they run the sirens the whole ride?

"I forgot," she said.

Loshak studied her with concern while she mulled these things over in silence. The hand on her shoulder squeezed.

"Why don't I take you back to the hotel?"

The thought of leaving alarmed her for some reason. She had to know that Agent Baxter made it through surgery. If he was going to be alright.

"I want to stay."

"Look, I know how this is gonna go. He'll be in surgery for a few hours at least, and after that, he'll go to recovery. The doctors aren't going to tell you anything since you're not family."

Violet started to protest.

"Listen! Let me take you back to the hotel so you can get cleaned up. You're a mess, kid."

Violet glanced down, noticed the dried blood caked around her fingernails.

"Shower, get some food in you, and then you can come back and check on Agent — on Ethan. I'll drive you back down here myself."

Somewhere in there, Loshak's tone had turned consoling, like he was talking to an ornery toddler who was refusing a nap. Violet didn't have it in her to complain about it. In a way, it was actually reassuring.

"OK," she said.

The blood on her hands caught her eye again as she stood.

"But first I want to go wash my hands."

Violet cranked the shower onto the hottest setting. Steam billowed past the vinyl shower curtain, fogging the mirror. She couldn't seem to focus enough to use soap or shampoo, so she leaned under the shower head and let the stream of hot water pummel her skin.

The white noise of the falling water made her feel like she was closed off from everything. A secure place where she could take her insides out and study them without worrying about being intruded upon.

She cried. Big, gasping sobs that heaved out of her chest with so much force she had to brace herself against the tiled wall.

When the tears had subsided, and all that was left were a few whimpering hiccups, she felt better. Lighter. Whether it was the release of pressure that had been building in her for some time or endorphins from the cry, she felt calmer. Actually, she felt tired.

She put on a clean pair of joggers and a loose t-shirt and wrapped her hair in a towel. When she exited the bathroom, Loshak bustled in from the hallway, tray in hand. He set it down on the bedside table.

"Ordered up a pot of tea and some toast."

"Thank you," she said, lowering herself onto the mattress.

She folded her knees to her chest and leaned back against the headboard.

Loshak unfolded a newspaper and read — or pretended to read — while she sipped at the tea. She sensed him watching her from over the edge of the paper periodically, though he did not press her to talk.

Rain pinged against the window, and Violet watched the drops pummel the glass, streaking it with wet, turning it into a smear of color and light.

CHAPTER 23

Her eyes were closed, but she knew she was in bed. She could feel the mattress beneath her, the pillow propping her head up. But something was wrong.

Wet.

The sheets were wet. And warm. And sticky. And that smell…

Blood.

The sheets were soaked in blood. Ethan's blood. He lay next to her on the bed, mouth gaping, eyes staring sightlessly. A fly buzzed overhead and then landed on his cheek. He didn't blink or twitch.

Ethan was dead, and she was lying in a pool of his blood.

Violet tried to scream and woke herself from the dream, her hands still clinging to the sheets that were not wet and certainly not drenched in gore.

It was a moment before she was able to catch her breath and reorient herself to her surroundings.

Her hotel room. In Atlanta.

The drapes were open, and she could see that the sky was tinted pink from the setting sun. A soft light filtered in through the window still streaked with rain from the storm earlier.

There was a strange weight on her head. Feeling with her hand, she found the towel still wound around her hair. She unwrapped it, freeing the still-damp tresses and combing her fingers through the tangles.

Violet inhaled sharply as a noise broke the silence: it sounded like a heavy piece of furniture being dragged over a slightly sticky wood floor.

She released the death grip she had on the towel once she realized what it was: Loshak had fallen asleep in the chair across the room, and now he was snoring.

She checked her phone. It was almost 7 PM, halfway through what would have been her shift monitoring the tip line.

Duty called.

While she changed in the bathroom, she debated waking Loshak. The chair he'd zonked in couldn't be comfortable, and it probably only made the snoring worse. Then again, if she woke him up, he'd insist on taking her shift. She knew that for certain.

She'd leave him there, then. A tiny vengeful part of her relished the notion of letting *him* sleep this time.

There was no line at security when Darger arrived at the Atlanta field office. Not surprising considering the hour. Even though the building was open 24 hours a day, most of the employees still worked a regular 9 to 5.

She greeted the two guards manning the x-ray scanner, and they waved her through. After passing under the arch of the metal detector and collecting her belongings, Darger took an elevator up to their makeshift call center.

Hushed voices emanated from the cubicles inhabited by the tip line operators. Among them, Darger recognized a familiar silhouette, the head adorned with sleek black braids.

Not currently on a call, Agent Dawson removed her headset and joined Darger at the coffee station.

"I didn't expect to see you here," Darger said, then held up a paper cup. "Coffee?"

"Please. I hung around the hospital for a few hours, but the doctors told Ethan's family it would be a while before they had any news. Once the story hit the five o'clock news, a big rush of tips streamed in. I figured I'd come down and help answer phones."

"Any updates on Ethan?" Darger asked.

"I got a text from his mother about an hour ago. He made it through the operation OK, but he's still in critical condition."

Darger nodded mutely and fiddled with her coffee swizzle stick.

"Have you been partners long?"

"About two years," Dawson said. "I know he's very intense sometimes, but he's so bright. And he wants the job done right. I owe you a debt of gratitude, you know? You saved his life."

Darger swallowed a knot in her throat, feeling a strange mixture of guilt and helplessness. If he died — she stopped the thought there.

He wasn't going to die.

"I've been meaning to tell you, I saw the story on you. The interview in *Vanity Fair.*"

"Oh. Yeah."

Darger never knew what to say when people brought the article up. The attention made her uneasy.

"I was glad to see the Bureau give the spotlight to a female agent for once."

This too made Darger a bit uncomfortable. She rarely thought about her gender when she was doing her job. Not unless someone else was pointing it out to her.

Dawson stifled a yawn.

"Oh goodness," she said. "Excuse me for that. I thought the coffee would help, but I think at a certain age your body doesn't give one iota how much caffeine you've had. Tired is tired."

Looking around the room, Darger could see that only two of the four operators were currently on a call.

"You should go, then. Get some sleep. It sounds like things have calmed down here. Thank you for coming to help."

Agent Dawson put a hand on Darger's shoulder.

"I should be the one thanking you. I mean that."

Darger held the other woman's gaze for several seconds before she lowered her eyes to stare into her coffee.

Agent Dawson set her cup down and stretched. As she collected her bag and jacket from the cubicle she'd been assigned to, Darger called out to her.

"Agent Dawson?"

"Yes?"

"Do you know what floor Ethan is on?"

"He's in the Pulmonary wing of Critical Care. Second floor."

They exchanged goodbyes, and Darger settled in behind her computer. She slid on a pair of headphones and clicked the first logged call highlighted in red to indicate that it had been deemed "High Priority." By the time she'd reached the third call, the outside world had faded from her awareness.

Darger had only been at it for an hour when her pocket buzzed. She knew it was Loshak before she even glanced at the screen.

"Where are you?" he asked, not even giving her a chance to properly answer the phone.

"And a good evening to you as well, Sleeping Beauty," she said. "I'm at the call center. It's my turn."

"Damn it, Violet. You know I—"

She interrupted.

"I know you would have insisted I stay back at the hotel to drown in my own guilt and self-pity, yes."

"Well, not exactly that," he grumbled. "But you could be resting."

"I don't need rest. I need work."

A sigh rustled out of the phone speaker.

"Just… don't overdo it, OK? I'd rather you not repeat my mistakes."

She went back to work, sifting through the logged calls. One caller insisted she'd seen a blue Ford pickup truck in the vicinity of the hilltop around the time Ethan was shot. But the very next caller swore she saw a man in a gray hoodie speeding away in a red Geo Metro near the Publix shooting. Yet another message contended that a spaceship was the madman's method of transportation. She sighed, feeling like they were grasping at straws.

The next time Darger glanced away from her screen, ASAC Fitzgerald was there. It was distraction after distraction tonight.

Darger refocused her attention on the screen, hoping Fitzgerald would be satisfied by quickly poking his beak into the room, seeing they were busy, and leaving them to it. She wasn't so lucky.

He hovered at the perimeter of her cubicle until she removed her headphones and gave him her full attention.

"Have you made any progress, Agent Darger?" he asked.

"We've got a couple vehicle descriptions for the various crime scenes. But most of them conflict with one another, so nothing solid yet."

He gave a curt nod.

"Keep at it. I want results."

Results, she thought sourly. Like she could make a solid tip appear out of thin air. Too bad she forgot to bring her magic wand.

She knew what he was really saying, of course. When tragic things occurred, people had a tendency to short circuit. They wanted an explanation. And so they cast about, searching for someone to hold accountable. Or more often, someone to blame. There had to be a "reason" after all. Bad things couldn't just *happen.* The truth was bad things "just happened" every day. Chaos was all around them, all the time.

But the public demanded answers. They looked to the police and the politicians — the men in charge — to tell them *why.* And one or more of those men was surely breathing down Fitzgerald's neck at this very moment. That shit trickled down.

Fitzgerald would breathe on Darger, and Darger was supposed to breathe on the operators and analysts, and it all accomplished nothing. Tip lines were all about the random luck of someone calling in with a piece of valid intel. No one had any control over that. No one could push people to call in with better information.

Only after he departed did it occur to her that he hadn't mentioned what happened with Agent Baxter. Did he even care?

CHAPTER 24

The ding of the elevator sounded particularly shrill in the quiet of the Critical Care Unit. It was late. Too late for visiting hours. That was what she'd been told by the woman at the information desk downstairs. Violet didn't care about their rules right now.

She paced the halls until she found the room Ethan Baxter was in. All of the CCU rooms had large sliding glass doors. Easier for the nursing staff to keep an eye on patients that required round-the-clock care, she supposed. Each room also had a curtain that could be closed for privacy or to cut the light from the hallway. Some of the rooms had the curtains thrown wide. Others were pulled closed.

When Violet found Ethan's room, the curtains were shut. She only wanted to see him for a moment. To see with her own eyes that he was alive. And to promise him that she would find the man who did this.

Her hand reached for the door handle, sliding it to the side with only a vague whooshing sound. The curtain fluttered around her as she stepped through. Her head cleared the billowing fabric first. She blinked, expecting her eyes to need to adjust to the darkness inside. But the blinds over the windows were open, and the lights of the city gave off a yellow glow.

A man stood before the window, a silhouette in the dimness. He turned at the sound of Violet coming into the room, and she stopped. Her breath caught in her throat.

It was him. It was Ethan. He was… standing. On his own. He looked unscathed. Healthy.

"Violet?" he whispered.

She couldn't answer.

He took a step forward and smiled, and she thought: No. He looked better than healthy. He was more relaxed than she'd ever seen him. There was an ease to his movements now. And his hair was different. Longer, falling in waves over his forehead and ears. The stubble she'd noticed earlier was now cropped into a short beard.

Her eyes flicked to the right, saw the man in the bed. Face swollen almost beyond recognition. Tubes at his mouth and nose. This. This was the Ethan she'd expected to see.

The other Ethan was close enough to touch now. He reached for her hand.

His ghost, she thought. I'm seeing Ethan's ghost.

She closed her eyes and willed herself to wake up. It was a dream. It had to be.

The fingers that enclosed around hers were warm and dry.

Her eyes snapped open. Ethan's ghost frowned down at her, still holding her hand.

His lips parted, and she wondered what he might say. What words from beyond would he impart? Wisdom or resentment?

"I'm Owen," he said. "Ethan's brother."

CHAPTER 25

Owen, who turned out to be not only Ethan's brother, but his *twin* brother, insisted on buying her a coffee in the small 24-hour cafe on the ground floor of the hospital.

"You know, we used to pull all kinds of Doublemint shenanigans when we were kids. But we never thought of trying the whole ghost angle. I can't wait to tell him," Owen said, chuckling.

Darger pressed the styrofoam cup to her lips and sipped her coffee to stifle a groan. She still wasn't sure why she'd told him, and she regretted it more every passing second.

"The doctors are optimistic?" she asked.

He folded his arms behind his head and stretched out against the back of the chair.

"Eh, you know what they're like. They're still saying it's too early to tell. But I know my brother. I mean, you've worked with him, right?"

"I only met him a few days ago, actually. I don't know him all that well."

"Yeah, but I bet you got a taste of Ethan Baxter in only that short amount of time," he said, then leaned across the table and gave her a sly look. "Kind of a prick, right?"

"I..." Darger struggled to find the words.

"It's OK, I take no offense. He sure doesn't. He's a stubborn son of a bitch. That's why I know he'll pull through."

He flashed her a wicked grin. It was infectious, and she couldn't help but smile back.

"Uncanny resemblance aside," she said, "are you sure you're

brothers? You seem nothing like him."

"I appreciate that."

When she'd finished her coffee, Violet stood to dispose of her cup.

"Will you come back upstairs before you go?" Owen asked. "Mom was sleeping when you came in before, but I bet she's awake now. She'll want to meet you."

"Why would she want to meet me?"

"Because you're the one who saved Ethan's life."

"But I didn't do anything," Violet said, feeling an intense pressure in her chest.

"That's not what the attending physician in the ER said. And the pulmonary specialist. They said if you hadn't improvised that dressing, Ethan wouldn't have made it."

Violet looked down at a spot of light bouncing off the polished tile floor, not sure what to say. It felt wrong to be lauded as a hero like this when she was at fault.

"Weren't you afraid he'd shoot you, too?"

"He tried. I figured once he missed he'd give up, knowing I'd call for help. But mostly I was in panic mode."

One of Owen's dark eyebrows arched into a quizzical expression.

"Doesn't sound like you panicked to me. Not at all. Sounds more like you kept your cool, despite everything that was happening."

She swallowed against the lump in her throat. She started to protest, but Owen was already pulling her into the elevator.

"I figure you came down here to see him, right?"

"I was told that visiting hours don't start until morning," she said, suddenly wishing she hadn't come. She'd only wanted to look in on Ethan for a moment. Quietly. Having all this unearned gratitude heaped on her from his family was too much.

Owen squinted at her, amused.

"Yeah, you seemed very concerned about visiting hours when you poked your head into the room a few minutes ago," he said.

The doors of the elevator clattered open, and he beckoned her to follow. With a sigh, Violet gave in.

She paused again at the threshold. Owen placed a hand on the small of her back and propelled her into Ethan's room.

Constance Baxter was short and full-figured, with round cheeks and big Southern hair. Despite her small stature, there was a brightness in her eyes that told Violet where Agent Baxter got his determination from.

"I'm sorry to intrude so late," Violet said after Owen had made introductions.

"Don't you dare apologize," Mrs. Baxter said. "You are welcome to visit anytime, day or night."

Mrs. Baxter nudged her closer to the bed. These Baxters were an insistent bunch. And more hands-on than Violet was used to.

"We'll give you a little privacy. Go ahead and talk to him. It helps," she said. "I know it does."

The curtains over the door swished as Owen and his mother passed through them. Violet took a step closer to the bed.

Ethan was almost unrecognizable. Darger counted six separate IV pumps leading to the PICC line below Ethan's collarbone. His face was swollen from the amount of fluids he'd been given. The features that had always seemed so hard before looked soft and puffy. There was a feeding tube in his nose, and a ventilator tube running into his mouth. On the side opposite her, she could see where the doctors had inserted a drainage tube for his chest wound.

Violet took his hand in hers, his fingers limp and fleshy.

"It was my fault," she whispered. "I shouldn't have—"

The words caught in her throat as fresh tears burned her eyes. She gripped the side of the bed, feeling like the floor might drop out from under her feet at any moment.

Why had she asked him to take her up there? Why hadn't she considered the risk they might be in?

She couldn't have known, that's what everyone kept saying. But the truth was, she could have. The DC snipers said they wanted to shoot a cop and then plant bombs at the funeral. Maybe that had been the ultimate goal here as well. And she should have seen it coming.

If that had been the plan, the shooter had failed, at least. Ethan was alive. There could be no funeral to booby trap.

She wondered if he'd try again but thought not. Not the same way, anyhow. The crime scenes were more securely locked down after today, and they would be closely watched going forward.

One of the monitors blipped, interrupting her thoughts. She took in all of the machines and bags and tubes currently keeping Ethan alive and had trouble catching her breath for a moment.

Breathe, she thought to herself, not wanting his family to see her so emotional.

She inhaled, counted to three, and then let the air out in one big sigh.

"I'm going to get the son of a bitch that did this, Baxter. I promise you that."

She gave his fingers one last gentle squeeze before she stepped away from the bed and passed through the curtains to the hallway beyond.

CHAPTER 26

When Darger awoke the next morning, she felt surprisingly refreshed. Then she remembered the events of the previous afternoon, and her mood tanked. She tugged at the rough motel sheets and wished she were home where she could stay in bed and mope. She did not want to hike her butt down to the call center where she'd spend eight hours sifting through nutjob phone calls. She wanted greasy pizza and ice cream straight from the carton and something mindless to binge-watch on TV.

Her eyes flicked over to the screen on the dresser. The only mindless TV she'd find today would be more coverage of the shootings. At least the busy work would take her mind off of… well, everything.

Remembering Loshak's pearl of wisdom about keeping their team motivated, Darger called in another Dunkin Donuts order. The boxes of coffee and assorted lumps of fried and glazed dough were ready at the counter when she went in.

Like a bloodhound scenting a fox, Loshak spied her as soon as she stepped through the door. He spun out of his chair and strode over. She suspected it was the donuts and coffee that drew him more than her person.

Loshak lifted a dough ball from the box and popped it in his mouth before she'd even set everything down.

"I stopped over at the hospital after I left here last night."

He gave her a disapproving look, not needing to say a word. She knew what he was thinking and was glad his mouth was full.

"It was a short visit," she insisted, waving a hand around her face. "Note the distinct lack of bags under my eyes. The fresh, rejuvenated appearance of my skin. Surely all of this evidence attests to the fact that I got a solid stretch of sleep."

"You see Baxter?" he asked through a mouthful of donut crumbs.

"Two of him," Darger said, then explained about meeting his twin brother. "He said the doctors weren't ready to make any predictions about Ethan's recovery, but Owen was optimistic."

Violet left out the part about thinking she was seeing Ethan's ghost. She wouldn't want Loshak to die laughing, a Dunkin Munchkin lodged in his throat.

"You're supposed to sleep after this. Shouldn't you be drinking the decaf?" she asked.

Loshak lifted the paper cup to his lips and took a long drink. "I thought I was the mother hen in this partnership."

"Cock-a-doodle-fuck-you," she answered.

He smiled, unperturbed.

"One more for the road," he said, picking up another donut hole. "I'll see you this afternoon. Oh hey, when you order in for lunch, we got some dynamite Greek food from a place across town yesterday. The gyro was excellent."

"Duly noted," she said, pouring herself a coffee before ducking into her cubicle.

Darger scrolled through a list of high priority calls that were marked "unplayed." The mouse clicked, and the first file opened and began to play.

By the lack of operator prompts, Darger gathered that this call was a message left when the lines were busy. It was a man's voice, gruff and blustering.

"You people think we're all sheep. Just simple pawns to push around the board."

Darger held her breath.

"But I know what's really going on. Me and other people like me, we see. Our eyes are open."

Could it be him? The paranoia, the thing about sheep and pawns — those were two of the keywords straight out of the profile.

"I seen the news footage. And I know when I'm being lied to. There wasn't no dead body under that sheet in the Publix lot. Not a real one anyway. It was planted. Clear as day. Blood don't move like that. You people think you're clever, but you're not even good actors. I see you smirking at one another. Laughing it up like it's all a big joke. My eyes are open."

She sighed. Another nut, this one apparently convinced that all of the shootings had been some kind of elaborate hoax.

It wasn't unusual, she knew. A certain small percentage of the population couldn't help but look for the most dramatic explanation. And what was more dramatic than an actual spree shooting? A *faked* spree shooting. Perpetrated by Zionists, the Illuminati, a secret class of lizard-people who ruled the world discreetly from their base deep within the Earth's core.

She forced herself to listen to the end of the call, to be sure. To check it off her list without feeling like she might have missed something.

In the next call, a man insisted the shooter was his father.

OPERATOR: Can you tell me your father's name, sir?
CALLER: George Blevins.
OPERATOR: And what leads you to believe your father is responsible for the shootings?
CALLER: They say he's dead, but I know he's not.
OPERATOR: Who's dead, sir?

CALLER: My father. He died in 1989. But I saw him at the Circle K the other day, getting a bag of peanut M&M's. He looked different... I suspect he went through radical plastic surgery, probably numerous surgeries, to change his face. A new identity, you see? But it was him. I know it was. He loves peanut M&M's. Always has.

Darger sighed and refiled the call as low priority.

After that, she played another message from the voicemail system.

"I have foretold what has come to pass for years, but no one wanted to listen. You can not abandon God without violent repercussions. We promote sodomy, abortion, idolatry, and degeneracy. The glory of the great empire of Rome was destroyed by its own depravity and wickedness. The West will face a similar fate if we do not heed the warnings."

She made a note and played the next call. Click. Play. Repeat.

Eventually, she glanced at the clock in the bottom corner of the computer screen, rolling her head from side to side to loosen her sore neck muscles. She'd barely been at it for two hours.

It was going to be a long day.

The morning continued to roll by in a series of clicks, recorded voices, and words on a screen. She was about to take a break when the tone of one call took an interesting turn.

CALLER: If you destroy a nation's culture and patriotism, then you will destroy their allegiance as well.
OPERATOR: I'm sorry... I don't understand.
CALLER: What's to not understand? Without a single unified cultural ethnicity, there *is* no country. The leftist, fascist,

globalist banker's white-genocide agenda is proceeding as planned. They want us on our knees. In slavery and servitude. But there are those among us who will not bow. We will not bow!

The line went dead. Darger blinked at the screen. Well, that one certainly had promise. It hit on about ten of the keywords she and Loshak had put together.

Darger made a few notes in her own file before she forwarded the call to a liaison at Homeland Security. It would take at least a few hours before she'd hear anything back.

CHAPTER 27

The numbness in Levi's hands threaded icy coils into his forearms, and that dead feeling threatened to spread, to freeze away all sensation. He balled his fingers into fists a few times, felt the cold as shards stabbing into the meat of his palms, though he couldn't tell whether the motions made things better or worse.

He looked at his reflection in the rear view mirror, made eye contact with himself, and he felt empty. He was a shell. A husk. A face with nothing behind it.

They drove without destination. The afternoon sun was bright and hot, and the air conditioner in the Jeep was no match for the humidity, but they couldn't sit still. They'd grown sick of the grubby motel room, sick of watching cable news, watching the pundits try to mythologize what they'd done and how it related to partisan politics.

Luke jabbered in the driver's seat of the Jeep. Smoking and talking. Talking and smoking. Levi only registered bits and pieces of it.

He could still see the FBI agent's head and torso as he'd looked through the scope of his rifle, could still sense the thrum of anticipation that had built in his chest as he waited for the man to keep still. And he remembered that incredible moment of emptiness before the muscles in his hand and forearm flexed, and he squeezed the trigger.

There was something clean about the way the bullet spun out of the rifle's barrel. It was different than the handgun, different from the shotgun. It was pure. True.

And after the man had toppled to the ground, he'd watched the girl — the female agent — scrambling away from the scene on hands and knees. He'd fired a round into the vehicle, not really going for her. He could have taken a shot at her as well. A real shot. But he'd hesitated, and by then she'd descended from view, disappearing behind the hill.

"You did good. You know that?" Luke said, his voice interrupting Levi's memories.

He didn't answer. Instead, he plucked the styrofoam cup from the beverage holder, brought it to his lips, sipped. The coffee had that burnt note to it, the blacker than black bitterness it got when the carafe had sat too long on the burner. He'd gotten so used to that acrid bite, though, that he couldn't really enjoy a coffee without it.

"It's happening now," Luke said. "It's all happening. Just like we talked about."

The Jeep wound its way through the suburbs. Brick facades and vinyl siding surrounded them.

"People will pretend like they don't understand it, like they can't imagine why someone would do these things. But they all know. Deep down they know. See, men play almost no role in creation. Only a woman can truly create life," he said, unlit cigarette twitching between his lips. "A woman creates, and a man destroys. That is the duality of our kind, you know? I kind of realized that in Iraq."

He brought the lighter to his face, flicked it, the little flame snuffling into the tube of tobacco, staining the tip black for a beat before it ignited into orange.

"Everywhere we went, everything we did, the threat of suicide bombers was all around us. Each and every time I walked into a building or rounded a corner, the fear was right there, hammering away in my chest. It could be anyone, you know? Man, woman, or child. Anyone. And this wasn't only an internal monologue of paranoia. The higher-ups reinforced the fear. We got warned about it constantly. I mean, these guys blow themselves to bits at the whims of their leaders, ostensibly for their so-called cause. But outside of the destruction itself, what were they accomplishing? The explosions were real enough — the human bodies liquefied to a bloody spray were *very* real — but there was no meaning in it."

He turned to look out the window, took a deep drag of smoke, and let it seep out of his nostrils slowly.

"It started to dawn on me that I was no different. I was following orders, too, wasn't I? I was watching my friends get blown up for nothing. I was putting myself in danger every day in a way that seemed just as meaningless as the suiciders, you know?"

He paused again, blinked a few times.

"It was like almost all of it was bullshit. Whatever meaning you tried to pin on it didn't quite stick. In the long run, only the destruction was real.

"And it's been this way for thousands of years. For all of human history. We fight. We die. We destroy each other and ourselves. Violence is in our nature, man. The bloodstains on our hands and teeth define us. Everyone knows it. Even if we pretend to be domesticated beasts, pretend to be good cattle chewing our cud, deep down we know it's true. And we want it. We want it more than anything."

Levi felt his thoughts spiral, his heart beat faster, that chaotic swirl of emotions that came over him whenever Luke talked like this. It was a language that got through to some part of him — a violent, frightened, angry part of himself that he didn't understand.

"Law enforcement is the living symbol of order. Of the status quo. The false security that keeps the machine functioning. It doesn't matter that none of us are actually safe. All that matters is that we believe that someone is keeping order, someone is keeping watch, manning the wheel. Someone is in charge. When you kill a cop, you knock the props out from under the whole fucking thing. You expose it for the sham that it is, the lie that it is. No one is watching over us. No one cares. The universe is utterly indifferent. At best."

He puffed on his cig, continued.

"Now, a pregnant woman? She is a symbol of life carrying on, of existence persisting indefinitely. When you snuff that out, you're really saying something. Now you're really speaking the truth of our kind. The awful fucking truth."

He smiled.

"It's a violent world, and it's inside all of us. You and me and everyone. We've proven it with bullets. Because power still grows out of the barrel of a gun. That's why we're here, I think."

Still smiling, he looked at Levi, made eye contact with him. His pupils were gaping black pits, demonic and strange.

"This is our legacy, brother. We were born to it."

CHAPTER 28

Darger slid the headphones from her ears. Break time. Turning her head from side to side elicited a series of borderline-disgusting cracks and pops.

Two of the trainees were chatting near one end of the coffee station, and Darger sidled up to refill her cup. She took the steaming brew out into the hall, preferring a few moments of quiet over joining in on the conversation. She was lost in a sea of her own thoughts. And besides that, she'd never been great at group dynamics. She had no problem with one-on-one interactions. In fact, she excelled at it. It was one of the things that made her good at what she did in Victim Assistance.

Drop her in a group, though, and she might as well be in the middle of the ocean without a life preserver. The problem, she thought, was that people in groups were always competing for attention. Because of that, the focus was constantly shifting. Violet was used to giving her undivided concentration to one person. The fluctuations in a group felt like a game of tug-of-war.

One of the analysts, she thought his name was Jerry — or was it Jared? — called out and waved to get her attention from his cubicle. Did he have something? A call she needed to hear? She stepped back into the room.

"Sorry to interrupt your break, Agent Darger, but people are starting to wonder about lunch. Agent Loshak had me order for everyone from Dimitri's yesterday."

Right. She was sort of the boss here, she supposed. Managing personnel wasn't something she was accustomed to.

And deciding what to eat was hard to give much thought to when they were hunting a psycho with a seemingly endless supply of both rage and ammo.

"If you guys are OK with doing that again, it works for me."

"Agent Loshak also had us stagger our breaks yesterday so the phones wouldn't be unmanned."

She gave a single nod. She wondered if Loshak mentioning the gyros was his way of hinting that she'd be expected to make this kind of decision. That or maybe the guy just really loved gyros.

"However you arranged things yesterday is fine."

"Would you like to see the menu?"

"Nah, you can order me the gyro."

Jared — she'd decided it was definitely Jared and not Jerry — joined her in the hall a few minutes later, phone pressed to his ear.

"They're saying it'll be an hour wait for delivery. Fifteen minutes if we pick it up," he relayed.

Darger was already heading back to her desk to grab her keys.

"I got it."

Darger cranked up the air conditioning as soon as she started the car. The earlier weather front brought rain but had done nothing to quell the heat. If anything, the humidity was even more cloying since the storm.

She'd volunteered to pick up the food for a few reasons. One, because she figured it was what a good manager would do. But two, she wanted desperately to get out from underneath the harsh fluorescent lights. She drove past a low hedge of gardenias, relishing the greenery after the dour gray of her cubicle.

The GPS in the car led her across town to the restaurant, and she slid into a parking space out front. As she stepped onto the curb, the growl of an engine drowned out most of the other street sounds. Darger glanced over to see a scrawny guy on a motorcycle rumble up to the traffic light. He stretched out a booted foot to catch his balance while he waited for the light to turn green. That was when she noticed the sticker on the rear fender.

It said: MY OTHER RIDE IS YOUR MOM.

Darger snorted, turning to enter the restaurant.

She was still thinking about the ridiculous bumper sticker a few minutes later as she loaded the food-laden paper bags into her rental. After everything that had happened in the last 24 hours, she'd forgotten about the Nameless Brotherhood and Ethan's mysterious contact outside of the FBI.

What if that person had tried to get in touch with Ethan? What if he or she had information that could lead them to the shooter?

Damn him for being so secretive about it. Why couldn't he have just told her what he was up to?

As Darger steered the car back in the direction of the field office, it occurred to her that maybe she didn't need to know *who* if she knew *where.*

CHAPTER 29

At the strike of four in the afternoon, a shadow fell across Darger's computer monitor. She spun around in her chair.

"Anything?" Loshak asked.

She pulled the headphones from her head and handed them to Loshak.

"This is the best I've got," she said, cueing up the flagged *Will Not Bow* call for him.

Loshak closed his eyes as the recording played out, then ducked out of the headset.

"Not bad. Though my gut says it's not him for some reason."

"Yeah, that was kinda how I felt," she said. "I forwarded the info to Homeland Security. This is what they sent back."

The file slapped onto the desktop, and Loshak paged through it.

"He used a traceable phone?"

Darger rubbed her eyes and tried to keep herself from yawning.

"Not exactly. The call originated from a computer with an IP address originating in Romania. Probably spoofed. But the same IP has a colorful internet history, as you can see from the file."

"A major connoisseur of white supremacy bulletin boards, eh?"

"Pretty much," Darger agreed. "I skimmed through it. It's pretty vanilla, really, at least compared to a lot of the rubbish on these forums. I get the feeling he's older than our profile says — in his fifties or maybe sixties. Look at how he types."

She pointed to a screenshot of posts made on one of the white pride online message boards.

"He either capitalizes every word or none of them. He'll go from six exclamation points at the end of every sentence to no punctuation at all."

Loshak pursed his lips and pretended to look insulted.

"Are you suggesting us fogeys don't know our way around a keyboard?"

She leveled her eyes at him.

"Only the racist ones."

That elicited a hiss of laughter.

"Alright," he said, swatting her with the stack of papers. "Get out of here. Go get some sleep."

Violet collected her things and made for the door.

"Hey, Darger?"

She turned back toward Loshak, and he stuck out an accusatory finger.

"Emphasis on the *sleep* part, right?"

Violet rolled her eyes and proceeded out the door without responding.

"What was that? I didn't catch your answer," he called after her.

She kept walking.

She did not plan on sleeping just yet, but she didn't need to tell Loshak that.

Instead, she fired up the engine of her rental and went off in search of the neighborhood of matching brick tract houses.

She remembered the general area, but it took some circling and a few U-turns before she zeroed in on it. Once she'd found the place, she worried she wouldn't be able to find the particular house she wanted. There had to be a hundred of the little brick boxes, and they all looked the same.

And then she saw it.

Rub-a-dub-dub. Mother Mary in the tub. She had never been so happy to see a statue in her life, religious figure or otherwise.

Violet parked on the street, undid her seatbelt, and wondered again at who she might find inside.

As she picked her way along the gravel driveway, she noticed a newish silver Honda CR-V tucked behind the house. It was a common vehicle and didn't give her much to go on from a profiling angle. If it had been something like a rusty pickup, for example, she might have anticipated that her "contact" was an older man. A minivan would have suggested someone with a family. A Toyota Yaris would bring to mind a college student, probably female.

The neighborhood was clearly working class. The houses were small, the yards sparse. The statue was what kept throwing her off. For all she knew, she was knocking on the door of Ethan's elderly aunt. Instantly a 65-year-old spinster with thirteen guinea pigs and a bad case of gout sprang to mind.

She hoped that wasn't the case. If this wasn't the contact Ethan had mentioned, Violet would be back to analyzing conspiracy theory phone messages. She had no idea how else she'd get information on the Nameless Brotherhood. Perhaps Agent Dawson would have ideas if this didn't pan out.

Violet went up the four steps that led to the screened porch and rapped the side of her fist against the door.

The crack and squeak of old floorboards preceded the home's occupant, and then the main door of the house popped open. Through the haze of the porch screen, Darger recognized the familiar figure.

"Oh," she said. "It's you."

"It's me."

Owen Baxter leaned against the porch frame, barefoot and wearing what she assumed were his pajamas: a pair of gray sweatpants and a threadbare NOFX shirt. Her first thought was that it was the middle of the afternoon, and he looked like he'd just rolled out of bed. Then she considered the fact that his twin brother was in a coma, and she should maybe stop being a judgmental bitch for two seconds. He'd probably been up half the night at the hospital, sitting with his mother.

He fixed her with an expectant look, no doubt wondering what she was doing on his doorstep. He didn't seem put out, at least. More like a combination of amused and curious.

Violet had moved down a step when she saw who was answering the door. Standing eight inches lower than him made her feel like a kid selling candy for a school fundraiser. She resisted the urge to fidget.

"I… must have misunderstood. Sorry."

"Misunderstood what?"

She brushed a strand of hair behind her ear and tried not to let her disappointment show. There was no contact here after all. Ethan had only been stopping by to talk to his brother. Damn it to hell.

"Nothing. Something about the case."

"Something my brother was working on," he said, and it was more a statement than a question.

She met his eyes. They were a stony blue-gray, just like his brother's.

"I can't really talk about it," she said. "I should go. Sorry to bother."

Whatever Owen's interest was — innocent curiosity, she figured — it wouldn't be wise for her to go blabbing about it. She'd already gotten Ethan shot. The least she could do now was keep her mouth shut about his blatant insubordination.

Violet turned and went the rest of the way down the stairs, the soles of her boots thumping against the concrete. Owen called after her.

"This is about the Nameless Brotherhood, isn't it?"

She stopped in her tracks, feet scuffing over the loose stones of the driveway as she spun to face him. Her eyelids squinted ever so slightly.

"What do you know about that?"

"I know that my brother came around asking if I had any information on them. Any contacts that might talk."

"And you'd have access to that kind of information because…"

He crossed his arms over his chest.

"Because I'm a private investigator."

"Huh," she said, struck momentarily dumb by the whirring of thoughts in her head. So his brother *was* the contact. Why hadn't Ethan just said so? Why the secrecy? Another question came to her.

"What would a P.I. know about the Nameless?"

"Depends on the skill of the P.I., I suppose. I happen to be one of the best, so…"

The corner of her mouth quirked upward.

"Certainly not one of the most humble."

"Humility is overrated."

Violet snorted. She was starting to see the family resemblance again.

"So what did you tell him?"

"I didn't have anything for him when he first asked. I needed to get in touch with some people."

"And now?"

"Now I know where the upper echelon Nameless guys hang out on Friday nights."

Bingo. Darger felt a sudden surge of adrenaline. She took a step forward.

"Where?"

"I'll drive," he said as if it were a legitimate answer to her question.

"Uh, I think not."

Now he was the one smirking. Maybe he thought if he stood there and looked smug enough, she'd change her mind. Fat chance.

"This is part of an official FBI investigation," she said. "You're a civilian."

Owen shrugged as if he really couldn't care less.

"Best of luck with your investigation, then."

With that, he slipped back inside. The porch door snapped shut behind him.

Darger's hands balled into fists. What was it with these arrogant, stubborn Baxters?

She strode back up the steps, holding her face an inch away from the screen. Owen hadn't bothered closing the door to the house, and she could see him inside, bustling around the kitchen. He bent down, hands shifting things around in one of the cabinets.

"Just give me the name of the place," she said.

"Sorry, Miss Darger, but either we go together, or I go alone. Those are the only two options."

Owen dumped a measuring cup full of kibble into a metal

bowl on the floor. Dog or cat food, she thought. Sure enough, a large black cat padded into the room a moment later.

"First of all, it's *Agent* Darger. And second, you're obstructing an ongoing investigation. I could have you arrested."

Owen stooped to stroke the cat as it mowed through the kibble.

"Could you now?"

She gave him her hardest stare.

"Don't try me, Baxter."

He returned her glare with a grin that reminded her of a cartoon wolf.

"I know you're bluffing. Ethan told me his boss didn't want him anywhere near the OMGs. That's why he came to me in the first place."

"Did you just say *OMG*?"

"Yeah, as in 'Outlaw Motorcycle Gang.' Not text lingo."

"Oh."

"See, this is exactly why you need me there."

She rolled her eyes. "I can handle myself, thank you."

"Look, all joking aside, I mean it. This isn't your run-of-the-mill street gang made up of juvenile delinquents. These guys are organized. A lot of them have military experience. They aren't fucking around," he said, and then his face hardened further. "Besides, Ethan is my brother."

"And what? You want vengeance?"

"No, I want to know that you're going to catch this motherfucker."

"We will," she said, adding a silent prayer that they'd catch him before more people died.

He straightened from petting the cat.

"Good," he said. "When should I pick you up?"

"I didn't say-"

"You can keep arguing if you want, Miss Darger. But we both know you're gonna go along with it."

"Oh, do we?" she said, overlooking the *Miss* for the moment. She had to pick her battles.

"You would have left by now if you weren't," he said, grinning in such a way that she was sure he was gloating. "Might as well come in. You're making me feel inhospitable hovering there on the front porch like that."

The hinges on the door creaked and groaned as Violet entered the house.

CHAPTER 30

Owen moved into a small room off the living room that turned out to be a rather untidy bedroom. The mess only helped in making it look smaller.

He stooped and lifted a crumpled pile of something from one corner. It turned out to be a battered pair of jeans. He brought them to his nose and sniffed.

With one surprisingly deft flick of the wrist, he dropped the pants he was wearing.

More surprising was the fact that he wasn't wearing any underpants.

"Whoa! Hey!" Darger protested, covering her eyes.

"It's OK." Owen stepped into his jeans looking unconcerned. "I'm not modest."

Darger pivoted so her back was to him.

"Yeah, I gathered that."

When she faced him again, he was pulling a plain black t-shirt over his head. He stepped from the room, leaving the clothes he'd been wearing on the floor. Darger considered her own housekeeping skills and figured she wasn't much better.

Owen was standing close enough to touch, studying her like there might be a pop quiz later. He paid particular attention to her chest and her ass.

"You don't happen to have any leather pants, do you? Maybe a matching fringed vest that shows a lot of cleavage?"

Darger felt her mouth pull together in a tight, disapproving pout she associated with elderly churchgoing women who made a lot of fudge and passed judgment on pretty much everyone.

She forced herself to relax the expression.

"I'm kidding," he said, squeezing past her on his way back to the kitchen.

He toed open the fridge and removed a carton of orange juice. After a long gulp straight from the carton, he paused to catch his breath.

"Thirsty?" he asked, and she shook her head. The fridge door hung wide open behind him, and she had a sudden glimpse of Owen and Ethan as boys.

Owen made messes and Ethan cleaned them up. Or perhaps, a little bit the other way around: Ethan kept everything tidy and ordered, and Owen came through like a tsunami disrupting the perfection with his chaos and irreverence.

She snapped out of it when she realized he was talking.

"Really if you just had a low cut tank top and some jeans, that should work."

He hopped up to sit on the counter, reaching over his shoulder to pull a box of Frosted Flakes from the cupboard.

"You do a lot of this in your line of work?" she asked. "Playing dress-up?"

Instead of answering immediately, he shook the box of cereal at her. Another offering, she guessed. Again, she declined.

"Hey, you gotta make an effort to blend in. And by 'you' I mean especially *you*," Owen said, gesturing at her with the cereal box.

"Meaning?"

"I can smell the bacon on you from a mile away. And if *I* can, you can bet the Nameless will, too."

She crossed her arms and repeated the word.

"Bacon?"

The box of cereal was already open, as he apparently hadn't

even bothered to tuck the flaps or roll the bag closed whenever he'd used it last. Owen thrust a hand inside and came back with a fist of Tony the Tiger's finest.

"Hey, be glad you don't have a law enforcement background like my brother. With those guys, it's practically baked in. You've only got a little of that federale pig-stank on ya."

"Thank you. That's… lovely."

He winked at her as he tossed the handful of dry cereal into his mouth.

She frowned then.

"How did you know I wasn't a cop before?"

He gave her a smug little grin while he chewed.

"I told you. I'm good at what I do."

He gave her another obvious looking-over.

"So, seriously. Got anything more casual?"

CHAPTER 31

She stomped out to her rental car, cursing the Baxter name.

Had he actually referred to her as *bacon*? Jesus Christ.

Sliding into the front seat, she glanced at her reflection in the rear view mirror. And did she really give off vibes of being a Fed that much?

Whatever. Screw him.

The clock on the dash caught her eye. 5:04 PM. She could squeeze in about four hours of sleep before she was supposed to meet Owen back here. That was if she hit the sack as soon as she reached her hotel room.

Her phone rang, and Violet glanced at the screen. Her mother.

"Hi, mom," she answered.

"Oh! You're actually there! I'm so used to it going to voicemail."

Violet sighed, sure her mother hadn't meant it to sound so much like a criticism. She felt a needle-prick of guilt anyway.

"How was the family brunch thing?"

"It was lovely. I wish you could have been there. Everyone missed you, of course. And the food was fabulous. They had lox and bagels, so I thought of you and how you used to just gobble it up when you were little. Do you still like lox?"

"Well, yeah."

Her mother chuckled.

"I was calling to see how your return trip went. You never let me know," her mother said.

Violet bopped herself in the forehead with a fist.

"Shit — I mean, crap. I forgot. I'm sorry."

"Oh, I know you probably ran straight off into some other pickle you can't really tell me about."

She didn't know how to respond for a moment. Her mother sometimes surprised her with little insights like that.

"And there was something else I wanted to tell you, and that is that I bought you a ticket."

Violet puzzled over this. For the life of her, Violet couldn't think of what her mother could be referring to.

"For Europe," her mother clarified.

Europe… Violet recalled her mother mentioning the trip: a two-week bus tour of Spain, France, and Italy. Violet also remembered telling her mom she'd think about it… not that she'd definitely be coming along. And certainly not that she should go ahead and buy a ticket on Violet's behalf.

"Mom, I don't even know if I can—"

"Don't fuss about it. I had the miles and needed to use them anyway. So I figured, why not?"

Violet could think of several reasons why her mother should not have booked a ticket for a trip she'd never agreed to go on, but she said nothing. Instead, she sighed.

"I have no idea if the Bureau would even grant me that much leave."

"But it can't hurt to ask, can it? The worst they could say is no."

Violet tried to imagine being gone from the BAU for two weeks.

"You work so hard for them, I can't fathom how they could say no. You deserve a little vacation. Some relaxation time," her mother said.

Trapped in a tour bus with her mother and two dozen other

bored, wealthy housewives sounded like the opposite of relaxing to Violet. She pressed her fingertips to her head and massaged the flesh over her temple.

"And when is this again?"

"End of September. You really should put in your request soon. You don't want to wait until the last minute."

"Yeah, yeah. I know. I'll take a look at things and get back to you," Violet said.

As they were saying their goodbyes, Darger caught another glimpse of her reflection in the car mirror.

"Hey, mom. If we didn't know each other, and you walked past me on the street, what kind of vibe do I give off?"

Her mother's musical laugh crackled over the line.

"What an odd question," she said. "I suppose I'd think you were… someone important. Someone with power?"

"Power?"

"Maybe that's the wrong word. Authority? But not necessarily because someone else gave it to you. More like it's something you possess all on your own."

"In other words, you'd think I was a badass."

Her mom laughed again.

"I just remember coming home from work once and finding you hunched over a book with the most intense stare on your face. I thought you were doing math homework or something like that. You looked like you were in the middle of diffusing a bomb. But you weren't doing math homework."

There was a stretch of silence.

"Hello? Are you still there?"

"I'm here. Sorry, I can still see you sitting there with your book."

"What book was it?"

"I don't remember the title, but it was a biography of Ted Bundy." Her mother sighed. "I suppose I should have known then how you'd end up."

"You make it sound like I'm some kind of freak," Violet said, more amused than offended.

"No, of course not." After a brief pause she added, "OK, maybe a little."

Violet pretended to scoff.

"You'll let me know about Europe?"

Violet nodded, then remembered she was on the phone. "Yep."

Violet ended the call and tossed her phone into the passenger seat. Her eyes filled with water as a tremendous yawn overcame her.

She steered away from the curb, thinking that her problem wouldn't be falling asleep once she got back to the hotel. The hard part would be crawling out of bed in less than four hours.

CHAPTER 32

Owen must have heard the gravel crunching under the tires of her car, because he was moseying down the porch steps before she'd even turned off the ignition.

He barely gave her a second look when she climbed out and followed him over to the CR-V, which irked her. Even though he'd only been teasing her, all that stuff about looking like a cop and showing some cleavage had made her especially self-conscious. She supposed it didn't help that Owen was the kind of guy that had always made her nervous when she was younger. The type that had a sort of offhand way of being charming and flirtatious, so she never knew how serious to take it. Plus, he was good-looking, and he knew it, unlike his brother who didn't seem to notice — or at least pretended not to.

The result was that it took her twice as long to get ready, despite the fact that she ultimately settled on a pair of jeans and an army green v-neck tee. But she had applied extra makeup and fiddled with her hair. Now she felt silly that she'd given his comments a second thought.

His thumb jabbed at the Engine Start button and the car came to life.

Like some kind of mind-reader, he turned his head and said, "You dress down well, by the way."

Irritated at the little thrill that ran through her at the compliment, she murmured a half-hearted, "Thanks."

He leaned across the center console and sniffed her.

"You smell good, too," he said and held his thumb and forefinger an inch apart. "Only the barest hint of slow-roasted pork belly."

Violet glared over at him.

"I'm armed," she warned. "It would be a shame if I had to shoot you."

Lifting her pant leg, she revealed her duty pistol. When she'd first gotten dressed back in her hotel room, she'd started to holster her gun at her belt like normal. But she realized that wouldn't do. The Nameless Brotherhood would make her for law enforcement and probably run for the hills before she got within spitting distance. Luckily, she found her ankle holster still tucked in one of the zipper pockets on the flap of her suitcase. Finally a benefit to being a mess when it came to organization: if you never fully unpack your suitcase, most of the stuff you need is already inside.

"No need to get testy, Miss Darger. Didn't your mama teach you that the appropriate response when a gentleman compliments you is to curtsy and say *thank you*?"

Not having any room to curtsy in the confines of the car, she thanked him with her middle finger.

The Tanglefoot Saloon was bustling with activity on a Friday night. Violet wasn't surprised. The parking lot had been jam-packed. There were plenty of bikes parked along the front walk, so she had high hopes that her quarry was inside, as Owen promised.

Passing through the front doors, she saw them immediately. A large group of maybe a dozen men in denim vests clustered in the corner of the bar nearest the pool tables, and each of them was boldly flying the colors of their club. Even in the dim light of the bar, it was easy to read the letters on the bold red and black patch: NAMELESS BROTHERHOOD. Beneath the top rocker was the club insignia, a humanoid skull with the curved horns of a goat or maybe a demon.

She had to admit, there was something ballsy about declaring yourself an outlaw so openly. Most criminals hid in the shadows. These guys literally wore their lawlessness on their sleeves.

Owen led her to a pair of open stools at the far end of the bar, giving Violet a chance to scrutinize the rest of the place. The decor matched the Old West-inspired name, with plenty of big game animal heads adorning the walls and exposed beams along the ceiling.

The wall behind the bar was mirrored, which meant she could keep an eye on the bikers with little chance of getting caught staring. The last thing she wanted to do was attract attention. Had Owen chosen these seats on purpose? She thought probably so.

"Beer?" Owen asked. She nodded.

An old Hank Williams song blared out of the overhead speakers. Combined with the chatter from the patrons, it meant they could talk about their task without much risk of being overheard.

The barman set a bottle down in front of each of them. As soon as he moved off, Owen leaned in.

"See the guy with the classic horseshoe mustache? The one sitting directly under the neon Budweiser sign?"

Violet's eyes flicked up and found the man in the reflection of the mirror.

"I see him."

"That's Donny Hardegree. President of the club."

Violet figured he was probably 55, maybe 60. He had thinning gray hair shaved close to his head. The mustache Owen had mentioned was well-kept, unlike some of the other men, who sported wild, unruly beards that made them look like Vikings and pirates.

Hardegree had the look of a man who had been heavily muscled in his prime but was now starting to go to fat. An aging bull. Violet stripped away the tattoos and earrings in her mind. Redressed him in a button-down shirt and a pair of chinos. He would have looked like any number of suburban men. Someone's dad, kicking back in a recliner on the weekends to watch the big game.

"The guy racking the balls at the pool table is Randall Stokes. Second-in-command and still one of their top enforcers. Also happens to be Hardegree's half-brother."

Stokes appeared about the same age as his brother, maybe a few years younger. He was wirier but by no means weak-looking. If Hardegree was a bull, this was the fox. He had a clever look to him. Violet played the same game, dressing him up in her head to play a new part, but unlike Hardegree, she couldn't make it stick. Something about his eyes, she thought. They were black and sharply focused, scanning the room often, fixing people with a laser-like intensity. There was a mischievous, possibly malevolent light in those eyes. Violet felt a chill run up her spine.

"Hardegree and Stokes paid for their power with blood. Back in the late 80s, they had a spat with the then-current president. He wanted to take the club in a more law-abiding direction. Cool it on the drug and gun-running. They apparently didn't agree. So they abducted him, drove him down to the Everglades, shot him, set his body on fire, and then left the barbecued remains for the gators. That's the legend anyway. Never found the body."

Stokes leaned over the pool table now, lining up his first shot. As he broke the stack, a loud whoop rang out from the table next to him. Stokes balked, and she could tell by the hard set of his mouth that he wasn't happy with his opening move.

He aimed a dark glare over at the inhabitants of the neighboring table. It was a group of four younger men, definitely not bikers. College kids, she'd guess. They barely looked old enough to drink. Judging from their boisterous behavior, though, they'd already had plenty. None seemed to notice the attention they were receiving from the dangerous-looking biker at the next table.

Violet sucked in a breath, hoping they weren't about to witness an all-out brawl. After a tense moment, one of the other Nameless guys clapped Stokes on the back, and his focus returned to the pool table.

She let out a relieved sigh.

"They've had a few run-ins with the Lost Horses lately. A rival club," Owen continued. "The Lost Horse boys run some action in Alabama, Tennessee, and South Carolina, and now they've got their sights set on parts of Georgia. Couple of Lost Horses ran a Nameless guy off the road in Marietta back in April. Beat him so badly the paramedics assumed he was dead when they first got to the scene. In retaliation, the Nameless crew in Marietta set fire to a pawn shop."

"In other words, a genteel and refined bunch," she joked.

"What I'm trying to say is that I deal with a wide variety of thugs, hustlers, and malcontents in my line of work. Nobody makes my ass pucker like the OMGs."

"On that delightful note, who should we approach first?" Violet asked.

"*We* shouldn't approach anyone. I'll do all the talking.

You're a silent observer. In fact, you should stay right where you are. Got it?"

"Then why did you even agree to bring me along?"

"I never turn down the company of a pretty lady," he answered, a mock serious look on his face.

She snorted.

"You think I won't argue with your plan if you butter me up enough? Is that it?"

"Actually, the thought of you rolled in butter hadn't crossed my mind before, but now… gimme a minute with that."

He closed his eyes and a grin spread over his lips. Violet kicked the leg of his stool, jolting him out of his daydream.

"You're awfully fucking flippant for a guy with a puckering asshole."

"For the record, I meant every word, Miss Darger," he said, taking a drink. "I suppose part of it is that mouth of yours."

She raised an eyebrow. "Is this going to turn into a Deliverance-type scenario?"

Owen had to pull the bottle away from his lips to let out a laugh.

"I hope not. I was talking about your colorful language. Something about a Northern girl that curses like a sailor always did give me a little thrill."

Violet blushed a little and took a sip of beer to conceal a smile.

"I don't know what part of that sentence to address first."

He made a face as if he were genuinely curious for her to go on.

"Is this a Catholic thing?"

"How'd you know I was Catholic?"

"Well, the giant bathtub Madonna in your front yard was a

hint."

He chuckled.

"That's not mine. I mean, I suppose it is now. But it was the previous tenants that installed it."

"And what? It would be blasphemy to desecrate a statue of the Holy Mother or something?"

"What? No," he said, shaking his head with amusement. "It turns out to be a good way to give people directions. I'm sure you've noticed that all the houses out that way look exactly the same. Now I just tell people to look for the house with the giant Mary."

Darger smiled, thinking that was exactly how she'd remembered which house was his.

"You know you could replace it with something else. A couple of pink flamingos. Or a collection of lawn gnomes," she suggested.

"Nah, I couldn't do that. Maybe at first. But now I've grown quite fond of her. Besides, Mary keeps the solicitors at bay. I'm spoken for."

Something near the pool tables caught his attention. Violet saw a younger looking guy in Nameless gear and a black bandana greeting his comrades.

Owen tilted his beer back to polish off the dregs at the bottom of the bottle. The empty made a hollow noise against the bar as he set it back down.

"Game time. I'll be back. Remember what I said about you sittin' tight, you hear?"

He planted his hand on the top of her head as if that might help root her to the spot. She swatted him away.

"I remember," she said through clenched teeth.

Violet tracked his movement across the room in the mirror,

doing her best to appear nonchalant. Inside, she was anything but. The idea of sending a civilian into the wide open jaws of the Nameless Brotherhood wasn't sitting well with her.

She supposed Owen would bristle at being called a civilian. And at her doubting his ability to handle himself. In truth, she didn't doubt him. She sipped her beer and glanced over to where the bikers clustered near the pool tables. She couldn't trust a group of men that sold drugs and illegal weapons for a living.

Owen was in their midst now, and Violet had to stop herself from chewing on her nails in suspense. He and the new arrival, Mr. Black Bandana, seemed friendly enough at least. Black Bandana grinned and clapped Owen on the shoulder as he approached. Owen said something into Black Bandana's ear and the grin widened. Both men turned and headed for the door, disappearing outside.

Violet sat tight, clutching her beer as if it were some kind of lifeline tethering her to the real world. She didn't like this. She'd been under the impression that she'd be able to watch Owen's interaction. If things went wrong, she could jump in to help. But from her seat at the bar, she had absolutely no idea what was going on outside.

She split her focus between the door and her watch. When Owen had been gone for about three minutes, she saw two more Nameless brothers rise from their seats and head for the parking lot. Violet *really* didn't like that. Not at all. She considered getting up and trying to peek out the door. She reminded herself that Black Bandana had been smiling. And Owen hadn't even given her a glance to suggest that anything was off.

When six minutes passed and Owen still wasn't back, Violet couldn't take it any longer.

Maybe she hadn't been close enough to notice that Black Bandana's smile wasn't a kind one. And now that she thought about it, hadn't he guided Owen all the way out with a hand on his back? Like he was marching him out to the firing squad or something? What if Owen was out there right now, going twelve rounds against three bikers? Violet imagined another trip to the emergency room and having to explain to Mrs. Baxter how she'd managed to get her *other* son a bed in Critical Care.

Violet released her grip on her beer. That settled it.

She was going after him.

CHAPTER 33

She lowered one foot to the floor. At the same moment, the front door of the roadhouse swung open. Black Bandana sauntered through first, along with the other two bikers. They appeared relaxed and in good spirits. But where was Owen?

A few seconds passed, and Violet's fingernails squeezed into the flesh of her palms.

The hinges of the door squeaked, and there he was, looking just as footloose and fancy-fucking-free as the other three men. Owen and his bandana-clad buddy paused and exchanged a final word or two. Owen's mouth moved and the biker threw his head back, guffawing. Black Bandana nodded, gave Owen a playful punch in the arm, and then the two parted.

Owen sidled over to the seat next to Violet, his body language as calm and serene as the ocean on a windless day.

Violet waited for him to say something, but he waved at the bartender and ordered two more beers.

She lifted hers to her mouth and used it to cover up a scowl.

In a low hiss, she said, "What the hell took so long?"

His head drooped near hers.

"Why, did you miss me?"

Her frown deepened, and Owen reached out to squeeze her shoulder.

"Relax, Miss Darger. The wheels are in motion."

He'd bent a little closer now, and she recognized a familiar glassiness in his eyes. She also got a whiff of something… particular.

Her eyes widened. She leaned in and sniffed.

"Are you *high*?"

Owen tried to stifle a giggle and failed.

"Jesus Christ! That's what you were doing out in the parking lot? Smoking pot?"

"Relax. I didn't inhale," he said, chuckling at his own joke.

What had she gotten herself into? She was already disobeying orders by investigating this lead. Now her accomplice was getting baked with the potential witnesses.

She clutched the neck of the bottle in her hand so tightly, she started to worry it might break. Owen let out another snicker.

"Now what's funny?"

"I was about to tell you to chill out. We don't want any of those guys to figure you out. But then I realized it's fine. Works out perfectly, really."

"What does?"

"You gettin' all bent out of shape. You'll read like the disapproving girlfriend."

She glowered at him.

"Good. Great. Keep making that face."

Violet had the overwhelming urge to punch him but resisted. Then again, wouldn't that be exactly the kind of thing a pissed off girlfriend might do? An evil smirk touched her lips.

Owen caught the change in her expression.

"What?"

She socked him in the arm. Hard.

"Ow!"

"Just playing my part," she said with an innocent batting of her eyelashes.

Violet took a drink and refocused her attention on the mirrored wall behind the bar. Black Bandana moved closer to the inner circle of the gang, nearer to Stokes and Hardegree. She forced herself to look away.

"So what exactly is the plan here?" she asked.

"I whispered a little something in my friend's ear, that I'm looking for certain information, totally off the record."

"And?"

"Patience, Miss Darger."

She wanted to explain that it was hard to be patient when there was a psycho gunman on the loose, but she figured Owen knew that well enough. Her mind went to Ethan lying in that hospital bed, clinging to life by a thread.

"Can I ask you something?"

"Shoot."

"I got the impression that Ethan was dead set on keeping his so-called source a secret. Why wouldn't he just tell me it was his brother?"

"Oh, Ethan doesn't exactly approve of my line of work. Kind of a snob that way. Always has been. Thinks P.I.s have a tendency to be a little too loose with the law. I doubt he'd want you other Feebs to know he has such a dubious and uncouth man as myself as his brother. His twin brother, no less."

Owen tried to keep the same jovial nature he'd had before as he talked, but Violet sensed something somber beneath it all. Bitterness at Ethan's disapproval? Or maybe worry over his brother's health? Possibly a little of both. Some sense of regret that they weren't closer after Ethan's brush with death.

Violet nudged the coaster under her beer with a fingernail.

"Does it bother you that he thinks that?"

"Why should it? I figure it's more his problem than mine," Owen said with a dismissive twitch of his shoulder.

He drank and then pointed at her with the business end of

his beer bottle.

"You a shrink or something?"

Violet noted that not only had Owen avoided answering the question, he was now redirecting the attention back at her.

"I used to be a counselor of sorts."

He nodded, smiling to himself.

"All the pieces are falling into place."

"Care to explain that?"

"You think it's your mission to save everyone, right? The problems of the world are somehow your responsibility."

"Where is that coming from?"

"Come on, you're a classic control freak. Gettin' your panties in a twist over a little bit of weed, for example."

"My panties," she started to say, but movement in the reflection of the bar mirror caught her eye, and she quit talking.

"Don't stop there, Miss Darger. What were you saying about your panties?"

She scooted closer, angling her mouth to his ear and keeping her voice low. By the satisfied smirk on his face, Owen must have thought all of his flirting was starting to pay off.

"I think your friend in the black bandana is heading over to us."

The pleased grin on his face faltered, but then he reached out and squeezed her thigh.

"Follow my lead, darlin'."

Owen spun around in his seat, lifting his beer in salute.

"Roach! I was just tellin' Violet here about the time Enzo peed on that electric fence and got shocked so hard it threw him on his ass."

Roach, she thought. Nickname or surname? Could be either.

"Owen probably left out the part about how he was the one

that dared Enzo to do it in the first place," the man said.

"Now, now, Roach. Don't you go tryin' to embarrass me in front of my lady friend."

"Owen, honey, you do a fine job of embarrassing yourself all on your own," Violet said, winking at the man formerly known as Black Bandana.

Roach's mouth gaped, showing off a collection of molars that glittered with gold fillings. A hoarse laugh emanated from his barrel chest.

"That's good," Roach said, then slapped Owen's arm. "Finally found a girl that can keep up with your horseshit, eh?"

Owen's eyes glinted as he regarded her. "She's got a PhD in horseshit."

Roach clapped a hand on Owen's shoulder.

"Hey man, I passed it up the chain, but it's not gonna happen. I'm sorry, man."

"That's too bad," Owen said. "But I understand."

"Yeah, it's nothing personal, you know. And I'm real sorry about your brother, really. I know he's Johnny Law and all, but I never had any beef with him. And I know you're cool. Some of these other guys, though, a pig's a pig. Sucks, but that's the way it goes, I guess."

"Thanks for trying, man," Owen said. "Can I buy you a beer for your trouble?"

Roach waved the offer away.

"Naw, man. You don't have to do that. It was your number in the parking lot," he said with a chuckle. "We're square."

After he'd gone, Violet's mouth pinched into a sour knot.

"It was *your* pot?"

Owen shrugged.

"That was the idea all along? To come here and get one of

your old buddies high?"

"Will you chill out? It was a solid plan."

"Solid?" she repeated the word with incredulity.

"You see that patch on Hardegree's vest, the one that says ACAB?"

"I saw it," she said.

"Stands for 'All Cops Are Bastards.' And that includes the FBI. I knew they were gonna be hesitant to even talk to me because of who my brother is. So smoking a joint works two-fold. It proves I'm not a narc," he gave her a pointed look, "and it loosens 'em up a little. Sets 'em at ease."

"You are unbelievable. Now I *really* can't believe you and Ethan are related."

She took a drink, shaking her head.

"And I assure you that is something we would both take as a compliment."

It sounded like a joke, but judging by the serious look on his face, it wasn't. Violet decided to change the subject.

"Well, seeing as your plan didn't work, now it's my turn."

Violet hopped down off the stool, and Owen seemed to choke a little on his beer.

"Excuse me?"

"I said it's my turn."

Owen snagged her by a belt loop on her jeans when she tried to step away from the bar.

"I hope you're not planning on just marching over there to chat with Hardegree."

"We can't wait around here all night," she said.

As she and Owen argued, her eyes darted over to the pool tables. Stokes was watching two of his fellow club members have a turn, but at that moment, his coal black eyes flicked up and stared directly into hers. She froze, feeling like an arctic seal caught in the sights of a killer whale.

"Are you listening?" Owen said, giving her elbow a tug.

The movement broke the spell, her focus swiveling back on Owen.

"Yes, I heard you," she said, though the truth was she'd heard very little. Being trapped in Stokes' gaze had rendered her half-stupid or something.

She was glad when she peeked back in the direction of the pool table and Stokes was no longer watching her. In fact, he wasn't even there anymore.

Violet frowned, scanning the crowd for him.

She found him at the next table over. The one with the obnoxious fratty-looking guys. Stokes was uncomfortably close to one of the bros. Like kissing close, though she doubted that was what Stokes had in mind. A lull in the music allowed Darger to hear a snippet of the exchange.

"Look, man. I'm not looking for trouble," the kid was saying. "We're gonna finish our beers and go."

"Yeah? Let me help you with that," Stokes said, shoving the kid's hand so it tipped his bottle into his face. Beer sloshed down the bro's chin and onto his J. Crew button-down.

The music swelled, drowning out their voices, but Darger could read the kid's lips easily enough.

"What the fuck, dude!"

J. Crew's hand balled into a fist. Stokes didn't move. He didn't even blink. He held as still as if he were made of stone. And just as the kid stepped within range, Stokes sprang to life, swinging a right hook into the kid's jaw. J. Crew stumbled backward but recovered quickly. Within seconds, he and his idiot friends were engaged in a full-scale brawl with the

Nameless Brotherhood.

"Oh shit," Darger said, standing so fast her chair tipped over.

Without her consciously telling it to, her hand reached for the ankle holster.

"Violet, don't."

Owen made a grab at her sleeve, but it was too late. She was already charging into the fray with her weapon drawn.

CHAPTER 34

There were shouts and the almost musical sound of glass shattering, and suddenly the whole place was in upheaval. People rushed for the exits, and the swarm of people between Darger and the pool tables meant she lost sight of the melee.

She dodged around the fleeing masses, trying to get a glimpse of Hardegree or Stokes. A waitress with a full tray of empty pint glasses crashed into Darger, terror etched on her face as she went down.

Darger kept her footing and shuffled away from the face-planting woman, watching a table flip onto its side right next to her, silverware and dishes clattering to the floor.

Finally, Darger reached the edge of the scuffle. One of the kids was on the floor, already out cold. Stokes had another up against the wall, forearm at his neck.

"FBI!"

No one reacted. Over the clamor of the fight and the rush of blood in their own ears, they probably couldn't hear her. She tried again anyway.

"FB-"

There was a crack as something collided with her forehead. An explosion of pink and white stars blotted out her vision for a moment. She stumbled backward, blinked, and turned her head in time to see one of the bikers holding a pool cue over his shoulder like a baseball bat.

He swung at her again. This time she ducked. She sprang forward in a crouch, coming up right in front of him and smashing the butt of her gun into his nose. He made a sound like a harpooned walrus as blood gushed from his nostrils. She shoved him away from her.

Darger barely had time to take another breath before someone grabbed her from behind, wrapping a thick arm under her chin in a chokehold. The hand holding the gun was pinned against her body. Useless.

She struggled, stomping down on his instep with the heel of her boot. If he felt it at all, his body language didn't show it. She changed tactics and tried to butt the back of her skull into his face, but he was too tall. Her head collided with a chest padded by years of greasy food and beer.

There was an odd sense of vertigo as he lifted her off the ground and body-slammed her into the pool table. The impact knocked the wind out of her lungs for a beat, but soon she was trying to squirm free again.

He pinned her to the green felt top, hands moving up to encircle her throat. They were face to face, and his mouth spread in a devilish grin. He was six-and-a-half feet tall, easy. Arms like tree trunks extended out from under his Nameless Brotherhood vest.

Gun. Where was her gun? She must have lost it when he'd dumped her on the table.

She kicked out, aiming for his groin, but he dodged to one side.

He removed one of the hands gripping her and pulled it back in a fist. He struck her once in the side of the head.

Stars again.

Violet stopped clawing at the meaty fingers around her neck and flailed out in search of something to fight back with.

Her fingertips brushed something round. The pool balls. They rolled away from her dancing fingers, but eventually she got one in her clutches. Just before the man's fist collided with her skull a second time, Violet smashed the ball into the wrist still holding her down. She felt the metacarpals in the back of his hand crumple. The man released her, howling.

"Bitch!"

Air scraped over her larynx as she inhaled the sweet, sweet oxygen. But before she could scramble down off the pool table he was on her again, back to using both hands to choke her. She tried to hit him with the ball again, but he batted her hand away. She lost her grip. Dropped it.

Her strength started to fade. She gathered herself for one last attack. Right when her vision began to blur, she bucked and kicked, more flexible than he was expecting. She knocked him off balance, his grip loosening slightly as he stumbled back in a stutter step.

Then she saw the legs of a chair raised high in the air. They hovered there, upside-down. Was she hallucinating? A mirage induced by the lack of oxygen?

The chair came down on the man's back and shoulder. She felt the collision jolt through his hands and into her chest, and then he went limp. He fell forward and on top of her. The big bastard must have weighed almost 300 pounds, but at least she could breathe again.

She coughed, breath rasping back into her lungs. The biker's weight shifted. At first, she thought he was getting back up. Then she saw that Owen had him under the arms and was rolling him off of her.

He pulled her down from the table, then plucked her gun from where it had holstered itself in a corner pocket and handed it to her.

"We better get out of here while we still can."

He looped an arm around her, keeping her steady as he guided her toward the exit.

Darger blinked, only vaguely able to make sense of the continuing chaos raging around them. Stokes had one of the college kids backed into a corner, raining down blows upon his head. Three brutes in Nameless vests huddled over a prone form on the floor, aiming kicks at the man's head and chest.

She didn't see Donald Hardegree anywhere. Probably his brothers insisted he escape in all the commotion. They would naturally want to protect their president from being arrested.

She hesitated at the threshold, her conscience nagging her for leaving the scene. For not doing more to break up the fight.

"Seriously, we need to go," Owen said, and she let him tow her through the door.

The red and blue flashers of a police car were visible at one end of the parking lot. Owen tugged her in the opposite direction.

“Shouldn’t we stay and give a statement?” she asked.

“Why would we do that? The whole point of this was to keep it quiet. Ethan made it pretty clear that if you got caught up in this, your ass would be grass, missy.”

As they reached Owen’s car, a bright beam of light flashed into Darger’s eyes.

“Atlanta PD,” a voice said. “I’d like to see some ID.”

The light flicked over to Owen’s face.

“Owen? What the hell are you doing out here?”

The cop lowered his flashlight, and Owen blinked a few times.

“Hey, Reggie.”

“Christ, man. I heard about Ethan. Saw it on the TV, too. Man, I’m sorry. How’s he doing?”

"He's gonna pull through. You know him."

Reggie nodded then inclined his head toward the bar. The authoritative voice of a police officer could be heard shouting orders inside.

"So did you see what happened in there?"

"That depends," Owen said.

He didn't look at Violet, but she knew enough to keep quiet for the moment.

Reggie rested his hands on his belt. "Depends on what?"

"On whether or not you'll insist on official statements."

"Come on, man," Reggie pleaded.

Owen only shrugged.

"Fine," Reggie said with a sigh. "Off the record."

Violet started to wonder if maybe Owen hadn't been exaggerating about being one of the best private investigators in Atlanta. Everywhere they went he seemed to know someone who was willing to do him a favor.

"Couple of college boys got in a scuffle with the Nameless Brotherhood."

"That's it?" Reggie asked.

"Far as I know."

"Man, how come when there's trouble, you always seem to be lurking around?"

Owen grinned. "Just lucky, I guess."

Reggie studied him for a moment, and then his eyes wandered over to Violet. His mouth hardened when he saw the goose egg on her forehead.

"And your friend here?"

"Where are my manners?" Owen said. "Reggie, this is Violet Darger. Colleague of Ethan's, as a matter of fact."

Reggie's face changed then, sensing he was onto something

bigger than a bar fight.

"Aw, hell. Does this have something to do with the sniper?"

Owen took a step forward and lowered his voice.

"We don't know. Could be. And that's why we'd appreciate it if you could keep our names out of any official reports."

Reggie inhaled and seemed to think on it. Finally he nodded.

"Alright, man. But you know how this works. If anyone in there brings up your name, there's nothing I can do."

He gestured back at the bar.

"Thanks, Reg. I owe you one."

"One?"

Owen winked.

"Put it on my tab."

As Violet lowered herself into the car, Reggie turned back to them.

"Oh, and ma'am?"

"Yes?"

He pointed at his own forehead.

"Probably should get some ice on that."

CHAPTER 35

"Don't think it'll need stitches," he pronounced.

Along with the bruising and swelling, the pool cue had left a small gash over Violet's eyebrow. Owen cleaned it up and applied a butterfly bandage.

"Well that was a bust," Violet said.

Her voice came out a little hoarse. She suspected her vocal cords were bruised.

Owen pulled a package of frozen corn from the freezer and pressed it to her face. She winced at the cold sting of it.

"The night is young, Miss — Agent Darger."

"What does that mean?"

"I mean, who knows what might shake loose when you turn the Nameless Brotherhood upside-down?"

Her brow furrowed as a suspicious thought entered her mind.

"The fight… did you know that was going to happen?"

He looked genuinely surprised.

"Are you kidding? If I'd known it was going to turn into an old-fashioned free-for-all, I would have brought my brass knuckles."

Violet lowered the bag of thawing corn.

"You don't actually have brass knuckles, do you?" she asked, then squeezed her eyes shut. "You know what? I don't want to know."

Peeling her eyelids apart, she glanced at the clock. The digital display on Owen's microwave revealed the time: 11:23 PM.

"I'd better go. My shift starts in half an hour," Violet said, standing and passing the bag of corn back to Owen.

"I'll walk you to your car," Owen said.

"I'm parked like ten feet from the door."

"And there are dangerous folk about."

Moths and other six-legged creatures fluttered at the windows of Owen's porch, a hushed patter of wings against screen. She followed Owen down the steps to the driveway. The hulking silhouette of the bathtub Mary cast a long shadow over the lawn.

Violet moved around to the driver's side of her car. Her thumb found the unlock button by feel.

"Well, I'll tell you what," Owen said. "You really know how to take a pool stick to the face."

"I'm gonna bring that up the next time my partner criticizes me for my thick skull."

Owen reached for her face, fingers brushing lightly against the bump on her forehead.

"You're bleeding again."

Her own hand instinctively went for the abrasion over her eyebrow. It stung when she touched it.

She realized how close he was then. Close enough that she felt the warmth coming off of his body.

"I sure would like to kiss you, Miss Darger."

"For fuck's sake, Owen. If you're going to kiss me, at least call me Violet."

He smiled. "There's that mouth again."

When he leaned in, she met him halfway. Their lips touched.

His tongue teased her mouth open, and she welcomed it, savoring the taste of him. The beer he'd had earlier left an almost citrusy tang.

Owen pressed against her, his hips pinning her against the car. His fingertips tickled over her scalp as he ran his hands through her hair and down to her neck. A warm tingle spread down through her.

Violet inhaled, taking in a breath filled with the scent of him. Not cologne or anything artificial. Just his innate smell.

What had he called it?

His natural musk.

No. That wasn't right...

Ethan had been the one who'd said that.

At the thought of Ethan, her mind flashed on the image of him lying in the dust on that hill. The pink, frothy blood oozing from the wound. The wet sucking sound of the hole in his lung.

Violet pulled away with a gasp, and Owen's eyebrows pulled together in concern.

"What's wrong?"

She felt light-headed and panicky. She tried to take a step backward, but the car was behind her. She bumped against it and wobbled off balance. Owen reached out to steady her with a hand on her shoulder.

"I saw... I thought you were..."

He stared at her, eyes wide. It took her a moment to find the words.

"I think what happened with your brother isn't quite out of my head yet."

Owen lowered his gaze, shoulders drooping as he exhaled loudly. Was he angry? Disappointed?

After a moment, he nodded.

"Yeah. I guess it's probably not out of mine either."

"No, you don't understand." She ran her hands over her

arms, trying to scare off the goose bumps prickling over her skin. "The shooting was my fault. The real truth is, your brother wouldn't have been on that hillside if it weren't for me. I was the one that dragged him up there."

"And that makes you responsible?"

Owen shook his head.

"You really must not have gotten to know my brother well, because everyone that knows Ethan Baxter knows that no one drags him anywhere," he said. "Besides that, I don't care if you're the best damn profiler in the world. That doesn't give you a crystal ball, and it doesn't give you power over every psycho with a rifle. Has it even occurred to you that if Ethan had parked in the opposite direction, or if you'd been driving that car, then you might be in his place?"

She swallowed.

"No. But I ran. He got hit, and my first reaction was to save myself."

Owen stared at her in disbelief, and she thought he was finally getting it. That she wasn't deserving of any gratitude for saving Ethan's life.

But then he said, "A crazy man with a sniper rifle was *shooting at you.* You're supposed to run."

He ran his hands through his dark hair, pushing the wavy locks off his forehead.

"This is exactly what I was saying earlier. You think the world is on your shoulders," he said with a sigh. "You're not a super hero, Violet."

She liked the way he said her name. The way his southern drawl softened the first syllable and dragged it out a little. It made her sad that things were always so damned complicated.

"I'm sorry," she said, taking his hand.

He gave her fingers a squeeze.

"Don't be."

"I do like you."

He leaned down and very gently kissed her brow, just above the spot marked by the pool cue.

"I like you, too. Miss Darger."

She smiled and let his fingers slide from her grasp. And then she got into her car and headed to the call center, still feeling the brush of his lips against her forehead.

CHAPTER 36

In lieu of a traditional greeting, the first thing out of Loshak's mouth when he saw her was, "Jesus, you look like hell."

"Yeah? Let's see how you fare against a biker that outweighs you by 150 pounds."

Loshak started to shake his head but stopped abruptly. He squared his shoulders toward her. His focus felt like a laser beam.

"Biker? Is that what you just said?"

Violet sealed her mouth shut. She couldn't think of anything to say that wouldn't get her in more trouble.

"Christ on a crutch, Darger. You can't help yourself, can you?"

"What?"

"Always stirring the pot."

"I was following a lead, Loshak. It wasn't like I went out of my way to be insubordinate."

That got a big enough laugh out of him that he was soon wiping tears from his eyes. She waited until he was through.

"Anything promising?"

"Agent Dawson stopped by with the forensics on the tire treads," Loshak said and plucked a sheet of paper from the desk. "Goodyear Wrangler TrailRunner AT. An 18" all terrain tire for trucks and SUVs."

"So he likes to off-road in his truck or SUV? Fits the profile," Darger said.

"Lab says they're close on narrowing that down further based on the tire tracks, which will give us the wheelbase dimensions of the vehicle."

He paused to peer at Darger's face.

"Man, he really got you good, eh?"

"Pool cue," Darger said. "But you should see the other guy."

"Yeah. Right. You put some ice on that?"

"Yes, mother," she said, waving his concerns away. "Are you gonna beat it, or what? It's my shift."

"About that… Did we or did we not talk about how it was eight hours on the clock, followed by eight hours for sleep?"

She grumbled something about sleeping when she was dead.

"You haven't actually slept since your last shift, have you?"

Darger knew better than to try to lie to him.

"I got a few hours," she mumbled.

"Here's what we're going to do, then. You are going back to the hotel, and you will sleep. I'll stay on until four."

"I thought you said twelve-hour shifts were inefficient."

"Not as inefficient as no sleep. Now go," he said.

His tone indicated there was no room for argument.

It wasn't until she was alone in the silence of the car that she realized how exhausted she was. Her joints felt loose, like she was a marionette in need of maintenance. There was also a possibility that she'd sustained a mild concussion during the fight.

On the drive back to the hotel, a sort of floating sensation took over. The lines on the road seemed to waver and undulate, as if she was seeing them through heat distortion, but she couldn't recall ever seeing heat distortion at night. She rolled the window down all the way, worried she might doze off at the wheel. As usual, Loshak was right. She really did need to get some sleep.

She drifted up to her room, the elevator seeming like a

portal to another dimension, the mouth of a machine that she was more than glad to walk into for some reason. When the door opened with a *ding* on her floor, she giggled. What an odd choice it was for a door to ding like that. Were they worried you wouldn't notice the door had opened when you reached your destination?

Down the hall she glided, barely feeling the floor beneath her feet. She reached her room, swiped her key card, and kicked off her boots at the end of the bed.

She was out before her head hit the pillow.

CHAPTER 37

Not all of the lights in Atlanta were turned off that night. Illuminated windows lit up many a neighborhood deep into the post-midnight hours. A number of residents chose to sleep with them on. To *try* to sleep, anyway.

Others didn't bother with this formality, pacing the floors instead, downing comfort beverages based on individual preference — mostly coffee or booze. Consciously or not, the community let the fear fully take hold and then tried to come to terms with the reality of what had happened in the past 96 hours or so.

The highway.

The grocery store parking lot.

The doorway in Pheasant Brook.

They tumbled these thoughts around in their heads, flung the paranoia every possible direction to find an angle that might make it make sense.

They grasped for some way — any way — to displace the terror.

Fear had a piss smell to it, however faintly. Tyrone Gwaltney had never considered it before now, but as soon as the observation occurred to him, it registered as something he'd always understood subconsciously.

He smelled it now, lying in bed, trying to sleep. Human terror. Was it a pheromone? Something that seeped out of the pores of his skin and filled the air? He didn't know.

He sat up, calmed a little when the silhouette of his blanket-draped wife took shape in the gloom next to him. He thought his movements might have woken her, but if so, she showed no signs of it. The blanket rose and fell, her breathing soft. Slow.

The urge to get up trembled in his chest and limbs, pricked the hairs on the back of his neck. He wanted more than anything to pluck the fire poker from its spot next to the chimney and walk the perimeter of his house, peering out of every window, ensuring that this swath of territory his family called home was secure.

He could imagine it all too clearly, spotting some figure lurking out there. Maybe wearing a ski mask like the one at the Publix parking lot. It occurred to him that there would even be a certain satisfaction to it. To trust his primal instincts and have them pay off to be correct. It would come with a flush of know-it-all glee, even if it only lasted for a split second before the real terror kicked in.

He knew the more likely scenario was that he'd find nothing stirring outside said windows. He'd find the same scenes he saw two hours ago when he took a peek whilst brushing his teeth — the empty street and driveway looking out the front and the rectangle of grass out back. Both utterly motionless. And that would be a good thing, of course, to find no murderers prowling around his house.

Even so, he hesitated to actually rise from the bed, listening for a moment instead and lowering his head to the pillow once more.

The trouble with looking out the windows was that the feeling of security only lasted for those moments he was looking. He knew this from experience. He could only feel OK when he saw with his own eyes that there was nothing to fear — when it was a concrete reality before him. As soon as he was back in bed, his security returned to being an abstraction. He'd revert to a state of uncertainty right away, a state that quickly devolved into paranoia.

He closed his eyes, listened to that slow in and out of his wife's breathing.

The night grew still once more around him. Quiet.

He slipped toward unconsciousness in stages, his mind circling back to that same thought over and over:

How could someone do these things? Just gun people down like that? Violence that was truly and totally random. Totally without meaning.

The trench of sleep finally swallowed him, but it remained a shallow and fitful slumber.

Two blocks down, Peggy Sanchez watched cable news all night for updates. She rocked in her recliner, the remote poised in her hands, aimed at the TV like a weapon.

With the lights out, the glow of the plasma screen provided flickering illumination to the living room. Light and shadow danced over the carpet, spasmed on the walls. Sean Hannity's face somehow glowed brighter than the rest, she thought. A fleshy pumpkin of a head, perpetually squinting. It cast quite a glare.

At least this squinting pumpkin was handsome, in her opinion. A hunky jack-o'-lantern.

She flipped back and forth, catching each network's take on the shootings. The pundits all talked about violent video games and the two kids who shot up Columbine high school some years ago. They used phrases like "violence as a spectacle."

Each time she changed the channel, there was a transitional moment when the screen went to a black glow. And even in the low light, Peggy could see her reflection in the glass during those times.

The clunky glasses sitting on the big nose. The tight curls of black hair that almost looked like a strange bush growing out of her head. It was somehow odd to see herself there on the screen, the theater stage usually reserved for the likes of Hannity and his ilk.

She guzzled Diet Pepsi all the while, the fake sweetener her primary comfort food over these past several years. She was out of real snacks now, but she licked her lips periodically. They still tasted like Dorito powder from the bag of Cool Ranch she'd finished a few hours ago.

All of this was very stimulating, and she found herself compulsively going over the events in her mind — the highway, the parking lot, the pregnant woman, the cute FBI man. Somehow this behavior made sense, like she was staying alert by dwelling on these things.

And then it hit her. She needed to take the garbage down to the curb.

Shit.

Normally, she might put it off, what with a psycho killer on the loose, but she'd missed it last week. The can was full, and she had two bags stinking up the garage. If she missed it again, she might as well give up her claim on the house and sign the deed over to the rats and roaches directly.

She stood, dusted Dorito crumbs from her shirt. She thought about flipping the TV off, but she decided she'd rather have it on. The noises and blinking lights provided a sense of comfort, a sense of not facing this alone.

Peggy peered out the window, finding the street vacant. Dead still. The strobe of the streetlight flickering two doors down was the only source of motion. Well, that was good.

A tremble overtook her chest as she made her way through the house. A throb like pins and needles that stabbed harder whenever she breathed in. It only got worse when she opened the door to head into the garage.

Again, she looked out at the street, this time gazing through the glass pane set in the door that led out to the driveway. Nothing. Nothing but that damn flickering light.

The odds of the killer happening by right as she rolled the can down to the curb were very, very low. And yet he was out there tonight. Somewhere. Probably somewhere in the city. Probably lying in wait to strike again and again, to cut short the lives of strangers — regular people just like her — for no good reason at all.

The chills throttled her, her shoulders rocking back and forth as they climbed into a shrugged position. Jesus Christ.

The smell of the garbage hit her then, and that steeled her resolve some. It smelled like wet dog, rancid peanuts, and a hint of that yeasty tang old bread sometimes got. She had to do this.

She took in a deep breath and held it, fighting against that quiver in her torso. The thrashing muscles steadied some, and her breathing grew easier, if only a little.

Her hand moved to the doorknob, hesitated just shy of it for a beat, and then clasped around the cold metal. She twisted it in slow motion, somehow compelled to get through this as soundlessly as possible. The door popped faintly as she pried it free from the frame.

And then she took those first two steps outside, enveloped by heavy night air, cool and thick. Her head went light as she moved into the open, swimmy and tingly and panicked. The scuff of her footsteps echoed around her in the quiet.

Sweat seemed to seep out of all of her pores at once as she closed on the garbage can. It made her whole body feel clammy, a little sticky. But it was almost over now.

Her fingers hooked around the handle of the trash bin, and she tipped it so all of the bulk rested upon the two plastic wheels at its base. Again, she hesitated, took a shaky breath. This was going to be loud.

As expected, the wheels scraped against the blacktop of the driveway, an excruciating sound that made her shoulders shimmy up into that shrugged position again. That faint feeling swelled in her skull — unconsciousness giving its final warning. Violent tremors throttled her now with every breath, her upper body flailing atop her legs. But she didn't slow. She kept moving.

Her eyes darted back and forth, scanning the shadows up and down the block for any movement, for any sign of the killer. Every silhouette threatened her, looking momentarily like a ski-masked maniac before it morphed back into a tree or bush or parked car. She saw nothing.

And then the curb was upon her. Just like that. She nestled the can into place and ran back inside, locking everything up.

She leaned her back against the door, huffing and puffing. Her body dripped with sweat like she'd run a marathon, but now euphoria filled all the places where the panic had pooled.

After a stretch of panting, she checked her watch. Good. The Hannity rerun was going to start in nine minutes, and she was excited to get back to him.

CHAPTER 38

Violet was startled awake by the sound of her phone chiming. Her mind struggled against waking, clinging to sleep. Her eyes, still not ready to function properly, were so blurry she couldn't read the screen on her phone to see who was calling. It didn't matter. The only person who'd be calling at this hour would be Loshak.

She cleared her throat and answered.

"Darger."

"Well you got your wish," it was Loshak, but the nonsensical greeting made her question whether she was dreaming the conversation or not.

"Huh?"

"City jail just called. They have someone in custody who says he has information on the gunman."

She sat up, suddenly fully awake.

"One of the bikers? What did he say?"

"I don't know yet. Guy says he'll only talk to you."

"Me? Why?"

Loshak exhaled into the speaker, creating a loud rustle.

"I don't know," he repeated, sounding a little annoyed. "That's all they told me."

"What about the biker's name?"

"Yeah, I scribbled it down somewhere. Hold on a minute," Loshak said.

Over the line, she could hear the crinkle of paper. She tried to guess who it would be. Maybe Roach had gotten tired of sitting in his cell and decided he'd talk now.

"You still there?" Loshak asked.

"Yes."

"Guy's name is Stokes. Randall Stokes."

Randall Stokes sat before a spare metal table in an interview room at the Atlanta Detention Center. She watched him through the small window on the door for a moment.

He held perfectly still, hands spread on the table before him, eyes downcast. His eyes barely even blinked. He almost appeared to be in a trance. She wondered if he was on something.

"Ready if you are," Loshak said.

Darger opened the door. Loshak had insisted on coming along, and honestly, she was glad to have backup with a guy like Stokes.

The biker's demeanor changed almost instantly when he saw her. He lifted his head and grinned, and Darger thought of the sharp rows of teeth ringing the jaws of a Great White shark. The smile faltered when he saw Loshak coming in behind her.

"Uh-uh. Just you," Stokes said, pointing a finger at Darger.

She and Loshak exchanged a wordless glance, and he put a hand on her shoulder.

"I'll be right outside."

She nodded and Loshak retreated, closing the door. Darger took a seat opposite from Stokes.

"I was starting to think you wouldn't come," he said.

His voice was raspy, almost hoarse. The raw sensation in her own throat led her to wonder if it was as a result of the fight, but somehow she thought not. She guessed it was his natural timbre.

"How did you know my name?" Darger asked. For the first

time, she considered the stupid *Vanity Fair* feature. She was starting to regret that more and more every day.

But he said, “I didn’t.”

“They said you asked for me specifically.”

“I did. The pretty Fed with the nice ass.”

Darger ignored the comment. He was testing her. Trying to push her buttons.

“For future reference, my name is Agent Darger. How’d you know I was FBI?”

He snorted.

Right. She made a mental note not to tell Owen about that. He’d only gloat.

“So what can I do for you, Mr. Stokes?”

“Randall.”

She sighed.

“Well, Randall, you’re looking at a whole slew of charges, including assault and battery, disturbing the peace, inciting a riot. I’m on about three hours of sleep, so either tell me what it is you want, or I’m going back to my hotel.”

“Don’t you get it? I started that brawl on purpose.”

“I gathered that you didn’t *accidentally* hit that kid in the face, yes.”

Stokes shook his head.

“No. I popped that pussy frat kid so that I could talk to you,” he said, eyes blazing with a manic glee. “I know what you want.”

“Yeah? What’s that?”

“Come on, Agent. Roach is a good soldier. He told me everything your little boyfriend said to him. That’s what you wanted anyway, wasn’t it? Roach is a grunt. He wouldn’t have that kind of information. But I do.”

Goose bumps prickled on her arms as a strange mixture of

hope and dread filled her. Like a genie was about to grant her three wishes, but they came with serious strings attached.

"Why help me?" she asked. "Doesn't that make you a rat in the eyes of your brethren?"

Clapping a theatrical hand over his chest, he said, "A rat! Agent Darger, you wound me. Besides, who said anything about helping? This is a trade."

"A trade? They're not gonna let me give you anything," Darger said, thinking about how ASAC Fitzgerald was probably already on the phone to Darger's superiors at Quantico informing them of her noncompliance with his orders.

"I think they will. They'll at least hear you out."

"And why is that?"

"Because it's a twofer."

"A twofer?"

"You know, a two-for-one kinda deal." Stokes held up two fingers. "I'm gonna give you two for the price of one."

"And what's your price?"

"Don't rush, Agent. You don't want to skip over the foreplay, do you?"

Darger raised an eyebrow. She wondered when he'd get the hint that the sexual innuendos didn't rattle her.

"Alright then. Why ask for me?"

"Because I know who can get a deal like this done in the shortest order. The slack-dick local cops always think small. But the Feds… you guys know the big picture."

Darger got another chill then, remembering that "big picture" had been the exact term ASAC Fitzgerald had used when he told Ethan Baxter to lay off the biker angle.

"And what's the big picture?" she asked.

"Catching these fucking psychos gunning people down in

the street."

"Are we talking about the sniper now? Or your Nameless compadres?"

His answer was a wordless smirk.

"Here's how this is gonna work," Stokes said. "I'll cop to the disorderly conduct. Thousand dollar fine. No jail time. Then you're gonna go to the address I give you, and you're gonna look underneath the kitchen cabinets. You know what a toe-kick is?"

"Yes."

"One of the toe-kicks has a false front. I'm confident you'll find quite a few treasures inside."

He flashed one of his predatory smiles.

"When that's done, and when the owner of said domicile is in custody, I'll talk."

"Who's the address for? A rival club member? One of the Lost Horse guys?"

Stokes didn't respond, and a small spiteful voice in her head said, *Fuck this.* She was done playing games.

"Forget it, then. We're not doing your dirty work."

Darger got up and was halfway to the door when Stokes spoke up from behind her.

"The address is for Amanda Russo."

Her fingers wrapped around the door handle.

"Who's that?" she asked.

"The mistress of one Donald Hardegree. And it's his name on the deed."

She squinted. He was giving up the club president? Why?

"You go to that address and do what I said," Stokes pressed on, "and I'll give you the name of a man that acquired a Glock-18c not so long ago."

It was an effort for Darger to keep her cool at that. Maybe he wasn't jerking her around after all. She circled back to the first question in her mind.

"Hardegree?" Darger repeated. "Why would you turn on him? He's your president. And your brother."

"Half brother."

"Half-blood isn't quite thick enough?"

She didn't know why she was badgering him if he was really offering to turn on Hardegree. That alone might be enough to stave off the shitstorm that Fitzgerald would want to unleash upon her.

Stokes shrugged.

"You go take that deal to your people. Get me something in writing that I can sign. Soon as I see Hardegree marched in here with cuffs on, I'll give you the name."

The adrenaline that kept her going during the interview with Stokes flagged when Darger was back out in the hallway with Loshak. God, she was tired. She rubbed her eyes, bumping the wound on her forehead as she did so. She winced at the sting of it.

"Why do I feel like we're making a deal with the devil?"

Loshak studied her for a moment, head tilted to one side. She thought she was in for some sort of lecture. To her surprise, he smiled.

"If it's any consolation, I think it's out of your hands now."

He nodded behind her, and Darger wheeled around to find Fitzgerald and another man marching toward them. Neither one looked pleased. Had they been asleep when they got the call? And who had called them, anyway?

"So you're not going to tell me something like: You made

your bed, now lie in it?" Darger asked, watching the men approach and knowing she was in for it.

"That works too."

Fitzgerald fixed his raptor eyes on her and bared his teeth.

"You're lucky you don't work for me, Agent Darger. If you were an agent in my field office, I'd slap you with a suspension so fast, the wind from the paperwork would knock you on your ass."

"Well then I guess that makes two of us glad I don't work for you," she said.

Out of the corner of her eye, she could see Loshak twitch at her mouthy retort.

The other man with Fitzgerald hooked a finger at her. He had sandy hair and the deep tan of a man that loved to golf and fish.

"This isn't just about you, Agent. You fucked up an undercover operation I've spent the last three years working on. All of it down the toilet now," the tan man said.

Well, shit. Ethan's theory had been right after all.

"That wasn't my intention, sir," she said. She didn't know his position or even what agency he worked for, but Darger figured he was probably a "sir" to her, whoever he was. "And if it's any consolation, he's offering to give us Hardegree."

Tan man brought a knuckle to his lips and seemed to ponder this revelation.

"Why?"

Her eyes flicked over to Loshak. They'd spent a few minutes mulling over that very question.

"Probably so he can take over the club. Stokes is second-in-command. With Hardegree out, Stokes would be an obvious choice to take over."

"That is neither here nor there," Fitzgerald said. "The fact remains that you deliberately disobeyed a command and—"

The other man interrupted.

"Take it."

Fitzgerald let out an exasperated scoff.

"Damn it, Jack."

Darger ignored Fitzgerald and addressed the other man.

"We'll need approval from the US Attorney's office for the deal Stokes wants."

"I'll take care of that. Tell him it's a deal."

Fitzgerald began to argue again, but Jack cut him off.

"I'm not wild about how this played out, either, Fitz," he said, shooting a quick, rebuking look in Darger's direction. "But if this is a chance to strike a big blow to the Nameless Brotherhood, I'll take it. It might be our only chance. Especially if he's giving us two for one."

Darger's scalp prickled. That was exactly how Stokes had framed the deal, and it felt like a bad omen for some reason. Stokes was too clever by half, and she didn't like the notion that he was several steps ahead of them.

She tried to figure a way that it could be a trap but didn't see how. Stokes would avoid felony charges and get to take a swing at running the Nameless. He wouldn't get that if he was setting them up.

After facilitating the deal with Stokes, he gave them the address for one Amanda Russo and reiterated his instructions.

Loshak was still waiting for her in the hall when she finished.

"What if he's playing games with us?" she said, feeling edgy and tired as hell.

There was a blip from where Loshak's phone hung at his hip. He reached for it.

"Who?"

"Stokes," she said. "What if he doesn't really know anything?"

Loshak's eyes were fixed on the screen of his phone.

"We might not need him."

"Why? What is it?"

"Text from Karla... Agent Dawson. They got the tire track analysis back. 95.4-inch wheelbase."

Darger raised an eyebrow. So Loshak and Dawson were on a first name basis now?

"95.4 inches? Is that supposed to mean something to me?"

"Only one type of vehicle has dimensions that match: Jeep Wrangler. 2007 through the current models. They've got one team going back through any matching Jeeps in the footage from traffic cams near the crime scenes to see if they can find a plate. Another group is going through the state registry vehicle by vehicle."

"Combing the registry is going to take forever if they can't get a plate from the video. We should go see if they need extra bodies."

"I'll go," he said, pocketing the phone. "You need to stick around to get that name out of Stokes. He seems set on talking to you over anyone else."

She rolled her eyes.

"Yeah, I noticed."

"I'll call if we come up with anything before then," Loshak said, giving her shoulder a squeeze. "When you talk to Stokes, don't let him get in your head."

"I won't."

Violet watched her partner retreat down the corridor. He turned a corner and was gone, and soon his footsteps receded as well. Left in the hush of the empty hallway, she suddenly felt exhausted. She was tempted to find a chair somewhere. A seat to catch a quick nap in.

Instead, she put her hand on the door of the interview room where Stokes was still being held. It wasn't the time for sleep.

It was time for action.

CHAPTER 39

The sky was gray. Dark. Drowsing on the cusp between night and dawn. And now that they'd turned off the Jeep and left it, the singing of birds seemed the only sound for miles.

They walked down a dirt driveway flecked with sparse gravel, something Levi only realized whenever a rock stabbed into the sole of one of his shoes.

Tall grass waved along the sides of the dirt path, some of it gone beige and crispy.

Levi surveyed the scene as he walked, not sure what to make of it. He didn't know where they were, and he was too tired to make any guesses.

A fence took shape ahead of them. The posts appeared first, growing solid and black in the shadows, and the chain link faded in some moments later like a spider's web stretched between the supports. A reinforced gate blocked the driveway, comprised of thicker metal bars.

Beyond the barricade, Levi could make out piles of rusted out cars, refrigerators, washing machines and the like. A junk yard? It seemed the only explanation.

Luke scaled the fence first. He kicked his legs up and over, and a cloud of dust fluffed up from his landing spot on the other side.

Levi followed, fingers hooking into the chain links, toes scrabbling for any kind of purchase. He didn't know why he was doing this or why they were here, especially at some ridiculous pre-dawn hour, but he was too tired to ask. He was here now. The explanation would arrive soon enough the way he figured it, with or without words.

The piles of junk cast long shadows, draping everything in inky darkness on this side of the fence. Levi could only really make out the white of Luke's t-shirt at times, but that was enough to keep going.

Hissing erupted somewhere before him, and the hair on the back of Levi's neck pricked up. He shuffled into something like a karate stance and snapped his head around to find the sound's source, fists raised.

When his brother turned to face him, he could see Luke's teeth exposed in a smile. Luke was giggling out an almost soundless laugh. Spitty. The whistle of air jetting through clenched teeth. It took longer than it should for all of this to register: Luke laughing was the sound that had startled him.

Levi let his fists fall back to his sides. At least the adrenaline woke him up a bit.

"What's your problem?" Luke said, still huffing out something like laughter.

"Nothing."

"OK. Just… you're standing like Captain America or something."

Levi looked down at his legs, watched his stance retract from something beyond shoulder-width to a more normal position.

Luke wheezed out additional laughter, enough moonlight catching his teeth to make them glow in the dark. The white hunks of bone in his mouth radiated purple against the black of the shadows around them, like this whole area was under black lights, and some raver dudes with glow sticks would pop out any second now when the beat dropped.

At last Levi mustered enough alertness to ask the question that had been on the tip of his tongue since they pulled off the road.

"So, like, what are we even doing out here?"

"You're about to find out."

Luke bent at the waist, one hand fishing into the cargo pocket of his shorts. He dug for a while before he retracted his fist, a ball of what looked like gray Play-Doh in it. It was small. Somewhere between the size of a golf ball and tennis ball from what Luke could see.

He fiddled with the stuff a bit, shaping it some with his fingers. It was still hard to see, but it looked like he jabbed a little pin of some kind into it, and then he either moved it or added a second pin.

"You ready?" he said, looking at Levi.

"Uh, yeah, I guess."

"Wait here."

Luke jogged some fifty feet to a rusted out El Camino and leaned into the open driver's side window. Levi could see that his brother's back and arms were moving a little, but nothing else was clear to him from this vantage point.

Levi's stomach grumbled, a rising pitch that sounded like it ended with a question mark. He blinked a few times, waited for some kind of clarity to occur to him, but none did. He figured he should probably know what Luke was doing by now, or at least be able to make an educated guess or two, but nothing came to him. His thoughts were still foggy with sleep — warm and slow and cloudy like a dream — even if he hadn't gotten much slumber of late.

The sound of Luke crunching back over the gravel brought Levi's focus back to the present moment. Again, he blinked a few times.

"Here. Put these on," Luke said.

He extended his arm, something clutched in his hand.

Goggles. Plastic safety goggles like something a factory or construction worker would wear. Levi took them and watched as Luke slid on a pair of his own, still grinning that purple grin. He followed his brother's lead and put on the goggles.

A strange sensation interrupted Levi's thoughts — an incredibly distant awareness clicking into place. Some part of him knew now what was happening. He was confident of that. It just happened to be taking a long, long time to make its way to his conscious mind.

Luke lifted one hand before him, a small black rectangle suddenly appearing there. It looked like a slender remote control and featured two red buttons.

His thumb slid to the top button, hesitated.

"You ready?"

Levi considered how to answer. He couldn't think of anything to say, so he shrugged.

The plum smile widened at this, lips quivering a little along the edges of the teeth.

The thumb flexed and pressed. The button clicked, and Luke yelled.

"Fire in the hole!"

The blaze lit up everything in angry reds and oranges. Fire licked out from the El Camino's windows. A flash. A whoosh.

The force of the shock wave slammed Levi in the sternum like a kick drum at an ear-bleeding concert, and he felt its rumble in his feet at the same time.

He could just barely see the gaping hole blown into the windshield and dash of the El Camino, all of it coming apart into tiny bits before the cloud of smoke and debris covered everything.

It was so violent. So loud.

So right.

Levi's heart hammered in his chest, and he felt his palms go cold with the surge of excitement. He was definitely all the way awake now.

After the incredible volume of the explosion, the silence seemed strange and empty. Almost eerie.

"C4?" Levi said.

"Shit yeah," Luke said. "Got a fuck ton of it. And this?"

He wiggled the remote control in his hand.

"The detonator works by radio wave. No wire or any hassles to fuck with."

Levi nodded, considering this revelation for a moment.

"So wait," he said. "What are we going to do with that?"

"You've never seen *Die Hard*?"

"Everyone has seen *Die Hard*."

"Well, what did Bruce Willis do in *Die Hard*?"

Levi thought about saying "walked around barefoot on broken glass, mostly," but instead he said:

"He threw a bunch of C4 down an elevator shaft?"

"He fucked shit up. And *that's* the plan right there. You and me? We're gonna fuck shit up."

CHAPTER 40

Mandy woke up, eyes blinking open gradually. Why? She'd been sound asleep and had a few beers in her, not to mention the good, hard fuck Donald had given her when he'd stumbled in after midnight. Usually that was enough to keep her in a deep sleep until morning.

He snored next to her in the bed. He'd been all worked up when she answered the door. Had a wild look in his eye like a grizzly or something. Practically had her right there on the kitchen table, but she'd managed to coax him into the bedroom. She was too old for that kind of funny business. The last time she'd let him do her on the sofa, her sciatica had acted up for a whole week.

She slid from the bed, still nude, and fumbled around in the closet until she found her robe. It was a silk kimono. A gift from Donald. She felt real fancy when she wore it. Like an old Hollywood starlet. Marilyn Monroe or Rita Hayworth.

Her bare feet padded out of the bedroom, down the hall, out to the kitchen. She'd make herself a cup of tea. That herbal stuff. Sleepyhead or whatever it was called. That would put her back to sleep.

The ceramic tile chilled her toes as she stood at the sink and filled a mug with water. She set the cup in the microwave and punched in three minutes.

Over the mellow hum of the microwave, there was another sound. The rumble of an engine as it rolled down the street. Slowly. Her heart beat quickened. It was a moment before she realized why that should bother her, and then Mandy remembered the woman on the news, the pregnant girl who had taken a couple of loads of buckshot in the face and chest right outside of her own home two nights ago.

A loud beep caused her to jump before she recognized it as the microwave. The water for her tea was ready. Good Lord, she was jumpy. Overreacting to every little noise. The odds of the car outside being the Georgia Sniper… well, there was simply no way. And besides, as long as she stayed in the house, she'd be fine.

Still, part of her wanted to go over to the window, to peek outside, just to be sure. She took a step that way and stopped herself. It seemed like too much of a risk. What if he was waiting there to see a face in the window?

She pulled the kimono a little tighter. She was being silly. She'd always been like this, scaring herself in the dark. Seeing things that weren't really there. She'd had terrible nightmares as a child. Night terrors her mother had called them.

Then she heard something else. The creak of a rusty hinge. Barely audible. Her breath caught in her throat and she immediately dropped the box of tea she'd been fumbling with. Another sound now, a soft clack. Yes. It was the gate. The one that led from the alley into the backyard. From the corner of her eye, a shadow passed by the kitchen window, and suddenly Mandy didn't think she was imagining things anymore.

He was here. Oh Dear Lord, Jesus, the sniper was here! Right outside!

"Donald!" she whispered, scared that if she made too much noise, the shooter would hear and know where she was and where to shoot.

She skittered back down the hall, hissing for Donald. Just as her toes met the rug inside the bedroom door, she heard the crash of a window breaking, and then there was shouting, and a loud crack — a gunshot? — and then boots stomping over the floors, and flashlights bouncing, and Donald was scrambling out of bed finally.

"Down on the ground! Hands on your head! Down now! Get down!"

It sounded like a hundred voices, all hollering at once, but she did what they said. She threw herself on the floor, hands on her head. With her cheek pressed into the rug, she peered up at the men in her house. They wore black vests emblazoned with bold white letters that spelled POLICE. Oh thank God, it wasn't the sniper. It was the police.

Donald was still completely naked, and Mandy noticed that his manbits were flopping about as he struggled with the policemen, like a damned fool. What did he think he was going to accomplish anyway? He had no weapon, unless he thought perhaps his nudity would keep them at arm's length.

It didn't. Two of the officers forced him face down on the bed and fastened cuffs around his wrists while Donald continued to cuss and squirm, his voice muffled by the bed.

The damned fool.

CHAPTER 41

Luke rummaged a hand around in the opposite cargo pocket, this time pulling out a bigger wad of the gray substance. This piece was longer, a semi-smashed rectangle with the corners rounded a bit from its pocket journey. It looked a little wider than a king sized Snickers bar. Luke molded it some with his fingers and stuck in a pair of detonator pins.

He couldn't keep that smile off his lips, teeth still glowing purple, though the darkness was receding to gray about them. Dawn would rear its head over the horizon within twenty minutes, Levi figured. Maybe less.

This time the explosive was placed under the driver's seat of the El Camino, and the brothers moved farther back from the doomed vehicle, kneeling to shield themselves behind a cluster of old refrigerators lying face down. The anticipation made Levi's chest tingle and his hands go cold, but he wanted it, he knew. He wanted to see what a bigger wad of C4 would do to this damn car as badly as he wanted anything.

Luke licked his lips, and let the silence grow awkward before he finally thumbed the detonator.

Again, the blaze flashed its orange fury, and in that instant, Levi felt its hatred in the way his jaw clenched and his nose wrinkled and his fingers curled into claws. And he liked it.

The boom was louder than before, a guttural blast with an incredible crack laid over top of it. He felt it from head to toe as much as he heard it.

The ground rumbled its excitement.

The glass exploded like crashing cymbals hitting a touch

after the big downbeat.

And the poor car came apart all at once.

The roof of the El Camino ripped off clean and blew 25 feet in the air, straight up, wobbling a little.

Both doors wrenched out of their frames and flopped to the ground, rocking a little on their rounded exteriors like box turtles trapped on their backs.

The roof tipped backward on its way back down and bashed into the El Camino's bed, wedging itself there partially upright.

Dust and smoke arose from the car and the ground as this transpired, the billowing clouds joining the flung shards of glass to obscure the scene little by little. It all sprinkled down in slow motion, pattering on the ground like rain.

All of this happened in the time it took to draw four breaths — that is, if Levi hadn't held his.

Again, the silence swelled into something uncomfortable. They stood and watched the scene go still as the last of the debris touched down.

"WWBWD, right?" Luke said, clapping Levi on the shoulder.

"Huh?"

"What would Bruce Willis do?"

CHAPTER 42

The observation room featured both a one-way mirror and camera feed displayed on a small black-and-white screen. There was nothing to see at the moment. The interview room was empty. But that would change. Soon, she hoped.

Stokes yawned from the seat beside her. She wasn't sure if it was theatrics or if he was genuinely tired. Darger stifled her own yawn, not wanting to share so much as a gesture with him.

The nerves were keeping her going at the moment, her mind filled with doubt. What if the stash wasn't where he said it would be? What if the drugs or guns or whatever illegal paraphernalia was there, but Hardegree wasn't? Or what if he managed to get away in the midst of the chaos?

"If you give me the name right now, you could be back in your cell, getting a few hours of sleep before you have to see the judge for the disorderly conduct charge."

He made a *tsk, tsk, tsk* sound with his tongue.

"You know the rules, Agent Darger. I want to see Hardegree in cuffs and Mirandized before I'll talk. But I admire your tenacity."

Darger's fingernails made tiny crescent moon indents in the flesh of her palms. She knew he was enjoying this part. The power he held over them, over her. Making them wait. Having everything done on his terms.

She'd figured out by now what Stokes was really after. He wanted his turn at the helm of the pirate ship. What she hadn't been able to puzzle out was why a man like Randall Stokes had ever allowed a buffoon like Donald Hardegree to run things.

Hardegree was surely a lesser breed of scumbag. Stokes was an apex predator.

She thought that maybe if she got him talking, he'd let something relating to the sniper slip.

"I know why you're doing this," she said, drumming her fingers on the table. "It's not a mystery. With Donald Hardegree out of the way, you can take over the Nameless Brotherhood. But why now? Why turn on him after thirty years?"

Stokes pressed his lips together, a sign that he wasn't going to take the bait, she thought. But after a few seconds, he croaked out an answer in that dry, husky voice.

"Donny got greedy and lazy. He doesn't care where the money comes from as long as it's green. That's a shit attitude. And well, shit trickles down."

"Are you trying to tell me you want to take the club in a more legitimate direction? The way I heard it, that was exactly what got the last president killed," she said, recalling Owen's story about Stokes and Hardegree feeding their former leader to the alligators.

"See, the problem with you cops is that you think being a one-percenter inherently means being a criminal."

"It doesn't?"

"It's a philosophy, Agent Darger. It's about freedom. It's about consenting adults being permitted to make their own choices without Johnny Law stepping in to say what you can and can't do."

Perhaps sensing that she remained unconvinced, Stokes shrugged.

"Honestly, I mostly hate the fucking Aryan Brotherhood. My two best friends growing up were a black kid and a Jew. The official policy of the club is that we don't associate with white supremacists, but the past few years, we've been doing more and more business with those neo-Nazi fucks. Had to bust up two younger members last month for sportin' 88 patches on their cuts."

"So… you're a criminal with scruples?"

"Everyone has principles, Agent Darger. The only difference between yours and mine is that you get yours from your FBI handbook, and I get mine from my own moral compass."

Darger had to bite back a bitter laugh. Moral compass. The way Owen told it, Stokes was the biggest bad in the group. If anything, the club would become even more ruthless with him at the wheel.

Before either of them could say more, a phone attached to the wall began to ring. Darger reached for it.

"Darger," she said, and relief flooded her when the desk sergeant informed her that Donald Hardegree was in the midst of being booked.

She thanked the sergeant, replaced the phone, and turned to address Stokes.

"Five minutes. I hope you're ready to give me that name."

"In due time, Agent Darger. Now how about you run along and bring me back a Coke?"

Hardegree sat in the interrogation room, his gaze pointed at the top of the table before him. All aggression — all the macho biker posturing — seemed to have drained from his being. A blank expression occupied the man's face instead, and his belly and shoulders sagged. He looked, Darger thought, almost comical in his melancholy demeanor, an exaggerated pathetic presence like a sad clown.

Stokes shook his head as he watched his half-brother

through the two-way mirror, his lips forming a crooked line of disgust. He took a swig from the bottle of Coca-cola, perhaps trying to wash the bad taste from his mouth.

"Look at him. An embarrassment. It's a shame. He's my brother, and I love him, but he's a fucking idiot."

Darger was staring at him, not interested anymore in anything he had to say about the Nameless Brotherhood or Donald Hardegree. She only wanted one thing. The name of the shooter.

He regarded her for a moment and then said, "The guy you want is named Luke Foley. That's the dude that bought the Glock-18, anyway."

"How do you know him?"

"I don't. One of the members set it up. Someone he went to school with or something."

"And you had no idea what he had planned?"

"Why would I? He bought the gun quite some time ago. When that detail got out in the papers, one of my guys just happened to remember it being specifically requested — a special order, you could say. Anyway, it's like I told you, I'm a proponent of personal responsibility. I am not accountable for the actions of another."

Darger scoffed, unable to hide her contempt.

"Right. I bet the victim's families would be quite impressed by your lofty ideals."

She stood, using her foot to kick her chair back under the table.

"Are you gonna take me back to my cell now?"

"An officer will escort you," she said, glad to finally be done with him. The whole arrangement was starting to make her feel dirty.

As the door was about to swing closed behind her, he called out.

"Agent Darger."

She caught the edge of the door before it shut.

"What?"

His black eyes bored into hers, full of amusement.

"Watch yourself out there. I'd hate to see this thing blow up in your face."

"I appreciate your concern," she said with no lack of sarcasm and walked out of the room.

She could still feel his carnivorous gaze on her long after she'd passed from his sight.

As Darger lifted her phone, intending to call Loshak with the name, it began to vibrate. Loshak was calling *her*.

"How did you know?" she asked.

"Know what?"

"That I got the name? Are you developing psychic powers on me now?"

"No. I called because we got a hit on the Jeep."

A fist tightened around her guts.

When she didn't speak, Loshak said, "You want to go first? Or should I?"

"Luke Foley," she said.

Now his end was silent.

"Loshak?"

"I'm here. The name we got on the vehicle is Levi Foley."

"Father and son? Brothers? What?"

She could hear muttering and typing in the background as Loshak directed someone — probably Rodney — to enter the names into the computer.

"The birth dates are a little over two years apart. Brothers. Now we just need to figure out which one it is."

"No we don't," Darger said, the realization suddenly hitting her. "It's both of them."

"What?"

"Two shooters. They're working together."

CHAPTER 43

Soaring tones screeched in Levi's ears — the remnants of whatever temporary damage the concussive blasts had done. Maybe it was his imagination, but it seemed to be affecting him physically. Each ear canal felt pinched, like the tube had somehow closed up. Or maybe they'd been clogged, long strands of cotton shoved in, everything all congested, weeping thick yellow wax in protest. He swiped his pinkie fingers at the openings, but it didn't help. There was no evidence of weeping wax, at least.

After running a few more tests with the plastic explosives — taking out the windshield of a Buick Skylark and employing a bigger chunk of C4 to obliterate a Maytag dryer almost entirely — Luke seemed satisfied. They'd walked back to where the Jeep was parked in the tall grass along the side of the road, and here they still sat.

Explosives. Jesus. It made him nervous. Even more confused than before. How far was Luke going to push this? And how far was Levi willing to go in helping him?

He didn't know. Nothing made sense anymore.

Before they started — back when it was all a plan — it seemed like vengeance was a noble goal. Psychotic, yes, but with some underlying honor attached. Like they could prove something to someone. Make something right.

But it wasn't a plan anymore, wasn't an abstract concept. It was concrete. Made real with guns and bullets. Etched forever into flesh and bone and blood.

And it was all different now.

In the violence itself, he found only meaningless destruction. No sense of vengeance. No sense of honor. No sense of anything beyond the brutality itself.

He licked his lips. Thought about saying something to Luke about it. But the words didn't come. There was no way to express the mixed up way he felt inside.

And yet, he had to admit it. There was an allure to the sheer force of the explosions he'd witnessed. A raw power that pulled him in like a magnet. Something primal. Aggressive. Cathartic in its hateful fiery glow.

Something that whet his appetite for destruction.

They were going to fuck shit up. That's what Luke had said. And when he said it like that, maybe things did make sense, if only partially.

The world had beaten them down, used them up, made them feel worthless. And now? Now they were standing up.

The wind picked up outside, swishing through the brush and whistling a little where it blew through the Jeep's open windows.

Blades of grass laid flat for a beat whenever the air moved through them, popping up moments later. This dance rippled through the field in segments. It looked organized, almost like a crowd doing the wave.

Now Luke brandished the tiny remote in his hands once more, wiggling it to get his brother's attention. Levi shook himself into the moment, focused on the little black rectangle in his brother's mitt. He had no idea how long Luke had been talking.

"You listening to me? The remote detonator here works by radio wave. Additionally, it is fucking awesome."

"Radio wave?"

Luke nodded.

"It sends a coded radio signal on a specific frequency to tell all the charges to fire at once, right? I bring this up because if I get taken out of the game, and I happen to have the remote on me, you might need to resort to a backup method of detonation. To finish the project, I mean. Just felt like it was something we should go over."

Levi thought about it for a second.

"Couldn't I just shoot it or something?"

Luke lit a cigarette, the lighter's flame flickering orange against his face. He shook his head.

"C4 is pretty stable stuff. You can throw it against the wall as hard as you can, and it won't detonate. Shoot it full of bullets, and it won't detonate. Light it on fire, and it won't detonate. It'll burn, but it won't detonate. To get it to blow, you have to trigger an electrical charge. That focused, intense burst of heat makes it explode."

He took a long drag from his Winston, held it, exhaled smoke from his nostrils.

"I thought about mixing up some ammonium nitrate and diesel. That's what the terrorists use, you know? But it's volatile stuff, and I figured we might as well use what the army uses, right? After all, this is still America, by God. Anyway, you've probably been wondering where my money's been going these past couple years? Well, you saw a little of it out in that junkyard. I've been stocking up, little by little. My whole life has built to this moment, to this project."

"How'd you get it?"

"Oh, don't you go worrying your sweet, little head over these things. I've handled it, acquired more than enough for our purposes, and I know just where we're going to use it."

Levi scratched his chin before he responded.

"And where is that?"

"What did I fuckin' say? Don't worry about it. You promised to help me finish this. And finish it, we will. Soon. Until then, the less you know, the better. In case things go south."

They fell quiet. Luke flicked his cigarette butt into the grass and lit another.

The sunlight had crept the rest of the way over the horizon at some point, but Levi had barely felt the passing of the hours. It was a gray day, overcast and dreary. It smelled clean, though. The green of the grass hung in the air around them. Alive and fresh.

Luke cleared his throat and spoke again.

"This is going to be it, man. The big one. My magnum opus. And I can't do it without you. Nor would I want to."

Luke smiled at Levi, and things once more made sense. As much as they could, maybe.

"Now let me show you how the backup detonation method works."

CHAPTER 44

The entire task force convened within the hour to plan the apprehension of the Foley brothers. Darger stood off to one side of the large room with Loshak, leaning against the wall for support. She was bone-weary, but there was no way she could sleep now. She wasn't stepping foot in her hotel room until the two men wore matching sets of handcuffs.

Driver's license photos for both brothers flashed onto a screen at the front of the room. Darger had to blink several times to get her tired eyes to bring the pictures into focus.

Luke, the elder brother, was on the left. He had pasty skin and greasy hair the color of porridge. His gaunt cheeks and dead eyes gave him an almost skeletal appearance.

Younger brother Levi was on the right. He looked an awful lot like Luke. His hair was a little darker, his face a little fuller. He was Luke without the flat gaze and emaciated lines.

Atlanta Police Chief Terry Hogaboom was laying out the preliminary measures of their plan.

"Names and photographs are being circulated to all area law enforcement agencies," the chief said. "The boys have been added to the no-fly list, and there's an APB out on the Wrangler."

He raised both hands in the air, revealing a wet patch underneath each armpit. Darger wondered if he was nervous, or if he was just a heavy sweater.

"Now I want everyone to listen, and listen good: we are waiting to release the names to the public. That means not a word of this to reporters, to your wives, to your goddamned priests. I don't care if Christ himself comes down from Heaven. These. Names. Do. Not. Get. Out."

Chief Hogaboom emphasized each word by hammering his fist into the podium. His cadence was starting to remind her of a football coach giving a pre-game speech.

"We only get one chance to get the jump on 'em, and our colleagues at the FBI have assured me that taking them by surprise is in our best interest."

She had to give him credit, he did a decent job selling it despite the fact that she knew he had reservations. He'd resisted when she and Loshak first recommended holding the names back from the press. Both he and Fitzgerald wanted to plaster the faces of the brothers Foley on every newsstand and morning live show possible. But the last thing they wanted to do was push whatever plan the brothers had into the next phase. Hogaboom and Fitzgerald eventually agreed to withhold the names for 24 hours. If they didn't have the brothers by then, they'd make their identities public.

Satisfied that everyone was on the same page in terms of keeping their mouths shut, Chief Hogaboom moved on. He brought up a picture of Luke Foley. This time it was a candid shot, probably from his Facebook page or elsewhere on the internet. In it, he wore a white tank top over a pair of camo fatigues and was giving the finger to whoever was operating the camera.

"Luke Foley. 30. A respectable rap sheet going back to age fifteen. Several assault charges which led to his expulsion from Fort McPherson High. A handful of alcohol-related charges: Driving Under the Influence, Public Drunkenness. Criminal Trespass and Damage to Property. Also, a history of domestic violence calls from his ex-wife, but no charges were ever filed."

A photograph of Levi, hood pulled up over his head, giving a half-smile, half-scowl to the camera.

"Little brother Levi, on the other hand… 28, clean record aside from an alcohol charge back in his late teens."

Hogaboom loaded the same map Darger had memorized over the past few days: an aerial view of Atlanta with the crime scenes marked with red dots. A blue dot now marked an apartment building on the east side of the city.

"Levi's driver's license and tax returns list this as his current address in Kirkwood. I just got off the horn with the manager of the complex, and the address appears to be up-to-date. We've got unmarked eyes on the house as we speak. They've reported a light on inside and a car parked in the assigned space — not the Wrangler, but a Hyundai. It's possible they dumped the Jeep."

One of the detectives sitting in the front row raised a hand. "What about the other brother?"

"Luke's last known address is down in Griffin, about an hour out of town. The house belongs to his ex-wife, Shelly Webb. Local guys are sitting on the house while a unit heads down to check it out, see if maybe the boys fled south, but our profilers think that's unlikely," Hogaboom answered, glancing over at Loshak and Darger.

He left out the rest of what they'd speculated: that *if* the brothers were found at the ex-wife's house, then she was probably already dead.

"Could be that Luke got his own place and never updated his info. Or maybe he's been couch-surfing with Levi or living in his car. In any case, we figure they're together now."

Hogaboom marked a second blue dot on the map.

"We've got another car sitting on the Fed Ex sorting facility on Shoals Road, Levi's place of employment. The office won't open until eight, and we don't imagine he's been showing up to work with all this going on. Obviously, we're keeping an eye on it regardless."

"No job for Luke?" the same detective asked.

"Hasn't filed a tax return in three years."

"What about parents? Or other family in the area?"

Gesturing at the map, Hogaboom said, "We got an address for the mother over in Sylvan Hills. Father is deceased."

Darger squinted at the map, trying to sense a pattern or logic to the location of the crime scenes and the places Luke and Levi might have connections to. For example, they'd discovered that Luke's ex-wife had once worked at the Supercuts that shared a parking lot with the Publix. She wanted to believe that wasn't a coincidence. But if the other sites had any particular meaning, they hadn't been able to connect the dots yet. It was likely they'd only figure it out after they'd apprehended the men and talked to them. If they even got that opportunity. She knew there was a very real chance the brothers would go down shooting.

Hogaboom clapped his hands together, wrenching her from her thoughts.

"Alright, everyone knows where they need to be, and I know I can trust you all to keep your lips zipped until tomorrow morning. Let's go bust down some doors."

CHAPTER 45

"Diddly-fuckin-squat."

Detective Horst was a burly man in a bright blue shirt. Most of his head was shaved except for a longer tuft of platinum hair on top that reminded her of a swirl of vanilla ice cream. He stood inside the door of Levi Foley's apartment when he made his pronouncement. Darger wasn't sure if it was for the benefit of her or everyone or maybe just for Horst himself.

The apartment was about what she'd expect from a 28-year-old guy living alone: thrift store furniture, carpets pocked with cigarette burns, a flat screen TV with a gaming system and a stack of games piled beside it. The walls were bare except for an Atlanta Braves pennant hanging over the only window in the room.

Darger crossed the living room to look closer at a small table next to the couch. It had casters on the bottom so it would slide under the couch, almost like the bedside tables in hospital rooms. She ran her finger through the layer of dust on the surface, noting a dust-free rectangle in the center, roughly 11" by 16".

"Looks like he took his laptop with him," she said.

Aside from the fact that he was a bachelor in his twenties, Darger wasn't getting much of a read on the place. It didn't have a ton of personality. In the kitchen cabinets, she found a few boxes of cereal, some energy bars, and a can of potatoes, which she hadn't even known was a thing.

She paused in front of the refrigerator, tilting her head to one side. Written in words from a magnetic poetry set was the phrase: MY POLE BLOWS A CHAIN.

She sensed someone looming over her shoulder and turned. The fleshy lips of Detective Horst bunched into a pout.

"The fuck does that mean?"

Darger shrugged, jotting the phrase down in her notes, just in case.

"No idea. I mean, I assume it's dirty."

She opened the fridge and found it similarly barren: a jar of pickles, off-brand steak sauce, and an orange so old and shriveled she thought it was some kind of strange mushroom at first. There was a fifth of cheap vodka on top of the fridge, 3/4 empty.

Someone's phone rang, blasting out the theme from *The Good, the Bad, and the Ugly*. Detective Horst answered and began an obnoxiously loud conversation.

"Horst here. Uh huh. Yeah. Well, shit. I know, right?"

He bellowed with laughter.

"No doubt about it. I'm cryin' my fucking eyes out over here. Yeah. Alright. Talk to ya."

He hung up and addressed the room.

"That was Reggie," he said, and Darger wondered if it was the same Reggie she'd met after the biker brawl the other night. "They knocked on Mama Foley's door. Young couple answered, say they bought the house last year. Apparently, Mrs. Foley has early-onset dementia. Had to be moved into a nursing home. Very sad, blah blah blah. Anyway, another dead end."

Darger ran a knuckle over the scabbed up wound on her forehead. His empathy knew no bounds.

Around 3:30 in the afternoon, Loshak convinced her to take a break.

"Let's go get a bite to eat. It'll help clear our heads."

Darger didn't want to leave, didn't want to risk missing some minute detail that could clue them in on where the brothers could be or what person or place they might attack next.

But she was starving, and he was right. A moment away from the dingy interior of the apartment might bring the clarity she needed to put the pieces together, even if those pieces felt a little sparse at this point.

Outside, the day had turned warm and bright. It was hard to believe that most of the day was already gone. Between sifting through junk in the apartment and filling out additional paperwork, she knew the rest of it would blur past with similar speed.

They passed a taco truck a few miles from the crime scene. Loshak pulled over, and they each scarfed three tacos a piece. Even though she couldn't see his eyes behind the mirrored lenses of his sunglasses, she could tell Loshak was studying her from across the picnic table.

"Maybe we should go back to the hotel. Get a few hours of sleep."

"Fuck that," she said and sat up straighter in an attempt to appear more vigilant. "These guys aren't done. It's only a matter of time before they strike somewhere else."

"On that, we can agree."

"We can't quit until we figure it out."

On the ride back to Levi's apartment, Darger let out a colossal yawn. The food had made her sleepy. She let her eyelids droop closed for a moment. It felt good to rest her eyes. Better than good. It was as luscious as eating a sun-warmed peach straight from the tree and letting the juices drip down her chin.

A car door thunked shut, and Darger startled awake. She spent several disoriented seconds trying to figure out where she was before she realized she was still in the car.

But the car was off, the driver's seat empty. Loshak was gone. They were parked across the street from Levi Foley's apartment building, under the shade of a sprawling live oak. She must have dozed off for a few minutes on the way back.

It wasn't until she stepped out of the car and saw how long her shadow was, noted how low the sun hung in the sky, that she glanced at her watch. 8:17 PM? She'd been asleep for hours.

She burst into Levi's apartment and found Loshak poking through a closet in the bedroom. An open shoe box rested near his foot, overflowing with a mishmash of cords and chargers for various electronic devices.

Violet stood there, arms crossed over her chest, until he turned to look at her.

"You look grumpy," he said. "Bad dream?"

"You could have woken me up. Who just leaves someone sleeping in a car like that?"

"The windows were cracked."

"I'm not a fucking dog, Loshak."

His trademark breathy laugh filtered out from the closet.

"Is this going to be a thing now? I fall asleep, and you go gallivanting off on your own?"

"If you'd slept a little longer, I bet you wouldn't be so crabby," he said, ignoring her question.

She sighed.

"Find anything in there?" she asked, examining the sleeve of a letter jacket. An embroidered patch on the shoulder read *Fort Mac Marauders* and featured a pirate clutching a knife in his teeth.

Loshak tossed out two pairs of shoes.

"Size 12, which matches the boot prints they found at the first crime scene."

She figured that since they were in Levi's apartment, they didn't have any of Luke's shoes to compare. Could Levi have been the shooter in both sniper attacks? She'd been operating from the assumption that Luke was the sniper, the leader. He was the one with the extensive criminal record as well as the military history.

The revelation that they were looking for two men instead of one had thrown her off her game. She felt like she was sprinting after a loping gazelle that kept getting farther and farther away.

Two shooters wasn't unprecedented. The DC sniper attacks were perpetrated by a two-man team. So was the Oklahoma city bombing and the Columbine school shooting. Hell, a pair of brothers had been responsible for the Boston Marathon attack.

The question shouldn't be *why* it was throwing her off. She should be asking herself why she hadn't thought of it before.

"What else?" she asked.

Loshak motioned to a pile of old newspapers on the bed.

"Those were probably the most enlightening thing I found so far."

Darger moved over to the stack of yellowing newsprint. She lifted one by a corner, studying the masthead. The name of the paper was *The Nexus.* A familiar image of a pirate caught her eye in the upper right-hand corner, and she realized it was a newspaper from Levi's high school.

Flipping through the pages, she stopped when she reached a block of text outlined in permanent marker. Darger brought the paper closer to her face, studying the byline. Sure enough, it read "By Levi Foley."

"So Levi was a budding journalist," she said.

"It would appear so. Did you notice how he used a Sharpie to draw a box around all the stories he wrote?"

"I did," Darger said, noting two more of Levi's bylines as she thumbed through another edition.

She knew what Loshak was thinking. The fact that he'd kept the newspapers at all suggested they meant something to him. That he'd gone through them and highlighted his work said it even louder. Whether that meant anything now, she had no idea. But he'd cared about something once, and that fact reminded her that he was human.

Darger moved over to a bedside table and rifled through the drawers.

"Also," Loshak said, "Agent Dawson stopped by with a juicy nugget."

"What's that?"

"One of Luke Foley's army buddies jumped off the Lake Street Bridge a few months after their unit returned from Iraq."

"The first sniper crime scene?"

"The very one."

"Huh," she said, pausing in her search of the nightstand.

Suddenly she felt on the brink of some epiphany.

"That's it, then."

"What?"

"That's the personal connection. That's why they chose that spot. The second attack was in the Publix lot, right where Luke's ex-wife used to work."

"You think he thought she still worked there?"

"Maybe. But even if he knew she didn't, it would have been a familiar place."

Loshak crab-walked out of the closet.

"OK. And then when they shot Ethan… that was a return to the first crime scene in a sense."

She nodded and watched her partner ponder this revelation.

"I think you're onto something. But what about Carol Jones? The pregnant gal."

Darger gnawed on her thumbnail before admitting she was at a loss.

"I don't know."

Her gaze fell onto the open drawer, where she spotted a small electronic device. It was rectangular, perhaps three-by-five inches, and sported a handful of buttons beneath an LCD screen.

"Hey."

Loshak's response was muffled by the closet.

"What?"

"You still have that box of cords?"

The shoe box skittered over the floor, landing with a bump against her toe. It was another few minutes before she had untangled the nest of wires enough to find the correct cable.

Abandoning the closet, Loshak came to stand behind her as she connected the cord to the old Flip camera.

"Whatcha got?" he asked.

She pointed the lens at him and waggled it back and forth.

"Video camera."

Loshak followed her out to the living room where she hooked up the other end of the cable so they could watch on a screen larger than the tiny LCD. After exchanging a suspenseful glance with her partner, Darger pressed the PLAY button.

CHAPTER 46

Blurry forms took shape, sharpening as the camera's autofocus made adjustments. It was Luke Foley's face that emerged, filling the screen. The date stamp on the video would have made him fifteen or sixteen. He wore a black Metallica t-shirt and had the same gaunt face with the hollowed out cheeks, but his hair was longer and his complexion was spotted with acne.

The shot pulled out and swiveled over to a glass jar on a kitchen counter top. The label said, "Pickled Jalapeno Slices."

"How much will you give me?" The question came from a boy in an Atlanta Falcons hat. He looked to be about the same age as Luke.

"I've got two bucks," Luke said. "Levi's got five."

"Why do I have to give him five bucks if you're only giving him two?" From the proximity of the voice, Levi was the one manning the camera.

"Just do it," Luke said.

In the background, two other boys removed rumpled bills from their pockets.

There was a sigh from off-screen. The camera shifted as Levi handed it off to Luke, who zoomed in on his brother's hand dropping the five-dollar bill to the pile. It was mostly singles, maybe fifteen or twenty bucks all together.

"Seventeen bucks," Luke announced. "That means seventeen seconds."

"Seventeen seconds of what?" Darger wondered aloud.

And then the boy in the Falcons cap unzipped his pants. Darger groaned as her brain did some quick math and figured out where this stunt was headed.

Loshak's voice came from over her shoulder. "Ah yes, the old wanger-in-the-pickle-jar routine."

She took her gaze from the screen long enough to frown at her partner.

"It's really a wonder that our species has survived this long," she said. "What is it about adolescent boys being so enthusiastic about performing parlor tricks with their genitals?"

Loshak held up a finger.

"*Some* adolescent boys. I prefer to keep spicy food above the waist."

"Good to know," Darger said.

The voices on the video counted down from seventeen, with Luke waving his arms like a maestro conducting an orchestra.

"Seventeen! Sixteen! Fifteen!"

The kid performing the act appeared fairly unperturbed thus far, aside from complaining about the coldness of the liquid when they'd first begun. But when the countdown reached ten, his face changed. His eyes suddenly bulged, revealing too much of the whites. Wrinkles formed on his brow, and his jaw dropped open.

He inhaled sharply. His feet did a little jig, reminding Darger of a jointed puppet. The boys had only reached the number seven when he wrenched away from the jar with a shriek and ran for the sink. As he attempted to splash water on his crotch, screaming about how much it burned, the camera got a shot of his friends all buckled at the waist, laughing so hard some of them had tears in their eyes.

"Get him some milk!" Luke coughed through his glee.

Someone fetched a half gallon of skim milk from the refrigerator, and Falcons Hat proceeded to pour it down his pants.

"A bowl! I need a bowl!"

This made Luke laugh so hard he keeled over on the floor, grasping his sides. His laugh was high-pitched and reminded Darger of someone who had inhaled helium.

The video cut.

The next bit featured grimy walls, dim lighting, loud music, and people shouting to be heard over it. A house party. The camera wove between the churning sea of bodies. Every hand held a red Solo cup.

Through a doorway into a kitchen. A pair of legs in the air and voices chanting, "Chug! Chug! Chug!" The feet flailed and came down to meet the floor. The crowd cheered. Keg stands. The next person stepped forward, eager to demonstrate their chugging prowess. The clip ended.

Another party, or the same party, who could tell? Levi, eyelids drooping, speech slurred. Obviously wasted. He practically swayed back and forth where he stood. He and Luke in conversation that couldn't be heard over the music. Levi said something. Luke laughed and gave him a light shove. So drunk that a feather would have knocked him off-kilter, Levi stumbled a few steps backward and fell ass-first into a cardboard box. Luke and the other kids standing around howled with hilarity.

The scene changed again. A sixteen-year-old Levi perched on the roof of someone's house. Nearby, a metal slide led to a nearby pool. Bridging the gap between roof and slide was a length of plywood, forming a very sketchy ramp. Darger guessed he was considering running down the roof, onto the ramp, and leaping onto the slide.

Standing in the yard below, Luke egged him on from behind the camera.

"Come on, man. Don't be a pussy."

Levi called out something unintelligible in response.

There was more goading, and then a countdown. Ten down to one. And then Levi lurched forward, trying to stand, and Darger noticed for the first time that he had inline skates strapped to his feet.

"Oh, God," she muttered.

Levi tried to stand tall, wobbled, and then settled for a squat as the wheels rolled over the shingles with a *bump-bump bump-bump.*

Surprisingly, he made it all the way to the edge of the roof without incident. It was the makeshift ramp that tripped him up. The plywood must have been just a hair too high. When the roller blades struck it, the whole sheet shifted forward, uncovering the rain gutter. The front wheel on Levi's right foot caught in the empty space, throwing him off-balance. He catapulted over the roof several feet shy of the slide, spread out like a flying squirrel.

He hit the ground with a thud.

The camera shook wildly as Luke ran over to capture Levi writhing in the grass, holding his arm. He sat up, and Darger saw the sharp end of a bone protruding from his flesh. There were shouts, and the camera angle twisted awkwardly and went black.

Later, in what Darger assumed was the ER waiting room, an older woman with thick waves of brown hair ranted at whoever sat behind the camera. It had to be their mother. From the odd angle of the camera and the way her head was partially out of frame, Darger figured she didn't even know the camera was recording.

"Do you not understand how serious this is? Your brother is

in surgery right now, having his bones screwed back together. He'll have to wear a cast for at least six weeks. The doctor says there could be permanent nerve damage," she said, then jabbed an artificial fingernail into the Formica tabletop. "He could have *died*."

Luke didn't respond, and Mrs. Foley persisted.

"What the hell were you thinking? Do you have no sense?"

"I didn't know he was gonna get hurt," Luke said, his voice sullen and detached.

"Do you have a single brain cell left in that thick head of yours, or have you killed them all with your liquor and your drugs? What did you think was going to happen? Did you think your brother was going to suddenly sprout wings and take flight?"

Luke was silent for a time, and then he muttered, "I don't do drugs."

His mother scoffed.

"I am at my wit's end with you, Lucas. You lie, you cheat, you steal—"

"When did I—"

She cut him off with a chopping hand motion.

"Enough! It's bad enough the shit you pull on your own. You know you are *this close* to being expelled? And now you're dragging your brother into it? I am so disappointed in you."

The video cut off. A new scene took shape.

The point-of-view glided down a corridor bathed in harsh institutional lighting. The main sound was the loud slap and squeak of footsteps on the polished floor.

A large set of glass doors drew closer. In the reflection, Darger could make out Levi, fresh cast on one arm, camera clutched in the opposite hand. He hunched in a wheelchair with

Luke pushing from behind.

Instead of slowing, the speed of the footsteps increased.

"Don't crash me into the doors, dude," Levi said.

"They open automatically."

"Yeah, but — hey!"

It was too late. In the reflection, Darger could see Luke thrust the wheelchair forward and release it. Levi sailed down the remainder of the hallway, gasping as the glass barrier drew near. At the last moment, the doors opened, and he sped through. On the other side of the doors, a man walking up the sidewalk stood directly in the path of the chair.

"Watch out!" Levi yelled.

The man dove out of the way, but now Levi was bearing down on the street. The camera tumbled from his grip as he released it to fumble for the brakes on the chair. There was a screech and then the world lurched and rolled, the rotating jumble of images on the TV screen looking like footage from inside a clothes dryer.

A loud clatter blotted out most of the other sounds and then a beat of silence. The camera was upside-down, the slowly spinning spokes of the upended wheelchair taking up most of the screen. There was a groan, and then Levi's foot kicked into view.

The thud of shoes clodding down the sidewalk got louder as they approached the microphone. The camera righted itself as Luke picked it up and focused the lens on his brother.

"Dude!"

Levi blinked up at his older brother.

"That was awesome. You totally bit it," Luke said.

There was a flash of anger in Levi's eyes, and then Luke burst into his tittering, chipmunk laugh. Levi's face softened. He grinned and chuckled along as his brother helped him to his feet.

"Hey!"

Both boys turned back to the entrance of the hospital where a large and furious-looking nurse in teal scrubs stood with her hands on her hips.

"Where did you get that wheelchair? You boys better—"

Luke did not wait for her to finish.

"Run!" he said and took off down the sidewalk leaving his brother to catch up.

The clip ended.

"Brotherly love," Loshak said, as the next video file began to play.

Luke hunched over Levi's cast, embellishing it with a black Sharpie.

"This thing smells like ass," Luke said.

"I know, man," Levi agreed. "Larry Green told me that when he got the cast off his hand, it was all skinny and weird and like, filthy."

Luke appeared to be a talented artist, if a macabre one. He had drawn a smiling skull with bulging eyeballs on Levi's cast, and around the skull, a halo of flames. Now he worked on another section of Levi's arm. It was on the back of the cast, currently out of Levi's view. Eventually, it became clear to Darger that he was drawing a large penis with testicles. He snickered to himself as he drew. Finally, Levi figured out something was going on.

"What are you drawing now?"

"It's not done yet, dickface."

"Let me see it."

"When I'm finished!"

Levi, much too suspicious now, finagled away from Luke's grip and angled his arm to get a look.

"Luke! You asshole!"

He lunged at the camera and the video ended abruptly.

Darger skipped through the files until she found one dated several years later.

The shot was unfocused at first, but from the murmur of voices, it was clearly footage of a crowd. As the frame sharpened, Darger made out the familiar scene of people milling about the baggage claim of an airport.

The camera swayed ever so slightly from side-to-side, as if the person operating it was nervously stepping from one foot to the other.

An elderly man in a raincoat stepped aside, and a man in full combat uniform approached the camera. Darger squinted, almost not recognizing him.

It was Luke, but he was changed. More serious. A haunted look in his eyes. He was no longer the laughing class clown. The court jester.

A young woman with curly auburn hair stepped into the frame. Darger knew from the meeting that it was Luke's ex-wife, though in the video, they would have still been married. The couple hugged and kissed and then parted.

"Hey, man," Levi said, and the camera shifted as the brothers embraced.

When they pulled back, Luke asked, "Where's mom?"

"She couldn't come," Levi said.

Luke's nose twitched once, the only sign that he'd even heard Levi's response.

The screen went black and the blue menu screen appeared. There were no more files to play.

CHAPTER 47

A single bar of light slipped through a crack between the curtains, and Levi stared at the spot where the glowing sliver wrapped itself from the wall onto the ceiling. His eyes felt glassy now, several steps beyond the sand flung feeling he'd experienced earlier. Even so, he looked into the light.

He still couldn't sleep. He wasn't sure how long it had been anymore. It was too confusing to try to count the days at this point. His brain wasn't up to it.

Confusion. That summed up his feelings in general. If the disorientation had truly seeded itself with the pregnant woman, it had blossomed into something more with the introduction of the explosives. His mind circled back to the same questions over and over.

Who or what was Luke targeting?

And how much C4 did he have?

Based on how willing he'd been to use up a couple pounds of the stuff on their tests in the junkyard, Levi suspected his brother had quite a lot stashed somewhere. Ready to do mass destruction.

He could still feel that rattle he'd felt in his sternum when the El Camino got its roof and doors blown off. Could still see the ball of fire and the glimpse of the damage done before the smoke closed around it. They'd moved even further back for the bigger blast that took out the washing machine, and Luke had used a couple of hunks of plastic explosive, each the size of a foot-long from Subway. That was a massive overkill, of course. Luke said he wanted to see it obliterated into bits so small you couldn't tell what color the thing had been.

According to Luke, the conventional wisdom was that a lump the size of a potato could take out a normal suburban home, and that a single one of those foot-long sized chunks could take out an I-beam if positioned correctly and detonated with a ribbon charge. Mulling over the amount of mayhem Luke could cause with these explosives made Levi's belly knot with dread.

He rolled over, thought about getting up for the millionth time. But no. What use would it be? It was 1:26 AM according to the alarm clock on the night stand. There was nothing to do, nowhere to go.

Luke's breathing filtered into Levi's consciousness then, slow and deep and even. Regardless of his surroundings or circumstances, his brother slept without issue. He always had.

An hour seeped past like that. He tossed and turned in bed, and his thoughts did the same, making less and less sense with each passing minute, slowly devolving as the lack of sleep won out over his ability to reason.

Confusion gave way to delirium, a strange fever dream logic overtaking his thinking as he lost his grip on reality.

Again, he watched that sliver of light where it peeked through the crack in the curtains, but now it danced on the ceiling, undulating like a glowing tentacle.

He was losing his shit.

And he was up now. On his feet. Moving quickly. Quietly. Gliding across the room to the door. Scooping the keys along the way.

It didn't fully occur to him that he'd left the room until he felt the carpet change to wet cement under his bare feet. It had sprinkled on and off all evening. Slicked the sidewalk and parking lot. The streetlights gleamed off of the places where puddles formed among the lot's gravel.

He eased the motel door shut behind him.

The road and parking lot were empty. Utterly still. And silence sprawled in all directions to smother the scene. That awful kind of silence that made him feel vulnerable and small right away, made him hold his breath, made his eyes swivel for signs of danger. The kind of silence that made him feel alone.

He staggered. His balance wobbling. He felt drunk. His thoughts and motor skills breaking down due to exhaustion.

And now he moved from the sidewalk down two steps onto the gravel, the texture once more transforming under his feet, going rougher and wetter, almost slimy.

The thick night air swirled around his body like fog. Heavy and chilly, like walking into a damp basement. Something about it was too cold to be normal, though. It constricted his chest and gave him goose bumps.

He looked down at himself for the first time and noted that he wore nothing but boxers. He hadn't realized that. Most of his body was exposed to the night, that wet air moistening his skin, making direct contact from head to toe. But it didn't matter now. Get on with it.

Levi climbed into the Jeep, fumbling in the dark to find the right key and insert it into the ignition. He got it. The dash lights lit up, their green glow shattering the darkness, illuminating everything before him. The starter grated and whined a little before it caught.

His eyes lingered on the door to their room as the engine came to life. He half expected Luke to come busting out with a shotgun or something, racking and firing wildly, flames and buckshot raining out of the barrel in waves. But nothing happened. Not so much as a twitch of the curtains over the window.

The Jeep eased out of the parking lot, the tires making that wet sound against the ground. He felt better once he was away from the motel.

Driving seemed easier than walking, more automatic somehow, less concentration necessary. His hands and feet just knew what to do.

He didn't see a single car on the back roads. Only the thicket of green running along each side of the blacktop. A tangled up mess of stalks and stems, indecipherable.

Headlights made their appearance once he merged onto the highway, though. Mostly semis at this hour. Trucks hauling crap around the country. Beer. Livestock. Machinery. Tankers of milk and oil and other chemical sludge.

In America, business never sleeps.

He took the third exit, spiraling onto the ramp. He suspected the Marathon station up here would have what he was looking for, though it was hard to be sure these days.

There was one other car in the lot — a purple PT Cruiser with a crinkled fender. The long haired guy pumping gas into the tank didn't look his way, though, so that was good.

As he pulled up to the payphone, the notion of security cameras occurred to him, and that gave him a jolt of adrenaline. His alertness surged, revealing how much his mouth tasted like dog. He craned his neck to look around the lot, unable to spot any cameras, though that didn't make him feel any better. They were probably there, he figured.

And then he realized that what he was doing didn't make a lot of sense. He wanted to call the tip line — the 800 number soldered into his brain after hearing it over and over on the news. Some part of him felt that if he called the police and told them about the explosives, he might be able to get some sleep. He needed to pass the responsibility on. Let someone else figure out what to do about it so he could rest.

But it hadn't occurred to him fully that doing so would very likely get Luke and himself caught. He didn't care for that notion much. He didn't want either one of them to go to prison. But he needed help in wrestling this project to the ground. He couldn't stop Luke alone.

He eyed the black phone resting in its chrome holster. He knew he was lucky to have found one on his first try. A lot of the payphones had been ripped out of places like this now that everyone had a cell phone. He'd half expected to find an empty shell here — a bare steel post where the phone used to be, maybe some wires hanging out.

To hell with it.

He reached his arm out the driver's side window, plucked the phone from its holder and brought it to his ear. A calm came over him as he did so.

His fingers punched the little metal squares, dialing the tip line number without thought.

The ringing gurgled that land line ring in his ear — a sound that triggered some nostalgia, reminded him of that weird series of chirps made by dial-up internet modems and fax machines.

A voice spoke on the other end of the line. Even. Mechanical. It was an answering machine.

He didn't know what he would say until the thing beeped, and he started babbling into the mouthpiece.

"My brother has explosives now. Plastic. I didn't know. He's going to kill a bunch of people. A whole bunch of people. And I guess I… I mean… I promised."

He laughed a little, a breathy chuckle to himself.

"I don't know what he's going to do, but I promised I would help him, you know? I promised."

CHAPTER 48

Luke is dreaming.

Some distant part of him remains aware of the weight of his hands folded on his chest. Vaguely conscious that his body lies still in slumber.

But the bulk of his imagination plunges deeper into the dream.

Machine gun fire clatters in his sleep. This is the music that hangs in the air of his dream world. The endless beat of automatic weapons rattling on and on and on.

The desert sprawls before him. Sand blowing everywhere. The grit clings to his chest. Crusts his chin and cheekbones.

He is confused. Alone. It's always this way in his dreams. He's been separated from the other men. Lost in the endless sand. Unclear on what he's supposed to do. This time he has no shirt. He does have his gun, though.

It feels like cigarette filters have been jammed into his ears. His fingers swipe at the congested tubes out of custom, but he knows he can't unclog them. He never can.

The sun bleaches everything out here. Drains all color. Drains all life. Dries everything out and blows the dust around for eternity. If he stays here long enough, it will drain him, too. It will blow him away.

He follows a beaten place where the sand has packed into something cakier. A path. A one lane road, maybe.

He walks. The wind whips sheets of sand at him.

A gray object emerges on the horizon. Indistinct. Blurred by heat distortion. He squints to try to see. Eyes focusing like binoculars to look through the haze.

It's a structure. A ramshackle home. It seems odd.

Something flits in the lone window. A flutter of shadows. His pulse quickens.

He waits. Watches. Not sure what he will do until his hands get to doing it.

He empties his machine gun into the little shack. He doesn't know why. Some distant part of him thinks he's supposed to. It's not a thought so much as an urge. A quiver in the gut. A flash of heat in the head that makes his jaw clench tight.

He sprays the little building with bullets until he's certain nothing could have survived, and then he keeps spraying. Waves the gun back and forth like a fire hose.

The fever blocks out all reason. He knows no objective but destruction. None. It is his purpose, his religion, his everything.

His breathing is slow. Too slow for this violent scene. He can hear it inside his head, inside his face. The way things sound underwater, when all hearing retracts, draws up inside, the water cupping his ears to make that ocean-in-a-shell sound happen within his skull. The air sucks in and out. Slow, slow, slow.

He doesn't wake when Levi sneaks back into the motel room.

CHAPTER 49

Loshak and Darger logged and bagged evidence in the apartment deep into the night. She could hear a cricket somewhere in the closet. The steady chirp provided a sort of white noise that she only truly noticed when it stopped for a beat now and then.

"They're going to release the names in the morning," she said, her chest filling with a frantic dread.

"I know."

"I hate that. If they see their faces on the news, plastered on the front page of the local newspaper… they're gonna bolt."

"I know that, too."

She slammed her fist into her thigh. No matter what they accomplished, it seemed too little, too late. They were going to lose the brothers. Or maybe even push them into escalating their rampage sooner rather than later.

The scraping sound of Loshak scratching the side of his neck drew her gaze over to him. By the far-off, glazed look in his eyes, the gears were turning.

"What?"

His eyes flicked to his watch.

"Only a few hours until the first news cycle."

Darger stared at the clock on the kitchen wall, stunned at how much time had passed. And then she realized what Loshak was hinting at.

"You think we can find something before then? Something that will lead us to them?"

Loshak shrugged.

"All we can do is try. We can search the database Rodney set up. Go back and sift through the tips with fresh eyes. We have names now, relevant places, the Jeep. Maybe we can shake something loose before the media gets those names."

Darger nodded, and they headed for the car.

"Gonna need more coffee," Loshak said as he buckled his seatbelt.

"Yeah."

"I'll call Agent Dawson. See if she'd like to lend a hand."

"Don't you mean *Karla?*" Darger asked, waggling her eyebrows.

"What?"

"Nothing."

"Are you trying to tease me?"

"Perish the thought," she said with a smirk.

"Because you're wasting your time. I'm unteasable."

"Unteasable?"

"Yep. Comes with old age. Once you hit about 45 or so, suddenly you don't give a shit what anyone thinks. It's pretty great."

"I can't wait," Darger said.

A giant light-up donut glowed over the Dunkin Donuts parking lot like a halo.

Darger hopped out but leaned back in before closing the door. "So I should grab three coffees?"

"If you would."

CHAPTER 50

Loshak had to squint to read the time in the bottom corner of the screen. 3:49 AM. He yawned and swiped a paw down his face. The casters on the bottom of the office chair squealed as he shoved off from the desk, propelling himself out of the cubicle.

He used his feet to scoot a half-foot at a time, feeling like some kind of crustacean on the ocean floor. Finally, he reached the next office cubby. He knocked his fist against the carpet-like surface of the wall, eliciting a dull thud. It was oddly unsatisfying.

Darger thrust the headset down around her neck and turned in her chair to face him.

"Wanna take a listen?" he asked.

"You have something?"

"That's what I need you to tell me. I'm so tired I think I'm starting to hear voices… and I mean in addition to those recorded for the tip line."

"What's the call number?

"2-1-8-7."

He watched her fingers dance over the keyboard. Damn kids and their fancy typing skills. Loshak still did the majority of his typing with his two index fingers.

Replacing the headphones on top of her head, Darger played the call. The chair back creaked as she leaned against it, listening with her eyes closed.

"My brother is…" she started to repeat the call, then stopped and shook her head. "I can't tell what the hell he's saying after that. He sounds like he's talking through a mouth full of potato salad."

Loshak was too tired to laugh. He settled for a sleepy smile instead.

"Yeah, plus the sound quality is shit, so that's not helping anything. Sounded like traffic noise in the background. Could be a payphone."

Darger unplugged her headphones, turned up the speakers, and played the call again. Her face scrunched up, a little tic she had when she was really trying to focus on something.

"*My brother…* something, something… *explosives.* Something *classic*?" she guessed.

"Huh. I hear: *My brother has sex robots. How nasty,*" Loshak said. "Check out the text version."

Darger read the words on the screen out loud.

"My brother Isaac's placid now. Placid. I didn't know. He's one of cabbage people. Overture people. And a guest of a mean apprentice."

Rodney's speech-to-text algorithm was supposed to be one of the best, but from time to time, it rendered the calls into gibberish. Especially if the audio quality was poor.

His partner replayed the call twice more before groaning in frustration.

"I think he's forgetting to even speak into the mouthpiece half the time," she said.

"Wouldn't surprise me. He's obviously drunk or high on something. And that's probably reason enough not to waste any more time on it."

Darger rested her elbows on the laminate desktop and cupped her chin in her palms. The blue-white light from the screen lit her face with an eerie glow.

"We're running out of time," she said.

He knew she was taking it personally. Not only this call, but all of them. Part of him wished she wouldn't internalize the work so much. And at the same time, he knew it was why he'd chosen her to be his partner after so long flying solo. They were alike that way.

Loshak bent forward and put a hand on her shoulder.

"I know, kiddo," he said. "I know."

CHAPTER 51

For the first time since all of it started, Levi slept. A dead sleep — utterly uninterrupted — that lasted a few minutes less than five hours. He did not dream. He did not stir. He was out.

When he woke, the tip of his nose was icy cold and something was making an awful grinding sound, somehow throaty and metallic. He blinked a few times and looked for whatever the hell was making the noise.

Of course.

The air conditioner unit rattled like crazy — a little window unit mounted on the wall next to the door. With a wood paneled grill, it looked like it was installed circa 1986. Still, it chilled the room surprisingly well, even if it wasn't so quiet about it.

He forced himself to get up and walk the seven steps to the bathroom so he could relieve the ache in his bladder. After that, he went right back to bed, draping himself in two blankets and a sheet.

It felt incredible to sprawl like this, relaxed, the weight of the blankets somehow comforting. He couldn't imagine a scenario where he'd want to leave this.

He remembered his excursion last night like it was a fever dream. Flashes of it came to him, distant and blurry. The drunken stagger out to the Jeep. The jumbled message he'd blurted into the payphone. Would it even mean anything to the police? He didn't know.

But he felt calm for having done something, and he was thankful for that relief, even if what he'd done was half-assed. It was better than nothing.

He closed his eyelids, took a few deep breaths, felt the cool of the sheets go warmer and warmer against his skin. He was drifting again when Luke gasped.

Levi opened his eyes, saw his brother seated on the foot of the opposite bed, face glued to the TV.

"Oh, shit," he said, cigarette flopping from his lip.

"What?"

Levi's head swiveled to follow Luke's gaze to the TV screen, and there it was.

His own face, the same sleepy expression on it that he wore now. He recognized the shot. The photograph from his driver's license filled the screen, and the graphic displayed his name below that in all caps: LEVI FOLEY.

Speechless, they watched as more photos came and went in a slideshow. One showed Levi smiling at a party, a silver can of Coors Light in his hand. The next showed him taking a big bite of a chicken sandwich from Chick-Fil-A. Then came a selfie, a dour expression on his lips, his eyes totally vacant, a little bloodshot.

They were pictures from his Facebook account, he realized. It seemed so strange to see them on television. Little slices of his life being broadcast around the globe, Wolf Blitzer's voice droning over them, calling him a "domestic terrorist."

Now Luke's driver's license photo occupied the screen. His face looked much bonier than Levi's, sharp angles forming his jaw and chin and cheek bones. A slight smirk curled his lip on one side, but his eyes were dead.

And a slideshow of Luke played as well: a photo of him in the crowd at a Falcons game, plastic cup of foamy beer in his hand, everyone smiling and red-faced. The next three featured him in his army days: sunglasses, fatigues, M4 in his hands. He looked skinnier still in these. Young. Maybe a little scared.

Levi's vision went blurry along the edges, and it felt like his chest was caving in. He knew he must be in shock, if only mildly. He glanced at his brother out of the corner of his eye.

Judging by the way his hands were shaking, Luke must be feeling something similar.

They sat there frozen even after the screen had gone back to the faces of the various pundits who would now chime in at length. Both of their mouths hung slightly agape. The smoke spiraling from the tip of Luke's cigarette in slow motion provided the room's only movement. That wall unit blowing cold air upon them, grinding endlessly.

Levi's chest jerked, finally, air rushing to fill his lungs, and it occurred to him that he'd been holding his breath. He swallowed. It went down funny, saliva drizzling into his wind pipe, and that got him started coughing.

Luke did a double take, seeming to remember the tube of tobacco smoldering in his fingers. He took a final puff and ground the butt out in the ashtray.

"What do we do now?" Levi said. Even to himself, his voice sounded small and tight and far away.

"Well..." Luke said, standing. "We should think about our options. I guess the next phase starts now."

He moved to the bed, pulled the suitcase up off the floor and began rifling through it. There was a jerkiness to his movements, and he kept licking his lips in a way that Levi could only think of as spastic.

The younger brother found himself standing as well then, somehow unable to keep still. He ran cold water in the bathroom, splashing cupped handfuls over his face and head.

Eventually he stopped and looked at himself in the mirror, droplets of water weeping down his face, collecting and dripping from his nose and chin. He was panting a little, mouth still open.

Could this have had anything to do with the message he'd left on the tip line answering machine? He didn't think so. But he wasn't sure what to think.

If the next phase really was starting now, it meant the plastic explosive would play its role sooner than he'd anticipated. Whatever just happened, the police had sped things up, had put people more directly in danger.

He left the bathroom and found Luke fiddling with something on the bed.

"What's that?" Levi said.

His brother looked up at him, smiled.

"Let's just say it's a tribute. A little taste of what's to come."

Once more the TV screen cut away to a graphic - a pull quote from Levi's last Facebook post, dated six nights ago. The big white type stood out from the blue background. Bold. A little shiny.

It read: "God forgive me."

CHAPTER 52

Agent Dawson pressed a pair of binoculars to her face.

"Sniper teams are in place."

Darger leaned forward to get a better view from the backseat of the Suburban. She could just make out a set of helmeted heads perched high on a nearby rooftop: one spotter, one counter-sniper. There were four of the two-man sniper teams at various vantage points surrounding the Forty Winks Motel. But the others weren't in her line of sight.

Their last-ditch effort to comb the tip lines for a clue as to the whereabouts of the Foley brothers was a bust. Less than an hour ago, Chief Hogaboom released the names. The media went wild with it, and within minutes of the broadcasts, the cable news channels had a troupe of psychologists and pundits analyzing everything from a tweet Levi made about the future of the Star Wars franchise to Luke's Reddit account name, which was Saint_Anger_666.

Less than twenty minutes after the news hit, a call came in from a motel manager claiming the brothers were currently renting a room in his establishment. When the operator asked if he knew what type of vehicle the brothers were driving — a detail they had not released to the press yet — the manager promptly identified the black Jeep Wrangler.

They were taking no chances with the motel room. In addition to the sharpshooters, three police helicopters were standing by in case the brothers attempted to flee. For the moment, everyone simply hoped they would take the Foleys by surprise.

The radio on the dash crackled and spit out a burst of chatter from the approaching SWAT team.

"You go to Sammy's last night, Ron?"

"Nah, not last night. Phoebe had a dance recital."

Despite the mundane topic, Darger heard the tension in those voices. The men were charged, practically hyper. It wasn't a wonder why: The men they sought had killed a dozen people now. She hoped this would be the end of it, with no more bodies added to that toll.

Dawson had passed the binoculars to Loshak who now handed them off to Darger. She adjusted the width of the eyepieces to fit her face. Holding the lenses up to her eyes, she spun the focus until the features of the motel were crisp. Each room had a single window, a wall-mounted air conditioner, and a bright blue door. The units appeared identical apart from the brass room numbers. She scanned down the row until she found it. Room 113.

Through a crack in the shades, she could see that a lamp was on. And was it her imagination, or had the edge of the curtain fluttered slightly? Her skin prickled with anticipation.

The voices of the SWAT team filtered through the small space of the car.

"Gettin' close, boys."

"Yeah. Real close."

"Hand me that flashbang."

There was a sound like two pieces of Velcro being ripped apart. The yammering slowed now that they drew near.

"Alright, boys. Bring 'em in."

In her mind's eye, Darger saw them all putting their fists together like a football team huddling before a game.

"You know the drill. Focus. Watch each other. Stay safe."

"Make sure you're chambered."

The armored BearCat rolled into view and halted two doors down from the motel. Darger lowered the binoculars.

"Game time."

The team hopped out, outfitted in their vests and helmets and other tactical gear. Each man carried an M4 carbine.

They formed a line on the sidewalk, each touching the shoulder of the guy in front of him. One man toted a Blackhawk battering ram.

"Let's go."

Each lifted his rifle, and they skulked toward the motel in single file.

"I got left," one voice said. "Eyes on the left side."

The group converged on room 113, and the man closest to the door hammered a fist against it.

"Police department! Search warrant!" A voice barked.

The officer at the door turned and nodded at two team members assigned to the window.

"Bust it."

With a glassy explosion of sound, the front window burst into a thousand shards.

"Hit 'em, Ron!"

One of the SWAT officers tossed something through the broken window. There was a loud pop and then a bright flash of orange light. Darger gasped until she remembered it was only a flash grenade.

"Go! Go! Go!"

The battering ram splintered the flimsy motel room door with a single blow.

Darger held her breath as the first member of the SWAT team stormed over the threshold.

CHAPTER 53

What seemed like more voices than went inside were suddenly shouting over the radio.

"With you!"

Another crash sounded inside, along with the thud of boots on the ground. Darger hated not being able to see what was happening. Were the brothers there or not?

"Bedroom's clear!"

Her hopes sank a little, and then a frantic voice over the radio called out, "Get that door. Somebody get the bathroom door!"

"Right behind! I got it."

A pause. Darger's fingertips gouged divots into the padding of the seat in front of her.

There was another loud thump.

"Clear!"

Her chest constricted. Please at least let there be something they could use. A clue. Anything.

"One more."

She sat up a little straighter again.

"Look right, I've got left."

After what seemed like an eternity, the words came over the radio:

"All clear."

"This is McIntosh. Place is clear. Oh! Dear God…"

Darger sprang out of the car. She couldn't wait any longer.

The brothers weren't there, but it was clear that SWAT found something in the motel room. What was it?

It occurred to her then that maybe they'd found no one *alive* inside.

Maybe they'd found their bodies. It would be over then.

That possibility propelled her over the parking lot with extra vigor. It felt strange for the prospect of finding corpses in the room to give her hope, but it would mean an end to the bloodshed.

As she approached the door, she heard the voices of the SWAT team still milling around inside.

"Thought you said it was clear, Bobby."

"Huh?"

"You missed Andre the Giant over there."

Several men laughed.

"Missed what?" one of the younger voices said.

Darger reached the door in time to see one of the men gesture toward the double bed with the stock of his rifle. In the center of the floral bedspread was a pile of human feces.

She wanted to scream. And to punch something. She settled for kicking at a dandelion sprouting up from the sidewalk. The fluffy seedpods took flight, floating through the air like miniature parachutes.

A hand clapped on her shoulder. She turned, and Loshak gave her a commiserating frown.

"Why's it called a Andre the Giant?" the young man said.

"You've never heard of that?" Loshak asked, stepping up to the threshold.

The man's black helmet shook back and forth.

"Well, there's a famous story from years ago, back when professional wrestling was first taking off. Hulk Hogan and Andre the Giant were staying in the same hotel, and one day Hogan got an urgent sounding phone call from Andre, demanding that he come to his room. When Hogan got there, he found a mammoth turd resting in the center of the bed, and there was Andre the Giant, rolling around on the floor laughing about his… output."

Darger leaned against the white siding of the motel, crushed by defeat. They had failed again. Luke and Levi were on the move, planning their next attack. She knew it.

On the stoop, she could hear that the topic had moved away from the soiled bed. Now the SWAT guys were teasing the one who'd manned the battering ram.

"I thought you were gonna dive right on through with the ram, Jeff."

"Yeah, I didn't expect it to break so easy like that," the man chuckled.

A third voice chimed in.

"Fifty-pound ram ain't no match for a shitty particle board door like that. Might as well be taking a sledgehammer to a piece of cardboard."

"Would've been hilarious if it just bounced off."

More laughing reverberated in the small room.

"In other words, you get razzed if it's fifteen hits to take down a door or one. You can't win."

Darger understood why the SWAT team was in high spirits. Their missions generally had one simple goal: get in and secure the scene without losing any of your guys. Having done that, they were in a celebratory mood.

It was another story for the investigators. They had reached yet another dead end.

Echoing in her mind were Detective Horst's words from the previous morning.

Diddly-fucking-squat.

CHAPTER 54

Once SWAT had cleared out, Darger joined her partner and Agent Dawson in the dank little room.

Loshak pulled a tape recorder from his pocket, and she couldn't help but raise an eyebrow.

"Started taking my notes dictation style," he explained.

"Boldly leaping into 1986 technology, I see."

He pursed his lips into a scowl.

"I don't know what you mean by that."

"I mean you could use your phone like everyone else," she said, wiggling her cell in the air.

Loshak smirked.

"Thing about the phone is that then people call me and want to talk to me."

She didn't follow his logic. He still carried a phone. And he answered when she called. Usually.

"Does that mean when you don't answer my calls, you're ignoring me?" she asked.

He answered without hesitation.

"Sometimes."

Darger scoffed, feigning offense. His face didn't show an ounce of remorse.

Loshak pressed a button on the recorder, held the mic input to his mouth, and began to speak.

"We are in room 113 of the Forty Winks Motel just outside of Atlanta. It is four minutes after 8 AM on Sunday, July 30th."

Loshak sniffed.

"Note the smell of charred paper intertwining with that of

human feces."

Darger turned, wrinkling her nose.

"Charred paper?"

"You don't get a faint smokiness?"

She had been breathing through her mouth since they came in, trying to avoid any revolting odors. Now she inhaled fully through her nostrils. It was there, though. That acrid, ashy smell of burnt pulp.

A brief search revealed a metal garbage can next to the bed. There were scorch marks inside, along with bits of ash. And something clinging to the side. Darger called one of the techs over, and he removed the scrap with a pair of tweezers, placing it in a plastic baggie. She waited for him to enter it into the evidence log, and then he handed it back.

Darger, Loshak, and Agent Dawson clustered together, examining the shred of paper.

"Newspaper," Loshak said. "Look at the perforated edge."

"Why burn a newspaper?" Dawson asked.

"Maybe they were looking at their coverage, got sheepish."

Darger met his eyes, and they exchanged a glance. No.

There were a few words visible beyond the blackened edge, but most were partial. She could read: "-ation" and part of a dot-com address. Nation? Population? Darger noticed something else about it, too.

She pointed out a thick line of ink that had soaked through both sides of the paper.

"Whatever it is, they circled it with a marker. Like the school newspapers we found in Levi's closet."

"We need to get copies of the local papers for the past few days so we can figure out what the hell they were so interested in," Loshak said.

"I'm on it," Agent Dawson said. "I'll send someone to find a newsstand."

From her pocket, Darger's phone vibrated against her hip. She checked the screen. It was Owen Baxter. Impeccable timing.

She swiped the screen, ignoring the call. She needed to think. To focus. To figure out what the hell they were going to do next, because she was out of ideas.

The phone droned again, and it took every ounce of her willpower not to borrow the SWAT team's battering ram to smash it into pieces.

Christ, she needed coffee. And sleep.

When the phone began to buzz a third time, she caved. She took a long, slow breath to keep from screaming an expletive into the receiver instead of a greeting.

"Owen, I'm a little busy right now."

"I know. Come outside."

"What?"

"Come outside the motel."

She stepped to the door and saw Owen waving from behind the line of police tape. She hung up and crossed the lot.

"What are you doing here?"

"That's a hell of a question. Why didn't you call me and tell me you got a name? Or should I say *names*? I had to see this shit on the news this morning."

He held up his phone with a story from one of the local papers.

"What was I supposed to do?" she asked.

"We both know you wouldn't have gotten that name without me. You're supposed to keep me in the loop."

"When did I agree to that?"

"I thought it was unspoken. Damn it, Violet! I helped you

out."

She couldn't deny that. "So what do you want from me now?"

"I want a peek inside that motel room."

"You're a civilian, Owen."

"And these assholes shot my brother. I'm not looking to meddle in the investigation. I just… want to know nothing gets missed. I thought you of all people might understand that."

She did, of course. And it wasn't necessarily against any particular rule, a civilian being present at a crime scene. Fitzgerald wouldn't like it, but fuck him. She could trust Owen to be discreet. Besides, another set of trained eyes couldn't hurt.

Sensing her hesitation, Owen crossed his arms.

"If you won't let me in, I'll go ask Agent Dawson. You think she'll be able to say no to this face?"

He blinked with wide-eyed innocence. Darger rolled her eyes, but she couldn't help but laugh a little too.

"Alright. But keep a low profile."

She held the tape for him, and he ducked under.

"Much obliged, ma'am," he said, flicking his fingers over his ear in an informal salute.

Darger led the way through a throng of law enforcement personnel, and Owen stuck close, not wanting to be separated.

They passed Loshak and Agent Dawson, who were huddled together over her phone. Still trying to figure out what newspaper the clipping in the trash can had come from, she figured.

Loshak glanced up at Darger, and she wondered what he'd think of Owen's presence. But he only nodded absently at her and fell back into his conversation with Agent Dawson.

When Darger reached the motel room door, she paused at

the threshold. There were two crime scene techs still working on lifting prints while Detective Horst directed a third technician in bagging the remaining evidence.

She swept a hand in front of her, gesturing for Owen to enter as if it were some kind of theme park attraction.

"After you," she said. "And remember what I said."

"Right, right. No touching, no pictures, no real names… oh wait, those are strip club rules."

She scowled at him, and he responded with one of his devilish grins.

Owen stopped a few paces into the room and put his hands on his hips.

"You didn't tell me there was an Andre the Giant in here."

She snorted, wondering if she and the rookie kid on the SWAT team were the only two people on the planet that hadn't heard of an Andre the Giant.

The heel of Darger's boot had just made contact with the grubby motel carpet when room 113 exploded.

CHAPTER 55

The first sensation Violet felt was the spasm of her chest as she coughed followed by a choking dryness in her throat.

Thirsty.

She needed water.

Her eyelids fluttered and immediately closed again. Something like sand scraped over her corneas, and the sting caused her eyes to fill with tears. What the hell?

She swiped a hand over her cheek. She was covered in a fine layer of grit. And now it was in her eyes.

Violet looked down through the tears and noted the red-black smear of soot mixed with blood on her hand. And then she remembered the explosion.

The scene came into focus all at once, the surge of adrenaline clearing her head.

The bitter smell of burning carpet. The patter of debris falling back to the ground. And above all, the stifling cloud of smoke and dust that hung about her.

She recalled something else then, and all thoughts of water or the burning of her eyes left her.

Owen. Owen had been right in front of her when the explosion knocked her flat.

Violet tried to move for the first time. She was on her side, snugged up against the tires of a police car. A chunk of foam from a mattress or maybe a couch lay across her legs, along with a few scraps of the bright blue door. She kicked the refuse away and rolled onto her stomach. The movement sent a sharp, blinding pain through her head, and she had to crawl forward instead of walking until it passed.

A car alarm blared somewhere off to her right, but her ears were ringing, making everything sound distant.

She pushed to her feet finally, still hunched against the throbbing sensation in her head. She found a pile of rubble. Boulders of concrete and bent lengths of rebar. A hand protruded from the wreckage, and Violet ran to it. She pulled away some of the smaller pieces of material, gasping at the sight she found. The right side of the body was a mangled horror show of blood and tissue. His arm was gone, as was most of his leg. The sticky pink coils of his intestines spilled out from his belly. And the blood. So much blood. The man's face was unrecognizable, burned and battered beyond recognition. But it wasn't Owen. By the vanilla swirl of hair on top of the head, she knew it was Detective Horst.

He was dead, she knew, but Violet checked the side of his neck for a pulse anyway. Nothing.

Moving on, she scrambled from one pile of ruins to the next. She found an arm. Only an arm. She tried not to panic.

A few feet away, a leg protruded from beneath a panel of drywall, still swathed in yellow insulation. The leg was clad in denim, and Violet knew it had to be him.

Clearing away the flotsam, she prayed the leg was not another severed body part, that Owen would be alive. The sheet rock thunked to the ground. Owen lay flat on his back, eyes closed. Instantly the image of Ethan in a similar position sprang to mind, and she dove to his side.

A metal rod jutted from his abdomen.

"Owen!"

She put a hand on his chest and then reached up to feel for a pulse. His eyelids fluttered open.

"Oh, thank God," she said.

"No, ma'am," he croaked. "I know I have the face of Adonis, but I am just a mortal man."

She hacked out something between a laugh and a cough.

"Can you help me up?"

Darger figured he must be in shock. She'd heard stories about people not knowing they were gravely injured until they saw the seriousness of their wounds, and then the pain came all at once. She scooted forward and leaned in such a way to hopefully prevent Owen from seeing the rebar impaling him through the belly.

"I think it's better if you lie still for now."

"Bad?" he asked.

Tears blurred her vision again, but this time it wasn't from the dust.

She wasn't good at lying about this stuff, and he'd probably know anyway.

"Pretty bad."

"My leg hurts something fierce," he said, and she turned.

She saw where the denim was torn and bloodied a few inches below his groin. Using her fingers to widen the rip, she found a long gash on his thigh. An alarming amount of blood was pouring from the wound. Too much blood.

She pulled her suit jacket off, glad she wasn't wearing one of the FBI windbreakers. She couldn't imagine they were very absorbent. Not wanting to contaminate the wound with all the particulate on the exterior, she turned the jacket inside out first. Something flopped out of the pocket. It was Ethan's silk tie.

Briefly, she considered a tourniquet but remembered how they'd been warned against them in her first aid class. She rolled up her jacket and pressed it to Owen's leg. But the wound was so large, she had a hard time applying pressure to the whole thing, even using both hands. Blood continued to seep from the laceration.

Darger scooped the fallen necktie into her hand and began to wrap. She was able to loop it three times around Owen's thigh and tie it off, just tightly enough to help keep steady pressure on the improvised bandage. That seemed to slow the bleeding enough that the pool of red forming beneath him stopped growing in size.

The ringing in her ears dampened the shriek of the sirens, but they were definitely there. Violet pulled away, intent on grabbing the first paramedic she saw and dragging him back here. But Owen caught her wrist.

"Don't leave me, Violet. Please."

Noting the fear in his eyes, she settled back beside him. She waved with her free hand but kept the other fingers entwined with Owen's.

"I need help over here," she called.

She was sure she was yelling, but her voice was small and removed in her own hearing. She continued screaming until she saw a silhouette approaching through the haze of smoke.

It was Loshak. A flicker of relief crossed his face when he saw her, and then his gaze fell to Owen. He stopped in his tracks, eyes wide. Then he turned and ran back the way he'd come, shouting for a medic.

Violet squeezed Owen's fingers and wiped a smear of blood from a slash on his cheek.

"Hang on, Owen. Help is coming."

CHAPTER 56

Ethan looked much the same as when Violet had visited the first time. Puffy face and bruised-looking eyes. And in the background, the beeps and whooshes and whirring of all of the machines keeping him alive. The only real difference was that he'd been taken off ventilation and was now breathing on his own, which everyone said was a good sign.

"I really fucked the poodle this time," she said, squeezing his fingers. "Pardon my French."

Violet had promised to stay with Ethan while Mrs. Baxter went downstairs to monitor Owen's emergency surgery. She'd gathered by now that Constance had raised the boys alone — their father had taken off when the brothers were young, and he stopped getting in contact for visits by the time they were in high school.

Mrs. Baxter had gotten in touch with her sister, but the flight from Tallahassee wouldn't arrive for several hours. And so Violet agreed when Constance asked her to keep watch over Ethan.

Violet couldn't fathom being in her position… to have both sons here in the hospital in critical condition.

It was as they loaded Owen onto a backboard and into the ambulance that she remembered the mumbled tip line call.

My brother has explosives now.

It was him. Levi Foley. It had to be.

And she'd missed it. They both had. Written it off as another drunk. She'd fucked up and now Owen was downstairs with a hole punched through his guts.

They sifted through all those calls only to misunderstand the one that mattered. All that work for nothing.

Her head hurt, ears still ringing. She had about two dozen minor cuts and abrasions from the glass in the explosion. And her face felt strangely hot. Like she'd been at the beach all day and forgot to put on sunblock.

"I never should have let him into that motel room," Violet whispered.

She swallowed against the lump in her throat, and tears stung her injured eyes.

"I'm sorry," she said, though her voice was so choked with emotion that she mouthed the words more than spoke them aloud.

One of the monitors seemed to come awake then, the screen flashing, the blipping loud and fast and no longer the two-beat rhythm of a steady heart beat.

It startled her, and she dropped Ethan's hand, as if her words or her touch had brought on the change.

The beeping stopped for several seconds, and a new alarm started to blare, an unmistakable harbinger of bad things. Darger had the sudden feeling of being trapped in a dream. A nightmare. Two nurses sprinted into the room.

One of them yelled, "V-tach, no pulse." And then, "He's not breathing."

She immediately began compressions on Ethan's chest.

The other barked at Darger to move and hit a button on the wall over Ethan's bed.

An automated voice sounded overhead.

"Code blue. Code blue. Room 204."

A doctor in a white lab coat and five more nurses bustled into the room, one of them pushing a cart.

Someone grasped Violet's arm, maneuvering her toward the door. She didn't see who it was. Her eyes never left Ethan's face. Not until she was in the hallway and the curtains were yanked shut to block the view of his room.

CHAPTER 57

Violet watched them work through a gap in the curtains, not understanding. He'd been fine five minutes ago.

Eventually, they wheeled him out, no longer doing chest compressions, but there was a nurse holding and squeezing some kind of bag over his nose and mouth. That gave her hope. Violet grabbed one of the nurses.

"Is he going to be OK? Where are they taking him?"

"He's being taken for an EEG. Are you family?"

"No, I'm… a friend. His mother is downstairs, she—"

"It would really be best if I could talk to a family member. What's her name? I can page her from here."

"Constance Baxter," Violet said.

The nurse walked to the nearest phone and called Constance Baxter to the second floor Pulmonary unit.

Violet paced the hallway until one of the elevators opened its jaws and spit out Ethan's mother.

"What is it? Did something happen?" she asked, clutching Violet's arm with surprisingly strong fingers.

Violet shook her head.

"They won't tell me anything, except that they took him for some kind of test."

The same nurse from before guided Constance into a private waiting room. The iron grip Constance had on Violet's arm did not let up, and so she followed obediently.

"Dr. Ogletree will be in to speak with you in a moment," the nurse said before she closed the door behind them.

Violet tried to remember what EEG stood for, but she

couldn't seem to focus.

She gripped Constance's shoulder and realized the woman was trembling.

"It doesn't seem real," the mother said to no one in particular. "I'd give anything for my boys, but there's nothing to give."

The door opened and two doctors strode in, one female, the other male. The woman's name badge read Karina Ogletree. She could not read the man's badge.

"Has anyone briefed you yet, Mrs. Baxter?" Dr. Ogletree asked.

Constance shook her head.

"No one has told me anything. Please. Please tell me what's going on."

"A few minutes ago, Ethan's heart stopped."

The hand on Violet's forearm grasped a little tighter.

"Oh my God."

"He also stopped breathing. We began CPR and used a defibrillator to get his heart started again, but it took quite a long time."

"But you did get it started? He is alive?"

"Yes, but Mrs. Baxter, I was concerned with how long he went without a normal heartbeat, and so I sent him for some tests to measure brain function."

Violet swallowed, sensing where this was headed. She stared at the stretch of carpet between her feet until her vision blurred.

"Ethan is brain dead, Mrs. Baxter. He will not recover."

There was a very long pause, and then Constance spoke, her voice wavering.

"I don't understand. You said you got his heart started again."

"Yes, but when circulation stops for any length of time, there is something called ischemic injury..."

The words all ran together for Violet from there. She wasn't sure they really meant much to Constance either.

It wasn't until Violet heard the male doctor say Owen's name that her conscious mind snapped back to the conversation. Constance was squinting and shaking her head.

"Wait, who are you, now? And what about Owen?"

Dr. Ogletree put a hand on Constance's knee.

"This is Dr. Nazarian. He's the head of our transplant team. He's been consulting with Dr. Arora downstairs in Trauma."

The man cleared his throat, as if to start over from the beginning.

"I don't know how much Dr. Arora has told you, but Owen has extensive liver damage. We feel the best course of action is a transplant, as soon as possible. Do you know if Ethan is a registered organ donor?"

"What? I don't know... I... Are you saying that you could use Ethan's liver for Owen?"

"I understand Ethan and Owen are identical twins. Is that correct?"

"Yes."

"Then Owen is a very, very lucky man."

"But Ethan would... I'd have to... I have to choose between them?"

Dr. Nazarian licked his lips.

"Normally we would do what's called a living-donor transplant. But given Ethan's condition, it is unlikely that he'd survive the surgery. And the fact remains that he is beyond the scope of recovery as a result of his own injuries. He is brain dead, Mrs. Baxter, and actual clinical death will follow. Probably in a matter of days. The longer we wait to harvest the organs, the more chance they will be rendered unfit for transplant."

"But you need my permission?"

"If Ethan is not a registered donor, yes, we will need your permission. But if he's already a donor, you do not have legal cause to override that decision. I know this is difficult, Mrs. Baxter. But I want to be clear: this is a very unique opportunity for Owen. People often wait for months or even years for a suitable transplant. The fact that Ethan is his twin brother means he is a guaranteed match. It also means there is no risk of organ rejection. Unlike other transplant recipients, Owen will not have to take immunosuppressants for the rest of his life. Furthermore, if Owen doesn't receive a transplant very quickly, he may not recover from his injuries."

Tears streamed down from Constance's eyes, and Violet didn't realize until she shook with a series of choking sobs that she was also crying.

"How long do I have to decide?" Constance choked.

"As long as you need. But for Owen's sake, the sooner the better."

CHAPTER 58

A swarm of nocturnal insects buzzed in circles around the overhead lights in the parking garage stairwell. It was gloomy and smelled of piss.

Violet checked the text from Loshak again, letting her know which section he'd left her car in. 7F.

Her boots scuffed up another flight of stairs, and then she saw the sign marking the seventh floor. Her jaw ached and her tongue felt swollen and sore. She must have bitten down on it during the explosion. Adding to her list of aches and pains was a pulsing headache and the fact that she was so tired she would have gladly curled up in a corner of the funky, urine-soaked stairwell and slept for a thousand years.

Constance Baxter's sister had arrived only minutes after Owen was wheeled into a surgical suite for transplant surgery. Marylou was an older, big-boned version of her sister, with a matching halo of frothy gray-blonde hair. Violet offered to stay through the surgery, and Constance thanked her but said Violet had been dragged into enough Baxter grief for one night. She promised to call with an update when Owen was out of the operating room.

As for Ethan… Darger swallowed, not even able to think the name without tears welling in her eyes. Ethan had been taken off life support not long ago. He'd been a registered donor after all, sparing his mother the weight of that decision, at least.

Ethan was dead. And the men responsible were still out there, planning some new terror to unleash upon the world.

Darger reached the seventh-floor door and pushed it open

with a metallic screech. It clanged shut behind her, and she followed a stencil on the wall that indicated section 7F was to the right. A moment later, she heard the stairwell door squeal and clunk as someone else entered the area.

Another set of footsteps echoed behind Darger, mirroring her own. It occurred to her that there were very few cars on this level at this hour. What were the odds that someone else was parked here and just so happened to be heading to their vehicle at the same time?

Some animal awareness prickled, sending goose bumps over her skin. Forgetting her fatigue, she dodged behind a corner, flattening herself against the wall, and drew her weapon.

When the person rounded the corner, she sprang out, pointing her gun.

It was dark and the man was hooded. She couldn't see his face in the dim lighting, but the build could have matched either of the Foley brothers. Long and lean.

She hoped for Levi. She'd had a lot of time to think about it over the last day, and she'd come to believe if she'd been there to answer his call, she might have been able to prevent this.

She'd suspected it before, but it was crystal clear to her now that Luke was the mastermind. Levi was the automaton… the good little soldier. The little brother not wanting to let big brother down. If she could only talk to him, she could get through. She could convince him it wasn't worth it. He knew what they were doing was wrong, but he wasn't strong enough to resist on his own.

"Who are you?" she asked, gun leveled at the man's chest.

He reached up, slowly, and pulled the hood down.

Amusement glinted in the coal black eyes. Randall Stokes.

Darger didn't lower her Glock. In fact, she brought it up a

little higher, in line with his forehead.

"Why are you following me?"

"Following you?" he rasped in his odd, hoarse voice. If snakes could talk, it was how she imagined they might sound. "I came down to say thank you."

"At this hour?"

He shrugged.

"I'm a night owl. Always have been," he said, tilting his head to one side. "Are you gonna keep pointing your gun at me? I thought we were allies, Agent Darger."

"You knew it was two gunmen."

"I did?"

"When you first told me what you were offering, you said, 'these psychos.'"

Stokes looked away, pretending not to notice that she was still sticking a gun in his face. Or maybe he really didn't care.

"I don't recall that. The last few days… they've been a bit of a blur. Lot of activity, you know?"

He turned back and fixed her with his viper's stare.

"By the way, I heard what happened at the motel. The big kaboom. I hope your boyfriend's gonna be alright."

The hair on the back of her neck stood up as she realized what he was suggesting. He was referring to Owen and the explosion. The bastard. She gripped her Glock a little tighter and took a step closer.

"You knew about the explosives, didn't you?"

He didn't budge. Didn't even flinch. Just stared down at her with that piercing predator's gaze. She pressed the gun to his forehead and still he didn't bat an eyelash.

"Is that why you came down here? To gloat?"

She jabbed the gun a little harder into his flesh to punctuate her words.

“You can keep poking me with that, but we both know you aren’t gonna shoot. You’re not the killin’ type.”

“I wouldn’t count on that. I’ve pulled the trigger before, and that guy ended up floating face down in a river,” she said.

“So I read,” he said. “Thought about bringing that magazine article down here for you to sign, as a matter of fact.”

“It’s a good thing you didn’t, because then I definitely would have shot you,” she said.

He laughed, a dry, scratching sound that brought to mind raking up leaves in the fall. For once his eyes didn’t have that vicious gleam. Darger lowered the gun but did not return it to her holster. She pointed it at the ground, fingers still clenching the grip.

“What do you want?”

“I wanted to make sure the explosion hadn’t messed up that pretty face of yours.”

She scowled but thought he might be telling the truth, at least in part. He was checking up on her. Why he’d want to do that, she didn’t know.

“If you cared about that, why didn’t you warn me about the C4?”

Stokes gestured at his head.

“My mind is a mystery to me sometimes. Pulls me one way and then the other. It’s like those old cartoons… an angel on my right shoulder and a devil on the left. You might be too young to remember those,” he said.

“I know what you’re talking about.”

“Well, sometimes it’s hard to decide which one to listen to.”

“Does that mean I’m talking to the angel right now?”

“I hadn’t thought about it like that,” he said with a smirk, "but sure."

"Do they have more?"

"How much did they use in the motel room?"

"Bomb squad estimated around a pound."

"I would guess they have more, then."

"How much?"

"A lot."

Darger suddenly felt very, very tired. She turned to leave. She wasn't entirely sure how wise it was to turn her back on Stokes, but she was too exhausted to care. He wouldn't hurt her. She was fairly certain of that. He liked playing games with her too much.

"Where are you going?"

"To sleep," she said, recognizing her car a few yards away. Her fingers wrapped around the door handle as he called out to her.

"It's a nice picture of you in that article. Thinkin' about cuttin' it out and havin' it framed."

"I can still shoot you from here, you know," she said.

His shark-tooth grin was visible in the rear view mirror as she rolled away a few moments later.

CHAPTER 59

Darger woke the next morning with no recollection of the night. She'd collapsed into the sleep of the dead. If her mind had conjured even a single dream, she didn't remember it.

The first thing she did was grab her phone and check for messages. There were two. One from Constance Baxter, letting her know that Owen was out of surgery. He was recovering in the ICU and would be sedated for the next day or two.

Darger felt so relieved she started to cry again, and then she felt guilty that she'd insisted Constance call her with an update when she had so much else on her plate. Ethan's funeral to plan, for instance.

Sniffling, she listened to the next message. It was Loshak. He and Agent Dawson had matched the newspaper clipping found in the motel room. It was a copy of the Atlanta Journal Constitution from earlier in the week.

"The remnant we found was from a page listing local events for the next month. The section outlined in the black marker is a schedule for the Braves."

She dialed Loshak, and he answered on the first ring.

"How ya feeling, partner?" he asked.

"Fine," she said. "What's happening down there?"

"I assume you got my message about the newspaper scrap?"

"Yeah."

"Everyone's mostly focused on beefing up security at the stadium, right now."

"They're not canceling the games?"

"It was discussed. Ultimately it was decided that this could be the way we get them. They've got a team of bomb-sniffing dogs in there now, and we're calling in more."

"There are three home games this week," Darger said, looking at the schedule online. "How do we decide which one?"

"We don't. We stake 'em all out. Keep running the dogs through. And hope to get lucky."

She sighed.

"I ran into Stokes last night."

"Ran into him?"

"More like he waited for me in the hospital parking garage."

Loshak swore under his breath.

"It's alright," she assured him. "He didn't try anything… shady."

Scoffing, Loshak said, "That guy craps shady. What did he want?"

"To play mind games with me. What else? He was being pretty coy, but the suggestion was that they have quite a bit more of the C4. I think a *lot* more."

"Figures, I guess. Did he give you anything else?"

"Not really. Where are you?"

"Right now I'm downstairs in the task force meeting room. But I've been running upstairs to check in on the tip line when I can."

"I can be there in thirty," she said, glancing at the clock on the table.

"Oh no, you don't. You're on light duty."

Darger's fingers tightened around the phone.

"The fuck I am."

"You have a concussion, Violet. Doctor's orders. And FBI policy," he said, then softened his tone. "I promise I'll let you know if anything new comes to light."

She didn't say anything.

"Alright?" Loshak said.

"Sure."

Darger hung up and headed to the shower.

Thirty-four minutes later, the elevator deposited her onto the fourth floor of the Atlanta field office in Chamblee. The conference room was filled with activity — phones ringing, people talking, at least half a dozen TVs, all tuned to a different channel. One of the monitors played the footage they'd found on the video camera in Levi's apartment.

Loshak scowled when he saw her.

"I thought we agreed that you would stay put, and I would keep you abreast of the investigation."

"You mean when I said, *sure*?" she smiled. "That was sarcasm. Didn't you hear the telltale inflection in my voice?"

"I must have missed that."

"You're getting rusty, partner," she said, clapping him on the shoulder. "Anyway, I'm not working, technically. I'm here in a consulting capacity. How is Agent Dawson holding up?"

Darger left the second half of the question unspoken: How is Agent Dawson holding up *after learning about Ethan's death?*

"She went home to freshen up. Change clothes. Insisted on working through it, though. Karla's tough, but you can see in her eyes that she's hurting."

Darger nodded. She couldn't imagine — didn't *want* to imagine — what it would be like to lose a partner. Not quite a year had gone by since she first met Loshak, but she'd come to depend on him for so much in that short time.

"I've had all our people downstairs listen to the Levi Foley call a dozen times, in case he tries again. Assuming it was really him, of course. I sent a recording of the call and a copy of the videos to the speech recognition experts in Quantico. They gave me a bunch of guff about the fact that he was obviously intoxicated when he called, says it messes with the algorithm."

Loshak shook his head and raked his fingers through his hair.

At his mention of the home movies, Darger's eyes floated up to the big screen at the front of the room. Teenage Levi was on the roof again. She shuddered, recalling the sickening sound of his arm snapping when he hit the ground.

"As if I got him loaded myself and then had him make that call," Loshak was still grumbling.

Her eyelids fluttered, Loshak's voice drawing her gaze away from the images on the screen.

Darger frowned. Something was bugging her, a gnat buzzing around in the back of her mind.

What Loshak just said?

No.

Her head snapped back to the TV screen.

"Go back," she said, not even sure who she was addressing. She waved a hand at the television. "Which computer is running that footage?"

An unfamiliar young woman pointed at a laptop in the corner of the room.

Darger stalked over and backed the video up, rewinding to when the camera first swung up to show Levi perched on the peak of the roof.

There. In the background. Something she'd missed before. She paused the playback.

"Loshak," she said, hypnotized by the glowing pixels.

"Hm?"

He stepped forward, squinting so hard his eyes looked closed.

"What does that say? My eyes are shit."

"Pheasant Brook," Darger said, reading the gold letters on the sign. "This is it. The house in the video is maybe half a block from Carol Jones' subdivision. I bet this is the house they grew up in, but…"

She brought up the map on her phone.

"It doesn't match the mother's address. Before the nursing home, I mean."

Loshak held up a finger and got on his phone.

"Karla? It's Loshak. Do you still have the school records for the Foley boys on your laptop?" There was a pause. "No, I only want the home address listed on the records."

He reached for a pen and scribbled something on a pad of paper.

"Yeah, I'll see you then," he said and hung up.

Darger was already entering the address he'd written down into her phone. When she finished, a marker popped onto the map and zoomed in on that section of the city.

"Bingo," she said. "But the house isn't there anymore. Looks like some kind of grubby little strip mall now."

Loshak sighed and swiped a hand down the side of his face.

"Now we just need to figure out how in the hell to use all this to guess where they are. Or where they'll hit next."

He was right, of course. But she was 100% certain now: the victims may have been random, but the sites were personal. And Luke and Levi were brothers. Bound by blood.

"I have to talk to the mother," she said, the words coming out before the idea had really solidified in her mind.

"From the sound of it, she's pretty far gone."

"I know that. But you know whoever talked to her would have been asking the wrong questions. She might be able to tell me things about them," Darger said, already grabbing for her bag.

"You want me to come along?" Loshak offered.

"No, I think you should probably stay on the stadium detail and the tip line. Just in case."

He crossed his arms. "Call me if you get anything."

"I will."

"I mean it."

"I said I will."

"You better. Because if you run off on your own like you did in Ohio…."

Darger paused outside of the room.

"That wasn't on purpose."

"Right."

"You're quite the nag, Loshak. You know that?"

"Right back at you, Violet."

CHAPTER 60

An instant, uncomfortable feeling welled in Violet's chest as she stepped through the doors into the KindHeart Nursing Home. It was the smell, she thought. Floor wax, stale urine, and medical-grade disinfectant.

Violet showed her badge at the front desk, and a nursing aide named Tiffani offered to show her to Barbara Foley's room. The name tag clipped to the girl's scrubs had hearts drawn over each letter "i". Tiffani with an "i" and two hearts, Violet thought to herself.

"Did either of the boys come visit, that you know of?" she asked.

"The younger one did. For a while…" Tiffani said, frowning a bit at the memory. Perhaps realizing for the first time that she'd met and possibly spoken to a mass murderer.

"Levi?"

"Yes. But in the past six or eight months, I think he's only been here maybe once. He was pretty regular before that."

"What about Luke?"

Tiffani shook her head.

"I don't remember ever seeing him. Other than the stuff she has in her room. Family pictures, you know? We have little plaques on all the residents' walls that have photos of close family and friends. Early on, it's an easy way to remind them."

"And how long has Mrs. Foley been here?"

"A little over a year," Tiffani said. "It's one of the few times it's almost seemed like a blessing."

"What's that?"

"The dementia. She has no idea what her sons… what's been happening. We've made sure to keep the news footage off her TV, off all the TVs, actually. But even if she saw it, I don't know if it would register that those are her boys."

Tiffani paused in front of an open door, and Violet could hear low television sounds coming from within. Tiffani knocked her fist against the wall anyway.

"Barb? You have a visitor."

Violet recognized her from one of the videos: the clip where she berated Luke about his involvement in Levi's rooftop rollerblading stunt.

Barbara Foley was smaller now. Frail and withered. The woman in the video had possessed flowing waves of mahogany hair. Today those waves were wispy and streaked with gray. She hummed and talked softly to herself or perhaps to the TV. At the sound of her name, though, she turned her head.

Barb blinked a few times, eyeing Violet and the nurse with a vacant expression. Then she frowned and bowed her head, picking at the hem of her blouse.

"This is Violet. She's come to talk with you, if that's alright," Tiffani continued.

Barb returned her attention to them.

"Hello," she said, then trailed off with a few nonsensical mutterings.

"It's nice to meet you," Violet said.

Barb tried a smile. Licked her lips. Touched a finger to her chin. On the way back down to her lap, her hand stopped to tug at the collar of her blouse. Both hands began to unbutton her shirt then, making surprisingly quick progress. She'd managed to expose her bony chest and the top edge of her bra before Tiffani stopped her.

"No, no, Barb. Here, why don't you change Dolly's outfit?"

Tiffani pointed to a baby doll on the bed. It was frighteningly realistic and wore a pink frilly dress.

While Barb reached for the doll and began fiddling with it, Tiffani explained.

"She's a disrober. It's not uncommon with dementia patients."

It felt strange to talk about her as if she wasn't in the room, but Barb barely seemed to notice them. Her attention was now entirely focused on the doll in her hands.

"Yes, I recall my mother having to invest in some of those special jumpsuits with the zipper down the back for my grandmother."

Tiffani nodded.

"We tried the jumpsuit, but she seemed more agitated. We're trying to give her something else tactile to focus on when she gets that urge to start undoing buttons."

They watched Barb pull the pink dress over the doll's head.

"She used to be a walker. She could do ten miles a day, indoors, bare feet. I put my Fitbit on her one day, and she logged 25,000 steps. That's three times what I get in a shift. She never stopped moving. The undressing seemed to start as soon as she needed some help with walking. I think all that nervous energy needs somewhere to go. If it can't come out with the walking, it finds another way."

Barb hunched over a shoe box, pawing through a pile of doll clothes.

"I bet Violet would love to help you pick out a new outfit for Dolly."

Violet had never been a doll person. In fact, she found them quite creepy, even as a child. But she aimed a friendly smile at

Mrs. Foley and said, "Absolutely."

Tiffani turned to address Violet then.

"You're not going to get too… specific, are you? I mean about the murd— umm… the crimes? We're concerned that the details will upset her."

"I understand," Violet said. "And the answer is no. I'm more interested in who they were before all of this. I'll keep it purely academic."

Satisfied, Tiffani headed for the door and said, "Let me know if you need anything."

Violet sat on the edge of the bed and watched Mrs. Foley tug a lace-edged sock from the doll's foot.

"Does she have a name?" Violet asked. She'd heard Tiffani refer to the doll as *Dolly* but Violet wanted to get Mrs. Foley talking.

"This is Dolly," the woman answered.

Her voice was soft and high, almost girlish. Very different from the stern voice Violet remembered from the video.

"Tiffani told me that you have two boys. Is that right?"

Barb's eyes lifted and circled the room, as if she were following the flight path of an invisible insect. Her gaze landed on Violet.

"You have two sons?" Violet repeated a simpler version of the question.

Barb smiled then. "My boys? Do you know them?"

"I don't, but I'd love to hear about them. Can you tell me their names?"

The woman's mouth worked like she might be sucking on a piece of candy. Her claw-like fingers picked through the box of doll clothes before settling on a pale blue dress with a white pinafore that reminded Violet of Alice in Wonderland.

“What about Levi, Mrs. Foley? Can you tell me about him?”

Barb bobbed her head up and down but didn’t say more. Violet was starting to think coming here had been a waste of time. And then Mrs. Foley spoke.

“Levi’s a good boy. A smart boy. Always writing.”

She lifted a skeletal hand and pretended to scrawl something in the air. Violet scooted to the edge of the mattress.

“Yes, I heard he wrote for the school newspaper.”

“He won an award!” The old woman beamed.

“What about Luke?”

The woman’s face darkened, and her chin dipped to her chest.

“Naughty.”

Violet held very still.

“Luke is naughty?”

Mrs. Foley nodded.

“Bad boy,” she said and spanked the doll. “Bad, bad boy.”

CHAPTER 61

Darger called Loshak as she pulled out of the nursing home parking lot and filled him in on her plan.

"When you get back to town," he said, "do me a favor? Go back to the hotel and get some sleep. You shouldn't even be out driving with a head injury."

"Loshak," she started to say. She was thinking back on the very first time they'd met. He'd been violently ill. When she suggested he see a doctor, he'd essentially told her to mind her own damn business. But somewhere in the midst of her pause, she had a change of heart. Maybe it was the recurrent thought of Agent Dawson and Ethan Baxter. And for the mostly unspoken fondness she'd come to have for this strange man.

"What?" he asked, waiting for her to finish.

"This might sound weird, but I love you." She said it quickly, before she could second guess herself and chicken out.

She thought it would throw him off. But his response came without hesitation.

"I love you too, kiddo."

The drive to Griffin was uneventful, a mostly straight shot south on US Highway 41. She passed quiet little one-stoplight towns with names like Bonanza and Sunny Side.

Though they slept in the shadow of the city, Darger suspected these people thought of the recent events up north as something that might as well have happened the next state over. It was an urban problem. The kind of thing that "happened" in a place where people lived stacked on top of one another like sardines.

Shelly Webb lived in a small house with a U-shaped driveway bordered by a thicket of rose of Sharon bushes.

As soon as Darger pulled into the drive, a man came barreling down the front steps with a shotgun in hand. A woman followed behind, hollering at him to get back in the house.

Darger had her badge out already, and she did her best to appear unperturbed by the big man with the big gun.

"I'm from the FBI," she explained. "Are you Shelly Webb?"

The woman nodded. She had sleepy brown eyes and a mass of curly hair held back from her face with a red plastic hair clip.

"Go on back inside now, Tommy," Shelly said to the man. "You're only makin' a fool of yourself."

Shelly gestured that Darger should follow her around the side of the house to the backyard.

"Tommy's my brother. He looks mean with the gun, but he don't got the balls to actually pull the trigger."

"Press has been bothering you, I take it?" Darger asked.

"Yeah, they were calling so much I unplugged the house phone. I suppose it's only a matter of time before they find my cell, too. And there's been one or two knockin' at the door every day since… since they showed Luke's name and photo on the news."

"I'm sorry. It's unfair that you've been dragged into all of this."

Shelly settled into a faux wicker chair and fumbled at a small end table. She lifted a black cylinder that Darger thought was a pen at first. When Shelly put it to her lips and exhaled a puff of smoke worthy of a fairytale dragon, she realized it was an electronic cigarette.

"I guess that's the price you pay for gettin' involved with

Luke Foley."

"I take it you're not on the best terms?"

Shelly scoffed, another cloud of blue-gray haze obscuring her face for a moment. When it reappeared, she wore a frown.

"In some ways, we were never on the best of terms."

"Meaning he was abusive?"

Shelly licked her lips.

"It wasn't always physical. We started dating in high school, and all my friends tried to warn me about him. He was always gettin' in fights then. Got himself kicked out of school junior year."

Shelly paused to shake her head and expel more smoke.

"He never took responsibility for any of it. Anything he did, he'd have a list of excuses a mile long. But if you crossed him, did him wrong? Forget it. You had an enemy for life. I broke up with him one summer. It only lasted two or maybe three weeks, but he never let it go. We'd have a fight five years later, and he'd bring that up. Carryin' on about me sleepin' around for those three weeks, wantin' to know who and how often. Buncha nonsense. I didn't see anyone those three weeks. I just cried over him."

She crossed her arms over her chest and shook her head.

"What a waste."

"Did he ever mention doing something like this? Anything violent?"

"No. I mean, in a general way he said some things that I look at differently now that all this happened, but nothing specific."

"Things like what?"

"Oh, that all the people that done him wrong would come to regret it. That someday they'd all get what they were owed. But he was usually threatening to kill himself in the same breath, so

I always figured...."

Shelly shrugged and sighed instead of completing the sentence.

"Did he do that often? Threaten suicide?"

"When he first got back from Iraq, yeah. We were already pretty much apart by then. Separated. But things were pretty bad. He had nightmares and mood swings. Worse mood swings than before, I mean. And he was drinking a lot. He'd get rip-roarin' drunk, and he'd start threatening to drive up to the overpass. To jump like Wade Iverson did. Levi was the only one who could ever calm him down when he got like that."

"How well did you know Levi?"

"That's the real surprising part for me. Luke doin' something like this... well, I guess I find it hard to be shocked anymore at his behavior. But Levi? He was the sweetest kid. Got good grades, even had a partial scholarship for college. When things got real bad with Luke, sometimes I used to think: I chose the wrong brother."

There was a clinking sound as Shelly tapped the e-cigarette against her teeth.

"Guess I was wrong on all accounts. It's a horrible thing, but..."

She trailed off again, seeming to change her mind about finishing that thought.

"What?"

There was a hole in the knee of Shelly's jeans, and she picked at the frayed edge.

"Now I think maybe everyone would have been better off if Luke had gone through with it one of those times. Just ended it and left everyone else out of it. Why's he gotta drag everyone down with him?"

Shelly turned to look at Darger. Her eyelids fluttered a few times before her brow furrowed.

"I'm sorry. I don't know if any of that was helpful. I kinda… went off there."

"No, it was very enlightening," Darger said. "Really. I had some sense of who Levi is by looking through his apartment, going through his things. But Luke has been sort of a mystery until now."

Shelly's face brightened. She chewed on the end of the cigarette for a moment and then gestured over her shoulder.

"You know, I have a box of Luke's old stuff in the house."

"You do?"

The red hair clip and the curls bounced as Shelly nodded her head.

"Can I take a look?" Darger asked, sitting forward in her chair.

A little snort of a laugh preceded Shelly's answer.

"You can take the damn things for all I care."

"I don't necessarily need—"

"Let me rephrase that, then," Shelly said. "I'd *prefer* it if you took them. I'd like it very much if I never had cause to think about Luke Foley for the rest of my life."

Shelly Webb, Darger decided, had been through enough. Not wanting to intrude any further, she thanked her and carried the box of Luke's things out to her car before she poked through them.

It looked like it was mostly junk: some old, yellowing copies of Rolling Stone magazine. An ancient iPod with a shattered screen. A pair of beat up Converse sneakers.

She sighed, not feeling like she'd made any real progress.

Levi was the good boy. Luke was the naughty one. And she still had absolutely no idea if the investigation was heading in the right direction. She hated the idea of waiting around for the brothers to show up at a baseball game. Or somewhere else.

They'd been blindsided over and over, hadn't they? What if they were looking in the wrong place yet again?

Darger pressed her knuckles to her temples and massaged the flesh there for a moment. A persistent dull pain in her head had plagued her all day. She glanced at the clock on the dash and figured she ought to get back to her hotel and do what Loshak had recommended earlier. Get some damn sleep.

It was after ten when Darger got back to her room. She carried the box up with her, not willing to leave the evidence in her car overnight. She dropped it on the end of the bed and went to the bathroom to get cleaned up.

Teeth brushed and pajamas donned, Darger hoisted the box. It smelled faintly of stale cigarette smoke. Something metallic caught the bedside lamp and her curiosity.

It was a thick, hardcover book. A yearbook from Fort McPherson High. Darger did the math and figured it would have been Luke's Junior year, but Shelly had said he'd been expelled that year. Would he have wanted a keepsake like this, even after being kicked out? Darger thought not.

She flipped open the front cover, and among the scrawled messages wishing a "kickass summer vacation" and "see you in the fall!" was Shelly's name spelled out on the fly page in sparkly silver alphabet stickers. Shelly's yearbook, not Luke's. So why was it in the box?

That became clear as Darger continued paging through it.

On the first page, the name of the school was crossed out

and changed to "Fart McQueerson High."

The margins in the next few pages were filled with drawings of skulls, guns, snakes, and knives. She recognized the style of the doodles from the video where Luke had been decorating Levi's cast with a marker.

As she'd noted then, the kid possessed some artistic talent even if he had no taste at all.

Most of the photos of teachers were scrawled over. Some were silly: an eye patch, hoop earring, beard, and parrot added to the photo of Mr. Pitkin. Mrs. Franco had been given the hinged jaw and vacant eyes of a porcelain doll. Others were pornographic in nature: the vice principal performing fellatio on a horse, for example.

Most of the Varsity Dance Team had been defaced. Huge block letters scrawled across the top labeled the girls "WHORES."

On the next page, he'd rendered an elaborate Nazi imperial eagle.

Further in, Darger noticed that Luke had gone through and labeled many of the students with racist or homophobic slurs.

So much anger, she thought and then yawned.

She needed sleep. Analyzing Luke Foley's adolescent scribbles could wait until morning.

Snapping the cover shut, she replaced the yearbook in the box and shut off the lamp.

CHAPTER 62

The warmth of sleep still clung to Levi's flesh. He felt it deep in the meat of his cheeks, in the faint itch plaguing the folds of his eyelids.

The morning of.

That phrase kept turning over and over in his head. This was the morning of.

Morning it may be, but the sun hadn't shown yet. Darkness still shrouded all things.

It was before dawn, and the brothers sat in the beat up Ford Focus. Waiting. Watching. The engine was off. They were parked on a dead end street, looking at an overgrown lot through the windshield. They paused here, Levi supposed, to collect themselves before the next of Luke's nightmares transformed into a reality, this time with the help of the 70 pounds of C4 stacked neatly in the trunk.

He swallowed, his throat clicking. He took a drink of watery gas station coffee. It wasn't enough to help wake him up. Not yet.

The morning of.

He thought about the roof of the El Camino thrust into the air, the doors thrown out of their frames, the flash and incredible bang that rattled his bones and made the earth quake beneath his feet. He thought of these things, and he swallowed again.

Levi read the name tag on Luke's jumpsuit. Leroy. The name on his own jumpsuit was David. Janitors. That was the ruse. The costume. That was what would get them through the door. Luke had apparently tested it multiple times without issue.

"Remember, if anything happens, we meet at the Jeep. It's parked a couple blocks from the old house. Behind the vacant Blockbuster on Mosel Street. OK?"

Levi hesitated a moment, then nodded.

Luke squinted at him, demonic wrinkles spreading over his face.

"Tell me where it is."

"Behind the Blockbuster. On Mosel."

"Good."

The muscles in Luke's face relaxed, a little at first, then all the way, and he looked like himself again.

"I showed you the backup detonation method, right?"

Levi nodded.

Luke placed a cigarette in his lips and took his zippo to it. The burnt butane smell of the lighter seemed sharper than usual somehow. Levi thought maybe his senses were heightened from the adrenaline.

"If something goes wrong with the detonator at the first location, I don't think there's anything we can do about it. There'll be too many people around to go in and wire it. We ditch it and move on. But we'll be able to wire the detonators up at the second location, if it comes to that."

Levi closed his eyes.

"Second location?" he said.

Luke scoffed, smoke shooting out of his mouth and nose.

"It wouldn't be much of a project if we only struck once, now would it? Shock and awe, baby bro. A spectacle is all about the element of surprise. The magnitude. The sense of grandeur. You hit 'em, get 'em lookin' one way, then you blindside 'em even harder from the other direction. Harder than they could have dreamed. The first blast is the shock, and the second is the awe."

He puffed on his cigarette and chuckled to himself before he went on.

"And I have to say — me, personally? I like the awe. I really do. Always have."

Even when he laughed he looked devilish in the green glow of the dash lights. His mouth looked too big, and his eyes looked dead as always.

The faint smell of the plastic explosive filled the car. It seemed to arrive just then, to make itself known all at once. Luke must have noticed it as well.

"Stuff's supposed to be odorless, but when it's hot and humid out like this, there's a smell."

He dropped his stubby cigarette into the paper coffee cup from the gas station, and the cherry hissed as the backwash extinguished it.

"They say it smells like tar, but to me, it always smells like vinyl."

"Vinyl?"

"Yeah, like a new shower curtain, you know?"

Levi concentrated on the smell for a beat, the image of an off-white shower curtain conjured in his head.

"Yeah, I get that. Maybe with some Play-Doh mixed in or something."

CHAPTER 63

A door slammed somewhere down the hall. Darger blinked at the hazy gray light seeping through the gap in the curtains. Not quite dawn.

She settled back against the pillow, finding the indentation her head had made in the night. Her eyelids slid closed.

Her mind played over the previous day. Images and sounds coming to her clearly now. She was in that strange half-dream state that often came in the early morning. She'd always thought of it as the intuitive part of her brain being in charge while the rational part stumbled around still partially asleep.

Leonard Stump called it the Sensate State. The way he waxed poetic about it, Darger felt it was almost a sacred time to him.

In his journal, he'd written, "There is a clarity upon waking in the morning that can not be matched by meditation, psychotropic drugs, or any alignment of the supposed chakras. It is a time when our right brain is given free rein to explore and expound after a night spent conjuring dreams.

"I spend at least one hour each morning in the Sensate State, and I inevitably come out of it feeling razor-sharp and reinvigorated. If I do not take this time, the day is never quite right. My mind is foggy. My body seems weighed down by some invisible force.

"My mother thought me lazy. To her I was 'lying about in there.' But she was a fool and an idiot, so it is no wonder she did not appreciate my commitment to this ritual."

And so, Darger willed herself to lie there and let her mind *explore and expound.* She wondered what Loshak would think if he knew that she was taking advice from a serial killer.

Her mind wandered to Levi Foley's closet, to the school newspapers they'd found. Each article he'd written had been carefully outlined. He'd been a kid with dreams and ambitions. Pride in his work. How had it come to this?

Images flashed in her mind's eye. The newspapers. The letter jacket. The yearbook.

Darger sat up.

The box was close enough that she could lean out of bed and pluck the book off the top of the pile. She pawed it closer and skipped to the index of student names in the back. Her finger ran down the alphabetized list of people in the Junior class until she found "Foley, Luke … page 78."

The glossy paper swished as she flicked to the correct page and found Luke's class photo among the rest. She swallowed.

He'd used an eraser or something else to remove the rectangle of ink from the page. All that was left of his face was a hazy blur. No eyes, no nose, no mouth. Only the faint outline of shoulders, ears, and hair.

So much anger… that's what she'd thought the night before. But it was more than that. He'd felt invisible. Unwanted. Unappreciated. Marginalized.

His hatred for that place was more than just leftover adolescent angst. It was more than unpleasant memories of youth. More than a lack of nostalgia. The defacement of Shelly's yearbook was a personal vendetta, not only against Shelly, but against the school. The people in it. His classmates, his teachers.

That was it, she thought. She slammed the cover closed and read the name of the school again. Fort McPherson High.

She jumped out of bed so quickly her head pounded and swam. She grasped the dresser to steady herself until the dizziness and little bolts of pain subsided, and then she got herself dressed.

The fuchsia and turquoise carpet muffled her footfalls as she jogged down the hallway. She stopped past Loshak's door. She'd never hear the end of it if she ran off without him.

She hopped the few steps backward and knocked. Waited. Knocked again. Growing impatient, she tried his phone. There was no answer, and she didn't hear it ringing from inside the room. She gave up on him and proceeded to the elevator at the end of the hall.

As soon as the polished aluminum doors snicked shut, Darger wished she would have taken the stairs. On the third floor, she had to wait as an elderly couple shuffled in. On the second floor, a middle-aged woman in workout gear joined them. It was all she could do to keep herself from jumping up and down with nervous energy.

Her phone trilled as she reached her car. It was Loshak.

She didn't bother with pleasantries and cut right to it.

"I think it's the high school."

"What about it?"

"The next target. If you think about it, every crime scene so far has had a personal connection. The bridge, the Publix lot, Pheasant Brook. I know we saw that Atlanta Braves pennant in Levi's apartment, but that's not enough. Hell, I liked the Braves when I was a kid. But the high school… Levi still had his letter jacket in his closet. The newspaper articles he'd written."

"Right, but if we think Luke is the one orchestrating—"

"There's more. Luke's ex-wife gave me a box of his old stuff. His high school yearbook was inside. Actually, it was her high school yearbook, but judging by the amount of time and effort he spent defacing it, I'd say he has a lot of leftover bitterness about that place."

There was a brief silence over the line, and Darger imagined Loshak mussing up his own hair.

Finally he said, "I suppose I can see the appeal for him. If you're raging against all of the various societal ties that bind, why not direct it at a place you spent years being told what to do and how to act?"

"And it didn't sound like he was a star when it came to academics or extracurriculars. Unless setting a record for highest number of suspensions counts," she added.

"Is it even open?"

"What?"

"The school. Seems early."

"I looked it up. Classes start today."

"Cripes," Loshak said, and she knew what he was thinking: that perhaps the Foley brothers wanted to make this school year start with a bang. "You heading over there now?"

"Yeah, I'm two minutes away according to GPS."

"You call for backup?" he asked.

"Do you count?"

He snorted. "I'm on my way, I'll see if I can borrow some bodies from Atlanta PD."

CHAPTER 64

Loshak called again as Darger strode down a long hallway leading past the gym. Judging by the smell of chlorine in the air, the pool was also somewhere nearby.

"The main student and visitor entrances have a security checkpoint with metal detectors," Darger relayed. "I'm checking all of the other doors to see if any of them have been forced open or otherwise tampered with."

She reached a door at the end of the corridor. After a brief inspection, she moved on to the next.

"Agent Dawson and I thought we'd cruise around the parking lot, see if the Wrangler's out here."

"Good idea," Darger said. "Call me if you find anything."

"If you'll do the same," Loshak said and hung up.

Her shoes squeaked over the vinyl floors as she rounded a corner. Ahead, Darger could see a wheeled cart loaded with a metal trash bin.

As she passed by, a custodian backed out of an open door, nearly bumping into her. He startled and stopped short just in time, muttering an apology.

The janitor reached up to adjust the brim of his baseball hat. As the blue sleeve of his coverall slid along his arm, it revealed a long white scar that ran almost from wrist to elbow. That must have been a nasty surgery.

Not breaking her stride, Darger thought about how they had always been so strict about students wearing hats in school when she was a kid, which she'd never understood. Was it still like that?

Her eyes were on the door ahead, and something was nagging at her. She scanned the door itself, looking for something out of place, but there was nothing notable that she could see.

The janitor's trolley emitted a squawk that echoed down the passage, and she stopped. Turned.

He was pushing it down the hall in the opposite direction.

He didn't seem to be in any hurry. If anything, his sauntering gait was completely relaxed. She had yet to pin down what it was that was bugging her when he pivoted to follow the cart around the bend. And then she saw the rolled cuff of his uniform sleeve and remembered the scar, and it all came together.

Your brother is in surgery right now, having his bones screwed back together.

Levi's surgery after his ill-planned stunt on the roof.

The man in the janitor's uniform glanced back, saw that she was watching him. His spine went rigid, and then he took off.

"Shit," Darger said.

She sprinted after him, pausing briefly at the cart now laden with a single garbage can. It appeared empty aside from the plastic bag, but on a hunch, she ripped the plastic liner away.

Resting on the bottom was a brick of plastic explosives with pins protruding from it.

How many had they planted? They could have one in every classroom, on every floor. Near emergency exits. In stairwells.

Jesus God.

She had to get everyone out of the school. Glancing up, she saw the man she was now certain was Levi Foley heading for another set of doors. But she also couldn't let him get away.

Darger noticed the red rectangular box with white letters

protruding from the wall. She pulled the handle, setting off the fire alarm as she jogged past, immediately triggering a shrill siren.

Continuing after Levi, and dodging the students now crowding the cafeteria area on their way out of the building, she tugged her phone from her pocket.

As soon as she heard the click of Loshak picking up, she shouted into the phone. "Loshak! They're in dark blue janitor suits. I'm chasing Levi on foot, headed west, I think. I don't see Luke, but he's gotta be here somewhere. They've planted explosives all over the building."

"We're on it," Loshak said. "Be careful."

He hung up.

Levi bounded through a door that led outside, knocking into a woman carrying a stack of three-ring binders. As Darger hurried past, she called out to him.

"Levi, stop!"

He seemed startled by that, his head swiveling around to look back at her. She didn't know why. Surely he was aware they knew his name, knew all about him. He must have seen his picture plastered on the news and in the papers at least a dozen times by now. He and his brother were in the midst of their fifteen minutes of fame.

Because he wasn't watching where he was running, his foot caught an uneven seam on the sidewalk and he stumbled for a few steps. Darger held her breath.

This was it. He was going to fall, and she was going to capture him.

CHAPTER 65

Luke heard the fire alarm go off.

Shit. Something was very wrong.

He looked both ways, finding empty hallways sprawled out before him, and ran for the door.

The car was parked in the employee lot, and the remote detonator was wedged under the seat on the driver's side.

He had to blow it now, and hope that Levi was out in time. They both knew the deal going into this. Death was always a possibility.

No fear. No regrets.

When he jammed through the big steel door, he found a familiar face in the side lot, standing in front of the Ford Focus. It was the FBI Agent from TV, Victor Loshak. The one who wrote the book about serial killers.

Shit. Shit. Shit.

He slowed to what he hoped looked like a nonchalant walk and rounded the corner.

Loshak appeared to be fiddling with his phone. Luke didn't think the Agent saw him.

When he got to the front of the school, he stripped off his janitorial jumpsuit and ditched it in some bushes set in a bed of decorative gravel.

He jogged out toward the busy intersection, hoping to fall in with the growing stream of foot traffic and blend in. He suspected the Braves hat he had pulled down over his brow would make him nondescript enough to go unnoticed. Or at least he hoped.

CHAPTER 66

Ahead of her, Levi managed to regain his footing and kept running with renewed vigor.

Darger continued her pursuit, following Levi as he cut a path through a baseball diamond behind the school.

A part of her kept waiting to hear it. The big boom. Why hadn't they blown the school yet? Luke had surely heard the fire alarm. She supposed he might be worried that Levi was still inside, but that suggested they expected to… what? Get out of this alive? Or did they have more planned?

The thought spurred her forward, despite the ache building in her legs.

Levi passed beyond a copse of poplars along the edge of the athletic fields, disappearing from her view momentarily. When she crossed under the canopy, she saw him dashing down a residential street that backed up to the school grounds.

He glanced back, saw that Darger was still on his tail, and veered to the left. Without hesitation, he cleared the chain link fence in a single stride, like an Olympic hurdler. Darger did not have the same confidence in her vaulting skills. She put two hands on the top of the fence and hopped over, sprinting as soon as her feet hit the ground.

An elderly woman hunched over a patch of marigolds planted along the side of the house. She spewed a series of panicked bird-like noises with her mouth as they blitzed past. Finally, she managed to shriek, "What! What! What is this? Who are you?"

Darger ignored her, her focus solely on Levi.

He took a diagonal path across the next lane, slipping through the open gate of a very tall privacy fence.

If this fence goes all the way around, then I'll have him, Darger thought. He would have nowhere to go. She rounded the corner of the house, and her hopes sank. There was a cord of firewood at one end, stacked high enough to bring the top of the fence within reach. He could climb the pile and have no trouble hopping the fence. And that's exactly what he did.

It wasn't until Darger was in the middle of the yard that she saw the dog.

CHAPTER 67

Luke proceeded at what he hoped was an inconspicuous pace, disappearing into the throngs of humanity swarming over the sidewalk. It had been a long time since he traveled through the city on foot. It looked different from this perspective.

A pair of cop cars flew by. Sirens screaming. Lights twirling. It wouldn't be long before they circled back to patrol this area more thoroughly. Canvassing. Setting up roadblocks. He needed to flee this vicinity faster than walking.

He cut right, leaving the busier streets to look for a more residential area. The foot traffic waned. Within a block and a half, he was the only one walking. He felt exposed, but it was OK, he told himself. In a minute here, he'd have a car.

Peggy Sanchez headed out to her car, visions of Sean Hannity dancing in her head as usual. Right as she jabbed a thumb at the key fob to unlock her Saturn, a gruff voice spoke up from behind her.

"Give me the keys, and I won't hurt you."

She turned in slow motion, the faces from the news flickering where they'd been burned into her brain.

It was him. It was one of the killers. A baseball hat rode low over his brow, but she could tell.

She did not hesitate.

She doused Luke Foley with the small can of pepper spray on her key chain, her heart thudding.

The killer screeched and brought his hands to his face, dropping to the ground in agony.

She kicked him once in the ribs and ran inside, locking the door behind her.

Her thoughts were jumbled, everything aflutter, but she took a breath, counted to three, and moved to call the police.

CHAPTER 68

The dog caught up with Darger as she reached the woodpile and began clambering up the side. It had the perky ears and fluffy fur of a teddy bear and a tail that curled back on itself. The eyes were so deeply set in the fur that Darger mostly saw the face as a big snubbed nose.

A far cry from a snarling Rottweiler, but still, she could tell its intent was more than a friendly sniff of the crotch.

It was a Chow, she was pretty sure. She remembered hearing somewhere that it was the breed most likely to turn on its owner.

As that thought ran through her mind, it launched itself for the attack. Darger tried to pull her legs up under herself, but it was too late. She felt the bite of canine teeth sink into her calf, penetrating the fabric of her pants as if it were wet paper.

She tried to yank away. When that didn't work she gave the leg a shake, but the dog held tight, using its powerful neck muscles to wrench back and forth. Darger's hand strayed toward the holster at her waist. She didn't want to shoot the animal, but she wasn't sure what choice she had. Despite being half her size, it was strong.

It gave another tug and Darger slid a few inches down the woodpile. One of the logs came loose under her, rolling to the grass. And that gave her an idea.

Darger reached for a piece of wood, clutching it with desperate fingers. She hefted it over her shoulder and swung it like a club, catching the dog on the side of the head. The Chow emitted a high-pitched whine and unhinged its jaws. Darger lifted the wood again, but the dog backed just out of reach, growling.

Not releasing her hold on the chunk of wood, Darger scaled to the top of the stacked logs. With one quick glance over the side of the fence, she hopped down. The impact of hitting the ground sent an almost electric sizzle of pain up and down her wounded leg.

Ignoring her injury for now, she whirled her head around. She was in an alley, walled in by high fences with a dead end to the right. He could only have gone one way.

With a limping gait, Darger ambled down to the crossroad, hoping she'd be able to tell which direction he'd gone from there.

When she reached the street, she heard a car horn blare to her left, and then another. She took a guess at what they were honking at and veered that way.

CHAPTER 69

Luke scrambled. His eyes burned. Excruciating. The left one a bit worse than the right, a sting that stabbed somehow, an ice pick skewering his eyeball to the hilt.

He could kind of see out of the right eye, but barely. Keeping it open for more than a fraction of a second was a lost fight. Still, he had to move.

He jogged down what he thought was the sidewalk, hands bobbing in front of him to feel for obstacles.

Milk. That's what people dumped in their eyes during times like this. He didn't know if it really worked, but he'd be willing to give it a try with a gallon or ten, even if it only helped a little.

Sirens blared somewhere behind him. The mourning wail growing closer and closer.

He needed to get inside somewhere. Anywhere. For just a few minutes.

Maybe the adrenaline helped or something, but he could keep his right eyelid open now, looking at the world through one narrow peephole.

He swiveled toward the closest house, crashing through the bushes to get to a window.

His flattened palms butted up against the pane of glass, trying to force it open.

Locked.

Fuck.

He had to think. Heart beating so hard, so fast.

He stripped off his shirt and wrapped it around his left arm and fist the best he could.

He punched the glass, feeling that brittle sheet cave against his balled hand. The crash was so loud and sharp and musical. A glassy burst that made him shudder.

He cut the punch short and retracted his covered arm with care, managing to come out of it unscathed.

Shards of glass still hung in the window frame, so he poked out a couple of big pieces, snaking his hand through the opening to unlock the window.

The sirens wailed right on top of him now, and the twirling lights twinkled in the corner of his eye.

He ducked into the bushes and waited, expecting with all of his being to hear the cruiser slow when it got to him, but it didn't. It slowed at the intersection and then picked up speed again, zooming past.

He rose, threw open the sash and climbed into the house.

It took a second for his good eye to adjust to the shade inside the house. He found himself in a bathroom.

Tyrone heard the sirens first. Multiple sirens. Close. He sat up, checked the alarm clock. It was 7:44 AM — later than he usually slept, and for a second, a twinge of panic passed over him at seeing those numbers, but it was OK, he reminded himself. Today was his day off.

All of this killer stuff in the news had messed him up, and he'd been looking forward to sleeping in until 9:00 or 9:30. That didn't seem likely anymore.

He listened for a moment. The sirens grew louder, moved closer, but he didn't quite care enough to go take a look.

He let his head plop back to the down softness of the pillow, blinked a few times, and closed his eyes.

And then glass exploded somewhere on the other side of the

house. The impact sounded like a blunt stroke, maybe dampened somehow, but it was unmistakably a window in his home.

He extended his hand over the side of the mattress and fumbled around underneath until his fingers found what they sought — the fire poker. It felt right in his hands — heavy metal. Hard and cold. An instrument of death.

He cocked it in his arms like a baseball bat, ready to take the intruder's goddamn head off, and lifted himself from the bed to investigate.

CHAPTER 70

She caught up with him at the foot of the bridge, the central support arching across the water like a strange bent spine. Darger followed him up that subtle slope for a time, and then Levi slowed as they reached the midpoint.

He stood still for a moment, facing the water. And then he climbed up onto the rail.

"Don't," Darger said, only able to get out the single word between breaths. It had to be 200 feet from here to the river below.

He got to his knees at first and then stood, swaying a little. Gusts of wind battered him and let up, battered him and let up, seemingly determined to knock him off his perch, but he rode the turbulence out, his t-shirt flapping against his torso. His arms splayed to his sides like wings to help him keep his balance.

For the first time, Darger saw the gun in his hand and shuffled back a couple steps. Her hand went to her own holster, but she stopped herself. Pointing a gun at a suicidal man didn't seem wise. For the moment, he paid her no mind, so she side-stepped to the rail, still keeping her distance.

Dark water swirled below when she glanced over the edge. A churning, burbling place to die.

"You don't have to do this, Levi," she said. "You can come with me. This can end peacefully for everyone."

She raised her hands in front of her, wind whipping strands of hair into her face. The traffic roared behind her. All of the people hurtling past, indifferent to the dramatic scene.

His lip twitched, twice, three times, but nothing came out.

"Get down, Levi. No one needs to get hurt. Not you or anyone else."

And then he pointed the gun at her.

"Stay back," he said. "I don't have the detonator. I don't have anything for you. I don't matter anymore."

"That's not true."

Darger took a step forward as she spoke.

"Get the fuck back!"

Spit flew out of Levi's mouth as he growled, the gun trembling at the end of his arm.

"You think I'm fucking around? You think taking one more life makes any difference to me? You think anything makes a difference now?"

Darger froze, eyes on the pistol in Levi's hand. She wondered if she'd been wrong about him all along.

CHAPTER 71

Luke squatted in the bathroom. Waiting. Listening. He pointed one ear and then the other toward the partially open bathroom door, as though the second might hear something the first had missed.

Nothing. The house was quiet.

He shuffled forward a few paces, pulling alongside the sink, and he caught his reflection in the mirror, his one eye all squinched up into a mess of wrinkles. Angry red puffs of swollen flesh swaddled his face from his brow to his cheek bones — inflammation trying to fight off the acidic fury of the mace. He wondered if the swelling and redness would make him less recognizable and almost laughed.

Something creaked in the distance, and he snapped his head around to face the bathroom door again. His mind raced. It didn't sound like a floorboard, but it was vaguely familiar. He wanted more than anything to believe that it was the house settling, the old wood giving off a random groan, but he didn't think so. A bed, maybe, he thought. A box spring.

He held his breath and listened some more, sliding two paces to his left to conceal himself behind the bathroom door.

Another noise. Definitely a squawking box spring. Additional sounds followed shortly after.

Thumps. Footsteps. The slow, careful patter of someone headed his way. The floorboards whining a little with every step.

Luke scanned what he could see of the bathroom for a weapon. But he'd let Levi hold the pistol back at the school, leaving his own in the car. Now he was contemplating arming himself with a toilet brush.

The steps grew closer, and he held his breath. Whoever it was, they were in the hallway, and they were creeping this way with great care. Surely they'd peek into the bathroom, wouldn't they?

The shadow darkened the crack between the bathroom door and the frame for a moment. Someone moved past very slowly. He couldn't make out any details from where he stood, except that the figure was tall enough to most likely be a man.

And then the footsteps stopped. The creeper must be gazing into the doorway. Seeing the broken window. The shards of glass scattered on the throw rug in front of the toilet.

Blood roared in Luke's ears, and cold fear trickled outward from the center of his chest, flowing into his shoulders and spreading from there.

He tried to think of what he should do — what he *would* do — when the man entered the bathroom. If the man had a gun, it would be over quickly.

The creeper took a breath, air hissing out of his nostrils on the exhale. It sounded aggressive. Frustrated. Very ape.

Something clunked against the door, swinging it a touch wider in slow motion.

Luke turned so his shoulders were parallel to the wall, making himself as skinny as he could. The door's swing stopped just shy of his quivering chest.

Even without closing his eyes, he could picture it. The image of the gun rising, the blaze and pop of the kill shot exiting the muzzle.

But then the footsteps resumed, moving further down the hall.

Luke leaned to peer through the crack. He didn't get a very

good look, but he saw the man's hands before he moved out of view.

No gun. He had something thin and metallic in his hand. Maybe a crow bar or fire poker.

The whining floorboards trailed away, like a wave that had reached its furthest bit of beach and now receded, rolling back from the land to gather itself.

Luke took a breath, finally, concentrating on keeping it quiet. The relief he felt wasn't enough to squelch that cold trickle of fear in his torso, but he'd at least gained some time and options.

His mind spun through the possible ways to interpret what had just happened.

Had the guy not seen the broken window? Had he seen it but assumed the empty bathroom meant that the intruder had moved on? He suspected the latter, if only because of the way that angry puff of breath seemed to signify the moment he'd spotted the window.

Either way, staying put wasn't an option. Luke needed to move.

The way he saw it, he had a choice. He could scurry back out the window and be gone, or he could venture further into the house in hopes of finding a weapon. Armed with even a blunt object, he was reasonably confident he could handle things here and come out of this with a car. A car that could quickly whisk him away from this neighborhood where the police were searching for a suspect on foot.

He took another deep breath, the panic now fleeing his body, morphing into something more aggressive. The guy didn't have a gun. Luke could handle this. This fuck with the fire poker had no clue who he was dealing with.

He stalked forward.

Again he looked at his reflection in the mirror, his chest heaving, his face all battered looking. Maybe it was a trick of the shadow he was standing in, but the red splotching his eyelids looked darker now. Angrier. He made eye contact with himself — the eye that wasn't swollen shut staring straight into itself, a dead expression set in the flesh around it.

He crossed through the doorway, pressing deeper into the house.

CHAPTER 72

Tyrone saw it. Sunlight streaming through the gaping rectangle where the frosted bathroom window should be. It was wide open, and the bottom pane of glass was busted out.

Goddamn. After all of that paranoia, all of that lost sleep, it was really happening. Someone was inside the house. And with the sheer quantity of sirens blaring outside? It had to be something big. A serious criminal. Maybe even… He tried to stop the headlines about the snipers from flashing through his head, but it was too late.

He let his eyes fall to the floor where the broken bits of glass lay. They glittered a little when the clouds shifted outside and the light in the room changed.

Goddamn.

He let out a single angry breath and listened for a moment. Nothing stirred that he could hear. Whoever he was, the guy was running from the law. He was probably heading for the garage. For the car.

Tyrone headed that way, taking careful steps, quiet steps. The hallway opened up into the kitchen, and he could see the doorway into the garage ahead.

He changed his grip on the fire poker, bringing it up to rest on his shoulder like a baseball player stepping into the batter's box. The muscles in his arms rippled, ready to deal out some punishment.

He didn't figure this guy likely to drive away with his Lexus, what with the three feet of fire poker he was about to lodge in his ass.

Then something crunched behind him. A footstep from somewhere back down the hallway. It had to be him.

Tyrone turned.

Kitty litter.

Luke had stepped on a few granules of crystal kitty litter, grinding them into the ceramic tile floor with great gusto. After all of the quiet, it was loud as hell — a grinding noise mixed with a high pitched shriek. He thought it sounded like someone chewing on ice with just a hint of nails on blackboard blended in for good measure. He also thought he was about four seconds away from getting beaten to death with a fire poker.

He'd moved from the bathroom into a small office across the hall. He hadn't paid much mind to the litter box in the corner, though he could smell the cat piss faintly. He didn't actually see the litter on the floor until it was crushed into a fine white powder by the heel of his sneaker.

The footsteps heading his way made no attempt to conceal themselves now. They pounded out an angry beat, the volume swelling with each step.

Luke crawled under the desk, knowing it was useless. All he could see from this vantage point was the plain white wall, a brown filing cabinet, and the litter tray loaded with a couple of fresh clumps. He pulled the office chair close in an attempt to conceal himself, even if he knew the hiding spot would be short-lived.

Cold sweat slimed his body, and the pulse of the blood beating through his ears grew louder and louder. His jaw clenched so hard that the muscles twitched under his cheek bones.

He tried to think, but the panic overwhelmed his ability to

reason. Fight or flight were the only possibilities. He'd have to choose one any second now.

The footsteps entered the room somewhere behind him and got closer and closer until the man's legs walked into view.

Luke chose fight.

CHAPTER 73

Levi faced her now, extending the gun so it pointed at her chest. Cars ripped past on the asphalt behind her.

He watched as her gaze shifted downward.

Her pupils swelled. Her eyes locked onto the gun trembling in his hand, the barrel aimed straight at her. She took a shaky step backward, her pleading cutting off into silence, and fear flashed on her face for the first time in their encounter. Good, Levi thought. Perhaps it was dawning on her that she had no control here. That she wasn't going to save the day this time. Wasn't going to talk him down. They weren't going to fix this with pretty words.

He was lost. He was beyond saving now. It was too late to talk, too late to beg or plead. Too late to pray.

It was too fucking late.

Levi turned again and looked down at the river. He knew that jumping from this height would end it. It would be like landing on concrete. He tried to picture it, tried to imagine connecting head first, his skull shattering like a dropped jar.

The daylight reflected from the ripples on the water, shimmering white shards of light up at him. Between the glare and the murk of the water itself, he couldn't make out anything beneath the surface.

It calmed him some to watch the rushing river. He thought about all of Luke's talk about symbols. Pregnancy was a symbol of life persisting. The police were symbols of order. Water was a symbol of life, wasn't it? What did it mean to kill yourself in water, then?

And then it clicked. Water was the place the shadow went to die. Nothing could wash away what he'd done, but the river could sure wash him away. This was the symbol of life conquering death, for now and for always.

He closed his eyes. Took a breath, slow and deep.

Her voice called out from behind him, rising above the drone of the traffic.

"You're the only one who can stop him, Levi. Luke is going to hurt so many more people if you let him. I don't think that's what you want."

His eyes snapped open, blinked a few times. He didn't turn back to face her.

"Look, we can talk about this. Just hang out for a minute, and we can talk."

She didn't have a clue. And there was nothing left to say. Not to her. Not to anyone.

No more words.

He pushed one foot out into the void, almost testing the nothingness — the empty space that lay between him and death.

"You're not like Luke. I know that. He was nothing but trouble his whole life, but not you. You were a good writer. A good kid. And everyone knew that. Your mom. Shelly. They knew. And they know that all of this rage, all of this violence, that's not you, Levi. It's not."

The wind picked up, battering him in the chest once more, lifting him a little. It swooped under his shirt and inflated it partially, the front plastered to his ribs and the back billowing like a cape.

It was almost like something was easing him back, some hand of fate, some force of nature trying to talk him down.

He blinked a few times. The air dry in his eyes.

And then he jumped.

Empty. Weightless. Flying.

His field of vision tilted toward the water. The dark swirls coiling there. He could see the black give way to blue in them now as they grew closer, could see hints of the depths that lay below the shimmer of the surface.

The cold of the wind stung his eyes. But he fought it off, held them open wide, stared straight into the end.

The river rushed up. Anxious to meet him. Anxious to be done with it.

His breath caught in his throat as the collision neared, a little gurgle emitting from behind his tongue. He still didn't close his eyes.

Let it be over. Head fucking first.

Bright white shot all through him upon impact. Knotting his muscles. Clenching his jaw. Pain jolting everywhere as his body broke against the rock hard surface. A final sizzle in his skull.

And the dark water lurched once and swallowed him.

CHAPTER 74

Darger screamed for him to stop, but it was too late. He stepped into the open air beyond the bridge and disappeared from her sight.

A dream-like detachment came over her, as if she were watching the scene unfold from a distance versus actively participating in it. Almost an out of body experience.

Her feet moved the two paces to the guard rail. Her fingers wrapped around the cool metal, knuckles white with tension. Her eyes searched the swirling tumult of the water, waiting to catch sight of him. Nothing but the rapids marred the surface.

He was gone. One moment he'd been standing on the rail, and in the span of a single breath, he'd vanished, swallowed by the cold, black depths.

He hadn't even screamed. But the sound of his body hitting the water was as violent as an explosion. A hard, percussive *crack*.

She'd thought she could talk him down, but she'd failed.

Shelly Webb's words floated out from her subconscious.

Maybe everyone would have been better off if he'd just ended it and left everyone else out of it.

But Shelly had been talking about Luke. Levi, on the other hand… for some reason, Darger had been convinced she'd be able to get through to him.

And then it struck her: Luke. He might still be out there somewhere.

A sucking sound slurped in her shoe as she hobbled back the way she'd come. Blood from the dog bite continued dribbling down her leg, soaking into her sock. She got out her phone and called Loshak.

"Do you have Luke?" she barked into the mouthpiece as soon as he picked up.

"No."

"Fuck!"

"They're setting up roadblocks all around the area. They've got choppers in the air. He won't get far. What about Levi?"

Her rib cage shuddered as she inhaled, not wanting to give him this particular news.

"Levi's gone. There's a bridge a few blocks from the school. He jumped."

"Jumped? You mean…"

"Yeah."

Loshak sighed. "Well, I suppose that's one way to end it."

"I tried to stop him, he—"

"Shit, I know that. I didn't mean it to sound that way. I'm sorry. You did everything you could."

But she was angry with herself, no matter what Loshak said. She swallowed against bitter tears.

"Where are you?" Loshak asked. "I'll come pick you up."

"That would be good. I had a little incident."

"Levi?"

"No. A dog."

"Hell, Darger. You're like a shit-storm magnet, you know that?"

"Are you going to come pick me up, or what? I'm on…" she glanced at a street sign, "Carlson Avenue, right before the bridge."

"Hold tight. I'll be there."

CHAPTER 75

The office chair jerked away from the desk, wheels scraping over the ceramic floor. Before Tyrone had time to react, a blur of a human figure dove out from under it. A man. The shoulders connected with Tyrone's thighs.

He flung his arms out to try to regain some balance, but it was no use. The tackle uprooted him, smacked him ass-first into the wall, and then both bodies went down in a heap.

Tyrone was so stunned that his first instinct was to get to his feet. He struggled for a moment — both men confused, off balance, fumbling and bumping into each other. Then he remembered the weapon in his hand and took a couple of swings.

The hooked part of the poker raked the back of the intruder's head on the second strike, and the man screamed and scrambled back, hands clutching his punctured scalp. His voice seemed high. Almost shrill.

Now Tyrone had enough room to stand. He got to his feet quickly and stalked after the wounded animal before him. The panicked creature could only scuttle backward like a crab.

Tyrone stood over him, his muscles tightening as he prepared to destroy. This time he wound up for a bigger swing, two handed — somewhere between Bryce Harper and Tiger Woods.

Luke brought his head up just in time to catch sight of the iron rod racing toward his face. It caught him in the mouth — a clean, powerful stroke.

Everything went white.

The seconds stretched out, and he felt his teeth come apart in stages — the lightning flash of pain where the metal impacted his lip and mouth, the incredible pressure of all that force trying to wrench his teeth out of place, and then the tension releasing, and shards of tooth crumbling all over his tongue.

A sound came out of him, a throaty heave like a vomiting cat, and then pieces of his teeth spilled from his lips, clattering on the floor.

There was one big downbeat after that, a swoon of his consciousness into blackness, and then he bobbed back up into awareness and full color and a mouthful of pain. He spit out more bits of tooth, watching the white flecks skitter away on the gray tile.

The impact still reverberated in his skull, and he realized that he was now on his hands and knees facing the opposite direction. He'd been knocked into the doorway, so he took advantage and scrambled into the hall.

It *was* him. One of those snipers from the news — the sinewy one. Luke Foley. Even with the red splotches around his eyes, Tyrone was certain it was him, though he didn't fully grasp this fact until after he'd clobbered him in the mouth with a fire iron.

The force of the impact spun Luke around, and Tyrone circled his foe like a boxer working the ring, shuffling into position to get a look at the damage he'd done.

To Tyrone's surprise, Luke's eyes were open. Clear. Blinking away a little bit of daze. That was it? He'd taken a Mickey Mantle shot in the mouth with a piece of iron.

That blow should have knocked him out. *Should* have. Tyrone couldn't help but think of the story on the news, the guy who'd tackled Levi in the Publix parking lot and bashed his head into the blacktop a few times but failed to subdue him. Jesus, these maniacs were indestructible.

Luke spit out shards of teeth, and before Tyrone could react, the fallen figure got to his feet and catapulted out of the room. Indestructible *and* fast.

Tyrone gave chase for a few steps out of instinct, the fire poker ready to take another stab at amateur dentistry, but then he found himself hesitating just shy of the doorway. A thought descended upon him like a cloud: If he went after this guy, he'd have to kill him. A wanted murderer would be facing the death penalty. He wouldn't be detained until the police arrived or anything of the sort. Luke Foley would fight to the death right here and now. He was sure of that.

So Tyrone had a choice to make in the next fraction of a second. He could stop now and let the killer go, or he could press the chase, knowing he would have to bludgeon a man to death with his fire poker… or die trying.

His tongue flicked over his lips. Maybe he'd done his part, clubbing him in the face. Maybe he didn't need to risk his life further, being that the guy would surely leave as fast as possible now.

Or maybe those were excuses, attempts to cover the fact that he didn't think he could bring himself to go through with it. As awful as this guy was, Tyrone didn't think he had it in himself to kill him or anyone, to bash away at a human's head and face until the life force inside was stilled forever.

And then Luke was on him, spilling both of them to the ground, clawing, punching, fingernails raking over his face, thumbs jammed into his cheekbones, seeking his eyeballs. The killer seemed to appear there from nowhere, diving through the doorway. Something animal. Something evil. And it was on him, straddling him above the waist, its weight pressing him into the tile floor, kitty litter crystals gritting into his spine.

The arm holding the fire poker was pinned between them, so Tyrone threw a punch with his free hand, a short left hook that grazed over the front of Luke's face. He tried to pull his arm back to line up another blow, but Luke managed to get Tyrone's thumb into his mouth.

The killer bit down with what teeth he had left. Hard. There was a strange snapping sound when the jagged incisors pierced the thick skin at the first knuckle.

Tyrone screamed.

He wrenched his hand around, but the teeth wouldn't give. They bit down again. Piercing. Penetrating. Driving deeper into the joint. It felt like half of his thumb was about to pull free in some stranger's mouth.

Amidst flailing and wincing, Tyrone tried to knee Luke in the groin. He shifted his hips. Kneed. Bucked. Kneed again. Over and over, but his knee didn't find what it was looking for, pounding uselessly into the corded muscle of the killer's back and legs.

He screamed all the while. Full throated roars and sobs and yips, totally letting go of any control.

Luke's face was nearly expressionless. Just like the creepy photograph they'd shown so many times on the news. A little tension showed in the lines around his mouth, but his eyes were dead.

Tyrone's knee finally found the crevice it sought, and a softening of Luke's posture told Tyrone that he'd hurt him. The killer's jaw unclenched long enough for Tyrone to free his bloody hand.

He scrambled back, sliding his legs out from under his attacker, favoring the injured paw so his crawl curled awkwardly to the right like a rowboat with one paddle. His chest heaved. Breath and drool and snot and blood mixed in his mouth.

He crab-walked until his back collided with the wall, and he cowered there. He looked down at himself.

The fire poker still clenched in his right hand seemed so small now. Moments before it had felt like an invincible instrument of death. Now? Maybe it would allow him to hold the guy off for a while. A few minutes, perhaps.

The scream of the sirens outside swelled again, each of their voices shrill and excited as they passed, turning mournful as they faded into the distance.

And the killer was up, moving to the window. He parted the blinds with his fingers, angling his shoulders to peer out at the street.

Tyrone stirred, adjusting his feet as though to rise, but Luke spoke up.

"Don't move."

Tyrone froze. It felt like he had no choice.

The killer glared at him long enough to take two breaths, slow and even. His eyes were as dead as ever, and Tyrone's blood surrounded his lips. He stalked toward the frightened figure curled up on the floor. Slowly. With care. Each footstep clattering and scuffing against the tile. The little sounds only served to point out how quiet it had gotten in here. After all the yelling and struggling, the silence was uncomfortable.

The fear finally took hold of Tyrone as he watched the killer draw near. He couldn't move. The fire poker lay over his chest, his shaky arm holding it there as though it could somehow shield him.

Luke hovered over him now. So close.

CHAPTER 76

A groan escaped Darger's lips as she wrapped and tightened the sleeves of her jacket around her injured leg. Another jacket ruined, she thought. She put a little weight on the leg and winced at both the pain and the disgusting sound of blood splooging under her heel.

"Not to mention my boots," she muttered out loud, earning a sidelong glance from a woman in athletic gear jogging by.

The rhythmic pulse of a helicopter thumped overhead, aiming for the bridge. Loshak would have relayed the news of Levi's demise to the rest of the team by now. The crew in that chopper now had a singular, dismal task: to search for Levi Foley's body in the river.

A big black SUV pulled to the curb, and the window rolled down. Loshak leaned across the seat.

"Need a ride?"

Darger staggered across the sidewalk to the Suburban.

As she reached for the door latch, she said, "How do I know you're not some kind of sicko?"

Loshak peeked over the top of his sunglasses and gave her a wry smile.

"You don't."

"Where's Dawson?" Darger asked, glancing at the empty back seat.

"She wanted to keep an eye on the evacuation, make sure they got everyone out of the building and kept at a safe distance."

Darger nodded.

"They cleared everyone out pretty quick, all things considered. Bomb squad is going through the place top to bottom with their little robot doohickeys. We found a detonator wedged under the seat in the car parked out back, but just in case the boys had a backup somewhere, we're taking every precaution."

Loshak turned into the long drive that led up to the school, passing a line of yellow buses.

"They canceled school, obviously. Postponed the first day indefinitely."

Some of the kids filing into the buses were jostling one another and joking around. Others looked more grim, perhaps aware of how close they'd come to utter destruction.

"Was it the Jeep?"

"What's that?"

"The car you found here at the school?"

Loshak shook his head.

"Nah. It's an old Ford Focus with Alabama plates. That was what stuck out to me, you know? I'd expect damn near all the cars in a high school lot to be local."

Something about that bothered her. Ditching the Jeep made sense, of course. Once they'd seen their faces on the news, the brothers would have likely assumed the authorities knew about the car registered in Levi's name. But the vehicle description had been released yesterday, and so far, no one had reported it abandoned somewhere.

Loshak stopped where Darger's rental was parked next to the curb. She hopped out, forgetting the wound on her calf until the jolt of hitting the ground sent a new shock of pain through her leg.

"Son of a shitfuck," she hissed.

Loshak's gaze dropped to her leg.

"You need to report that so they can quarantine the dog," Loshak said.

"Yeah. Right. I know," Darger said, sliding behind the wheel of her car. "After we catch Luke."

She fired up the ignition and the radio on the dash began to crackle with police chatter.

"10-78. Witness at 301 Gladney has positively identified the SP. Says she got him with a can of pepper spray. Requesting additional units to set up a perimeter around 9th Street and Gladney Court."

The radio beeped and sizzled.

"Center, 23. Holding position at 9th Street and Gladney Court. 15, you wanna take the 8th Street crossing?"

"This is 15. I'm down the street at 414 Gladney. We've got a… well heck… this guy just came stumbling out of his house and says Luke Foley just stole his car. Guy says he tussled with him, knocked out the suspect's front teeth with a fire poker, but the Foley kid kept at him like a mad dog. Finally got away with the keys and tore out of here a few minutes ago in a gold Lexus. Plate number is Paul-Adam-Frank, Nine-Zero-Zero-Nine."

Darger typed the cross streets into her phone and then lowered her window, flapping her hand in the air so Loshak would do the same.

"You hear this chatter about a scuffle on Gladney Court?" She had to almost shout over the rumble of the two engines.

"Yeah."

"That's not far from where Luke and Levi grew up."

She knew she didn't have to spell the rest out for Loshak. Levi was dead, and everything was going terribly wrong for Luke. She had a feeling where he'd be headed.

"Let's go, then. I have to swing around the other side of the school to pick up Agent Dawson."

"See you on the other side, partner," Darger said, before speeding out of the lot.

One brother jumps off a bridge, the other is beat to hell, Darger thought to herself. *Where do you go when everything is going wrong?*

Home.

CHAPTER 77

Luke sat in the Jeep, occasionally peeling his lips open to look at the jagged remnants of teeth in the rear view. The swelling around his eyes still blushed that angry shade, all swollen and wrinkled, but it was nothing compared to the dental damage.

These were small prices to pay, he knew. He'd almost paid a higher one. He tried to stop himself from thinking it, but he wondered if his brother had paid that ultimate price. He'd be here by now otherwise, wouldn't he?

Maybe. Maybe not.

He felt nothing, either way. Felt nothing at all beyond the desire to move forward with things as quickly as possible.

He'd ditched the Lexus six blocks up and walked here. Parked it in the lot outside of an upscale apartment complex with a fountain out front.

He didn't know why he'd let the man live — the owner of the Lexus, the one who'd busted him in the teeth. Maybe there was some mutual respect there, for someone to fight back like that. Maybe he was just in a hurry, and there was nothing to be gained in taking the time to do it.

It made no difference now. None of it did.

That vinyl smell filled the car, even more than it had in the Focus this morning. Something about the odor cleared these reflective thoughts from his head, refocused him on the future.

He crawled into the backseat and sprawled out the best he could. It had been an early morning, and he'd gotten his ass kicked pretty hard. He'd sleep a while. A little rest would do him good.

He checked the time and let out a deep breath. He'd wait two hours for Levi. Maybe three. And then he'd proceed with the plan, with or without his brother.

CHAPTER 78

Levi crawled up onto the muddy riverbank. The icy cold of the water seemed to constrict his chest, to hold the muscles around his rib cage so tightly that he wasn't sure how he managed to breathe or move, though he did both.

He scrabbled up the slope of wet earth, gouging divots of black muck with his fingers. He needed to get away from the water. Far, far away from it. Needed to get onto the flat land, onto the grass, and then he could rest.

His body collapsed before he could get there, the tightened trunk of a torso plopping to the mud. Stiff. Rigid. It slapped the ground like a felled tree in the wetlands, and he laid still.

Something in his left shoulder had broken when he made impact with the water. The collar bone, maybe. He could wiggle the fingers on that hand, but moving the arm itself shot tendrils of pain into his neck and all through the upper arm.

He pushed himself up, propping his weight on the good elbow. The bad arm dangled at his side like a dead eel. He leaned that way, arching his back some, tilting the broken collar bone toward the ground. It seemed to hurt less that way.

His legs churned once more, feet sliding in the muck, his good hand seeking out some solid edge to pull himself up off of the bank.

He found it at last, pulled, feet still working, all of his muscles shaking. There was a moment of vertigo as his bulk shifted onto the new plane, and he was there.

He lay on his back, the grass cold against his wet body. His chest seemed to loosen some, his lungs taking advantage, sucking in deep breaths.

He didn't know how he'd survived. Didn't know how long he'd been unconscious or how long he'd been afloat in the river. Minutes? Hours? The gray sky above offered no clues.

If he'd wound up face down, he'd be dead. Drowned. He was pretty sure he'd been out long enough for that. But no. He was here. Wherever *here* was.

Levi added that to the list of unknowns. He must have floated some way away from the bridge as he could no longer see it. With the way the trees and brush cluttered the hill running up from here, he couldn't see much.

When his breathing slowed to something reasonable, he listened for a time. He didn't hear any traffic over the sound of the rushing river, but when he squinted he could make out concrete somewhere up the hill. The mess of branches obscured it to the point that he didn't know what he was looking at, but concrete meant he was still in the city. That was something.

He lay there for what felt like a long time. Breathing. Blinking. Staring into the heavens. His wet clothes hugged against him, pressing him down with all their weight.

There was much he didn't know for the moment. The where, why, and how of his situation concealed themselves from him.

But he did know one thing. He knew what he needed to do.

CHAPTER 79

The radio continued to babble and blip as the various police units relayed information between themselves and dispatch. So far there had been no further sightings of Luke Foley.

Darger balled her fist and slammed it into the steering wheel. Where the fuck was he? He couldn't just disappear.

She wanted this to be over already.

The image of Levi came to her again, balanced on the edge of the bridge, arms outstretched in a Christ-like pose. But there was nothing Christ-like about Levi Foley or his brother.

Still, some nagging sense of guilt pulled at her. That she hadn't convinced him not to jump? Or that they hadn't managed to stop them sooner?

And they still hadn't. Stopped them. Luke Foley was out there somewhere, prowling the streets.

The turn signal ticked away in a steady rhythm. She was close now. Close to where he'd been sighted. Maybe ten blocks from where the boys grew up. She let her foot off the accelerator, coasting down the street with her eyes scanning the sidewalks and yards and parking lots.

For no reason she could discern, her heart began to thud a little faster. A little harder.

He was close. She didn't know how she knew it, but she did.

Her chest swelled with a feeling of expectation.

She was going to find him and end this once and for all.

CHAPTER 80

Luke is dreaming.

The desert sprawls before him once more. Indecipherable sand in all directions. Unknowable. Barren.

Machine guns clatter in the distance. The sound is somehow welcome in this place. Familiar. Like an old friend.

He picks a direction and walks like he always does. A random choice. They're all random choices here. Direction holds no meaning in the sand. It all looks the same.

He grinds his molars together. The tension is unbearable. The dread of what waits where the land meets the horizon. Violence lurks out there. Waits for him to stumble near.

Most of his mind traverses the dreamscape. Not all.

Some part of him remains aware that his body reclines in the backseat of the Jeep. Hands fidgeting on his lap.

Even in sleep, he waits for Levi. For his brother. Waits for any sign of him.

It's time to finish what they've started.

Red rings circle his eyes. He can feel the hot pepper sting of it through the anesthetic of sleep.

In the dream, he climbs a dune, falling forward onto his hands to scramble up it on all fours like a dog. The hot grit of the sand flings everywhere. He squints to keep it out of his eyes.

Something stirs in the real world. A scuffing sound outside the car. Perhaps a rubber sole on concrete. He drifts closer to the surface of consciousness. Listens. But no further sound follows.

He smells the C4 now. Can picture the bricks of it stacked in the trunk. Just waiting to go off. He tries to remember how that image fits into his mission out here in the dream desert.

The silence drags him back down and these thoughts are forgotten. He sinks deeper and deeper.

In the dream, he descends the opposite side of the dune. The stench of smoke occupies his nasal cavity. More than a stench. A cloud. Something physical that takes up space. He smells it, tastes it, feels it with every breath.

It's all so real.

He doesn't wake when Levi climbs into the passenger seat.

CHAPTER 81

Levi climbed into the car, careful to close the door with only the faintest click.

Luke was sleeping, sprawled in the backseat, his chest rising and falling. He looked peaceful, although the skin around his eyes had a dark, irritated appearance.

Levi watched his brother for a time, considered waking him but decided against it.

This was it, after all. He knew what to do.

And it was better this way.

That vinyl smell of C4 was everywhere. The Jeep reeked with it. He could see how someone might compare the scent to tar now. It reminded him of playing basketball on the blacktop when they were kids. It was that smoother, shinier blacktop that got soft again whenever the sun beat down on it. Gooey and smelly, that shimmer of heat distortion blurring above it. It made their hands sticky. Used to smudge its black onto the pebbled surface of the ball.

When he was really young, he wondered if the whole parking lot might move a little bit over time, heating up into a liquid and oozing down that faint slope until their little basketball court had slid out into the street. He asked Luke about it, and his brother laughed for a long time.

He could still see it, still smell it, still feel its tacky residue on his palms.

His hands worked as these old movies played in his head, fingers pressing two bricks of the clay together. It still killed to use the left, but he'd reached a point where even the severe pain of a fractured collar bone had grown meaningless, a hurt without displeasure, almost morphing into a kind of distant ecstasy in its own excruciating way.

He mashed together two and a half pounds of the stuff. About five times what they'd used to blow out the interior of the El Camino. Levi molded it in his hands, sliding the first pin in slowly, carefully. He looked over his shoulder often as he worked, watching his brother's breath go in and out of his sleeping body.

Luke's nose twitched a few times, but he didn't wake. With the way his eyes wiggled beneath his eyelids, Levi thought his brother must be dreaming.

Now Levi unspooled a short run of wire, hacking at it with the blade of the Swiss Army knife he found in the glove box. There were probably wire cutters among the fold-out parts of the knife, but he was too keyed up now for any kind of work requiring fine motor skills. The blade would do.

The tension was unbearable. He wanted this to be over.

The roughly hacked wire twisted into place, and that was it. He was ready.

Levi peeled off his shirt. He didn't know why. He took a breath, let the wad of explosive rest on his chest. It was heavy and strange, a football-sized wad of gray clay — enough to reduce a small building into a fine powder. Enough to finish it.

It even felt like Play-Doh on his skin. Cool and smooth with a deceptive heft to it.

Weird how his thoughts could never stray far from childhood, one way or another. Play-Doh. Footballs and basketballs. The oozing blacktop on the little court near their house. Even here and now, the past was always with him. Always with both of them.

He closed his eyes, thumb trembling on the button.

CHAPTER 82

The car rounded the left turn, centrifugal force pulling Darger to the right. She barely felt it, all attention focused on her surroundings. The gold and green Pheasant Brook sign appeared, and she briefly considered veering that direction. But no. Something urged her past it.

The faded awnings of the abandoned strip mall loomed ahead, and she knew that was where her instinct drove her. If that was what propelled her at all. Darger toed the accelerator, the added force pressing her back into her seat.

Half a minute later, the tires bumped over the uneven lip between street and parking lot. Darger guided the car around what she thought might have once been a Blockbuster video outlet.

The place had a half-feral look to it. Overgrown shrubbery reached almost past the roof, largely obscuring the boarded up doors and windows. Snarls of grass and chicory sprouted up in the cracks and seams of the concrete. A single tire jutted from a bathtub-sized pothole filled with grimy water.

She steered around the side of the building, heading for whatever lay behind the vacant structure.

And then she saw it.

The black Wrangler.

Her foot jammed on the brake pedal, jolting her forward from the sudden stop. She clenched her teeth against the throbbing spasm in her calf.

Darger ignored the pain. She stared at the Jeep for several seconds, holding her breath for the duration, waiting for something to happen. For gunshots. For the engine to suddenly roar to life, tires squealing as Luke tried to flee. For even a flicker of movement.

But there was nothing.

She let herself exhale. The Jeep was empty.

It made sense. Why go back to the black Wrangler everyone was looking for when you'd just stolen a shiny new Lexus?

The gearshift thunked, and she skittered onto the pavement, limping toward the vehicle on foot. Sunlight glinted on the windshield, but as Darger moved closer and the reflection shifted, a silhouette took shape behind the glass.

She halted, her view into the car suddenly becoming clear. The Jeep wasn't empty after all.

Luke slumped in the back seat. Levi up front on the passenger side. Levi. How could that be? She'd seen him jump.

Her fingers went to her belt, gripped her Glock, and slid it from the holster. She was taking no chances this time.

"Out of the car with your hands on your head!"

The fine details were hazy behind the glare of the glass, but she swore she felt Levi's gaze on her. Sensed as his eyes met hers.

There was a beat of stillness. The silent inhale before a scream.

The bright sparkle of the windshield became a blinding flash of white light. At the same moment, a wall of heat smacked into her. It lifted her off her feet, throwing her back with the force of a high-speed train.

Everything went black.

CHAPTER 83

"Stupid," Loshak was saying. "I shouldn't have let her run off without getting that leg checked out."

"I'm sure she would have insisted on seeing a doctor immediately if it was that urgent," Agent Dawson said. She lifted one of the hands folded in her lap to secure a loose braid behind her ear.

Loshak snorted.

"That just shows how well you *don't* know my partner."

Agent Dawson only smiled and aimed a slender finger down the hill.

"It's a left at the next intersection," she said.

A flash of orange light to the west drew Loshak's gaze away from the road. A huge ball of flame surrounded by a plume of black smoke followed, billowing into the sky only a few blocks from their position.

People in the surrounding traffic whooped and pointed at the explosion, completely in awe.

Loshak veered to the curb and put a hand on Agent Dawson's shoulder.

"Brace yourself."

"What do you—"

The shock wave hit with a low, sternum-rattling boom. The ground shook, rocking the vehicle like an earthquake. Instinctively, Loshak raised his arms to shield his head.

"Oh God," Dawson stuttered. "Oh my God."

There were screams from people on the street around them. The woman in the BMW directly in front of him got out of her car and ran for cover.

Loshak blinked a few times after the burst had passed, and then he fumbled to put the Chevy back in gear.

He uttered a single word.

"Darger."

CHAPTER 84

Darger woke in the ambulance, Loshak bent over her, gripping the fingers of her right hand. The look of frenzied panic on his face dissipated when he saw her eyes open. His mouth moved, but no words reached her.

She squeezed her eyes shut, as if that might clear the blockage in her ears.

Every bone ached. Every rib, every tooth, every metacarpal. The skin on her hands and face felt scalded. Her head killed, and she thought her ears might be bleeding. Something sharp and made of glass that emitted a high-pitched whine must be lodged in her skull somewhere. It was the only explanation.

When she opened her eyes again, she tried to gesture at her ears, but found her arms strapped to a gurney.

Loshak's lips flapped again.

"I can't fucking hear you," she mumbled.

Watching him laugh with no sound was a strange thing. Like someone had pressed "Mute" on the whole world. He patted her hand and then gave her fingers another squeeze.

The attending physician in the Trauma Center insisted Darger be admitted.

"You have sustained two concussions in a very short period of time. It puts you at grave risk for something called second-impact syndrome," the doctor said.

"But I feel fine."

Loshak scoffed loud enough that she actually heard it.

"Fine *enough*, all things considered," she said. "I just want to go back to my hotel for a long, hot shower and about twenty hours of sleep."

"You're in luck, Agent Darger. You can get all that right here, under the careful observation of trained healthcare professionals," the doctor said, then paused to scribble something in her chart. "And also an MRI."

By the time they finished with their needle pokes and brain scans and moved Darger to a regular room, she had most of her hearing back.

She peppered Loshak with questions. Had they found remains of either Luke or Levi after the explosion? Was there anything at all left after the Jeep exploded? Did they know what they'd planned to do with the C4 in the vehicle?

"You're supposed to be resting," Loshak said.

She flopped her arms in the bed.

"Fuck off, Loshak. If I start doing cartwheels around the room while I ask questions, then you can give me grief."

"You're just crabby because the doctor scolded you for running around with a concussion."

"I'm crabby because I don't have a single jacket left that isn't completely ruined," she said. "I fucking hate shopping."

A laugh wheezed out of Loshak before he stopped abruptly and pointed a finger at her.

"Don't forget in all the excitement that we still need to track down the dog that bit you."

"Right. The *excitement*," Darger muttered.

A light knock announced Agent Dawson's presence.

"I just came from a visit downstairs," she said.

"Owen?" Darger asked. "He's awake?"

Dawson's braids swayed as she nodded her head.

"Groggy, but awake. And demanding to know why *Miss*

Darger hasn't come visit him yet."

Darger tried to snort, but it hurt her throat. There didn't seem to be a single body part that wasn't sore.

Loshak put up a half-assed protest when Darger demanded that she be allowed to go downstairs to see Owen.

"I know you're only pretending to object so you can tattle on me when the doctor checks in," she said.

His eyebrows raised in unison.

"That's right. I'm finally figuring you out, Loshak. You're a kiss-ass."

He pursed his lips and said, "How do you think I get all those favors at the Bureau?"

In the end, they reached a compromise. Darger could go for a visit, but she had to go in a wheelchair. Loshak himself rolled her to the elevator.

Constance Baxter came to the door when Violet arrived and kissed the top of her head.

"He's been so anxious to see you," Constance said, then stood aside to let Violet go in alone.

Owen sat up in bed, thinner and paler than she remembered. But he was alive.

"Well, lookee what the cat dragged in," Owen said, clicking his tongue. "I thought maybe you'd forgotten about ol' Owen."

"I've been a little busy."

He dropped the surly tone and gave her a weary smile. "So I heard."

His hand flapped in the air like a caged bird.

"What are you sittin' all the way over there for? Come closer."

She gave the wheels of her chair a downward thrust until her knees bumped the side of his bed. He reached for the side of her face, fingertips brushing over her cheek.

"Are you OK?"

"Only a couple of concussions. But I'm fine on account of my extra thick skull," she said, not quite thunking her knuckles against her head. "What about you?"

Owen stared into her eyes for a moment before blinking.

"I'm… glad it's finally over. Happy as hell that you're OK."

She felt herself flush a little at the affection in his voice.

He swallowed and folded his hands in his lap.

"Ethan's funeral is next Wednesday," he said. "Mom waited until she knew I'd be ready for discharge."

Violet nodded, the warm, fuzzy feelings replaced by heartache. She considered Owen's loss. His twin brother. A person split from the same original cell. An exact genetic replica. Gone forever. It felt like some universal unfairness had played out here, and she wondered at her own part in it.

Owen cleared his throat and then spoke again.

"So I was thinking you could be my date. Assuming you'll still be in town."

"Your date?"

"For the funeral."

She cocked her head to one side. "Who brings a date to a funeral?"

"Well in truth, I need someone to push the chair and hold my piss bag."

She rolled her eyes. "Oh, that *does* sound romantic. Always the gentleman, this one."

"If you wanted a gentleman, you saved the wrong brother."

Violet's smile vanished, and she lowered her gaze to her hands.

He reached for her. "Now don't do that, Violet. I was only

kidding around."

"I know, but—"

"But you're still set on thinking you're Super Girl or some such nonsense?"

Her lips pressed together in a thoughtful line.

"I always thought of myself as more of a Wonder Woman type."

"Did you now?"

"She's got that lasso thing," she said, pantomiming a whipping motion. "Brings lying men to their knees and forces them to tell the truth."

"You want the truth, Miss Darger? I'll give it to you."

He suddenly looked very grave. It was not an expression she was used to seeing on him.

"If I know you, then you've been giving yourself hell about what happened in that motel room. Worryin' over how if you'd kept me from going in that room, then I wouldn't be in this position."

Violet held very still, not trusting herself to do much more than breathe.

Owen spread his fingers wide and stared down at his palms.

"This probably sounds strange, and maybe quite a lot of it is the morphine talking, but…" his voice grew husky and strained. "If this is how things had to happen, my brother dyin' and all, well, there is an odd kind of comfort in knowing that part of him will be with me forever."

He placed one hand on the soft place beneath his rib cage. Underneath the blankets and the hospital gown and the dressings, Violet knew there was a large wound just beginning to heal.

Owen cleared his throat and blinked a few times.

"Besides, I'm gonna have one heck of a time taking Ethan's liver on all manner of adventures. Do you know, I don't think my brother had ever been drunk once in his life?"

Smirking, Violet wiped the corners of her eyes.

"Maybe he had and just never told you?"

"Please. I knew about every cookie Ethan ever stole," he scoffed, then waggled his eyebrows. "I'm the one with secrets."

"What kind of secrets?"

"I can't tell you. It would ruin my irresistible mystique."

Violet squinted over at him.

"Sounds like I might be forced to use my Wonder Woman whip on you."

He caught her by the wrist and pulled her closer.

"Promise?"

CHAPTER 85

Violet wheeled Owen to the head of the chapel. Parking his chair next to the front pew, she locked the wheels and moved to sit in the row behind. He snatched her hand with lightning speed.

"Now where do you think you're off to?"

He nodded toward the pew, indicating that she should sit next to him.

"That's for family. Your mother—"

He gave her arm a little tug, so she had to bring her ear closer to his face.

"Sit your butt right there, or I'll pull you into my lap and make a real scene. If you think I'm about to sit through this pageant on my own, you got another thing coming."

Studying him, she wondered if he was having some breakthrough pain. She noticed he got more lippy when he was hurting. He did have that glassy sort of look in his eyes. Or maybe his flippant attitude was the result of extra painkillers. It would not surprise her to find out he'd been doubling down on the Vicodin just for kicks. Violet plopped down next to him.

"Don't you have any friends? People you've known longer than two weeks?"

"Of course I do, but they're all ugly as hell. I need something pretty to look at when Father Pascal starts pontificating on my brother's many virtues," he said with a wink.

"Owen Baxter, you hush your mouth and wipe that indecent grin off your face this instant," a voice hissed from over Violet's shoulder.

Constance Baxter slid in beside her and shot a withering look at her son.

Violet wasn't sure if Constance was half-teasing or not, but she turned to give Owen a gloating smirk anyway.

She felt odd and out of place at the start of the service. Like she was an outsider given a close-up view of a family's grief. She couldn't stop thinking of all the people sitting behind her, wondering who she was. This stranger in their midst.

Father Pascal's words filtered through her thoughts.

"Let us not forget Ethan's family — his mother, Constance, and his brother, Owen. They will surely need their time to grieve, but too often our reaction is to pull away, not wanting to intrude. For while they need those quiet moments for thought and prayer, they also need to feel the warmth of communion and community."

Violet glanced at her hand, clasped in Owen's, and suddenly the awkwardness was gone.

Maybe that was all that was required to make it right.

Owen needed comfort, and he'd chosen her.

The funeral-goers converged on the home of Constance Baxter, dressed in their Sunday best, casserole dishes in hand. Violet gnawed on a piece of fried chicken, seated in a tufted wingback chair across from Owen.

"You ever been down to Lake Anna?" Owen asked.

"No. Why?"

"Friend of mine has a place there. A little cottage right on the water. I've been thinking… I have these damn weekly check-ups with the transplant team for a while, but after that, I thought I might head out there. Take some time away from everything."

"Sounds like it would be a nice place to do that," she said, wondering why he seemed to be seeking her approval for such a thing.

He stared down at his plate, nudging a pile of macaroni and cheese with his fork.

"Lot of tourists in the summer, but they start thinning out over the next month or so. The changing leaves reflecting on the lake can't be beat, or so I've been told. It's only about an hour south of Quantico, you know. "

The realization hit her like a slap across the face. He wanted her to come stay with him. And he was being almost bashful about it. She couldn't resist drawing it out a little.

"Are you trying to ask me something, Owen?"

"Maybe."

"So ask."

He gave her a flat look, and then, seeing that she really was going to force it out of him, he closed his eyes and sighed.

"Would you like to join me some weekend, or perhaps a week, if you could get the time away?"

She speared a chunk of potato salad, popped it in her mouth, and smiled.

"Is this your standard routine for picking up women? Rescue her from a bar fight, get yourself blown up, invite her up to your cabin for a romantic getaway?"

"Believe it or not, usually I don't have to work quite so hard. I mean, the bar fight is pretty standard, but…"

"Oh? So I'm special?"

She waggled her eyebrows.

"Very," he said, no hint that he might be teasing.

"Of course I'll come. I would love to."

"Good," he said with a nod, then leaned forward. "Now my

next question is: you wouldn't happen to have any skimpy little Wonder Woman outfits lyin' around, would you? After our talk the other day, I just can't seem to get that picture out of my head."

Violet used her elbow to reveal the gun holstered on her belt.

"Do I have to remind you that I'm armed?"

EPILOGUE

Her footsteps echoed down the long, empty corridor. Darger passed the indoor firing range, usually a source of endless noise, but today it was silent. It was Friday afternoon, and most people had already left for the weekend.

Darger's heel caught on the floor as she rounded a corner, emitting a high-pitched yelp. Stupid squeaky soles. She missed her old boots, all worn and perfectly conformed to her feet. She should have sent the bill for the new pair to the owner of that damned blood-thirsty Chow.

As she turned another bend, Darger caught sight of the elevator ahead. A man hurried to slip through the wood paneled doors, and they clunked shut behind him. Darger inhaled sharply.

The man stepping into the elevator had looked exactly like Casey Luck. She only caught the side of his face from an angle, but he had the same height, same build, same meticulous hair.

By the time she reached the elevator herself, she realized it wasn't possible. Casey lived in Ohio. What would he be doing here at Quantico? The DOWN button lit up as she jabbed it with her knuckle, shaking her head. With the week of vacation time she had planned, she supposed her mind couldn't help but wander to whatever nook held the memories of lovers, both past and present.

Darger glanced at her watch as the elevator droned down to the ground floor, noting that it was a few minutes past 5:30 PM. Owen would be getting antsy, especially after spending the last five days on his own. A little smile touched her lips. He didn't strike her as the type that spent a lot of time reflecting in solitude.

Her car hummed to life, and she pointed the unlit headlights toward her apartment. She needed to grab her mail before she headed south.

The cottage was unlocked when Darger arrived. She elbowed her way inside, both arms hugging grocery bags, and nudged the door closed behind her. Depositing the bags on the kitchen counter, Darger was about to call out when something moved in the reflection on a nearby mirror. It was only a dark blur streaking past, and before she could turn around she felt the presence behind her. The gentle current of an exhale of breath on her neck.

"What the hell took you so long?"

Owen buried his face in her hair and then began to kiss her, working his way around to the soft spot under her chin.

She leaned back, pressing into him, and he nibbled at her ear.

"Are you going to help me unload this stuff, or are you just gonna gnaw on me?"

"Can't help it. You left me in such a state after last weekend, I don't know if I shall ever be able to let you out of my sight again."

"Some of us live in the real world and have something called a *job*," she teased. "Loshak says hello, by the way."

"Now hold on a minute. Before you start besmirching my name, let me clarify something: I *have* a job."

"You're in Virginia."

"So?"

"So, you're not licensed to investigate in Virginia."

"Well that may be true, but I don't recall you complaining the last time I was investigating your priv—"

She spun to face him and clapped her hand over his mouth, cutting off the words.

"You swore you wouldn't make that joke anymore."

Owen feigned an innocent look, and she removed her hand.

"What joke?"

She squinted at him with distrust and then returned to tucking groceries into cabinets.

"Anyway, I thought my job was as your manservant-slash-concubine?"

She snorted. "Shouldn't the manservant be putting away the food?"

"Ma'am, I am far too delicate for that kind of manual labor."

Owen twirled her around and kissed her full on the mouth, moving her across the kitchen until she was backed up against the refrigerator. When he released her, he gazed into her eyes for a long time, and she had the sense he was about to say something serious for once.

"Mrs. Kleinstubel was out pruning her roses yesterday. She gave me some very wanton looks. I think she noticed that you went away and decided to make her move."

Mrs. Kleinstubel lived in the house next door to the cottage Owen was renting, and she gave them dubious looks every time they happened to cross paths outside. Violet suspected the old lady might have caught a glimpse of a midnight skinny-dipping session Owen had talked her into the first weekend she'd visited.

"I don't think Mrs. Kleinstubel sees all that well. She is 82, you know. She probably thought you were a sasquatch," Violet said, running her fingers through his shaggy hair.

One of Owen's eyebrows rose a few degrees.

"If so, she was having some very bawdy thoughts about Bigfoot." He squinted over Violet's shoulder. "And I must confess, I considered it."

Violet bit down on her cheeks and attempted to appear sullen.

"Now you're just trying to make me jealous."

"Is it working?"

"Maybe," she said, her mouth disobeying and pulling into a smile. "And as punishment, I don't think I'll be showing you the special underwear I wore just for you."

Owen's eyes sparkled.

"The what?" he said, reaching for the waistband of her jeans. "Let me see!"

Violet dodged away from him, laughing. She took off for the other end of the house, knowing he would chase her.

Before he could catch up, she shut herself in the little bathroom off the master suite. The box spring squeaked as Owen bounced onto the mattress.

"Don't lollygag in there, you hear? If you make me wait too long, I'll have no choice but to trot over to Mrs. Kleinstubel's house."

Violet came through the door wearing only a thin white t-shirt and the underwear.

Owen looked her up and down, grinning ear to ear.

"Wonder Woman panties. Why, Miss Darger, you know

exactly how to push my buttons."

He was leaning up against the headboard, and he pulled her closer by the waist until she knelt on the bed next to him. He pressed his lips to hers, and he tasted like milk and honey. His hand snaked around the back of one thigh and tugged it over his lap until she was straddling him.

"You like?" she asked.

"I like," he said, his voice raspy with arousal.

She shivered as his fingers slid under her shirt, up her spine, then around her rib cage to her breasts.

She leaned into him — the feel of him — and the rest of the world dropped away.

They lay in bed after, tangled up together in a cocoon of sheets. She ran a finger over his surgical scar, and he trembled under her light touch.

"It's funny," he said, "but sometimes I almost feel like he's in there a little bit."

"Ethan?"

"Yeah. More like there's part of him in my head, I guess. Not always. Just sometimes."

"Like when?"

"Like now."

"And what is Ethan thinking now?"

Through half-closed lids, he studied her.

"He's thinking all manner of virtuous and honorable thoughts about what a fine woman you are, and how it would be a shame to let you get away."

Violet propped herself up on one elbow.

"And then your response is… what? *Fuck 'em and forget*

'em?'

His mouth spread into a wicked grin.

"Now Miss Darger, what did I tell you about that salty language and the effect it has on me?"

He disappeared under the sheets with a ravenous look.

Owen collapsed onto his back with a contented sigh.

"Well after all that, I am just about hungry enough to eat a damn sea cow."

"They were fresh out of sea cow at the supermarket," Violet said. "How about regular cow?"

"Regular cow will do just fine."

He finished dressing first and went out to fire up the charcoal grill in the backyard. Violet followed a few minutes later, bringing along a sack of sweet corn and her pile of unopened mail.

Owen popped the cap off a bottle of beer and handed it to her while she shucked corn.

"Got an email from someone at HarperCollins yesterday," he said.

"Really?"

"They want me to write a book about my *experience*." He used his fingers to put air-quotes around the last word.

"Does that mean you don't want to do it?" she asked, ripping the husk away from an ear of corn.

She didn't see why he wouldn't. He hadn't shied away from making guest appearances on several cable news shows since the events in Atlanta, not to mention the dozen or so newspaper and magazine interviews. Owen Baxter was not a shy man.

"I don't know. Writing a book is more the kind of thing Ethan would do. He was the book-smart one."

Violet rolled her eyes.

"Quit doing that."

"Doing what?"

"Selling yourself as the dumb one. Besides, didn't you say that he's in your head? Tell him he's gotta earn his keep."

Owen pointed a grill fork at her.

"I never said I was the dumb one. I said he was book-smart. Me? I'm street-smart."

He stabbed the sharpened tines into a tenderloin steak and slapped it on the grill with a sizzle.

Violet finished wrapping the corn in aluminum foil and handed it off for Owen to put on the grill. Then she turned to her mail. She fished through the pile with a fingernail. Junk. Cable bill. Junk. Junk. At the bottom was an envelope addressed by hand.

She plucked the letter from the stack, thinking at first that it must be something her mother had sent from Europe, but after a closer glance, she knew that was wrong. The handwriting was not her mother's. But it was familiar.

Her finger slipped under the flap, and a small shock of pain went through her hand.

"Ouch."

Owen turned from the grill, fragrant smoke coiling behind him like a cape. "What?"

"Paper cut," she said, popping the fingertip into her mouth for a moment.

Then, more carefully this time, she ripped the top of the envelope open and shook the letter free.

Her body went rigid as she read the opening lines.

Dear Violet,

So many times over the past few weeks I thought of writing this letter and stopped myself. You see, I am retired (both from my work and from the world) and have been for a very long time. But when I saw your interview in *Vanity Fair* and read all of the interesting things you had to say about me… well, it awakened something. Something that lay dormant for so many years, I thought it might be gone forever. Dead.

But we all have a calling in this life, in this world. We all have a gift, a purpose, a job that we alone are meant to do. Not everyone can find theirs. Most people never do. You have to look through things, squint your eyes just so to see past the surface and stare upon that ugly beating heart in the middle there. The wad of misshapen meat that pounds out the rhythm of your existence, makes you tick, makes you who you are.

You have found your gift, it seems, and if I genuinely helped steer you toward it, I am glad for it. I suppose that, in turn, you have helped me rediscover mine.

And I get the feeling, just now, that our paths may cross again. Perhaps soon.

-Leonard Stump

Owen was talking to her, but she didn't hear. Finally his voice broke through as she tore her eyes from the blue ink scrawled on the paper.

"Vi," he said, frowning at her, "what's wrong?"

She dropped the letter on the table and went into the house. When she came back out, Owen waved the paper at her.

"What is this? Some kind of joke?"

"No. And don't touch it so much. They'll have to dust it for prints."

"But this letter is signed Leonard Stump. Like the serial killer?"

"Not *like*. It's him."

Her voice came out sharper and higher than normal, like an overtightened string on a violin.

"Come on, it's probably only someone playing a trick. And not a funny one, I might add."

She brought up a scan from the Stump journal on her phone and laid it side by side with the letter.

"Where'd you get this?"

"The journal? He wrote it in jail. Before he escaped. Loshak gave it to me."

"You don't think Loshak would—"

Owen trailed off when she started to shake her head.

"That's not his sense of humor. Not at all."

"Who else would have access to that journal?" he said. His private investigator mind was kicking into gear now.

"As far as I know, only FBI personnel. And even then, I got the impression that the journal's existence is mostly secret. They don't want the press getting a whiff of it and slapping them with the Freedom of Information Act."

He stared at her for a long time.

"I suppose this'll sound real selfish of me, but this is gonna royally fuck up all our plans for the week, isn't it?"

She sighed.

"Probably," Darger said. "Loshak needs to know about it as soon as possible. I should probably call him right now."

Owen nodded.

"I don't know how he's going to react," she added.

"How do you *think* he'll react?"

Her eyes spun up to the sky. It was a clear sapphire blue, with a hint of pink beginning to show on the horizon.

"Helicopters, National Guard, Witness Protection. No big deal."

COME PARTY WITH US

We're loners. Rebels. But much to our surprise, the most kickass part of writing has been connecting with our readers. From time to time, we send out newsletters with giveaways, special offers, and juicy details on new releases.

Sign up for our mailing list at:
http://ltvargus.com/mailing-list

SPREAD THE WORD

Thank you for reading! We'd be very grateful if you could take a few minutes to review it on Amazon.com.

How grateful? Eternally. Even when we are old and dead and have turned into ghosts, we will be thinking fondly of you and your kind words. The most powerful way to bring our books to the attention of other people is through the honest reviews from readers like you.

ABOUT THE AUTHORS

Tim McBain writes because life is short, and he wants to make something awesome before he dies. Additionally, he likes to move it, move it.

You can connect with Tim on Twitter at @realtimmcbain or via email at tim@timmcbain.com.

L.T. Vargus grew up in Hell, Michigan, which is a lot smaller, quieter, and less fiery than one might imagine. When not click-clacking away at the keyboard, she can be found sewing, fantasizing about food, and rotting her brain in front of the TV.

If you want to wax poetic about pizza or cats, you can contact L.T. (the L is for Lex) at ltvargus9@gmail.com or on Twitter @ltvargus.

TimMcBain.com
LTVargus.com